American Family

BOOKS BY FAITH BALDWIN

Three Women
Departing Wings
Alimony
The Office-Wife
The Incredible Year
Make-Believe
Today's Virtue
Skyscraper
Week-End Marriage
District Nurse
Self-Made Woman
Beauty
White-Collar Girl
Love's a Puzzle
Innocent Bystander
Wife Versus Secretary
Within a Year
Honor Bound
The Puritan Strain
The Moon's Our Home
Private Duty
The Girls of Divine Corners
Men Are Such Fools!
That Man Is Mine
The Heart Has Wings
Twenty-four Hours a Day
Manhattan Nights
Enchanted Oasis
Rich Girl, Poor Girl
Hotel Hostess
The High Road
Career By Proxy
White Magic
Station Wagon Set
Rehearsal for Love
"Something Special"
Letty and the Law
Medical Center

And New Stars Burn
Temporary Address: Reno
The Heart Remembers
Blue Horizons
Breath of Life
Five Women in Three Novels
The Rest of My Life With You
Washington, U.S.A
You Can't Escape
He Married a Doctor
Change of Heart
Arizona Star
A Job for Jenny
No Private Heaven
Woman on Her Way
Sleeping Beauty
Give Love the Air
Marry for Money
They Who Love
The Golden Shoestring
Look Out for Liza
The Whole Armor
The Juniper Tree
Face Toward the Spring
Three Faces of Love
Many Windows
Blaze of Sunlight
Testament of Trust
The West Wind
Harvest of Hope
The Lonely Man
Living By Faith
There Is a Season
Evening Star
The Velvet Hammer
Any Village
Take What You Want
American Family

Poetry
Sign Posts
Widow's Walk

American Family

By

FAITH BALDWIN

HOLT, RINEHART AND WINSTON

New York | *Chicago* | *San Francisco*

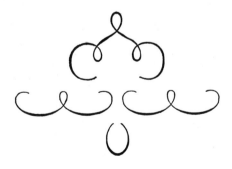

Published simultaneously in Canada by Holt, Rinehart and Winston of Canada,
Limited

First published in book form in January 1935
New Edition 1972

This novel was originally serialized in *Cosmopolitan Magazine*

ISBN: 0–03–00016–0
Library of Congress Catalog Card Number: 72–78110
Printed in the United States of America

CONTENTS

FOREWORD

FOREWORDS to novels are written in order that the reader may have something he can skip without the least self-reproach. However, there are one or two things I want to make clear and a foreword remains the only medium.

In the first place this story is fiction. The characters in it are figments of my imagination. Where I have occasionally mentioned a person who actually lived and had his or her being, by name, it is because in writing of the years between 1862 and 1917 I have been unable—and unwilling—to escape a slight tinge of contemporary history.

The surname I have used to indicate my fictional American family is in my own family. My great-grandmother was born Abby Eliza Condit. I selected the name because I like it and because there is a certain danger in the christening of book characters. Even when one "makes them up" there are always a hundred people of the same name to arise and demand "why?" My why is partly caution, partly sentiment. And I do not believe that any of the living Condits, of whom there must be many, will question my right to employ a name which is set down in the family annals.

The other names, save for one or two which also have come down through collateral branches of my family, have been chosen at random; and none have any reference to any living person.

In the matter of locale I must admit that New York City and Fuhchau, China, exist. The other towns in Fukien Province and the villages and towns of northern New York are likewise realities. No one is likely to cavil at my choice of an American or a Chinese metropolis but there may be some who will voice objections to the other settings. To them I can say this, in extenuation . . . northern New York has long been to me one of the very loveliest sections in my country. I have for it as deep a devotion as if I had been born in one of its counties. But the acquaintances I have among its population are all of recent years. So far as that goes, I know no one in Carthage or its environs. I have not endeavored to draw of this section a picture that is historically correct; nor have I "fictionized" any person who once lived or now lives there. It has been my good fortune for the last eight years to motor through this part of New York twice during each summer; and it occurred to me that if I were David Condit, intent on acquiring a country practice, I could do no better than to select the little town of Natural Bridge.

A great many people have helped me to write this book. I would like for my own satisfaction to set down their names, a roster of good friends, known and unknown. First of all my deep gratitude must go to Mary Brewster Hollister, who, it appears to my vanity, was born and lived, for many years, in the south of China solely in order to become of most invaluable help to me in the writing of this story. For her advice, criticism and editing, her loyal friendship and unremitting aid, my thanks.

My thanks are due also to Dr. Milton Charles Winternitz, Dean of Yale Medical School, and to Miriam Kathleen Dasey, Registrar, and to Dr. Harry Burr Ferris, Professor Emeritus; and to Basil Lubbock for his book *The China Clippers,* and his letters of encouragement; to Carl Price, historian of Wesleyan University, and his book *Wesleyan's First Century;* to Stephen Mapes Ruden, for his help in tracing that vanished ship, the *Hotspur,* to her brave beginnings and braver end; to Dr. Robert Carlisle, authority on Bellevue Hospital; to Stephen B. Early; to Alfred B. Carhart; to Carl Smith, and many others. I wish also to thank my friends in the nursing profession who read my manuscript with editorial eyes and to those of my immediate family who suffered hearing me talk about it for months on end. And also my agent and my publisher for their patience and assistance.

Many books have helped me also. It seems extraordinarily pretentious to list them. I shall do so, however, to some extent—in the back of the book where such lists really belong. Many of the volumes consumed were read for sheer enjoyment and included contemporary history in the form of contemporary novels and diaries; travel books; costume books and others too numerous to mention. In addition I have in my possession certain family journals, scrapbooks and letters which helped me materially.

American Family is just a story. It propounds no problems and sets no match to controversial tinder. If I like some of my characters better than others, that is my own affair. If I have suggested that all missionaries to China are not the inhuman and rigorous fanatics certain fiction cycles have led us to believe, that is merely my belief.

I have in no way attempted to draw an accurate or serious portrait of the fifty-five years which this story embraces. If I have omitted "significant" trends or erred in the cut of a gown or the curling of a tress of hair, I am sorry. But I am no historian, I am merely a teller of tales; and I wanted very much to tell this one.

FAITH BALDWIN

PROLOGUE

Eastern Passage

1862

WHEN, in the winter of 1861, Tobias Condit, taking his courage and his heart in both hands, asked Elizabeth Lewis to become his wife and to go with him to China, as his beloved co-laborer in the, as yet, scarcely furrowed field of foreign missions, she stammered—"Yes!" in that quick impulsive way she had, her great black eyes, radiant with happiness, bravely meeting his pleading earnest regard. For she loved him with an intensity which seemed to her almost indecorous. A moment later, she had remembered that the responsibilities of a minister's wife are heavy, and those of a missionary's wife even more grave. China was five months away, and on the other side of the world. Elizabeth in all her twenty years had only once left her native town of Carthage, when in 1850 she had been taken, a tremulous child of nine, to the great City of New York in order to hear Jenny Lind sing at Castle Garden.

Therefore, even as she stood and faced him, her heart pounding painfully beneath her tight bodice, her hands clasped so tightly that the palms were wet and the knuckles white, she begged him—realizing the full enormity of her alteration—to release her from a promise given a scant sixty seconds before.

She was most sensible, she told him, very low, of the honor he had done her. He must believe that she held him in the highest regard. But she was not fitted, she was, she concluded, on a wail of pure grief and humility, entirely unsuited . . .

His eyes, almost as black as her own, were very tender but there was also in their eager and intelligent depths that spark of mischief which on their first meeting, over a year ago, had so captivated her. He said merely, "Suppose you allow me to be the judge of that, Elizabeth," and took her, without further ado, into his arms.

Now it seemed really as if her heart must perish in her side of a new and frightened rapture which drove everything before it. Not so long ago she had heard Tobias preach . . . "perfect love,"

3

he had quoted, "casteth out fear." While it was undoubtedly sinful to apply to her purely emotional exaltation the beautiful words of the Scripture, she felt that she had never before fully understood them. And felt, too, that wild, amazing sense of strength and adventure which had driven the Bourbon ancestors of her mother across the seas, over sixty years ago, in order that, in a wilderness, they might find healing and tranquillity.

Then she ceased to think, for, if his first kiss bestowed its devout benediction upon the wide brow, beneath the bands of darkest hair, his second found, and held, her mouth.

He said, a moment later, as men have said since time immemorial and will say until time ends, "I shall be so good to you, my dear," and he added that, with her beside him, his approaching exile, longed for and yet in some measure dreaded, would be merely a coming home.

She was never to forget that evening in the large, austere best parlor of her aunt's frame house, with the wind from the mountains at the windows and the soft sound of the snow slurring against the pane. The lamplight made strange shadows on the patterned walls and a fire burned in the grate. The sound of a coal falling was no louder than her heartbeat.

Presently they were sitting side by side on the hair-cloth sofa, handfast, and Tobias was making their plans. They would be married in the sweet early spring, he told her, and would sail in the early summer. Listening, it was like a dream. She scarcely heard his words, important as they were; she listened merely to the tone, the inflection of his compelling voice, and felt his nearness as a bright sword in her breast, with a pleasure that was pain. And listening, she studied every lineament of his face, which for months had been engraved upon her heart. The broad brow from which the dark hair curled, the rather arrogant nose, the strong carved lines of bearded mouth and chin.

A moment later her mother came in with a steaming pot of coffee and a plate of recently baked cookies. Tobias rose to help her and Elizabeth's eyes were gratified by his great height and appearance of supple strength. A tall man, Tobias Condit, and, in this eager youth of his, as lean as a race horse. Elizabeth thought, suddenly, he needs good food, and plenty of it. She wondered briefly how one cooked in China, and again the sense of inadequacy overcame her.

Her mother was as small and dark as Elizabeth herself. She was fifty and looked older. She had the compressed but resigned appearance of the good woman who has lived through much sorrow and who, in accepting it, has not lost the capacity for suffering. She was a widow, these many years; Elizabeth was the only child of a short and happy marriage.

Tobias set the tray down upon the round table. He said, as Mrs. Lewis murmured, with her eyes questioning first one and then the other, that she regretted not having any loaf sugar, "Mrs. Lewis, Elizabeth—subject, of course, to your approval—has done me the very great honor to promise to become my wife."

Mrs. Lewis' hands shook a little. The fine porcelain cups, the worn silver spoons set up their musical clatter. She reminded him, after a moment, bending her graying head under the widow's cap which, although fashions were changing, she would not lay aside, "Elizabeth is very young, Mr. Condit."

Time, he told her in his eager, laughing way, would alter that. He looked at Elizabeth, sitting very still, very erect on the sofa, her small slippered feet crossed, the best dress of tan barege billowing about her, over the crinoline. Mrs. Lewis saw that look and noted as well her daughter's answering regard. It was, she told herself, God's will.

Lizzie came in now, in her spare bustling manner. She was the aunt for whom Elizabeth had been named, and with whom they lived. A brisk and forthright spinster, she took the intelligence of her niece's betrothal without astonishment, but with outspoken misgiving. "I must say, Mr. Condit," she admonished, "I trust you have given this matter long and sober thought. Elizabeth, while a woman in years, is still a child in many ways. She has lived a sheltered life. Is it not a grave undertaking to take her from her home and friends to a savage country, among heathen people?"

He admitted it, frankly, stirring his coffee. His fine young face was rather pale above the severe black broadcloth of his best coat.

But, he assured Miss Lewis, the country was not, after all, savage. It had possessed a culture for thousands of years. And it was because the people of that country were heathen that he—and, he believed, Elizabeth—had been called to work among them and to bring them, in friendship and with unceasing devotion, to the worship of God.

This was an argument which Lizzie, an outstanding member of her church, could not deny. Had she not for some years superintended the packing of the missionary boxes and barrels? Had she not, also, seen from their very first meeting that her niece and the young preacher from New Jersey were attracted toward each other? She, too, told herself that it was God's will, with, however, considerable doubt, not of the clarity and wisdom of the Divine decision, but because of the frailty of human flesh, so much weaker than the spirit.

She allowed, however, with much of her customary briskness, that perhaps, after all, Elizabeth might be made useful in the Lord's work. Had she not taught Sunday School since early girlhood and, for the last two years, common school as well?

During the next hour as her mother, her aunt and her betrothed discussed, practically, and with no show of emotion, the plans which were to change the entire course of her life, to deflect it from its narrow and sheltered bed and send it down the wide, unknown channels, Elizabeth sat, quite still, and was suitably silent. But this talk of ships and passage, of household goods, of household furniture and linen and garments to last, at least, five years, reached her only dimly. She was thinking that nearby sat the man she loved and whom, very shortly, she would marry; with whom she would spend the rest of her days; upon whom, and solely, she must depend for kindliness and warmth, comfort and sustaining strength. And curiously, as this realization came to her, she ceased to be afraid.

Later, just before he left for his lodging at the home of the reverend gentleman with whom he had been staying in order to preach from the Carthage pulpit last Sabbath and at the midweek service, Tobias suggested, as a matter of course, that they unite their hearts in order to ask guidance and to assure the success of this coming voyage, and of their mission. He did not ask that they pray for his happiness and for Elizabeth's. God's soldiers did not pray for personal happiness. And perhaps, too, he felt it unnecessary, looking at Elizabeth, the pure, sweet oval of her face, the bright crimson of the mouth he had kissed, the shining black eyes.

So they knelt and prayed. I am, thought Elizabeth, her head bowed on her clasped hands, a wicked woman. But while she might ask forgiveness, she could not believe her sin so heinous. Surely God would pardon, being her Father, the fact that the content of Tobias' petition meant less to her, kneeling there, than the sound of his voice?

Afterwards she went to the melodeon, and played a hymn. It was the hymn which once she had heard the Swedish Nightingale sing to the thousands of silent people in great Castle Garden. It was . . . "I know that my Redeemer liveth . . ."

They were not alone again that evening. Together with her aunt and her mother she saw Tobias to the door, opening on the swirl of snow, the biting wind. She saw him sheltered in his overcoat, the gray shawl about his throat. His last look was for her, laughing, and yet not wholly merry, pledging her some word which, as yet, she could not interpret but in which she fully trusted.

Later, in her small, cold bedroom, with the lamplight flickering, she laid aside the tan barege and ran her hands gently over the corded silken stuff. She would always love this dress, every button on the pointed bodice, the round collar, the length and breadth of it. It had been an extravagance, she had believed, when she commissioned a relative to buy it for her in Albany. For she had saved the money, knowing that Tobias Condit was coming back to Carthage.

Stepping out of her crinoline, she was tiny, very slight, delicately, exquisitely made. Her shoulders rose round, olive skinned, smooth as satin. For a moment she stood looking into the round, dimmed mirror, seeing herself, flushed, the black eyes wide. Her thoughts were reverent and modest, yet they served to quicken her pulse. She was kneeling, later, in darkness, by her bed, in the white, long-sleeved, high-necked nightgown, when her mother came in, a lamp in her hand.

She set it down on the bureau. She waited. She could not, if her life depended upon it, kneel beside her child. Her own praying would be done—as she must live—alone.

Elizabeth rose from her knees. Her mother advised, without visible tenderness, "Get into bed, Elizabeth, you will take cold."

She was obedient. She had always been docile, if not without spirit. Her mother stood by the bed, and stooped to draw the covers about the girl's slim throat. She asked:

"You are satisfied that you are taking the right course?"

"Yes," said Elizabeth, and, abruptly and completely, was.

Her mother did not ask . . . you are happy? Happiness had little place in her personal scheme of things. She had once been very happy. She was so no longer. The Lord giveth and the Lord taketh away.

She was silent a long moment. Elizabeth inquired, timidly:

"You—you like Mr. Condit, mamma?"

"He is," replied her mother, "an upright young man." She rose and looked down upon her child. Flesh of her flesh. How dearly loved only she and her God might know. She bent and kissed her cheek briefly. She said, "You will be in my prayers, always."

She took her lamp and went, walking very straight, through the connecting door. Elizabeth lay in a cold darkness. She neither felt the cold nor saw the dark. She lay enwrapped in a warmth and radiance which glowed through her mind and body. She loved, she was beloved. The future, however strange, would be companioned.

In her own room Elizabeth's mother set down the lamp. She looked at it idly, the clear yellow flame blossoming within the glass, the reddened wick. She did not see it. She was thinking . . . It is too much to ask.

It was not too much to ask. If this sacrifice were required of her, she would make it. It did not occur to her that there could be any other course.

She had never admitted to herself that she had hoped Elizabeth would not wed, but would stay on in the frame house, set in lawns and trees, in the quiet, lovely town; would stay on until the time came for her dutiful and loving hands to close her mother's unbetraying eyes. Or that, if she chose to marry, her husband would be one of the young men with whom she had grown up, whose families were neighbors, who were like sons about the house. No, she had not dared pray—*Let her not marry, Lord!* It was a woman's duty, her mission, even, to be given to a man in wedlock, to keep his house and bear his children, to share his burdens. Not that her own marriage had not been more than that. Sometimes she thought perhaps because it had, too soon, ended it had been God's way of reproaching her for her mortal happiness. There was that small strain of Latin blood in her veins which had troubled her pulses and coaxed a thoughtless song to her lips. But her other blood was of New England, the blood of men who had come the hard, long way from Vermont and settled here in the foothills of the Adirondacks. The blood of men who had gone to the French and Indian wars, who had plowed their lands, who had knelt in church, and who had bequeathed to her her stoicism, and her conception of a just God to whom souls were of great concern and bodies of no moment; to whom mortal happiness mattered not at all, but righteousness, deeply.

She thought, lying straight and alone in bed, of the farmhouse and the hills and the little brook which had made music all day long, and of the great trees which had whispered to her, on the sunny day when, in agony and silence, she had been delivered, after ten years' barrenness, of a girl child. She thought of her husband's eyes as he had bent over her, and anxiously searched her drawn and sweating face for a smile of reassurance. She had given him that smile and it had cost her almost as much effort as it had to give him a daughter.

That was all over now. Elias Lewis had died when Elizabeth was four, of an accident . . . a nervous horse bolting at the lightning flash . . .

They had brought him back to the farmhouse, the great limbs crushed, the eyes indomitable. He had commanded, clearly, "Do not grieve." He had advised faintly . . . "Teach Elizabeth—"

That sentence was not to be completed. Just at the end he had promised, "I'll be waiting. . . ."

It had not killed her, that lightning flash. It had not killed her because she knew that he would be waiting and that one day she would put her hands in his again. Only to her would the intervening years seem endless and sterile.

She turned her thoughts from the farmhouse and the stained parlor sofa . . . he had been a heavy man, and there had been, moreover, no time to move him that he might die decently in his bed. She turned her thoughts from the stillness and the people who had touched her shoulder and from the memory of her own startling, stricken cry which still rang in her ears. She thought of Elizabeth, sleeping next door, whose slender feet were already set on the long road, across the world.

It was, Mary Lewis told herself, a suitable match. Tobias Condit's background left little to be desired. He was New Jersey born and bred, as his forebears for generations had been. His parents had died within a year of each other, when he was very young. Like Elizabeth, he had been an only child. He had lived with an uncle, a prosperous merchant from whom, quite recently, he had inherited a comfortable sum, in trust for himself and his issue. He had studied in the Newark Wesleyan Institute, and had preached his first sermon during his studies. Later, he had graduated from the Biblical Institute in Concord, New Hampshire, and had had a year of circuit preaching. His first appearance in Carthage had been through the invitation of the son of Mrs. Lewis's pastor, a classmate at Concord of young Condit's. He had returned, for a visit, during the past summer. Between then and his present appearance he had felt the clear call of the Spirit urging him to go to China, a call of which his bishop had approved.

It had not all been an open way for him. Men were fighting on bloody battlefields. His own countrymen waging a bitter war, brother against brother. He had been troubled, and he had told her so, during the summer. He was young, strong, vital. It was not fitting, because of his calling, that he should bear arms. But there must be work for him to do, comfort brought to the dying, strong hands to lift the sick and wipe the death sweat from their foreheads, prayers to be said to help the soul, so terribly and suddenly reft from the broken body, on its true course, to its ultimate destination.

This he had had to face. Mary Lewis, talking to him one day in her own lovely garden, had said so. No one could help him, not herself, to whom, believing in her wisdom, he had come, not his friends, not even his revered bishop. It lay between himself and his God. And before he could decide word had come that the mission ranks in Fuhchau had been thinned by a death and he must be ready to sail in June. The issue seemed clear.

He would marry Elizabeth; they would go out to China, and she, Elizabeth's mother, would be alone and would suffer. But she would be silent. It was like giving birth, all over again, the tearing and the pain and the lips bitten to keep back the shriek. But there would be no end to this delivery, she thought, and turned her head on the great, soft pillow and wept, in bitterness and in silence.

Tobias Condit and Elizabeth Lewis were married, on Thursday, May 1, within the quiet walls of the church in which Elizabeth had been baptized and which she had attended from earliest remembrance. If she wept when the time for parting came, it was to be expected, and if others, who had long known and loved her, also wept, that, too, was as it should be. However, her aunt Lizzie reminded her, brokenly but undaunted, it was not as if this were to be the final farewell, as she and Elizabeth's mother would make the trip to New York to see them sail, and to wish them Godspeed.

Mary Lewis said very little. There was, after all, nothing to be said. Presently she would be with her sister-in-law in the frame house and stubborn life would go on, as it always does, no matter if the heart writes Finis.

On their leisurely way to New York Tobias and Elizabeth stopped in Albany to visit members of the Lewis connection. There they were well and soberly entertained, and there, too, Elizabeth sat in a bigger church than the one in Carthage and listened to her husband speak from its pulpit. He had a warm, friendly way of speaking, a little informal to conventional ears, but he made friends. The Lewis connection approved of him and said so, congratulating Elizabeth on her choice.

She listened, grave and composed, and made her stately replies. But her cousins could not know how the heart within her danced in her breast at the mention of his name. No one knew save herself, the scarcely sounded depths of his tenderness, his gentleness and his forbearance. She had come to him in ignorance and unconfided terror and he had brought her the beautiful marriage gifts of pity and comprehension, and a young passion burning in purity.

Their way to New York City lay by water and it was fitting that this should be so, that this stage of their journey should lead them, by water, to the sea on which, presently, they must embark. The white steamer with her great side wheels and her gay flags flying, red and blue in the May sun, her comfortable stateroom, her gilded, ornamented saloons, pleased Elizabeth. This boat, her husband assured her, was the Queen of the Hudson, the *Mary B. Powell,* the finest of the fleet and one of the newest. He was intensely interested in her every aspect and led Elizabeth from one place to another so rapidly that she could hardly keep up with his long, much less hampered strides, exploring deck and accommodations and even engine room. But by now she had come to know something of his interest in everything, in places and people and things.

She had little time to marvel at New York, its growth and alteration since her dazzled child's eyes had first seen it twelve years before—even Castle Garden, firmly entrenched in her memory, had ceased to be a place which housed great music and fairs and amusements, and had become a receiving station for the increasing tide of immigration. But she had scant space in which to exclaim, for they went, almost directly, to New Jersey to pay their duty visits to various of Tobias's friends and relatives.

They returned to New York ten days before they sailed, as stipulated by Tobias's instructions. As a rule the Board found suitable lodgings for its departing missionaries but Tobias and Elizabeth were housed, very pleasantly, far uptown, on Murray Hill, with two spinster cousins of his mother, who maintained an exclusive boarding establishment. These ladies, Abigail and Permelia Smith, took Elizabeth to their hearts and arms. She was, they thought privately and afterwards informed Tobias, far too delicate and young to make this great sacrifice of home and people in order to follow her husband across the world. They did not tell her this, being gentle women, and fearing to dismay her. They simply set about to make her feel at home in the best front bedroom reserved for temporary honored guests, occupied themselves in taking her about the city, whichever one of them could be spared from the household duties, while Tobias was busy with conferences in Mulberry Street, in superintending the packing of the household things, in procuring passports and receiving final instructions.

Under Abbie's, or Permelia's, guidance Elizabeth was taken to call on family friends downtown, especially upon a Mrs. Martin, who lived in an elegance far beyond any Elizabeth had ever encountered in the "Oriental," in Colonnade Row, La Grange Terrace. Through the amiable offices of this lady Elizabeth went driving in Central Park, at an hour during which the finest horses and carriages were to be seen with their drivers in dress livery and glimpses of their owners, certain and exciting. For the Misses Smith, as well as Mrs. Martin, had all the great names at their fingertips, and by craning her neck Elizabeth could see this lady or that . . . magnificently dressed, a little bored, driving through the sweet spring sunlight. There was So-and-so, Elizabeth was told, she had been at the ball for the Prince of Wales . . . Mrs. Martin had also attended this ball, and her description of it was spirited in the extreme . . . the ravishing gowns, the uniforms, the flowers, and the jewels; and how one was permitted, alas, only twenty minutes in which to partake of a sumptuous supper, because only in that way might the vast assemblage find space to sup with His Highness!

Elizabeth listened, enthralled. She did not, of course, dance. She had never attended a ball, and never would. And she wondered if she were not perhaps too worldly to be a missionary's wife because her heart lifted as if to music, listening to Mrs. Martin's entrancing stories, and, yes, her downright gossip.

Later she unburdened herself to Tobias and confided in him that she feared herself much too superficial to fulfill the mission laid upon her, but taking heart, thereafter, at his great shout of laughter, she fell asleep in the huge carved bedstead to dream of music and fair women, uniformed escorts and torchlight processions.

Other novelties awaited her; the sight of the great hotels, the Metropolitan and the St. Nicholas and the Fifth Avenue; the glimpses of the mansions downtown, such as the De Rahm house, for instance, on quiet Fifth Avenue, and the country houses out of the city, as far even as Jones' Woods. Broadway was particularly gay and delightful, with its green trees and bright awnings, its traffic of carts, of carriages, stages and buses, its shops and people. But here a note of warning was struck . . . in the recruiting stations.

During this time, Elizabeth experienced the novelty of reading her first metropolitan newspaper. To be sure it was the New York *Herald,* a publication of which her mother—and others—would not have approved. But the Misses Smith, who prided themselves upon being modern, assured her that Mr. Bennett's once rather despised sheet was now to be found in all the best houses. And the paper, to Elizabeth, was the harbinger from a new, unknown world, for in it she saw the close-columned advertisements of amusements, of Niblo's Garden, of the Academy of Music, which was presenting Italian opera on the Castle Garden plan, and of Barnum's huge Baby Show. Reading, she puzzled a little over the statement, "the most beautiful children are reserved." For whom? she wondered. Or did it, she asked Tobias laughing, refer to their dispositions?

It could not and must not concern a minister's wife that Maggie Mitchell was playing in *Fanchon the Cricket* at Laura Keen's theater or that on June 14 at the New Bowery, Adah-Isaacs Menken would appear in *Joan of Arc* and *The French Spy.* Nor should the advertisements of frocks and bonnets hold her attention for a moment, yet they did. Here were materials of which she had never heard, "illuminated poplin," for instance, while Lord & Taylor's advertised in their three stores the sale of mozambiques and alpacas.

Well, her own traveling dress was of alpaca and had been made by the best dressmaker at home, from a style shown in *Frank Leslie's Weekly,* which, if sedate, was at least sedately in the mode.

Tobias, finding her poring over various items, teased her a little, and she submitted to this, not in the least affronted. "But do you," she asked him gravely, "really believe there are women who would pay eight dollars for silk scarfs and mantillas?"

Tobias replied as gravely, that probably there were. He said, drawing her up and into his arms from the deep tufted chair in which she sat, that all the mantillas in the world, at eight, yes, and at eighty dollars, could not make her more beautiful in his sight.

She was both entertained and shocked by the matrimonial advertisements, one of which ran, "The advertiser, a pug-nosed individual with orange-colored hair and lemon-tinted beard will receive and consider prepaid proposals for matrimony addressed to Nobody's Nephew, Williamsburg Post Office, New York. Preference given proposals accompanied by carte de viste," and she was sincerely sorry for the poor man who advertised that, on the 6th of June, there had strayed from his home in Fortieth Street, between Ninth and Tenth Avenues, "A low-sized red cow having two white spots on her side." It was absurd, yet long weeks later she thought of John Hawkins of Fortieth Street, and wondered if his cow had been returned to him.

The guests of the Smith establishment were for the most part elderly people, retired business men and their wives, schoolteachers and some, very few, young students. They were most amiable and before the week had ended she felt that she had made some friends. Toward the end of their stay, the Misses Smith held an At Home "to meet the Reverend Tobias and Mrs. Condit." The best silver was on view in the long double parlors, with their cut velvet draperies and fine solid furniture—among which were two graceful mauve upholstered settees which had been made by Duncan Phyfe—and their walls crowded with paintings, and their ornaments of shell and waxen flowers under bells of glass, and big stuffed hassocks.

It was the most beautiful room Elizabeth had ever seen, the great gas chandeliers flooded it with light, and there was plentiful tea served in the finest porcelain cups, and cakes and cream and a hundred delicacies. Mrs. Martin, sitting very straight, and sipping her aromatic beverage, commented on its fragrance. "You, my dear," she told Elizabeth, "will soon be taking China tea as a matter of course."

It didn't, somehow, seem possible.

The talk was light and dignified, and ranged from the recent publication of Mrs. Southworth's new book *Love's Labor Won*— a topic of conversation in which Elizabeth, owing to her lack of acquaintance with novels, could not join—to the record voyages of clipper ships in the old days. For was it not well known that since the depression of the year 1857 few great ships had been built? And in that year only ten had been launched, of which the ship on which the Condits had passage was one. Steam was rapidly coming to the fore, and there was talk of a great transcontinental railroad, although that, most of those present believed, was a wild and not to be realized dream.

Elizabeth was flooded with advice on every topic, from wearing apparel to remedies for seasickness. Mrs. Martin, whose late husband had been a clipper captain on the California run in the tremendous forties and who had herself accompanied him more than once on that desperate and dreadful voyage around the Horn, was both practical and discouraging. "You'll have," she submitted, "enough water to last you the rest of your natural life."

Elizabeth was not alarmed. It was a curious thing but as soon as people, well-meaning enough, began to warn her, she was not in the least afraid. She smiled at Mrs. Martin, sitting there in her afternoon best, the heavy bracelets and necklace of intricate mosaic about arms and throat. She said, still smiling:

"Mr. Condit has seen our ship. He says she is beautiful, has most superior accommodations and a very admirable captain."

"His name?" inquired Mrs. Martin.

"I believe, Captain Bennett."

However, Mrs. Martin did not know Captain Bennett and her headshake said plainly that, not knowing, she could not answer for either the ship or her master.

Two days before they sailed they were joined on Murray Hill by Mrs. Lewis and Aunt Lizzie who, also coming via Albany, had traveled down on the *Daniel Drew*. To Elizabeth there was something strange in seeing them again, so far from their natural setting. It was as if the real good-bys had been said, back in Carthage, and as if, in a way she could not understand, there was a gap between her and them, a widening gap, not yet of water. Yet she had never loved them as much.

On Monday, June 16, the clipper *Hotspur* sailed for Hong Kong, taking the Eastern passage. South Street was alive with color and noise, with the odors of tar and spice, with people hurrying and with shouts of workmen. The great bowsprits were like the branches of a forest, reaching across the street, almost to the windows of the ship chandlers and warehouses. The *Hotspur* had been built, and beautifully, by Roosevelt and Joyce of Houston Street. Her lines were lovely and slender, her bow sharp for cutting through the water. Her brasswork shone in the June sunlight, and she was, thought Elizabeth, clinging to Tobias' arm, like a great black swan, with snowy pinions.

Around her hull was a bright stripe, and she flew the burgee of her owners, Francis and Thomas Hathaway, with its great white H upon a deep blue ground.

There were many to see them off, members of the Mission Board, a kindly bishop and friends of Tobias', some of whom had come from New Jersey. There were the Misses Smith, smiling and weeping, there was Mrs. Martin, her eyes remote and wistful, there was Aunt Lizzie, moved to rare tears, and Mary Lewis with hot, dry eyes. There were the last embraces . . . China was so far away . . . missionaries' wives had died, ere this there were little distant churchyards filled with their sacrificial dust and that of their children . . . there were disease and famine in China, there were rebels and bandits, there was annihilation perhaps by torture, perhaps by a swift and more merciful fever . . .

So far away . . . some went and never returned.

Those who had come to say good-by thought these things; and Elizabeth thought them too, but briefly. For was not Tobias' arm around her, before them all, strongly, sustainingly?

Good-by—Good-by—God bless you—

They were singing on the piers, they were singing "Abide with Me." The voices came clear, a little unsteady, over the widening water. And the bright tears poured down Elizabeth's cheeks, but she was singing too.

It had been high tide at Governors Island at 11:43. At 2 P.M., the flood tide would be slack, turning toward the ebb. There was a strong northwest wind. The *Hotspur* would get under way, she would drop down to Battery Park and take on her crew and their dunnage and she would spread her great wings, yard on yard of spotless canvas, and put out to sea.

At Battery Park crowds of people were watching, listening to the chanteys, calling out and cheering. There were the green trees and the old houses and beyond the lift, to heaven, of Trinity's slender spires.

Her canvas filled, a shudder ran through the ship as if she braced herself for whatever awaited her beyond the Hook, her ensign dipped, and she was running down the harbor, a beautiful ship which had, in her short life, shown some of the larger, more notable clippers a splendid record, and with the sunlight hot and golden on the blue waters of the harbor she was off to meet the chance of her voyage.

At the Hook something over an hour later, the observer, Jim Fayton, watched her pass, bird swift, arrogant with beauty, crowding her canvas, the white water curling against her sides. And so, in the line of his duty, reported her passing.

Elizabeth, standing on the white deck beside Tobias, felt under the soles of her small stout boots the life and pulse of the ship. It was awe-inspiring yet somehow not frightening to know that all that stood between them and eternity was this solid, yet fragile structure of wood; that trees had been torn and hewn, screaming and rebellious, from their strong thrusting roots in earth to build this ship, which now ran before the wind, hull down on the horizon, and met with thrust and heave, with fortitude and faith, the onslaught of the Atlantic Ocean; this ship whose restricted confines must be their home for months to come.

She said something of the sort to Tobias, drawing close to him, feeling his strength as a cloak about her, shielding her from wind and leagues of water, from terror and adversity. And he told her with his hand in her own, gravely, "Wherever you are, that is home to me."

Later, beyond the Hook, she went to unpack in the small shining cabin which would house them during this voyage, and still later to make more than casual friends with the other missionary family aboard, a Mr. and Mrs. Henderson, who were returning to China after their first furlough. Elizabeth had met them before, she had heard Jonathan Henderson speak on his work in Fukien province. And she had been drawn to him and to his competent, pleasant wife. She would grow to know them very well indeed before the voyage was over, and, in a lesser degree, the other passengers. There were not many of these and they were for the most part business men, with connections in China.

In their room the chairs, which had been presented to them by friends in New York, were new and comfortable, a reminder of people whom Elizabeth scarcely knew yet whom, in some measure, it had been a wrench to leave.

With the moon nearing her third quarter and favorable winds, the *Hotspur* went fleetly about accomplishing her first day's run. And in the darkness of that first night Elizabeth Condit lay close in her husband's arms, and listened to quiet words of comfort and high-hearted words of hope. For with night's coming, homesickness had taken her by the throat and shaken her with sobs and she realized perhaps for the first time, now that the excitement of departure was past, all she was leaving. She was a little girl again, wanting to run to her mother, wanting to hide her eyes against her mother's arm.

Now it was Tobias' arm against which she hid them, drenching his sleeve with tears. Presently, as her sobs shuddered into silence and her swollen lids closed and she slept, exhausted, he lay there, very still in order not to disturb her, and watched the dim, gray patch which was the porthole and felt each separate effort of the ship along his nerves. He prayed, his arm cramped and his eyes heavy with weariness, for guidance not alone in the new life of labor which lay before him, but in the care of this unique human being entrusted to him. Although he was not much older than his wife, as years are counted, he felt toward her not only a love both rapturous and grave, but a deep responsibility.

Down and across the Atlantic Ocean ran the ship *Hotspur*, driven by the favoring winds which filled her canvas, foam at her heels, a bone in her teeth, the dancing waters chuckling blue and sun-gilded beneath her. Elizabeth, to her infinite distress, proved in the beginning a poor sailor. She had awakened from that first strange sleep to the forlorn misery of those who go down to the sea in ships. Tobias had been patient with her, and tender, nursing her as skillfully as a woman, his big hands gentle. But for days she lay supine, too ill to dress and far too ill to receive with any show of enthusiasm the meals sent in to her and brought to her bunk by a solicitous, very black steward. She lay and thought of her home and of the waste of water she must traverse before once more she might speak of home, and of her trepidation and her anxiety lest she not prove worthy of the task her God and her love had laid upon her. Once Tobias found her kneeling, in her straight white nightgown, her arms outflung and her black hair, released from its smooth, parted bands, falling over her shoulders. She was trying, she explained, gasping, to pray. Tobias lifted her and laid her softly down and drew a blanket over her and sat beside her, her hand in his, talking of all they would accomplish. That they would accomplish much he had no doubt. Had he not faith, and great strength of body and a compelling purpose? . . . and had he not her beside him, not only to this journey's end, but to the end of that longer journey?

Perhaps it was this buoyant belief which served to help her. In a few days she was able to be on deck, very pale and with her limbs not accustomed to the sway and quiver of the scrubbed white wood beneath her feet, but glad, weakly, of the sun's shining and the wind's free blowing.

And so little by little she found her sea legs, and long before they had reached the calms of Cancer, she was a seasoned sailor.

Tobias was restless, active, imperative. The *Hotspur* was too small to hold him, he could have taken the seas in his stride with the seven league boots of his burning impatience. He swarmed halfway up the mainmast, sitting astride the yardarm to watch the sunrise, to shout a greeting to the dawn, from a full throat and heart. He was popular with the passengers and with the crew. With Mr. Henderson, he held services in the cabin every evening and they were, he wrote back to the Corresponding Secretary, "very well attended." And when Elizabeth was up and about and able to share the cabin meals he dominated the talk, firing questions at Mr. Henderson and at Captain Bennett, learning all he could; learning even a few first phrases of Chinese from Henderson and poring over the books with which he had been able to supply himself.

The table talk was varied and sometimes breath-taking. There was mention of the pirates in the South China Sea, an ever-present menace. Elizabeth, listening and shuddering with visions of brown, naked bodies swarming over the decks with bright-edged menace held in sinewy brown hands, was somewhat comforted by the Hendersons' matter-of-fact attitude. On their first trip out they had actually lived through such an attack. But the *Hotspur,* as were all the clipper ships, was armed . . . with muzzle-loading Enfield rifles and smooth-bore muskets, with broadswords and cutlasses, and ample powder, while the captain and mate possessed Colt revolvers.

Ella Henderson and Elizabeth Condit became good friends before a quarter of the voyage had passed. Mrs. Henderson, a quiet woman with deep brown eyes, was cheerful and practical. Yet behind her cheerfulness there was a still place dedicated to grief. She had taken her two children home and left them with her people, in Ohio, for their education, and now she was sailing back again to take up her work where she had left it, while her heart was oppressed with the most poignant of all longing and the most pitiless of all fear. More than once Elizabeth had found her weeping soundlessly, and something in the still quality of that sorrow frightened her. She had not thought . . . nor realized . . . that this, too, might be required of her, on some unknown, never-to-be-forgotten day.

Children, of course, she would have. Marriage was ordained for their procreation. This she knew. She would bear strong straight boys to Tobias Condit, and small, enchanting girl children. Yet somehow she had never thought deeply about it, had never visualized fully that these would be born in a far and certainly dangerous land and that one day she would be called upon to relinquish them, to banish herself, to remain in exile without them, for perhaps many years.

There was none to whom she might bring her new awareness and her instant terror, unless it be Tobias, and least of all to him, for tradition sealed her lips, even when in the month of August she became aware that she would have a child.

Seasickness had passed but that other illness seized her by the throat and shook her, leaving her faint and alone. She longed, with a longing she thought must surely kill her, lying awake in the darkness, listening to the thousand and one small sounds of the ship, for her mother, her cool, swift hands, her utterances, which if they lacked tenderness and softness bespoke something dependable, stable, a shelter and a refuge. She longed, too, for the feeling of green summer earth beneath her feet and the solidity of the frame house from which one might look at the foothills. And sometimes she prayed and sometimes she wept, yet she was not rebellious, she was merely frightened.

As time went on and she became more certain, she still said nothing. She did not know how to go about saying it. She would not, could she have spoken, add the taint of terror or the heaviness of concern to Tobias' glowing happiness. For he was happy. He was informed with health, with the compulsion to arms, the urge to battle. He was brown with salt and sun and easily moved to laughter. He was like the wind itself, like a great breath of keen cool wind, blowing through her heart. She could not, would not distress him. This burden was hers, to bear in silence, until the time came when she must speak. Yet, regarding him, she wondered that, thoughtful of her as he was, he had not guessed. Sometimes lying close in his arms while he slept, she seemed to draw courage from that immense vitality which even in sleep did not slacken. A vitality which drew the other passengers, men and women alike. Now and then Elizabeth saw Mr. Henderson, a little gray and drawn and very thin from past fevers, looking at her husband with a certain wonder, a queer, brotherly pride and something which was, perhaps, compassion.

And so the days passed.

Tobias was keeping a letter-journal which would be sent back to the people at home, and passed about among the friends and relatives. On the twenty-fourth day of September—two days after, had he known it, the President's first proclamation to free the slaves was issued—he wrote:

"So far, a splendid voyage. Captain Bennett has been very kind and attentive to all our wants. We have maintained family prayer in the cabin every evening which has been attended by passengers and officers. We have had public service on the Sabbath and I have thus been permitted to preach ten times to such of the sailors as chose to attend. One old sailor has been sick for some time and is now evidently near his end. I have frequently conversed with him, read to him from the Scriptures and sung some of our familiar tunes in his hearing. He is a Roman Catholic and wishes to die in his faith, yet takes my services kindly. Yesterday after I had read to him the Twenty-third Psalm and the fifteenth chapter of First Corinthians, he expressed his gratitude and said, 'These are good words and comforting.'

"I have been blessed with good health and Elizabeth, although not an accomplished sailor, is holding her own bravely. She is a great favorite with passengers and officers and crew alike, as well she may be. Affable, engaging and refined in her manner toward all, gracious without ostentation in her air, and commanding without pride; in her deportment perpendicular, and in her friendships devout and sincere, beautiful in body and in soul, I do not let a day pass without thanking my Heavenly

Father for the companion and helpmeet it has pleased Him in His infinite love and wisdom to bestow upon me. But enough of this, or my pen would run on all day.

"We have enjoyed, you will be glad to hear, more comfort than most people ashore would imagine to be possible at sea. Some of you in whose minds sea life is always associated with salt beef and hard biscuit would be surprised to see us faring sumptuously on fresh pork, string beans, tomatoes, cranberry sauce, lima beans, etc., with cucumber pickles for a relish, and apple or peach pie for dessert. Let no one imagine that missionaries going to China in an American clipper are in any danger of arriving at their field in a starving condition. We have a constant reminder of the pastors of the Central and Twenty-seventh Street Churches in the elegant and comfortable ship chairs which their kindness placed in our room. May they live to breathe into many congregations the missionary spirit which fills their hearts.

"For the rest, Brother and Sister Henderson have been most kind and friendly. I am making a little headway with my few common Chinese phrases in the Fuhchau dialect, under the guidance of the former, and his wife spends many hours with Elizabeth, preparing her for the conditions she must meet and with which she must cope. Together we have seen many wonders of the deep; waterspouts, flying fish, porpoises, whales, the glory of tropical sunsets, gales and calms, have in their turn been the subjects of our observation. But of all these so much has been said and so well said that I shall make no attempt at a description. Twenty days ago our thermometer was below freezing point. To-night it stands at 83 degrees, so rapidly do we change our climate. We crossed the Tropic of Cancer July 10, the Equator July 23, the Tropic of Capricorn August 10; passed the Cape of Good Hope August 31, seventy-six days out; crossed the Tropic of Capricorn the second time September 19 and hope to cross the Equator again within a week. We are now just halfway round the world from you; and when the sun's last rays were departing from us to-night, they were shining on you as the first beams of a new morning. We are twelve hours ahead of you and you can't catch up with us except by coming this way. We hope to hear good news from the Union Army to-morrow. We have kept the flame of patriotism alive by singing 'Hail, Columbia!' and 'The Star-Spangled Banner' and 'America.' We hope to hear soon that McClellan is in Richmond and that the rebellion has given up the ghost. God save our native land is a most earnest petition. And now I must close for this day's writing. We look forward to our work with the grave hope of usefulness in the vineyard of the Lord and expect confidently the prayers of God's chosen people in our behalf. The Lord willing, you will soon hear from us at Hong Kong."

But long before Hong Kong had been reached much had happened.

Tobias' recountal had been sober indeed, thought Elizabeth, to whom he gave the journal to read before they spoke the shore at Anjer and sent letters ashore to find their long way home on a returning ship. There had been days of no wind, days when the ship rolled hopelessly becalmed on the glassy, golden surface of the water. There had been wild rains and sudden storms and tremendous heat, when it was an effort to lift a hand to arrange one's heavy hair, when it was a burden to breathe. There had been nights of such miraculous beauty that standing on deck with Tobias' arm about her shoulders she had felt helpless yet exalted, small as an atom in the face of Eternity and yet strong as a giant to do the bidding of the Creator of this blazing beauty.

In the Indian Ocean the monsoons were favorable, the winds were generally southwest to northeast but here occurred the heavy rainfalls in which the great slanting sheets of rain all but hid the water from their view and between storms there was an oppressive heat, as tangible as a clutching hand.

Elizabeth was better, however. After the first weeks had passed she had felt quite well again. But Mrs. Henderson had guessed; had drawn her aside with motherly questioning and Elizabeth had put her dark head against the frail slim shoulder of the other woman and had told her all that in her young ignorance she knew. And thus Tobias had learned, not from Elizabeth but from Henderson, who had told him gravely, the older woman's messenger. In so roundabout a way did Tobias Condit learn that when the lovely spring should come to China and the rice fields should be green as jade, when the time for picking tea was upon the hills of Fukien, his first child would be born.

He was inordinately happy. He took his wife in his great arms, chided her lovingly for not telling him, but perfectly understanding her reticence and promising her such care, such consideration. She said, a little unhappily, "But it is so soon, Tobias . . . I shall be of poor assistance to you, I am afraid."

That was, he assured her, nonsense. Just by being with him, close to his side, she was of invaluable help. She could occupy the long hours in which she would be convalescent in learning the language, the ways of the people to whom they were coming to bring the word of God, not as a keen, bloody sword, but as the loving gift of a friend.

And so he comforted and reassured her.

In the Indian Ocean the old sailor died. There was none aboard of his faith to read the service of his church. There was no priest to administer the last rites. But he died with his hand in Tobias Condit's and a look of peace upon his sharpened and sunken features. And was committed to the deep, with words of hope read over him, as the long stark canvas bundle was entrusted to the clean mercy of the waves. And Elizabeth Condit wept because a man must die so far from his home and from those who loved him. Not that Death seemed so great a matter to her, having lived always in the hope of a life so conducted that death would only mark the opening of a door into a more lovely country. Yet, since her marriage, during this voyage, since the knowledge that within her another life was slowly blossoming, her perceptions had sharpened and Death seemed less kind to her than heretofore. Not that she dreaded dying . . . for herself. But there was Tobias, whom she so loved, and so the last departure needs must take on a more personal aspect. . . .

In the China Sea, however, the winds were not favorable. They beat their way up, with caution and courage. The winds were northeast to southwest, driving directly into the keen slender bow of the ship, and the passage was one of difficulty and danger.

Difficulty for the men who manned the ship, danger for the ship herself, danger for the passengers.

They had warning of the typhoon. The barometer fell steadily, the wind was squally and the sky above the horizon a leaden gray. The Hendersons, who had experienced more than one typhoon ashore and at sea, looked anxiously at each other, and Mr. Henderson spoke to Tobias with as much cheerfulness as he could muster. "We're in for a blow," he warned, "by the look of things. Look to your good wife. You know, the first experience is always the worst," he added, and managed a smile.

Captain Bennett's orders were quick and terse, the ship was snugged down, the hatches battened down, fore storm stay sail set and stunsail booms got in off the yards. Topgallant masts were sent down on deck, sail much shortened, and all the usual precautions taken.

The middle watch was the worst, with the ship shuddering and groaning under the wind's driving weight. There was lightning tearing the horizon, rain of such force and quantity that it seemed the heavens themselves had been ripped apart, and, all through the noise and confusion, the desperate wallowing of the ship.

Sleep was impossible. There was the long night, and the still perilous morning. Fully dressed, her hand in Tobias', Elizabeth huddled close to him in the common cabin. The other passengers received the typhoon according to their divers characters. There were men who cursed and men who prayed, and men who asked Henderson and Tobias to pray for them.

Mrs. Henderson was very white but she made no sound of terror. In a flash of pure instinct Elizabeth knew with whom her thoughts were housed. Not here, not at sea, with the lurching ship and the screaming wind, but somewhere, across the world, in a tidy Ohio village.

Tobias had prayed. He had led in song, his raised, straining voice defeated by the crash and the clamor. And then, suddenly, because it was a time when all able-bodied men must do as they could, he had gone against all orders, fighting his way out on deck somehow, ready to lend a hand, to help where he could.

Elizabeth, very silent, waited . . . and the hands clasped in her lap were ice-cold and drenched with sweat.

Morning came. Leaden. The sudden calm of that morning was strange. The noise had ceased; yet silence was louder than noise. But it was only the interim. The typhoon rested, gathering its malicious forces.

Chips was busy, repairing, hammering, fastening. There were torn sails and broken rigging. And the "Doctor," staggering in the galley, managed somehow to make coffee. . . .

Then, the typhoon struck again.

As it did so Elizabeth was on her feet. There was in her be-numbed brain some idea of finding Tobias. If she must die, he must be with her. *Not alone, God,* she said in her voiceless anguish.

The ship gave a deep, sickening lurch to leeward. Elizabeth fell, from her full height, heavily, striking her head and wrench-ing her limbs. She lay unconscious.

They carried her to her room, and did what they could for her. There was no medical man aboard. The captain served as physi-cian and crude surgeon but he could not be spared. It was Ella Henderson who worked over her, with such remedies as she al-ways carried.

The cut on Elizabeth's forehead was not deep, it would not leave a scar. But she knew, waking at intervals during that next day, waking to a calmer sea and a brave ship which had outridden the storm, that she had lost her child.

On the twenty-fourth day of October, the *Hotspur* let go her anchor off Hong Kong—Fair Harbour, at the mouth of the Pearl River.

Elizabeth Condit, with the clear, dazzled eyes of one still weak from illness, looked her wondering first upon the shores of China. She had remained below decks during the up-coast trip after the typhoon, when the *Hotspur,* very little damaged, had steered steadily, yet with winds for the most part adverse, toward their destination. She had not been on deck when the first exultant cry of "Land Ho!" sounded, she had not seen the rigging alive with figures, nor had she been beside Tobias when the dim blue distant peaks had told him that the conclusion of their voyage was literally in sight. But he had come to their room shortly after, and lifting her in his arms, had spoken to her with exultation of their journey's end.

She had been very ill; shock and pain, seasickness and a growing terror as her body weakened had all contributed to a mental condition in which for some days she lay lax and quiet, scarcely speaking, moving her hands restlessly on the sheets. Ella Henderson was kind and Tobias, sitting beside her through the hours in which it seemed to her that sleep was a sort of fevered waking and waking a sort of troubled sleep, was a rock of quiet strength. The lanternlight flickered on the walls, and the ship spoke and the wind whispered in her canvas. There was a checkered darkness and a mindless peace. If she woke fully there would be pain and a strange, forlorn sorrow. She thought dimly of women who had lost children . . . small, quick-moving babies, children who staggered as they walked, and grown children with the eyes of perfect confidence. She did not see how they could endure such loss. She writhed, with Tobias' big hand touching her forehead, smoothing back the heavy plaited hair, and something within her spirit groaned and would not be comforted. For she, too, had lost a child, almost as soon as the knowledge had come to her that she had been chosen to bear one. A child that had possessed no breath of life, nor as yet within her mind and body a definite shape. Yet of whose loss one might easily bleed to death, in body and in spirit.

She said as much to Tobias, breaking a long silence, whispering in the little room so vibrant with the speaking voices of the ship, so vocal of the sea. And he comforted her as best he could.

There would be other children, he told her, strong and understanding, and beloved. Meantime she must rest, must wrench her mind from melancholy. It had been God's will: the confusion of wind, the blackness of sea, the rain which fell and the lightning which darted; these elemental things and the accident which had befallen her.

He felt very much her senior and terribly inept. Even his words, in which he believed, fell with hollowness upon his own ears. So little she looked, and lost, the great, dry, dark eyes, the plaits of blackest hair, the pale beseeching mouth. He put his hand over her eyes suddenly and covered them. He could not endure the look in them. Then as swiftly he drew it away, his gesture having wounded him with another thought, an image too dreadful to contemplate. In such wise did one close the eyes of the dead.

Now, of her own accord she closed them and slept. Big and bearded, his brown face somber, he sat, a little stooped, beside her and clasped his hands between his knees and looked dumbly into the flickering shadows. Thus far he had brought her to grief only. But, he told himself, there would be happiness too. There must be. Not the unthinking happiness of youth but the stern, austere happiness of work well accomplished, and love tested and proven.

Perhaps she felt something of this, perhaps a message reached her; surely she smiled as she slept? Or no, was it merely a trick of the shadows playing from the lamp as it swayed?

The ship was safe, the course ahead comparatively so, the sails set and the harbor not so many sea leagues away; Captain Bennett was once more able to concern himself with his passengers. Mrs. Henderson had been competent and swift with the few remedies with which she was equipped. There were others in the medicine locker. The captains of sailing ships must needs provide themselves against any emergency. More than one woman passenger had been delivered of a living child in a sailing ship and by the miraculously sure hands of seamen.

So, little by little, Elizabeth recovered. She was young and she was strong and all her twenty years had known little save good health. But while her body prospered, her mind was, for a little, sick . . . homesick, sick of sorrow, sick of an unconfessed fear.

This, too, passed. With returning strength, sanity returned. She had made her bed. She would lie in it. And seeking a little timidly the eyes of the man she had married, she knew, with a surety beyond words, that if that bed were to be fashioned of thorns, she would still choose to lacerate her delicate limbs upon it.

This was marriage, this sharing. No matter what one shared. These days and nights when she lay quite still beneath the coarse sheets, and was too weary to lift her hand to brow or lips; these days and nights in which, as in fever, things became distorted, familiar furniture, familiar faces growing enormous and terrifying, and then receding until one could no longer find them; these days and nights in which Tobias watched beside her and did the homely, necessary things for her easement and comfort, had married them . . . again . . . and forever.

And so it was with laughter, astonished laughter on lips which once more curved red, and wonder in her eyes that she looked upon the Middle Kingdom.

Here were the hills and the island, the granite hills and the mountain-guarded island, the place called Hong Kong. Here were the many ships lying at anchor, sailing ships, and the craft of the East, ferries, houseboats, junks, lorchas . . . sails like the bronze of a bird's wing, glinting in the sunlight. And at the foot of the sharp hills the houses, sheltering against the slopes, the warehouses, the dwellings.

Between the two islands, ferrymen steered and shouted. And Elizabeth's first impression of China was one of noise, an incessant weaving to and fro . . .

She had expected the Chinese people to look—stranger, more unusual. She had never in all her life seen a Chinese. She murmured and clung to Tobias' arm ". . . but . . . I could never tell one from another!"

She could see them closely, in the little boats which racketed around . . . broad, flattened faces, with the tilted opaque eyes. All alike, she thought, looking with eagerness and a little unconfessed dread.

"No," denied Jonathan Henderson, joining them and overhearing. "No, not alike. You'll learn soon."

She thought she would never learn. She was sharply disappointed. She had thought to see a tropical land of trees and sunlight and hot skies and people with yellow faces, dressed in silks and wearing curious jewels and carrying the fans without which one never imagined them. She had thought to find an even stranger architecture, something out of a dream, something keenly alien. And so she was disappointed.

Henderson was pointing out the various landmarks. Victoria Peak, towering up into the autumnal sky, almost two thousand feet in height. He was telling them that here was the mouth of the Chu-Kiang—the Pearl River . . . and that they were now ninety-one miles southeast of Canton; Canton, the very name of which must carry all the romance and the heavy spicy odor of the earlier trading days . . . and the allied name of Peter Parker, who "opened the gates of China with a lancet."

Ella Henderson stood beside them now. She said softly to Elizabeth, while Tobias gesticulated and questioned and demanded information, "It's not what you expected, is it?"

"No," agreed Elizabeth, "no, it is not."

"It never is," the older woman told her, "and when we reach Fuhchau—that will not be what you expected either. Then before you have had time to realize how strange, after all, it is, you will have settled down and become part of it—one of us."

Elizabeth said, Yes, not loudly but with determination. She thought . . . God helping me—

The *Hotspur* rested. She had met favorable and unfavorable winds, she had lain becalmed upon a surface of living glass, she had seen the sun rise and set for one hundred and twenty-nine days and she had seen the moon wax and wane, wax and wane. Sea fowl had followed her screaming, and fish had mocked her, leaping almost at her sides . . . had they not met the great white porpoise in the China Sea? She had outsailed the typhoon and she had carried death and sorrow as passengers. Now she was at peace, having crossed the harbor bar, having dropped her anchor.

Now there were farewells to say and people to thank and people whose faces one must engrave upon the memory, as it might chance that never again would one see them in this life. The captain's handclasp was grave and earnest. He wished them luck, he said, and his eyes were sober while his mouth smiled at them and spoke the words of parting. And presently they had left the sand-scoured decks, and taken their last look at the black ship, the lovely ship which had brought them thus far upon their journey.

Some time later the *Hotspur* would lie at anchor below
Fuhchau at Pagoda Anchorage, the captain told them, and would
load a valuable cargo for New York and then begin her return
voyage. Perhaps they would meet again then.

Victoria, Elizabeth found, was as British as the Union Jack and
here she and Tobias and the Hendersons were housed with mission friends of the people in the Fukien field.

Now Tobias went sightseeing. He strode alone or was companioned through the streets and amused himself and his new
friends by practicing the set Chinese phrases he had learned
aboard ship, upon the astonished and courteous and blankly un-
comprehending merchants, passers-by, beggars, children. *"Siah cha
lo mwoi?"* he would intone amiably, having learned that to ask
if one had eaten rice was comparable to a friendly good morning.
Incredulity greeted him, and in the case at least of the black-eyed
boy children with the round faces and shaven skulls, a scarce-
veiled merriment. Tobias shook his head, laughing and impatient. He couldn't grasp, as yet, that it might take him a lifetime
to master one dialect . . . and that he could hardly hope to be
fluent in several. Speaking, and not at all expertly, in the Fuhchau
tongue he could not be understood in Hong Kong.

Their short stay in Hong Kong passed swiftly. They had been
pleasantly welcomed and entertained, they had attended service
in the mission chapel, they met a number of amiable people. But
Tobias was restive; he wished to be immediately at the field of his
future activities. Elizabeth, wishing it for him, thought herself a
hindrance, chafed at the enforced rest prescribed for her by one
of the doctors from the hospital.

When shortly thereafter the doctor had pronounced Elizabeth
fully recovered, the last stage of their journey was at hand, and
they took their departure. It seemed to Elizabeth that much of
her new life was a series of good-bys. How many good-bys
would be said in the long years ahead, she did not know. She
turned her eyes resolutely away. Better not think of farewells. . . .

She, with her husband and the Hendersons, made the trip to
Fuhchau on board the small coastal screw steamer, *Undine,* under
the command of Captain Barker and a competent crew. Three

days were consumed in that journey along the rugged coast, and
there was a stop at Amoy. But at the end of the trip there was
Pagoda Anchorage.

Pagoda Anchorage, to which the clipper ships came, from
which the great tea races began. Captain Bennett had told her of
some of these, had rolled upon his tongue the names of beautiful ships which waited every year at the anchorage, loading their
tea, impatient to be off. And Captain Barker, coming to where she
and Tobias sat on deck, watching the coast line, deeply indented
and magnificently wild, had many such sagas to tell. Some day,
he prophesied, they would come to the anchorage and see the
most magnificent ships in all the world, the finest fleet since
time began.

Some day—

Then on the third day they came to the anchorage, nine miles
below the city, where the branches of the river Min united. Here
were river craft of every kind and in great abundance and here
again Elizabeth was struck by the clamor, the confusion. Here
were the boatwomen, walking lightly on their unbound feet, with
bright flowers in their shining black hair. Here were boats upon
which a man was born, lived, married, begat children and died.
Here were ferries and boats for trade and fishing craft . . .

And here was the Min. Yellow as gold, tawny as copper, the
teeming, tireless river, which flowed for more than three hundred miles, now contracting, now expanding, fortressed with hills,
bearing upon its deep breast commerce, and households, travelers
and house owners, making a land to be fertile, and affording a
people a living. Upon its banks stood seven and twenty walled
towns and of these Fuhchau was the greatest.

When the mission houseboat had met and taken them to the
jetty in the city, Elizabeth and Tobias stood, at long last, upon
the soil of Fukien, the Happily Established; while here, in its
great plain, surrounded by hills, its suburbs stretching three miles
to the river bank, was the port of their destination, the vineyard
of their labors, the end of their voyage, the Happy City, Fuhchau,
which Tobias would one day learn to call Hokchiu, after the
fashion of neighbors and friends.

Youth

1864–1894

CHAPTER I

DAVID CONDIT was born in Fuhchau, China, on the seventh day of February, in the year 1864. He was born, a lusty, nine-pound, strong-lunged baby in the missionary compound, on the hill overlooking the city, on the south side of the river, and commanding a view of Middle Island and the Bridge of Ten Thousand Ages. His mother was attended by the mission doctor and Ella Henderson. David, when it was found that Elizabeth was, to her great sorrow, unable to nurse him, was given into the care of an amah from the hills, a country woman, taller than the average, with unbound feet and strong, sure hands.

The day of his birth was auspicious. There was quiet in the streets, for the shops were closed and shuttered and enlivened with red banners of rejoicing. Prayer papers fluttered in the wind from the river craft, and in the fields from plow and tree, implement and dwelling. During the evening which preceded the New Year, Elizabeth, waiting in the torture of her labor for deliverance, heard the preparation for this holiday, the constant noise of firecrackers, the sound of gongs, the clamor of preparation. But with the dawn came quiet and David's first long, astonished cry.

This was his birthday. It was also the birthday of every man, woman and child in China. In so close a fashion was he to be identified with the people in whose country he had encountered life. It made him, he said in after years, half Chinese.

On this day debts were discharged, and houses swept and purified. On this day a man spoke in goodwill to his neighbor. It was the New Year.

A child is unastonished. He accepts the surroundings into which he is born. It is not until much later that he questions them or begins to imagine there may be a world other than his own. David's first unfocused gaze saw nothing. Later as objects began

37

to appear to him, as he began to recognize scents and sounds and even people, there was nothing strange in the large encompassing of his environment. All houses in the world must be rather like this one, verandaed, shuttered with bamboo, with the high, echoing ceilings. All furniture such a hodgepodge of new and old, the household things brought from the other-country, the willow chairs from Canton, the leftovers discarded by former residents, the common things of everyday use which might be seen in any mission house, and in any Chinese house as well, rich or poor.

His earliest remembrance, the furthest reaching back into the dawn of consciousness was not of Elizabeth, his mother, nor of Tobias, his father. It was of his amah, and wet nurse, Mi-daik, whom, almost from his first word he learned to call I-so, *Elder sister-in-law*. He remembered the smell of blue cotton and the clean smell of sweat. He remembered the shining blackness of her hair, the tint and texture of the face which bent over him. He remembered her quiet walking, and her ready laughter and the sound of her voice calling his name. She could not say "David." That was impossible to her and to his other friends. She called him "Dea-dea," as did the rest of the Chinese household. She adored him; he filled arms hungry for the child who had died at the time of David's birth. It was from her lap that he took his first enormous steps, his fat legs widely braced, his hands outstretched before him, and his blue eyes wide with excitement. For his eyes were blue, deep, astonishing, and his hair, during babyhood, a distinct red-gold.

This coloring, inherited from his paternal grandmother, had caused his father and mother a little laughing concern. They themselves were dark enough in all conscience. And David's hair at birth had been straight and black. But that had soon disappeared, leaving these absurd red-gold curls in its place. How to explain such a child to the Chinese, whose devils were always depicted as white of skin, red of hair, and blue of eyes? "He'll have to live it down," decided Tobias, when the black hair had departed.

"As if," said Elizabeth indignantly, "he weren't the most beautiful child in the world!"

It was well that she said it in English. Otherwise Mi-daik would doubtless have snatched the baby from her arms in terror and despair lest some evil spirit overhear this too-much praise.

David's earliest memory of his mother was of her eyes; next of her voice, and finally her hands. His father, for some time, appeared to him as a bearded giant, who laughed a great deal and spoke in a rumbling, as of thunder on the hills. But presently he accepted them all and their relationship to himself, but it was to Mi-daik that he went most often for comfort and understanding. It was she who consoled him when he exhibited his first bruise; she who put charms about his neck; she who watched him, chubby, perilously balanced, endeavoring to fly his first kite, before he was two.

On May 8, 1865, Tobias Condit wrote to his mother-in-law, Mary Lewis, in Carthage, New York:

"MY DEAR MOTHER:

"Yours of January 30, postmarked February 4, reached us on the 16th ult., in two months and twelve days. The afflictions to which you refer seem a long way back among the things now of the past; and we have reason to be thankful that during all the time that has elapsed since I wrote you concerning them, our dear little David has been blessed with good health. I do not think he has had a sick day since that time. He has sometimes been a little worrisome with efforts at teething but he gives very little trouble to anyone, unless it be by his incessant activity. During his waking moments he seems to think it necessary that he keep in motion. A friend, Mr. Bates, on leaving Hong Kong for home, sent his child's carriage to us for David; it is a very nice one and he has had many pleasant rides out on the hill in it, with his faithful Mi-daik. Captain Enright, an English Wesleyan, who was here with his ship when David was born and who saw him before leaving, brought him a pretty whistle with an India rubber ring on one end. He creeps a great deal, tries to stand, has even essayed a few steps. He continues to be a very sweet child, and, I dare to say, handsome, as he does not resemble me in the least.

"Elizabeth has been quite well, and since I got over my itch, or whatever it was, I have had no unusual ailment. We are all in good health and spirits.

"Our work goes on as usual with no diminution of effort and enthusiasm. Forty members were received during the last year and our church now numbers about one hundred and forty. The openings for labor seem to be abundant on every side. The rebels, who were driven away from Nankin, now have possession of Chang-chow, a large city about thirty miles from Amoy. It seems probable that they will soon be driven from there. There has been talk at various times about their coming to Fuhchau, but I do not believe they will ever come. It seems to me they must be pretty nearly played out. But there are some who think otherwise. Meantime our news from America is very encouraging. I hope we shall soon hear of the capture of Richmond and the downfall of the Confederacy.

"Hoping that you speedily recovered from the sore throat which afflicted you when Aunt Lizzie finished your letter for you, and with love, from all of us, to both of you,

"Yours affectionately,

Tobias"

Writing his mother-in-law, he recalled how Elizabeth had trembled when the letter addressed in her aunt's hand had reached them. If—if—something had happened to her mother? They were so far away, mail took so long. It was, moreover, costly. The people at home paid forty-five cents to send a letter of half an ounce in weight; over that, it cost ninety. They wrote, therefore, seldom.

As time went on and David's first words became sentences, he showed a marked preference for Chinese and Elizabeth complained often, half earnest, half in jest:

"He's very willful. He detests English. He won't learn it. He says it's a language for barbarians—!" she said once.

"What!" asked Tobias, amazed. "When?"

"This morning . . . I was teaching him a few phrases. He

screamed and stamped his feet, 'Won't,' he shouted at me, 'won't learn that foreign-devil speaking.' "

Tobias suggested discipline but he smiled and Elizabeth smiled back. Her face was thinner than it had been when she voyaged across the world, and more mature. She was very near to being a beautiful woman, in spite of her plain and drab-colored clothes and her lack of vanity. She said, gently, "He's really a good little boy, Tobias. Only sometimes I think he cares more for Mi-daik than for me."

Tobias reassured her, but without much conviction. And when she timidly broached the subject to Ella Henderson, that lady nodded in a complete understanding. "Why not?" she answered, "it's natural enough." And at a little sound which escaped the younger woman, she added, "My children were exactly the same. They outgrow it, of course. It's only at first."

If Elizabeth were, secretly enough, a little jealous of Mi-daik, she did not display it. She blessed heaven for her. Ignorant she might be, from Elizabeth's standpoint, woefully superstitious, and while she accepted their Heaven-Father as the most powerful of spirits, hers was still a demon-haunted world, still markedly heathen at heart, but barring a few details upon which their viewpoints were bound to clash, she was a treasure; and absolutely to be trusted. Elizabeth was a very busy woman. She had not come out to China to sit with folded hands. She had come out to work, and work had been given her, in full measure. At first she and Tobias, in the intervals of settling down to running a house and learning the mission routine, had studied the Fuh-chau dialect—for six hours on end, with a native teacher at the other end of a long table. They had learned also the two hundred and fourteen radicals, or mothers, as they are called by the Chinese. They had practiced painstakingly and painfully with the slender writing brush and the oblong brick of ink. Their teacher, Sia Ho-mei, had been enchanted by Elizabeth's aptitude with the brush. Then too, from the first, she taught in the girls' school, helped with the babies and the small forlorn orphans, sewed, played the melodeon, and made friends.

Tobias, long before his knowledge of Chinese was even adequate, went among the Chinese, convert and non-convert alike. He went with Jonathan Henderson and others of the mission on long trips by water or land, sleeping sometimes on the mission houseboat, but more often in temples or in the incredibly dirty common room of a provincial inn. He slept on floors of mud, on tables, in chairs. He tramped the hills and the steep roads with their climbing-upward steps. He talked to beggar and to thief, to priest and to scholar, to merchant and to farmer. And whether or not at first they understood him, whether or not they had any feeling of liking for him, something of his immense vitality, his strong, unsentimental friendliness reached them.

Before David was born, Tobias had preached his first sermon in the common tongue. Not, however, without trepidation. The inflections astonished but did not daunt him. Even though he had once requested some perfectly ordinary articles of household use and had been brought a basket of goat's tails after many hours! While he who brought it panted humbly that he could not procure the required number.

The inflections! The tones! Ask for a fork and they brought you a bundle of wood! The word was the same, the tone entirely different. It was enough to drive a man out of all patience with himself, and, in regretted moments, with his instructor. Rising, diminishing, entering, departing! There was no end to them. And now and then, even after he had mastered the language sufficiently to be comprehended whether he spoke, preached or prayed, he found himself regarding the small David with wonder mixed with envy. For David had no difficulty at all—with Chinese. His difficulty was with English. He continued to be reluctant to learn, even more reluctant to speak—and his father sternly required that at mealtimes only English be spoken among the three of them, and David was often full of laughter at the absurdity of his second language. "Butter!" It seemed to him an entirely idiotic word. *Ngu neng iu,* on the other hand, *meant* something. It gave you the picture. It said plainly and comfortably, "cow's milk oil." And that was that.

If as David grew into a more independent childhood his far-reaching cry for Mi-daik—"I-so! I-so!"—became less frequent, it was still to her that he went with his questions and perplexities. It seemed to Elizabeth sometimes that with the rich plentiful milk of the country woman David had taken into his being an insatiable curiosity about the people and the life of the place in which he lived. And by the time he was three they had been removed to the country.

The distance was not far in mileage. The village lay back three miles from the Min, and was twelve from the city. Still, the communication, by water or by bad road, was not easy. Tobias, as a reward for his unremitting labors, was to be sent to Ngu-gang to open one of the early outstations.

Elizabeth, after her first breathless questions, was silent and acquiesced. Tobias was extraordinarily happy to make the change. He liked Fuhchau, he had made friends there among the mission members, the American and European colony, the Chinese in every walk of life. But he felt that in the village he could perhaps come closer to the people and be of more service to them. To that end, before their departure, he spent as many hours as he could spare with the mission doctor, that fine, overworked, always worried man, learning the principles of first aid, learning to administer familiar remedies, to bandage, to make splints. In that way, too, he might be useful, he said, and pointed out that a missionary in a village station should know something of medicine just as a ship's captain must.

Elizabeth nodded. She retained a very grateful memory of Captain Bennett of the *Hotspur,* but of the *Hotspur* she rarely spoke nowadays. For, pursuant to his promise, Bennett had sought them out while the ship lay loading off the anchorage, and had taken tea with them and with them attended worship, shortly before he sailed for home. Elizabeth had entrusted him with gifts for her mother and aunt and for Permelia and Abigail Smith, brassware and silken goods, a charming fan, a chest of tea, a pot of ginger, and some long, embroidered coats. He had pledged himself to deliver their presents to the Smith sisters in person and to mail the rest on his arrival in New York; but this he had not been able to do.

On the seventeenth of February, 1863, the *Hotspur* ran on the

Paracels Reef in the South China Sea. In the long boat that put off from her in her death struggle were Captain Bennett and eighteen others, and the two mates, each commanding a boat, had seven passengers apiece. They endeavored desperately to keep together, but failed. Those in the long boat were seen and rescued by a junk and taken to Bangkok. The second mate's boat also reached shore, where the weary and frightened occupants, many of them ill, were kept prisoners for seven days. But, after many hardships, they escaped and boarded an English vessel from which they were landed at Saigon. The third boat reached shore in safety, but a woman passenger died during the trip.

It was long before the news reached Fuhchau. And even now, several years later, Elizabeth still dreamed of it. She saw the *Hotspur* foundering, thrashing, struggling, a live thing, a black swan with white wings, wounded and dying, her beautiful pinions futile, her life ebbing. She would dream that she stood, safe, a great distance off, and knew Tobias was on the ship. She would dream that she was on board and could not find Tobias. Of David in this connection she did not dream, but when the nightmare rode her she would wake drenched with sweat and sobbing.

It was in the spring of 1867 that the Condits removed to Ngugang, where they remained for several years. Mi-daik went with them, as did their cook and one houseboy. Other servants, as needed, they would procure in the village itself. And with them went Sia Ho-mei, delighted at the opportunity. For was not his ancestral home in the village, did not his father still reside there? Moreover, he had become deeply attached to Tobias Condit, and as his personal tutor would have felt it his duty to follow him wherever he might go.

Sia Ho-mei was a scholar—and a gentleman. Slight almost to emaciation, with a great bald forehead and sagacious eyes, and skin the color of old ivory stretched tightly over his bones, wearing the long coat and round cap of the scholar, he looked twenty years Tobias's senior. But he was the same age as his other-country friend, and as Tobias's knowledge of the language increased, so did their understanding of each other.

The furniture had gone on ahead, as had the servants. The

Condits followed on the next day by boat, David almost out of his mind with excitement, watching the life of the river during the three-mile trip. Mi-daik was very nearly out of hers. The child, she declared, was like a fish for slipperiness, and her strong brown hands clutched him firmly to her breast despite all his wriggles and commands and even beatings. For beat her he did, and lustily, about the face and head until his mother intervened with a sharp, quick word. But Mi-daik was not perturbed. Ai—a man child, and a strong man child!—born, thought Mi-daik proudly, to have his own way and to beat women when he couldn't get it!

Sedan chairs waited on the landing. David found himself in one, on his mother's lap. He nearly broke his neck looking at the strange new country which surrounded him, as the bearers carried them along the narrow trail through the paddy field, lush and green with the new upspringing of the rice. Mud was on every side. If a bearer slipped and fell . . . Elizabeth shut her eyes and then laughed, opening them into David's face. He was pulling at her lids with strong baby fingers. He didn't like her eyes shut, he complained, in Chinese.

"Oh, David, do talk English!"

"No," said David, in English, "won't," and shut his lips firmly.

He was, she knew, a singularly headstrong child. But looking at him, the deep eyes, the clustered copper curls, her heart melted within her and she snatched him so closely that he grunted with a mingling of pain and anger and tried to release himself. Suppose, she thought, suppose he were to become ill, at this outstation? So far from doctors, so far from the mission.

There were tears in her eyes. She would miss people so much, people she had grown to love. Ella and Jonathan Henderson. Others . . . There were some for whom she had mere liking, some for whom she had only respect. But the Hendersons and Dr. Jasper and his family were close to her heart.

I'm a coward, she told herself. After all the thousands of miles she had traveled, must she rebel at twelve more? But her heart went back to the compound on the hill, to her friends and to the brown bodies of her Chinese babies, who had taken, with laughter and with solemnity, her ministrations of soap and water, her care; to the older children who listened to her teaching, faltering and uncertain at first, then firmer and more sure, and to the people of the hills and the shops, the country and the town, who had grown as familiar to her as her own face in a mirror. She would be homesick for the house itself, even the bed upon which she had slept these many nights and on which she had suffered childbirth; the hard bed, with the mosquito netting . . .

But the bed, she reminded herself, had been transferred to Ngu-gang with other household goods and chattels. With the kitchen god too, she thought smiling, for here, as in the mission, her cook would paste a poster of that plump gentleman to watch over the servants' kitchen.

The sedan chairs went on. Not the luxurious chair of an official, of some high mandarin going to and from his yamen but the straight and exceedingly uncomfortable chairs of lesser folk. Now the ground rose, slightly, now the way became steeper and the bare feet of the bearers were on the rough stone steps. Sweat drenched their blue cotton blouses. And with them walked Mi-daik, a little apart, conscious of her position of trust and responsibility in the house of her master.

Behind David and Elizabeth were the chairs of Sia Ho-mei and Tobias. Tobias, reflected Elizabeth, must be a burden!

Here stood a great banyan, its branches wide and spreading, and beyond, the small chapel and dwelling in which they were to live.

It had the hipped roof of all the houses of the district. The floors were of mud and so were the walls. There were five dwelling rooms, a kitchen and the chapel, the central room. Within, the furniture already stood in its proper place, the round and merry face of the cook beamed from the doorway, where the houseboy also waited, smiling a welcome. On the house itself were pasted the new red posters with *Fu,* the happiness character, in black upon them and upon the wishes for longevity, prosperity and many offspring. Firecrackers sounded, and a new lantern, gift of the servants, swayed above the door.

The sedan chairs were set down. David, running, shrieked "I-

so, I-so!" imperiously. He was in the country. He loved it. The
village was a cluster of tumble-down houses, not far distant.
There was a smell of spring in the air, of blossoms, of things
green and growing. That there were other odors did not affront
his young nostrils, he had been born into a city of odors, and it
was to him entirely a matter of course that the green rice fields,
the grain fields, the orchards, every inch of cultivated Chinese
land, should be fertilized by the night soil of city and town and
village. Why not? Waste became plenty; plenty became food;
and food became waste. It was a proper cycle, never ending.

He was like a small colt to catch and bring into the house. He
was not concerned with the house. Once he saw his familiar bed,
his few toys, the books from the other-country, which interested
him chiefly because of pictures, his kite, and his personal belongings, he was content and at home. "I-so! I-so!" he shrieked again
. . . and ran out and ran . . . and ran, until for lack of breath
he stopped.

A black and white magpie spoke from a tree. The bird of happiness. David watched it with amusement. He liked birds. When
he was older he would have pigeons, many of them, as the
Chinese boys had. Pigeons with whistles skillfully fastened to
their tails that in flight they might make a humming music. He
would have a lovely bird in a cage, as well, and go walking with
him. He would have fighting crickets too, in a little cage of bamboo. All these things he had seen and had coveted. But he had not
yet years enough, Mi-daik assured him when he told her of these
yearnings. The fact that time would cure this lack did not occur
to him. To be old in China was in itself desirable. Was not the
courteous greeting . . . "What is your honorable age?"

He sat down waiting for Mi-daik to pant her way up to him,
chattering and scolding, and put his round chin in his hands. He
wished he were grown up. One stayed a little boy so very long.

The hills were green, and the trees were in leaf. The sky arched
overhead, a soft and miraculous blue. Three miles away the river
whispered on the shore. And from the house his mother was
calling him. "Come home, David," she was calling. "Come
home."

The villagers clustered about the new door and a great, white goose was waddling about the steps, ready to "watch house" and give warning of marauders.

His hand in Mi-daik's, David went home.

CHAPTER II

THE Condits remained in Ngu-gang for seven years. They did not at the end of their first eight-year period in the mission field avail themselves of the customary furlough. For in this year Elizabeth carried and bore her second child, a girl, Lydia. When the time for her confinement approached, the little house in Ngu-gang was closed and they went back to Fuhchau, returning to the village in less than a month.

David had forgotten the city. It was new to him, all over again. The narrow, filth-running streets, which were never straight because of the known fact that evil spirits cannot turn corners and therefore the crooked street is safest; the shops, the traveling cobbler and dentist and sweetmeat-seller. The hills and especially Black Rock hill from which, with his Chinese companions, he flew kites on fine windy days, and sometimes, when evening came on, attached tiny lanterns to their tails and watched them sail like fireflies. But these late home-comings were not greeted with enthusiasm on the part of his parents.

Interested as he became in Fuhchau, the month was lonely. For in Ngu-gang, David had made a close friend, one with whom he had even performed the ceremony of blood or "dry" brother. This lad, two years older than himself, known to him therefore as Elder Brother, was Sia Heng-ong, nephew of the Condits' personal tutor, and son of a prosperous merchant in Fuhchau.

Heng-ong spent a good deal of his time in the clan house in Ngu-gang, ruled by his grandmother, a small upright woman who, when David was small and had the run of the women's quarters, very much frightened him. She walked on the tiniest of golden lilies, supported by her stalwart women. She smoked incessantly, a tiny, precious pipe. And her eyes were as black as night and as keen as a sword.

The clan house itself was especially lovely, with a stream flowing by, a lovely garden reached through a moon-gate, and numerous heaven's well courts, with spirit screens and flowers and plants in tubs, with small pools in which the lazy fat goldfish flirted their colored tails. There were other buildings, servants' quarters and guest houses, there were latticed walls and some of the windows were fashioned of pearl shell. And there was also, of course, a room set aside for the school in which the various children of the family studied under a tutor and, "backing their books," presented their solemn little rear-ends to their teachers and, standing, recited the classics. There was also a great hall of ancestors where David more than once saw his friend perform homage to the spirits of the honorably departed.

For the rest, during the time Heng-ong lived in the clan house, the two boys were much together. Heng-ong was a short, stocky boy with a fine-textured skin and intelligent eyes and brow. He was dignified and courteous, and a favorite of his grandparents and, indeed, of the entire household, uncles, aunts, husbands, wives, secondary wives, servants. He had a number of fine clay toys and a notable collection of kites. He had pigeons and crickets and caged birds, and everything he had he shared with David.

So together they played and ran and shouted and got into mischief exactly as two boys will do anywhere on the face of the globe.

Heng-ong, while resident with his family in Fuhchau, attended, after he was seven, the mission school, where the Chinese classics were taught as well as a great many other things not included in the Chinese curriculum. This came about through the fact that his mother was a convert; a little later her husband also became one. Heng-ong's mother had been seriously ill of smallpox; and all the prayer papers burned to the gods of small-pox did not do any good; nor did the frequent visits of the Chinese doctors, one after another, who took her pulse, made wise pronouncements, left medicine compounded of very strange ingredients, and ceremoniously departed. In despair, her husband appealed to the mission and their doctor was dispatched. And presently Heng-ong's mother recovered with very little marring of her beauty.

Heng-ong was going to be a doctor too, a doctor trained in Western medicine. He announced this to David when David was nine and he was eleven. His father, who had hoped that his son would be a scholar, and thus attain to the real aristocracy of China, was quite reconciled. For Heng-ong's heart was set upon it. He spoke seriously to David of the great need, of the beggars, the lepers, the opium addicts, the blind and the halt. To learn all that he could, perhaps in Europe, and then to come back and work among his people. Such was his ambition and David, listening, felt his small heart swell.

His, too, he declared suddenly.

They were on a hill above the village when his decision was reached, looking down upon the clustered houses. David had always taken it more or less for granted that he would be a missionary but even at nine he was questioning blind faith. He had not forgotten the time when, at the age of four, he had been alone with his mother and the servants during a preaching trip of his father's, and the great wind had come, the typhoon . . . He had prayed, the little boy, with his craven head beneath the covers . . . that God would stop the wind. But He hadn't stopped it. And so, when the worst was over and the rain fell through the broken walls and the partly denuded roof, he had gone to his mother to ask why. And she had not been able to tell him. Therefore, he reasoned. His parents had an unquestioning belief which, at nine, he had not attained. They looked upon the most hideous suffering, the most indescribable squalor with pity, yet with acceptance. To be sure, they tried to relieve it as best they could. But to David, listening to Heng-ong announce that his life would be dedicated to medicine, it seemed that medicine, combined with faith, was perhaps the broom which would really sweep out the ancient accumulated disorder of superstition, ignorance, ill health, horror . . .

He asked Heng-ong, "But won't it be hard? It takes years, Dr. Jasper says."

Heng-ong nodded. His reply was measured and stately.

"With diligence nothing is difficult," he reminded his Younger Brother.

That evening David went home to supper and bowed his curly head during grace over the rice and pork, and the salty sauce of the soy bean. Elizabeth during the first months of her residence in China had cooked, as best she could, American food on the cumbersome brick and plaster stove; and had tried to instruct her kitchen boy in matters of American diet. But she soon found that she liked Chinese food. Of course, there were cakes, and pies and even flapjacks for a special treat, and the menu was as varied as possible. But often, after a strictly American meal, to which guests were bidden, she would discover David out in the kitchen with a dish of the servants' rice in his lap and wielding those nimble lads, the chopsticks, with the ease of long practice.

Little Lydia Condit was less than four years old when she died, of a swift fever. David, his life long, was never able to forget her. The transformation in a few shocking days from round chubbiness to emaciation, the thin high cry rising above the wailing of the women servants, Mi-daik's, whose charge she had been, loudest, most keening of all. Nor did he forget the village people clustered outside the house waiting for news. The death of a girl child in their stoical eyes was perhaps not so very important, but this was the child of people they loved, to whom they came for help, themselves, as trusting as children.

Elizabeth was very white, very quiet, with blazing, rebellious eyes. A messenger had been sent to the mission, the doctor would come as soon as was humanly possible. But it would not be soon enough. She told herself that and then tried desperately to believe that she simply lacked faith. She and Tobias worked with tender and frantic hands over the burning, pitiful, small body. Often they prayed, not always in words, although once Tobias tried . . . "Spare her, God," he implored simply, "if it be Thy will," and David huddling in a corner of the room, waiting, his heart beating in his throat until it seemed to him that he could taste blood, waited for the miracle which must occur, as the dreadful sound of despair forced its way past his mother's set lips. But there was no miracle and before the mission boat had made its way down the river, Lydia, having lived so briefly, died.

David, running from the house in a blind rebellion of grief, went alone and unnoticed. If Heng-ong were only there! But Heng-ong had gone back to the city home a week before.

Lydia was buried in the mission graveyard in Fuhchau. She took up very little room. And the Condits did not return to Ngugang. After the child's death Elizabeth was very ill of an ailment which doctors refused to diagnose. And for a time, listless. Then she asked Tobias, "If we could stay here . . . ?" At first she had believed that the sight of the orphanage babies would tear her into minute and quivering pieces. But that had passed. There were more babies to care for here than in the village. And she knew that she would never have another child of her own. David, dearly beloved, had grown away from childhood. He was a tall, sturdy boy, the copper curls darkened, the square-jawed, wide-browed face tanned to bronze, the eyes incredibly blue. She loved him deeply, and he caused her considerable concern. He was, at times, both willful and stubborn and once his heart was set on something it was difficult to move him from his purpose.

She was closer to him than the average mother is to her son. She had been his first teacher, and he came to her, during the first ten years of his life even more freely than he approached his father. Not even Lydia had taken David's place. But Lydia had had her own. She had filled arms which had lost touch with infancy. And now Lydia was gone.

Some months after the intelligence of Lydia's death had reached Mary Lewis, she wrote to her daughter Elizabeth, at the top of four close-written pages of family recipes:

"Dear E. I would like to write you a letter to go with the recipes but have very little time. I have been as well as I could expect and your aunt continues in good health. Your last letter caused me much concern and I must remark that you had a remarkable and pretty dream about your little Lydia, but now try to let her rest with her Heavenly Father and console yourself with the thought of how much she has missed of affliction and sorrow that the wicked world would have afforded her under the best circumstances.

"Tell little David that Grandmother would write him to-day if she could, but will do so presently. We send love to Tobias and yourself.

"Your affectionate mother,

MARY LEWIS"

Elizabeth read the note in silence and, in silence, gave it to Tobias. She had not told him of her darling dream which was that Lydia was alive, and running about the house on small, dancing feet. He looked at her under his eyebrows when he laid the letter down. It did not seem a cruel letter to either of them, and to one, at least, it appeared a brief and justified reproof.

"You did not tell me of your dream," Tobias said to her, after a moment.

Her face contorted momentarily. She said, low, "I have often dreamed it. I still do. Do not ask me, Tobias . . . I am a wicked woman," she said sharply, "rebellious, unresigned."

She looked out across the compound. He knew whither her thoughts, above which small mound they hovered. He rose and touched her shoulder in passing. He said quietly, "Life was not intended to be easy, Elizabeth."

The Hendersons took the Condits' place at Ngu-gang. And until David was twelve his parents continued to live in the compound in the city. Occasionally David returned to the Sia clan house on a visit with Heng-ong and was treated with a deference and civility, as an honored guest should be, which warmed the cockles of his young heart. And during the rest of the time he studied, played, learned to use the writing brush, learned, too, to chant the classics with the Chinese students, made friends and entertained himself hugely.

Once, he ran away. This was after he had committed a crime of an astonishing magnitude. It had to do with candy. A large wooden box of hard sweets had been sent the Condits by English acquaintances and was kept under lock and key by Elizabeth, who permitted David a given amount per diem. This restriction irritated him, as restrictions usually did, and once when his mother was busy with her school and his father off for the day, he looked for and found the key and amply filled his pockets.

Heng-ong assisted him in disposing of the sweets, remarking sententiously, if with his mouth full, "Though thieves infest the streets, if they have no stolen goods they can't be convicted."

But David's stomach convicted him. Heng-ong's was the stronger. David, suffering from surfeit and bellyache, made his way home from the special hideaway in which he and Heng-ong often convened to discuss important matters and in which he had, to earlier, swift disaster, smoked his first pipe. And having arrived at home his indisposition was noted, and the doctor summoned. After the diagnosis, the treatment proved more deadly than the disease.

He was whipped. Tobias, like his father before him, believed in physical chastisement and so, sore in person and affronted in dignity, David ran away after the supper hour on the following day. He took with him the proverbial handkerchief containing a few coppers, some bread, cheese, cold rice, and a hunk of fearful sweetmeat. And thus equipped, he departed, in the chill early winter evening, wearing the native clothes in which he most often rejoiced, including a long padded outer garment.

He made for the hills. On these, scattered along the higher, barren slopes, above the terraced cultivated fields, were the grave houses, in which the coffins of the deceased waited, until the auspicious day and place were selected for their delayed burial. Cold, tired, and more than a little frightened, David entered one of these huts and sat himself down on a moldering coffin to partake of the bread and cheese. The grave house was damp and dark. There was a stench which repelled him, accustomed as he was to stenches. But he was running away. He had no idea where he would run. He merely knew that with the sunrise he would walk on, perhaps he would learn what lay on the other side of the hill. Perhaps he could find employment in the fields. Perhaps, he thought with bravado, he might join a band of wandering robbers, bandits. Why not? He was a thief, he'd been told so by no less an authority than his father.

A small, tight sob escaped him, thinking of his father and mother. His mother would miss him, he knew, and Heng-ong would deplore his loss. Perhaps Heng-ong would even wear the white garb of mourning for his sake. He remembered something his friend had once said to him . . . "to be parted from each other while living and separated whilst dying is the greatest of all sorrows." A veritable howl of grief escaped David as he pictured himself stark and cold in some forlorn and far corner of the hills.

He was very sorry for himself.

He rose, and tying up the remainder of the food in the large square of cotton, decided to go home. For, he told himself, his mother's sake.

Listen! Wasn't that a sound . . . a rustle . . . the padding of stealthy paws . . . ? couldn't he see, peering from the entrance to the grave house, two strange green lights, wavering, far off . . . coming closer . . . like eyes . . . ?

That the hills were tiger-inhabited he knew very well. There were even tigers so near the city. There were tigers who came down from the hills into the villages and plundered and killed and destroyed. There were probably tigers waiting for him—outside, beyond the grave hut. They waited, closing in, in a circle about him, silently.

And it served him right, he thought glumly, with the acceptance which had been imposed upon him. Had he not lost his temper and shouted at his father, had he not twisted and turned seeking to escape that merited thrashing, had he not caused his mother concern and sorrow?

The rice and bread and cheese and sweetmeat had not been very filling. Better to die of damp and hunger among the musty odors of death than to be taken alive by a tiger, he thought.

The lights came nearer.

David clenched his fists. Terror muted his voice in his throat and dried his eyes. He waited. There was nothing to do but wait.

Five minutes, ten minutes of waiting, alone, in the darkness, for creeping fate on padded paws.

But the lights were the lanterns of searchers.

At home, warm, fed, he was the prodigal son all over again. They were so glad to see him that they couldn't, and didn't, scold him. Elizabeth took him, big boy that he was, in her lap and filled her senses with him, and rocked him to and fro and his father stood by, making funny sounds in his beard. And presently, not as ashamed of being babied as he would have thought, David fell asleep.

Later they stood beside his bed watching him, one brown arm flung out, the red curls riotous over his well-shaped head, the sleeping face hiding its secrets from those who loved him, the young lips set and the forehead frowning. Tobias said, low, sighing, "He must be taken back to the States."

Not because he had stolen the candy nor yet because he had run away. But because he was growing up. He must have the advantages they couldn't give him, the advantages of the other-country.

At the time of Lydia's death a furlough had been suggested to them. It had been rejected. Only in work, hard, unremitting work, could the agony of this sacrifice be somewhat ameliorated. But now, for David's sake . . .

His father talked to him the next day, in the bare, utilitarian study, with the old melodeon in one corner, the soberly bound books, the engravings and photographs from home upon the walls. "Why did you do it?" he asked gently.

David hung his head. Then he straightened and looked at his father directly. There was a marked resemblance between them in that moment, for all their difference in coloring.

"I was angry," he answered.

"Because you were angry you desired to cause your mother and me anxiety and sorrow?" the patient voice queried.

"Yes," admitted David.

"You thought you would perhaps—repay us . . . ?"

"Yes," said David again humbly.

"Come here," said Tobias, and when the boy stood beside him, in the Western clothes he hated, products, gleanings, of the missionary barrels, and far from satisfactory to their wearer, Tobias said, "You must learn self-discipline, David. When you do wrong, you will be punished, as surely as B follows A. That punishment you must accept. You must learn to accept it. We must all learn. I have learned."

"You?" David looked at his father with respect and astonishment. It seemed impossible to him that Tobias had ever done wrong. Yet that matter of the thrashing, for instance . . . he still could not quite see the justice of that. He said, "I thought preachers couldn't—"

There was a little laughter in Tobias' eyes. He replied gravely, "But they can, David."

David said, on a deep breath, making the confidence he had so far withheld:

"Then I couldn't . . . I mean . . . I couldn't be a preacher . . . for if you have a hard time being good, think how much harder it would be for me!"

Tobias smiled but his heart troubled him. Of course, David was only a little lad. He'd change his mind a thousand times before reaching manhood. He asked, however, soberly:

"What do you want to be—?"

"A doctor," said David eagerly. "Heng-ong too. He's going away to study some day. His father permits it."

"I see," said Tobias. "It is a fine profession, my son. But it requires patience and long years of preparation and quite," he added, smiling, "quite as much self-discipline and denial as that of preacher."

Later, after dismissing the boy, he repeated the conversation to Elizabeth and concluded:

"If this ambition continues, if it is not merely one of emulation, or a boyish fancy . . ."

She said decidedly:

"It would please me very much, Tobias."

It did not occur to either of them, nor to David, that if he became a doctor he would not return to China.

"There is enough money," said Tobias thoughtfully, "with the scholarships he would probably be offered—the funds would be ample."

Two years later, the Condits sailed on a Pacific mail steamer for San Francisco to take their first eighteen months' furlough. It had already been arranged that David live with Abigail and

Permelia Smith in New York and there attend school, after his parents had returned to China.

But for eighteen more months they would have him with them.

Leaving was hard. It was hard even for Elizabeth and Tobias, who knew that they would soon return. But to David, who knew that in the course of events it would be many years before he again set foot on Chinese soil, it was a raw, bloody business, this wrenching loose of deep roots. He felt flayed and quivering.

He paid his last visit to the Sia clan house in the village, and said farewell to the ancient lady who knew, as he knew, that there would be no more partings after this one; he bade good-by to Sia Ho-mei, who had returned with them to Fuhchau and who begged him in stately phrases not to forget his Chinese nor to let the writing brush lie idle for long; he said good-by to the Hendersons and to others in the mission, and to his many friends, stopping in at shops, thrusting his curly head inside and making his last set speeches . . . and adjured as he left to "Walk slowly! Walk slowly!" in the courteous regretful phrase of leave-taking. He said good-by to Black Rock, where he had flown his kites. He gave his pigeons, those he had tended, those he had raised, to Heng-ong . . .

Harder still, leaving Heng-ong.

Their speech was measured and brittle. Of the two David exhibited the more emotion. Heng-ong's bright, fine eyes were dry, and his face expressionless, merely a little paler than usual. When next they met they would be grown men.

Farewell. Farewell to Kushan, the mountain, with its fish pond and temple and chanting priests, where David had spent so many happy holidays away from the heat of the city. Farewell to Pagoda Anchorage, where on the houseboat of Heng-ong's father he had seen the start of the great tea races from Fuhchau to London. Farewell to the compound on the hill. Farewell to the Bridge of Ten Thousand Ages, to the chapels, to the people who wept to see him go. Farewell to Mi-daik, whose breast had nourished him, whose hands had tended him, whose feet had been tireless in his service. Farewell to the river, the fishing fleets, the cormorants, the houseboats, the lusty life of the boat people. Farewell to flowering plum and sweet-scented blossom, to orange groves, in fragrance, to the tall red pine and the pungent camphor tree. Farewell to tea in leaf and the green shoots of the rice in the mud, to water buffalo and water wheel, to the half-naked farmer toiling in the sun, shaded by his great straw hat. Farewell to a thousand scents and sights, to the high bamboo grove, the leaping waterfall, the magpie and the lark . . .

Farewell to China . . .

"I'll come back," he called, as the people waved and shouted from the jetty and the first stage of their journey began. *I'll come back!*

CHAPTER III

Not by a clipper ship, this voyage, not by a black ship with white wings, not by the long weary way of months, but by steamer, now that for some years the Pacific Mail ran upon a regular route. And in less than six weeks they landed at San Francisco, from which the journey led homeward by rail. For the dream had been completed and the vision seized and held and the long lines of shining steel stretched between the west coast of the United States and the east.

The Condits stopped long enough in New York to see the Smith cousins, and to present David to those fluttering kindly maiden ladies with whom he would presently make his home. They had, they said, found just the right school for him, the Collegiate School of the Dutch Reformed Church, now open to pupils of other denominations and situated at a little distance, on Twenty-ninth Street off Fifth Avenue. And to the school David was escorted, in order that he might meet the principal and his future teachers. But his studies there would not come yet a while.

For they were going to Carthage, to the Lewis homestead. There, in intervals of traveling and lecturing for the mission work, Tobias would rest. There Elizabeth expected to live for the most part, although she, too, would probably speak at various missionary societies, through New England and possibly farther afield. And there David would live and attend school until his parents sailed for China. There, even during his residence in New York, he would return for his vacations.

His first impression of New York was that it was very big, that it was very clean and that it frightened him. He met few children either on shipboard, or train, or in the city and those he did meet of his own age seemed to him childish and without dignity. They laughed at him too. His clothes were patently old-fashioned, cut down from the clothes of older men, or plainly unsuitable. There was a strange inflection to his speech and his English was stilted and rather elderly. Also he had lived in China, he had been born there, he could even talk Chinese. This made him a subject of curiosity and a foreigner. Was it true that he had eaten rats? Why didn't he wear his hair in a pigtail?

It took many months for the strangeness to wear off. At first he was much on the defensive. Later it amused him to break into fluent and, it is to be regretted not always translatable, Chinese when particularly tormented—not, may it be stated, within his parents' hearing. And still later, although he never completely forgot what after all he considered his mother tongue, he became ashamed of his oddity and unlikeness to other children and was stubborn when they asked him to speak or sing in the language or to teach them the Chinese games with which he had been familiar since babyhood. He was ashamed because, as time went on and he became more a part of the community, he felt his apartness. And children, naturally gregarious, cannot endure not to be one of the majority. So through that first summer he learned to play baseball and even a modified version of football; he went swimming—he could, as it happened, swim like a fish—played pranks, carried off gates at Halloween, attended the common school and was, outwardly, much as other children.

His grandmother had received him quietly. Emotion was not her way. But Aunt Lizzie, a more volatile individual, took him to her with open arms, spoiled him, kept the cruller and cookie jar filled, sweetened his oatmeal with plentiful maple syrup and defended all his mischief-making against her sister-in-law and the Condits.

His parents were, however, not in Carthage much or long. Even his mother was frequently away. In this way when the time for parting came it would not be so hard on him, they thought, resigning themselves. For little by little he must become accustomed to this life, must dig himself in, must learn to be happy.

Happy he was not, at first. But he was only twelve and he soon learned to be. For Carthage was beautiful, with its big frame houses set back from the street, its tended lawns with their imposing ornamentation, the iron stag, the hitching posts with the colored boys' laughing heads, or the curious animals with the rings through their mouths. There were the far hills and the Black River, welcome surroundings for a boy who had never in all his life lived far from hills or flowing water. There were boys to play with and there were disregarded and despised girls. He had, definitely, a rather low opinion of the weaker sex, and admitted few exceptions . . . his mother, the sister he had lost just at the time when she had come to lean upon him, Heng-ong's grandmother and beautiful mother, some of the mission women. But these small girls didn't matter. They were silly and stupid. They weren't the world's workers, or masters. Couldn't be. A mare is not fit to go into battle, he thought; this was one of Heng-ong's solemn pronouncements.

School wasn't hard. He was ahead of his grade. Painstaking lessons in his childhood at Elizabeth's knee had accomplished that, and the later sessions in his father's study where he had wrestled with Latin and Greek verbs years before an American boy at home would have attempted them. Spelling was his weakest point, handwriting his next. Curious that he who had shown a really amazing aptitude with the writing brush should fall so far short when it came to the ordinary pen.

But he accustomed himself to things; to the small schoolroom in which both girls and boys were crowded . . . much to his disgust, as he considered that girls needed little or no education in order to learn to keep a man's house and rear his children—the harried teacher with the ready, and stinging, ruler, and the long hours bent over a small battered desk. He grew accustomed also to the rich, hearty food, and to like it, although he did spend hours in the kitchen once trying to teach his entertained great-aunt to cook rice the *right* way, dry, flaky, every grain standing separate from its fellows.

And he longed for the tender bamboo shoots and the salty foods and the pungent sauces, with an unappeasable hunger.

During that first year he fought several epic battles. There were boys who chanted "Ching ching, Chinaman," when they saw him, and made fearful gestures, putting their thumbs in the cor-

ners of their mouths to stretch them into a flashless grin and
making their eyes squint and slant by pulling at them with their
first fingers. And thus did David acquire his first black eye, and
lose a tooth, to the distress of his grandmother who, after Aunt
Lizzie had clucked over him and had attended to his wounds,
took him into the dim best parlor and seated him on a hassock at
her feet, while, with her steel-rimmed spectacles perched on her
nose, she read "Blessed are the peacemakers" to his reluctant ears.

David never knew his grandmother very well. He was perhaps a little afraid of her. A small, dark-eyed, sallow woman
with hair which, in the years intervening since her daughter's
marriage, had turned completely white, she moved quietly about
the big house, took little interest in anything save church attendance, the reading of her Bible, and the meetings of various
women's societies. She was content to leave the conduct of the
household to its owner, her sister-in-law. Even the arrival of her
daughter and son-in-law and their child had not deeply penetrated her remoteness. The ailment from which she had suffered
for a decade and of which she had never written to Elizabeth was
slow, and increasingly painful and mortal. This she knew and in
this she rejoiced. Her family physician, Matthew Brent, came to
see her almost every day, in order to alleviate the pain. He had
told her the truth, she had forced it from him. But she wished it
kept from her kinsfolk.

Elizabeth, when she was at home, worried incessantly over her
mother's changed appearance and her remoteness. She seemed to
be withdrawn, as if the natural springs of her affections were forever frozen. Tobias consoled her, unaware of his mother-in-law's
illness. It was her advancing age, he explained, and the fact that
she had become resigned to separation from her daughter. Hers
was a nature, he elucidated, more keenly than he knew, which
was easily cast into a mold.

Dr. Brent, stooped, brusque, hearty, was a bachelor, and living
for some time in the village of Natural Bridge, some ten miles
from Carthage. He had removed there early in his practice and
had but few patients in Carthage itself. One of these was Mrs.
Lewis, to whom he was distantly related.

His own district consisted of the village in which he lived, the outlying farms, an iron ore mining town and several logging camps, and covered certainly an area of twenty miles. And there was nothing David liked better, in the summer or during holidays, than to be driven out to Dr. Mat's to spend a night or two, spoiled by the doctor's housekeeper, and going on the doctor's rounds with him. He had told him, early in their friendship, that he, too, wished to become a physician. "When you do," Mat assured him, laughing, "I'll retire and you can take over my practice. But," he added, "that's a long way off yet." It seemed to him that he could never retire so long as one person trusted and needed him. But then, he was in the prime of life, just turned fifty, a mountain of a man, tireless, a tremendous eater, a light sleeper.

The eighteen months during which the Condits remained in America passed swiftly. David had learned to overcome his first astonishment at a real snowfall, had learned to skate and go bellywhopping down hills, and had experienced the first thrill of sugaring off, when the sap runs in the early spring and the snow is still thick upon the ground, and when a small boy is permitted to lick the great spoon which has been thrust into the iron kettle. He had learned hard ciphering, and to recite the long, mournful poetry. He had outgrown the clothes in which he came to America. He was refusing, in summer, to wear boots. He had learned to go barefoot and overalled through the briar patches and undergrowth and to whip the trout streams with deft, careful hand, returning home before sunset with a string of shining beauties, his brown legs scratched and his darkening red hair tousled. He had learned to forget a great many things. Not his special friends, not the hills and river of the country which he still, in his thoughts, called home. "When I go home—" But the writing brush was growing idle and his last letter to Heng-ong, entrusted to his parents, was in English. And he no longer dreamed himself back in the compound and woke to strangeness. Waking in the small gabled room allotted to him, with the first rays of the sun in the eastern, small-paned window, was a familiar thing. He no longer said his prayers in Chinese.

He had long since stopped thinking in Chinese. His English was not now inflexible and it was interlarded with the strange ejaculations of his contemporaries. "Julius Cæsar!" was the strongest and most often used of these. He had become, in fact, an American boy of the later seventies.

A proper boy, thought his grandmother, although she did not tell him so, and despite his mischief. She would often stand where he could not see her and watch him, her small figure erect, carrying its burden of pain and its prayer for release and reunion without a sign. She still wore modified crinolines in a day when crinolines were outmoded. She wore black silk aprons with deep pockets and a lace collar about her shrunken throat. She wore her white hair neatly banded and knotted in the nape of her neck.

She wondered if after all it would not be better for David to make his home with them—she nearly said "with Lizzie—" for good, instead of going down to the city. But when she spoke of this to her daughter and son-in-law, they could not agree with her. If he were set on being a doctor, and it looked as if he were, he must get all the necessary schooling. He would go from the New York school to Wesleyan at Middletown, and thence to medical school. After which, they said, he would return to the mission field.

Mrs. Lewis agreed. She could not admit to them, and did not perhaps admit to herself, that she was jealous of the few remaining years . . . or was it months? . . . of David's boyhood. Remote as she seemed to others and often to herself, her heart, strangely imprisoned behind curious walls of glass, looked out and begrudged every minute of the boy's life, of Elizabeth's presence. Tobias did not matter. She admired him, he was as a son in his deportment toward her. But her voiceless affections were centered upon Elizabeth and Elizabeth's child, and, less strongly, upon her dead husband's sister.

Yet she did not weep when the time came for Tobias and Elizabeth to return to China. They had decided that, as it was autumn, David would travel with them as far as New York and they would see him safely established with the Smiths before they began the long train journey to the Coast. Thus in bidding them farewell, she was saying good-by to David too. David, taller than she, bent his head and kissed her cheek. He would be back for the Christmas holidays, he assured her; he would see her soon. Tears, partly of this latest wrench, partly of excitement, stood in his eyes. Hers were dry. She told him to be a good boy and asked that God might guide and bless him. Her lips on her daughter's forehead were hot and tremulous but so light their pressure that Elizabeth could not know, herself crying frankly.

"I'll never see them again," Mary Lewis told her sister-in-law after they had gone, and raised her hand to stem the younger woman's outcry. She was right. She never did.

Now there was another parting, more difficult for Elizabeth to face. It was their last night in New York and she and Tobias stood beside David's bed in the boarding establishment. He was sleeping, worn out with change and emotion. Elizabeth said slowly, looking down, "We'll never see him again . . . like this. We'll never see him a child again. The next time we see him, he will be grown, nearly a man."

Tobias said nothing, unhappily. He knew, they both knew. They knew what they were forfeiting, the years between, the changes of time, the growing from child into man. They were saying good-by to something they would never witness. And, as her mother had thought upon the night of Elizabeth's betrothal, so now she thought, *it is too much to ask* . . .

But it had been asked.

A slender woman, with quiet eyes, middle-aged at thirty-six, she knelt by the narrow bed and prayed that she might become resigned.

David, after they had gone, fitting himself into the ways of the big house with its many strange people, fitting himself into the ways of his new school, obeying, as he had promised to obey, his father's cousins in all things, was shaken, for weeks to come, by a homesickness so bitter that it was gall in his throat. It was not so much homesickness for the actual physical presence here in New York of his parents, but for his parents in the place toward which they were traveling. The nostalgia for China, which was never to leave him for very long at a time, was at its strongest and most agonizing during that autumn. Thus would the sky be above the mountains . . . Thus would Heng-ong look while flying his kite on Black Rock hill. And when the chill winter came, with frost perhaps, but no snow, would not Sia Ho-mei carry his little copper brazier with him for warmth? . . . would not Heng-ong's honorable grandfather sit long and with just such a contemplative expression over the delicately carved chessmen? Taking his bemused way through the city streets, it seemed to David that they closed in upon him, grew curved and twisted, that the brownstone houses vanished and the tentlike roofs sprang up on every hand. He could smell the noisome odors of the Fuhchau streets; he could hear the voice of the river. There was so much he was missing as the years went by, the Festival of Lanterns, the dragon boat races, the spring plowing ceremonies . . .

There the gongs were beaten and the temple bells sounded and the priests chanted . . .

"Look where you're going, Bub," cautioned the elegantly clad and bewhiskered gentleman with whose immaculate person he sometimes collided, his thoughts so far away. And one day, long after his parents' departure, a little girl wept and then laughed outright at him, as he almost overstrode her. She was a small child, some five years his junior, with golden curls, a furred coat and bonnet and a small muff on a long gold chain. He had knocked the doll from her arms.

"Mamma," said the little girl, "what a clumsy boy!"

Blushing to the roots of his hair, David made his apologies and picked up the undamaged toy. The little girl looked at him long and fearlessly. Then she laughed. "How red his face is!" she remarked, amused.

Her mother hushed her, smiled at David, and hurried on. David, standing quite still, conscious that he would be late in reaching home, looked after them. For the little girl he had little or no thought, save that she made him appear an oaf. But the lady . . . with her trailing skirts and her little bonnet and the odor of violets that emanated from her, was the most beautiful being he had ever seen.

China, for the moment, faded. And he was back again in the clear frosty air of New York, on his way home from school.

At Christmas he returned to Carthage for the holidays. His great-aunt had wished it so, for she was alone now in the frame house. Mary Lewis had died, quite peacefully and with a look of much rejoicing on her pinched features; it had stopped Lizzie's heart to see her. Her death coincided almost exactly with the arrival of her daughter and Tobias in China. David had not gone up for the funeral. He was himself ill at the time, with his first illness since coming to America. He had a sharp attack of la grippe and was nursed and tended by Abigail and Permelia with loving devotion. Only after he was well did they tell him that he had lost his grandmother. And were a little secretly shocked at his apparent lack of emotion. Although he had lived with Mary Lewis for eighteen months, he had never felt that he knew her; she was not real to him, somehow, and never had been.

During the following autumn, at the beginning of his second year in the Collegiate School, he wrote to his parents, who at the time of their last letter had been taking a brief holiday in the sanitarium at Sharpe Peake, completed shortly before David left for America.

"My dear Mamma and Papa,

"Your last letter was one to strengthen my faith in God. If He had permitted that ball of fire to strike a little to the left or to the right I might never have seen my precious father and mother again in this world. You do not tell me very much. Was the sanitarium severely injured?

"I have such a little time away from my studies that I do not write as long letters as I should. Since I wrote you, however, I have risen one class in school. I have no difficulty with the Latin, thanks to Papa and so could skip a grade. It seems so strange to think that I have been in this country over three years.

"I have made a number of new friends at school. We have a little club and expect, when weather permits, to go skating in

Central Park. Aunt Lizzie writes that she is very well and looking forward to my next vacation. I had the pleasure of seeing Dr. Mat last week. He came to New York and took me out to dinner at the Brevoort Hotel. It was perfectly splendid. I must tell you, I have become quite a carpenter. Cousin Abigail gave me a fine set of tools, worth twelve dollars, and the man of all work taught me how to make some pretty fair boats and the boys think them pretty splendiferous. Please thank Mrs. Henderson for the pictures she sent; I cannot write her by this mail but will by the next. Do you know, I wish I could come home to China every Saturday and stay over till Sunday and then come back to school on Monday. I sat for my picture last week and got them to-day. I am sending you one and shall send one to Aunt Lizzie.

"I have an autograph book which Aunt Lizzie sent. Will you write your names on a slip of paper, with verses or a text or advice, and send them to me, and ask the Hendersons too, please, and Dr. Jasper and the rest of the mission. And perhaps Mr. Angus and some of the other merchants. And dear Sia Ho-mei—

"I have not heard from Heng-ong for a long time. Is it true that he is going to start his medical training in China and perhaps go later to Scotland? I wish he would come over here.

"Cousin Permelia has a new dog. She says he is less trouble than a boy. He never has dirty hands or pants with no suspender buttons, and he don't wear holes in his pants knees and stockings. Well, he is a good dog, and I am not very jealous of him.

"Yesterday I went to a surprise party at Bertie Brisley's. He was fifteen years old.

"I wish so much that I could be with you. But I am trying to be contented with my lot. Everyone is very kind to me. There are several new boarders. One is a Miss English. She teaches music. She is about twenty years old and very pretty, and genteel.

"Give my love to everyone. I remain,
"Your aff. son
David Condit"

He had been reticent in his praise of Julia English. Miss English, engaged to be married to a former lodger of the Smiths', whose home was in the Middle West and who was teaching music in a fashionable girls' school in New York, was bored and lonely, waiting only, and in impatience, for her durance to end and her marriage to arrive, with the summer. David, for all that he was still a child in many ways, with childish turns of speech and, as is exhibited by his letter home, no master of the written phrase, looked older than he was. He was exceedingly self-reliant, his life having taught him that quality. And he was very personable, as tall as she, with broad shoulders and big, strong hands. It amused the young lady to turn the handsome boy's head—a little, and within the bounds of perfect decorum. She played and sang to him in the best parlor of the Smith establishment. She drew him out on his life in the East and cried, at intervals, with melting hazel eyes, "Oh, poor, *poor* boy!" when, feeling self-pity well in him at her sympathy, he stumblingly tried to sort out for her some of his emotions. It wasn't, he declared, that he was unhappy here—"particularly since you came, dear Miss Julia." He liked his home, his school, his classmates. But, after all . . .

Their friendship prospered. David had a very small allowance. From this he saved, heaven knew by what deprivation, certain small coins which he expended to do her homage . . . a box of sweets, a bouquet of posies, a bottle of scent with a cut-glass stopper. For her sake he dreaded the Christmas vacation which sent him back to Carthage, for had he not offered to teach her to skate on the Park lake? And as spring approached he gave her, at Easter, his most cherished possession, the carved ivory brush holder which had been one of Heng-ong's parting gifts, and over which the lady fell into a sincere rapture, for it was delicate and almost priceless, carved with little scenes and pictures, with verses from the poets and signed by the hand of a master.

But a month later David surprised her in the dimness of the parlor, in the arms of a gentleman with auburn side whiskers and a double-breasted frock coat.

Miss Julia, blushing, presented her affianced to "my little friend," and that was the end of David's first romance. It cost him some unhappy hours of a jealousy almost too sharp for boyhood to bear and a bitter remorse . . . had he not betrayed his friend Heng-ong for this despicable, this adored and forever lost, example of womanhood? He suffered a distinct loss of appetite for several days during which Abigail and Permelia exchanged secret and understanding glances and then, recovering, began to wish that he had once again the sums he had expended upon this falsest of her sex. To say nothing of the brush holder. Ivory brush holders were not common; most people were forced to be content with those of bamboo.

But by June David had recovered sufficiently to view without agony Miss English's pretty church wedding and to stuff himself with inferior tea and superior cake at the reception tended her and her bridegroom at the Misses Smith's on Murray Hill. But he was finished with women, and in fact so far immunized that he passed through his final two years' schooling in New York untouched by any return of the gentle passion. Nor did his vacations in any manner disturb his emotions.

In the early summer of 1882 David Condit, having graduated from the ancient Collegiate School, having received his presentation Bible and school history with his diploma, left the lachrymose Abigail and Permelia to summer in Carthage. And so, in the autumn, embarked upon his freshman year at Wesleyan University, in Middletown, Connecticut.

CHAPTER IV

IN SEPTEMBER of that year, David Condit traveled from Carthage to New York; after staying for a day or two with the Smith cousins—who assured him that his room would be kept in readiness for him, he boarded a train on the New Haven road for Middletown. He was at this time within five months of nineteen years old, and a big young man, as tall as his father and much heavier, with a shock of unruly dark red hair and extremely blue eyes. He was still growing, with the result that his wrists often protruded from his jacket sleeves, to his great-aunt's despair.

"Dear me," she would exclaim on each such occasion of their meeting at the beginning of a holiday. "If you don't stop growing, David, you'll never be able to keep yourself in proper clothes."

To which he merely grinned, completely unconcerned. He was never, his life long, to be convinced of the importance of meticulous dressing. To be clean, and to be covered, surely that was sufficient.

The Carthage summers had broadened him physically. He had spent a good deal of his last two long holidays with Dr. Brent at Natural Bridge. "For if," counseled Mat, "you're going to be a bonesetter—and, may heaven help you, it's a thankless task—you may as well pick up a little information. It will come in handy."

David ran errands, compounded pills under Brent's direction, groomed the two horses and made himself generally useful. On one occasion he decided that perhaps, after all, he wasn't suited to medicine. This, shortly before he left for college, was when he assisted, reluctantly, at an operation. The patient was one of the men in the logging camp; and the operation was an amputation. David administered, with a shaking hand and a reeling brain, the crude anæsthetic; and held the lamp during the later stages of the operation. After which he was very ill indeed. But Dr. Brent merely chuckled. "Shucks," he consoled, "that ain't nothing. I've been sick, times unnumbered. You'll be. A passion for healing don't always communicate itself to the stomach, Davy. Here, brace up and drink this."

"This" was David's first experience of brandy. He choked and sputtered and shook his red head. "You ain't," said Mat Brent, "breaking any temperance pledges. It's purely medicinal."

David's letter to China describing his initial experience in surgery was rueful. Tobias Condit, reading it weeks later, chuckled aloud. David, he assured Elizabeth, would come through all right. He'd merely permitted, for the time being, the flesh to conquer the spirit.

When he wasn't at Brent's, or in his great-aunt's house, David was out in the fields. Lizzie Lewis owned a farm, worked on shares, some little distance from town. During the last few summers David had spent no little time there. He liked farming. Perhaps it was a sense of the importance of the farmer to the nation, which had seeped into his blood, that gave him such a sense of oneness with the soil upon which his bare feet trod. He liked animals. He liked the stables in the yellow dawn, and the sleepy sounds of waking birds in the heavily foliaged trees, and the touch of horseflesh on his hard palms and the odor of straw and dung. He liked the feel of sweat running down his muscular back, and the scent of the hay, and the swing and thrust of the pitchfork. He wrote to Heng-ong, "There's something about waking to morning out here on the farm that makes you want to kneel down and give thanks that you were born a man into this world."

Now, on his way to Wesleyan, he found himself excited and a little frightened. This was really the beginning of the long road which led back to China. Whether he would safely travel that road and arrive at his destination was entirely in his own hands. He was, he knew, a good student, not, he knew also, a remarkable one. But perhaps if he gave his entire time to work and study, and never for one instant lost sight of his goal, he would reach it—eventually. Four years of college, two of medical school, an interneship in, he hoped, a great hospital—almost two years more; and then perhaps China . . . or first, England. Heng-ong had written in his black, exquisite hand and painstaking English, "It occurs to me that after medical school in America, a year's postgraduate work in England would be of great value to you, my brother."

Nine years, then. He would be twenty-seven before he again set foot upon that ancient soil. Almost an old man, thought David despairingly.

From New Haven he went in the same car by the Air-Line to Middletown. There were others who went with him, other newcomers to the university and with these he had fraternized before reaching New Haven. It was never hard for him to make friends and acquaintances.

"You're Chinese, Condit, aren't you?" one of the other freshmen asked him, solemn-eyed, and David, vastly astonished at the appellation, nodded. But the mystery wasn't a mystery very long. His new classmate, one Richard Wright, had "heard" of him through a cousin in David's class at the Collegiate School.

"I suppose you speak Chinese fluently?" young Mr. Wright inquired politely, but David shook his head. It was quite true. He no longer spoke his first tongue with ease. There had been a time in boyhood when, dreading to be set apart, he had tried to forget it entirely. He hadn't, of course, succeeded. Yet there was much that he had lost. Within the last year or so he had realized that he must not forget if he was ever to return, and so had tried to brush up on the language, even going so far as to invade certain dim laundry shops in New York in which the proprietors, polite if curious and unsmiling and bewildered, had listened to his halting phrases and regretfully shaken their heads. They were, these laundry men, for the most part Cantonese.

David had written his father, with the result that in the bags packed for college there reposed Baldwin's manual of the Fuhchau dialect, and a dictionary.

Young Mr. Wright was unburdening himself. No student, four years of incarceration in Middletown appealed to him not at all.

Also there were women in the university, as Wesleyan had been coeducational since the middle seventies. Mr. Wright deplored this deeply, caressing the chief pride of his existence, a drooping, chicken-yellow mustache.

David, whose skin, very fair under the overlay of bronze, had not thus far reached the dignity of daily shaving, looked upon the mustache and envied the possessor, and envied, too, a little, his extremely stylish garb. He asked, "You do not favor the fair sex, then?" On the contrary, admitted Mr. Wright with a groan, he liked them too well. That was the trouble. His china-blue eyes looked hopefully into David's and he waggled a long thin throat with its prominent Adam's apple caged behind a high, tight collar. Was—Mr. Condit—er—did Mr. Condit—in short, was David a ladies' man?

David disclaimed the honor, frowning.

Mr. Wright, eyeing David's physique and with a sigh for his own gangling build, inquired whether or not David would go in for athletics. David hadn't, he replied, thought of that. Football, declared Mr. Wright, was a glorious sport. That is to say, for those who liked it. Personally he preferred the light fantastic.

David, who had never in all his life danced, had nothing to say.

Other young men came up, made themselves known. And presently they were pulling into Middletown and David had his first glimpse of the beautiful Connecticut River. That there was to be a river near by for four years, and in the distance low and rolling hills, pleased him greatly.

In company with Richard Wright, who appeared to have taken a fancy to him, and with the others, David, after leaving his trunk to the tender mercies of the expressman, walked to the college, carrying his bags. The air was cool and golden, the beautiful trees were just beginning to turn, after a sudden, sharp frost. Later there would be Indian summer, and a purple haze on the hills and the trees would flame with the autumnal torch.

His way lay uphill. Despite the pleasant September breeze the sun was warm and now and then David put down his bags to wipe his forehead. His eyes were brilliant with interest and curiosity. Wright, panting along beside him, was full of information.

He had visited Wesleyan during the previous spring. He drew David's attention, gloomily, to the five cemeteries they passed on their walk. It seemed scarcely a good omen, he announced. And David laughed, deciding that his companion was a trifle touched in the head, but excellent company. Neither of them knew at the time that another freshman, many years before, had remarked of that same walk to his best friend, "George, if I ever get out of this town alive it will evidently be more than most people have done!" But it would not be very long before David and Richard Wright would recognize and love the features of that freshman, who had entered college about the time they were born, for they would attend the classes in English literature of Professor Caleb Winchester and, as long as they lived, they would be somehow under the spell of his charm and erudition.

At the intersection of Washington and High streets, David, looking southward, drew his breath sharply. This was the very spot on which Charles Dickens had exclaimed, "The most beautiful street in America," and David, gazing with eager eyes, saw peace and prosperity, and lawns shaded by magnificent trees, and beautiful houses. He said something, inadequately, but Mr. Wright tugged impatiently at his arm.

"Let's hurry," besought Mr. Wright. "I'm dead beat." He cast an uninterested glance at the magnificent houses. They said very little to him but later David was to know why the streets he had never seen appeared so familiar . . . and as if he had come home. For the fine houses and the acres of lovely estates had been built by men who had made their fortunes in shipping, and especially in the China trade. And in those houses were precious trinkets, and curios, there were carven gods, and pieces of jade, there were tea chests and mandarin coats and miniature pagodas; and in them, too, the very scent and feel of the sea traditions. Had not Samuel Russell of the great Russell company been born in Middletown?

Even now, in the eighties, there were still shipyards, still shipping on the river, if not as much as in former years.

Walking along High Street, two blocks to the south from Washington, David came to the head of College Street, where in front of the president's house, he saw, for the first time, the campus. Here was the broad lawn which occupied nearly seven hundred feet along High Street, and the beautiful, thickly-leaved massed trees, and in the background, the college itself, built of the Portland brownstone quarried across the river. And at the northern end, old North College, in which David was to live.

His room secured, on the topmost floor and adjoining that of Mr. Wright, who had little use for what he termed pitiful accommodations, David made his arrangements to take the entrance examinations.

He had decided to take the scientific course because of the profession he had selected. His freshman studies would include Greek, Latin, Mathematics, and Trench's *Study of English* under Professor Winchester. It was Wesleyan's inclusion of science in the curriculum, as well as his church affiliations, which had decided David's choice of a university, a matter which had concerned Tobias Condit since the day he brought his son back to America for his education.

David's means, while not ample, were adequate. The legacy inherited by his father would serve to feed and clothe him during his college years and would take care of traveling and other small expenses. He had, moreover, a seventy-five-dollar scholarship. During medical school and his later interneship, there would be a heavier drain upon the fund. Tobias wrote him in the first letter which reached David at Wesleyan:

"I desire that you have the normal opportunities for pleasant and proper social activities of any boy of your age and station. However, my dear boy, you must not lose sight of the fact that you are preparing yourself to be a worker in God's vineyard, and that your parents pray most earnestly that you will so conduct yourself. We expect good reports of your work, and we expect also that, in the larger freedom which college affords you, you will not for one instant lose sight of your early training.

"We are well here, and very much occupied. Three more out-stations have been opened, we are busy traveling on the district. The school and the orphanage grow, and your mother is hard put to it to find sufficient time for all her duties. I am translating the New Testament into the Fuhchau dialect, with the help of Sia Ho-mei, who remains our faithful friend. You will be sorry to learn that the head of the Sia house died last month. We had the funeral card. Although he did not die in the Christian Faith, I am sure that he has found peace and light in another world. He was a good man. Heng-ong, diligently pursuing his studies, is much affected by his grandfather's death and it is to be expected that the venerable wife will not long survive him.

"All here send love. Keep a journal for us of your activities, your friends and your studies. Write us as often as you are able to do so. You are constantly in our thoughts and prayers.

"Your mother will write you also, by this boat.

"Your aff. father

TOBIAS CONDIT"

Reading that letter, closely written on small, thin sheets of paper, in his father's spidery hand, David was seized by a nostalgia as acute as physical pain. He looked slowly around the small austere room with its battered second-hand furniture, its desk and books, which had by now become as familiar to him as President Beach's voice thundering from the pulpit in chapel, or "Winch's" rugged features with their slow, illuminating smile. And looking, the years ahead seemed intolerably long to his impatient youth and he was desperately homesick and unhappy. Only Wright's knock at the door and thrust-in, innocent face, oval as an egg and about as expressionless, saved him from an outburst of which he would have been inexpressibly ashamed.

David's class contained seven young women, only three of whom graduated with him. None were known to him, save by sight and word of greeting. He made a number of friends during his years at Wesleyan, none closer than young Mr. Wright of Philadelphia, who was languidly taking the classical course and who was dropped in his junior year. There were four other men in the class graduating in '86 who became physicians, all of them good friends of David's.

The four years were not, after all, intolerably long and, although David's application to his studies was noteworthy, particularly with the start of his sophomore year, in which the science courses began, they were considerably enlivened by unacademic incident and episode.

The freshman cane rush gave way to the moderate excitement of the freshman party in October at the home of a professor. It was at this party that David met Malvina Edwards, daughter of one of the richer men in town, and a rather beautiful little person. It was not Malvina so much as her home on High Street, which had been founded by the prosperity of the China trade, that attracted David who, on her parents' invitation, was formally asked to call and later to dine. He grew to know the Edwards' very well during his four years' residence in Middletown, and although the friendship between him and Malvina came to nothing—she was an exceptionally popular young woman—there were moments when she gave him a rather bad time . . . the turn of her head, the long, questioning glance of bright eyes, the pressure of her hand. But, he told himself sternly, he had no time for women.

David's four years were rather turbulent ones for student and faculty. The brilliance and intelligence of President Beach had not taught him how to control young men, in the mass. There were all sorts of antics and disturbances, the first of which took place in November of David's freshman year and was the burning of a negro shanty on the corner of High and College streets. It was a ruinous place, and an eyesore, and various attempts had been made to burn it. On this occasion the endeavor was successful although an adjacent billboard, with its posters of high-stepping ladies of the lighter drama in tights, a shocking sight to the staider students and the faculty, survived. The previous attempts had failed owing to the agility of the fire department, but on the night of November 15, the shanty blazed to heaven.

For the fire company's hose had been cut!

David had not cut the hose, nor had Richard Wright. But they were attracted to the scene of the fire, and not long thereafter found themselves in a riotous and magnificent fight with a town gang, led by a gentleman of most alarming proportions. Young Wright was the first to suffer a casualty, and as the press of "town and gown" grew greater, David fought his way into the firing line to effect a rescue of his friend, who was bleating feebly, one eye shut and bleeding copiously from the nose.

The fight was an epic one. "Here!" shouted the freshman, "here comes Chinese Condit!" David had not pitched hay for nothing. He laid about him lustily, his red hair on end, his eyes blazing with excitement, and his temper, never too solidly under control, rising. But he laughed as he fought, while Richard Wright crawled away to nurse his wounds and marvel at his friend, for, once the zest of battle seized him, David lost sight of the fact that the motive for this engagement no longer existed. The clean sweet smack of his closed fist or open palm on hostile flesh held a distinct pleasure for its own sake.

David spent the rest of the night, in company with half a dozen other freshmen, in the town jail, examining what was left of the new, low-crowned gray derby which had been one of his costlier purchases and wondering what would happen to him. His immediate fear was expulsion, and the consequent bitter disappointment of his parents.

He took his red head in his hands and groaned and even the sight of Wright, who had bribed his way in to speak to him, having himself escaped arrest, and all his proffered consolations and offers of help, spiritual and financial, were of no avail. He was ruined, and knew it. He had betrayed his trust. What of the conduct required of him, and rightly, by his people? He had become a roisterer upon the streets of Middletown.

"Well," said Wright in a piercing whisper, "the worst that can happen is six months in the county jail at Haddam!"

Six months!

"You didn't," asked Wright, trembling at the sight of his friend's misery, "*kill* anyone, did you?"

On the following day the bedraggled lot were tried, and acquitted. The judge was a Wesleyan man, the prosecutor also, and so was the lawyer for the defense. Go and sin no more, was the gist of the verdict; and the *Argus,* the college paper, published an extra.

And David found himself a hero.

Shortly thereafter he was elected to membership in Psi Upsilon.

David's first holiday was spent partly with the Smith cousins and partly in Philadelphia with Richard Wright and his very amiable family. Richard, a lackadaisical youth, timid in action and in speech inclined to smart-Aleckism, had, nevertheless, a stout heart for friendship and a gift for loyalty. He admired David tremendously, for his superior physique, his quickness at his studies, and for the varied experiences of a life which seemed to Richard much less narrow than his own. And David had for him a tolerant affection which he was always to bestow upon those weaker than himself. They quarreled occasionally, they disputed hotly often, but in the main they got along very well.

When his freshman year ended David returned to Carthage for the summer, dividing his time as usual between Aunt Lizzie, who seemed to grow no older, although she must, by then, have been sixty or more, and Dr. Brent, who listened to his saga of university life with interest and amusement. Brent's university had not been confined within a campus, his medical education had been bought dearly, and he had little use for new-fangled methods of education and said so frankly.

The shanty fire had been, of course, the outstanding event of David's first year. He had written his father, completely and truthfully, after an even harder battle fought with himself. He had even taken counsel of Richard, a more worldly soul, who had reminded him, "He'll find out anyway. There are always people who write . . . and it was in the city papers, David." So David took his pen in hand and wrote soberly and fully. And when the answer came, the long weeks between had served to dissipate his fear to some extent and to prepare him to hope for just what he received, a lecture on the control of one's passions and a full forgiveness contained in the post scriptum. "I hope, David, as long as you fought, that you acquitted yourself with some measure of honor and success."

There was no one quite like Tobias.

In his sophomore year the Sunday service in the chapel was discontinued and David attended church in town. In the same autumn he went out for football and proved himself a strong, if not spectacular, member of the team which closed that season with a record, the total scores being Wesleyan 90—opponents 78. His friendships prospered, his work went well, including the required courses in Evidences of Christianity and Ethics and other allied subjects which, as a medical missionary, he would be expected to have. His vacations passed swiftly and in 1884, returning for his junior year and finding the campus changed by the removal of the house belonging to the widow of the first president, deceased during vacation, David told himself in some astonishment that he was halfway to one stepping-stone, at least.

Halfway as well to seeing his parents again for they had promised that they would be home, on their second furlough, to see him graduate from Middletown and enter Yale Medical School.

In his junior year the college colors were changed from the lavender, which many of the students felt was too girlish a shade for their masculine university spirit, to the striking cardinal and black which was to soar victorious over many a hard-fought football contest. And in that year also Richard Wright, by advice of the faculty, decided to conclude his education elsewhere and so left Middletown, to David's whole-hearted regret, to begin a series of *wanderjahre* in Europe, which included Heidelberg among other landmarks of learning. "It's a good thing," said Richard sadly, on taking his departure, "that I don't have to earn my living . . . if your ability to do so is based upon your marks."

President Beach's discipline continued to be severe and unremitting. David met him more than once, face to face, in the halls of North College looking for possible offenders, and woe betide the boy who whistled at a town girl on the streets or otherwise conducted himself without dignity! He was a brilliant man and, to individuals, kind. But for the student body as a whole he had little tolerance. For a number of years the conversation—if a monologue can be called conversation—which David had with the president, after the shanty fire, remained almost verbatim, and most uncomfortably, in his memory.

One of David's good friends in the college was "Doc" Raymond, who had been janitor since 1865. Even Doc was not exempt from the humor of the boys who decided once to park his amiable and treasured cow in the North College reading room. And there was one night, after celebrating a football victory by a forbidden bell-ringing, when David was just one pace ahead of Doc, upstairs and down, in the darkened auditorium, and listening, as he urged his long legs to flight, to that gentleman's muttered adjurations.

If he was heart-whole during his university years, he was not entirely untouched. There was Malvina with her blond curls, and her lacy, elaborate frocks and her widened eyes . . . "Oooh—David, tell me all about China"; there was the dark girl who sang in the choir, whose name he never knew; and, more important than either, the daughter of a certain drug-store proprietor whom one mild and enchanting spring night he took for a ride in a hired buggy, along by the silvered river, and whose knowing, yet delightful, mouth pressed suddenly to his was infinitely, and initially, disturbing.

It was his inexperience, rather than his common sense, that set him walking the floor of his room late that night in something like pure terror.

Was he not pledged to this girl because, moved by her provocative presence and the spring night, he had taken advantage of her and kissed her?

He was in no position to marry. He had the rest of his college career and his medical school training ahead of him. Nor was it fair to ask any girl to wait so long, for him. And so, having reached this lack of conclusion, he sat down at his desk and looked with lack-luster eyes at the books strewn upon it.

For he did not love plump, giggling Sarah, and he knew it.

If Richard Wright had been there, and had come upon him in such a case, he would have wormed the truth from him and given sage counsel. But Richard wasn't there. Therefore, upon the following evening David presented himself at Sarah's modest home with a heavy heart and a dragging step. Letters, long and incoherent, to his father and mother lay unsealed on the desk in North College. After to-night, he would add the last, important line, seal and mail them.

But Sarah had an engagement to go driving—and not with David—and she misunderstood his first bungling sentence. She tossed her shapely head and put him properly in his place. She'd have him know that he wasn't entitled to all her time, she said. And presently David escaped, almost running down the graveled path, feeling that he could shout and sing for sheer relief. He was a free man. He had added something to his knowledge. There were nice girls who kissed lightly . . .

Half an hour later, the letters to China reposed in the wastebasket.

And so having gained something in book knowledge, having strengthened and broadened and hardened his body by exercise and training, he graduated from Wesleyan University on June 24, 1886. Meanwhile Elizabeth Condit's sunken dark eyes were so filled with tears that for a long moment she was not able to distinguish the tall red head topping the big young body, among all the others standing there waiting to receive, at the end of their four brimming and turbulent years, the coveted diploma.

CHAPTER V

FOLLOWING David's graduation came the summer in Carthage which he afterwards looked back upon and recognized as one of the happiest periods of his life. For Elizabeth and Tobias were with him and, although Tobias departed frequently on speaking trips, he returned home for long periods and enjoyed leisure to a much greater extent than upon his last furlough.

Elizabeth did not leave the Carthage house. She had not been very well and David saw, too often, the anxious regard which his father bent upon her, and the uneasiness he exhibited. Elizabeth herself was faintly amused, palpably irritated and, secretly, deeply touched. She would say, "Please, Tobias, do not concern yourself, I am perfectly well. A little tired, that is all." And when Lizzie would come clucking to her side with a new-laid egg beaten up in fresh milk and flavored with nutmeg, she would drink it dutifully but with a shudder of distaste.

"What's wrong?" David asked his father, when they were alone one day. They had gone fishing, with a picnic lunch, and plenty of bait, and were sitting on the overgrown bank of the trout stream. "I mean . . . *really?*"

Tobias sighed heavily. He had not changed, except to grow a little heavier and somewhat stooped, but the dark hair and beard were streaked with gray. He looked at his tall son for a moment, and replied presently:

"We do not know, David. Dr. Jasper says that her heart is a little—tired. She has been working overhard, you know, and after all these years, despite the respites at Sharpe Peak and Kuliang, the climate has told on her."

"She should see a doctor here," said David sharply, "in New York perhaps. Uncle Mat's a good man," David went on, "sensible and sound. If she'd see him . . . ?"

"She won't," responded his father, his line slack in the water.

"She becomes disturbed if I mention doctors. Of anyone with a less amiable nature I would say, almost irritable," he added thoughtfully. He looked out over the small, swift-running stream. There was a brief silence, while David frowned, jerked at his line, lost his fish and was indifferent. The hot mid-summer sun beat down in checkered light and shade. Leaves drooped, motionless. No bird sang, but the hum of insect life rose drowsy and insistent from the grass.

"I—I have wished for some time to retire from the mission field," said his father suddenly, "but your mother would not hear of it."

David turned and looked at him aghast. His shirt was collarless and open at the throat. He was deeply tanned, and the bridge of his arrogant nose, so like his father's, was freckled. His strong hands were freckled also. The dark red hair, damp with sweat, curled above his forehead. His blue eyes were intent. He repeated:

"Retire?"

"Yes," said Tobias. "I suggested to her that we come back home—for good. There would be a pleasant town somewhere, perhaps in this district, in which she was born and which she loves. And a church."

David still looked at him, the strong, wiry man, in the prime of his years, which were not yet fifty. It had never occurred to him that one day his father would leave the work which had been his life. His heart contracted as if a hand had squeezed it unmercifully. He said, low, "You must think her very ill."

Tobias did not answer immediately. Presently he said:

"I have asked too much of your mother, in my zeal and ignorance. She has given almost a quarter of a century to our work in China. She has sacrificed everything, her home, her people, the companionship of her only surviving child." He was silent a moment. Then he went on, "She has never intimated that the sacrifice has been too hard . . . there may have been moments of natural weakness—but they passed."

He broke off. David stated, frowning at the water running brown over the stones, and silver with the sun in the shallows:

"I shall never marry."

His father smiled at him, with his fine, firm lips under the graying beard, and with the deep hooded eyes. He said, "Better men than you have said that, Davy—"

David laughed, at himself. Nevertheless he thought, silently, he is right . . . it's too much to ask . . . in the best of circumstances. He said, aloud:

"But I don't understand. I mean, if you are willing . . . to come home . . . ? You *are* willing, aren't you?"

"Perfectly," said his father, "but your mother does not believe that. And she says, moreover, that she is not. She feels that she no longer has her roots—here."

At the quick alteration in the younger man's face, Tobias touched his shoulder, where the cotton shirt clung to the smooth wet skin. "I did not mean to wound you," he said gently. "How dearly your mother loves you only she and God may know. But—"

"I understand," said David with difficulty. It wasn't, he knew, that Elizabeth Condit loved him less and her work more. It was that he had grown away from her. Every day taught him that. Not in love, not in the deep intuitive understanding of the heart. He couldn't explain it, even to himself. But the years between, the formative years. Lost to them both. He thought, That's the harder thing, sending your children away, not knowing . . . waiting for mails . . . wondering . . . they might be dead and buried before word would reach you. Boyishly he wished, with a sharp regret which stung his eyes with tears, that he had written more often, during these last years.

"She was twenty," said his father slowly, "when we went out to China." He thought briefly of that voyage. Not even to his son, a grown man, could he speak of the storm and the agony and the loss. "Twenty," he repeated reflectively. "More than half her life has been spent in China. The mature half. Can't you see that, David? It is strange to her here . . . even in her birthplace, and with the people she most loves."

It was strange, David agreed, remembering his mother's amusing yet rather sad little efforts at housekeeping, in an attempt to relieve Aunt Lizzie of some of the burden and to keep herself occupied. She no longer knew how to keep house, in America. She was lost without her servants . . . she was lost in a maze of detail which she had forgotten.

David asked, "Mi-daik? Do you ever hear of her?"

His old amah had gone back to the hills, to the village in which she had been born. His father shook his head. "Not for the last year or so," he said, "I haven't gone back there. Brother Henderson saw her, two years ago, I think. She lives with her sons, respected, an autocrat. There are grandchildren. She told him then, David, that she would not die until you returned."

They spoke briefly of Heng-ong, studying medicine at Tientsin, under Dr. McKenzie at the school which had been opened five years earlier, with the patronage of Li Hung Chang. He had completed the first of his three years' course, and was planning to go to Edinburgh afterwards. David said slowly:

"He wants me to take a postgraduate in London, or Edinburgh, after I graduate."

"I know," his father told him. "I had a talk with him before we sailed, when he was home on a brief holiday. He is a very fine young man," Tobias went on, "you will be proud of Heng-ong, David."

"I am now," David told him. "I don't know about the postgraduate course. It will mean further expenditure. I intend, of course, to find work if I can during the summer holidays. As you know, my degree cuts my medical course to two years. But, if necessary to earn the additional money for the postgraduate work, I could take three."

His father said quietly, "I don't think it will be, Davy. Time enough when the time comes."

They were quite silent. The fish flickered through the brown and silver water, unmenaced. Neither of them made any further pretense at fishing.

Tobias said:

"Some things are hard to say, between father and son. There are questions difficult to ask. You have had comparative freedom, liberty even during the last four years. You have been your own master in a certain sense. The world is changing; standards have changed. I can see that, after eight years' absence. Over there, times move more slowly. Ours is a narrow world and, I believe, a wider life. But here— You are a man, David, strong, impatient, young. There are warnings I should deliver. I find it hard. Easier, if you were a friend's son. I have counted, perhaps overmuch, upon your early training and the influence of your mother, of myself. But you have been away from us for a long time. When we leave you we will not see you again until you come back to us, mature, to begin the merciful practice of your elected and noble profession. Medical school will be different from college. You will find it so. You will, you must, encounter many things which will shock you, appall you at first and then tend to harden you. If a word of mine—"

He stopped. It was too much. How to tell this son of his that the harder way is in the long run the easier? How to tell him that liberty is not license; that a man is not less but rather more a man if he preserves the sane mind in the sound body, the keen, unclouded intellect in the unblemished flesh?

"Chastity—" he began, and stopped again.

For him it had not been difficult. His body had been a temple to his God. He could not defile it. Nor was it expected of him that he should. He had thought since, anxious for David, and very far away, that the cloth of his calling had been more than an outward symbol of an inward striving after grace. There were certain things the world did not tolerate in a preacher. But David was not a preacher, and this was another generation. An era of luxury and spending, of extravagance, of, perhaps, something they called progress.

Tobias and Elizabeth Condit had married young and in innocence. But to his inexperience Tobias had added imagination and tenderness and the healthy blood of a normal, magnificent vitality. Since his marriage men who knew and loved him had made him the repository of certain stammered confidences. He thought they had been fortunate, he and Elizabeth. Their mating had been quite simple and unashamed. It had been a union blessed of God.

David said, quite simply:

"I understand. It hasn't always been easy . . . but—"

That was all, no word given and no pledge. Nor would Tobias ask it. He remembered his own father, when he was quite a small lad, and shortly before the elder Condit's death, thundering to him of brimstone and hell-fire. "Whose feet go down to hell!" Thundering, too, of strange women and their whoring. Warning, exhorting.

Such days were past. Tobias no longer believed, very firmly, as he had once believed, trembling and sweating over a minor misdemeanor, in hell-fire and lakes of flame. He had looked upon injustice and cruelty and had come to believe in justice and mercy. His conception of an austere, punitive God, who once said *Vengeance is mine,* had altered slowly over the years to a belief in heavenly kindness. He could not, therefore, exhort his son nor did he seek to terrify him. A grown man, of another generation, the boy sat beside him quietly and dedicated himself without words to an ideal, which did not after all seem so difficult to his father. And Tobias thought, *Blessed are the pure in heart, for they shall see God.*

It was growing late and the shadows fell long and golden across the grass, filtering through the green network of the trees. They rose presently and went toward the village, David carrying the poles, the can of bait and the lunch box. At the steps of the frame house he paused and addressed his father. "If we could persuade her to see Uncle Mat?" he said.

His father said, sighing, "I'll try, Davy."

There was supper waiting. The cuts of cold meat, the golden preserves in the old dishes, the homemade pickles. There was salad and spice cake and great pitchers of fresh buttermilk and milk. There was coffee. David, eating with a tremendous appetite which caused Aunt Lizzie to shake her head with pride, looked at his watch. He must, he said, be getting down to the drug store.

He was working that summer, nights, and sometimes week days, in the largest apothecary in town. In this way he would earn a little extra money. All in vain for his father to assure him that there were adequate funds. Tobias had not touched the legacy since the time of his marriage. It had been there all these years for David. But David was stubborn. He must earn some of his own. That night, when he was compounding prescriptions under the eagle eye of his employer in the heat of the small back room, in an atmosphere redolent of spice and medicine, cinnamon and quinine, Dr. Brent came striding in and clapped him on the back.

"How many folks have you poisoned to-day, Davy?" he demanded.

He swung himself up on a high stool, after greeting Mr. West, the druggist, genially. He said, his big fingers fumbling with a heavy watch chain, "Miss you, since you started out to be a druggist."

David laughed. He corked a bottle, wrote a label. He explained: "Can't spend all the holiday being idle, Uncle Mat."

"Maybe," suggested his old friend, "maybe next summer I could use you, myself. Had an assistant for a while, let him go, he was no good. But next year you'll know more'n he. First year men always do, I find. How about it, Davy?"

"You!" said David, in affectionate scorn. "When not half a dozen patients out of the lot pay you—except in potatoes and cider."

"You forget the load of hay now and then," Mat reminded him, his eyes twinkling, "and the crock of butter, to say nothing of six dozen doughnuts at a wallop."

David grinned. Dr. Brent went on:

"Well, if your aunt Lizzie can spare you next summer . . . there's your board and lodging in it, and a couple of dollars a week. Now and then a shin plaster extra, if you promise me you'll have a stronger stomach by then than last time you assisted me at an operation."

He remained in the store talking until it was time for David to go on home. They left the apothecary's with the red and green bottles in the window and walked through the soft, hot night to the Lewis house. David said, after explaining, "If you'd just look at her, Uncle Mat . . . I mean, perhaps she wouldn't know . . ."

"Who, Elizabeth Lewis?" snorted the doctor. "That little tyke . . . I've known her since she was knee high. There's nothing she don't know! . . . You think she's really bad off, David?" he asked after a minute, his good, pleasant face sober and anxious. If Tobias Condit hadn't happened along—but he had. So Mat Brent had put young Elizabeth Lewis out of his mind and that was that. Somehow there hadn't been anyone else he'd wanted, since.

Now he went up the broad steps a little wearily.

"Hard day?" asked David, following, noticing how he stooped.

"So-so. Two babies. I can't get used to seeing women suffer, David. And the new hand at Sims' broke his fool leg falling out of the haymow. And at supper time along comes Carter's young 'un with a toothache, bellering so's you could hear him over to Lake Bonaparte. And before that, that colicky baby of Mrs. Benedict's, and some others. There's a possible typhoid too— I dunno yet. No, average sort of day, Davy. Gets monotonous sometimes. If I were twenty years younger, I'd go out to China with you," he said, as they went in the front door, "blessed if I wouldn't."

When he left an hour or so later, and David stood with him in the porch, he shook his head. There was just enough light to see the gesture. He said, low, "I can't tell, David. She don't look good, and that's a fact. If you could coax her to let me examine her—?"

Persuasion wasn't, as it happened, necessary. A day or so later, driving his mother in the surrey over Natural Bridge way, she grew white and swayed against him, saying apologetically, "I'm so sorry, Davy—such a nuisance . . . it's the sun, I think—"

Her lips were faintly blue. He got her to Brent's big rambling house on the main street, and helped her in. The housekeeper, Amelia, voluminous in a blue apron, her hands white with flour, met them with clackings and exclamations. The doctor was in his office.

David lifted his mother in his arms and put her down on the horsehair sofa in the parlor. She looked very small in her summer frock of soft striped material, with its tight waist and small bustle. He unfastened her clothing and laid her big shade hat aside. She lay without speaking and presently Mat stomped into the darkened room, with its stiff furniture and heavy steel engravings and set his bag down on the round table and ordered David to pull up the blinds.

Then he sat down beside Elizabeth and took her hand in his own, watching the hands of his big gold timepiece. She said, after a minute, "It was the heat, Mat."

"Of course," agreed Mat cheerfully. "Just you lie here till I fix something . . . temperance, naturally," he added with a chuckle, not very authentic, at his little joke. David, watching him move away, saw, with a heaviness at his heart, that his back in the heavy black coat which despite the weather he always wore in office hours, had a defeated look.

Presently he was back again with a glass which he held to Elizabeth's lips. And after she had taken the medicine and, smiling faintly, had sunk back against the pillow Amelia brought, he looked gravely at David. Aloud he said cheerfully, "You'll be as fit as a fiddle in half an hour. You lie still and rest, Elizabeth. Try and sleep."

A little later David followed him into the office. Amelia was sitting beside Elizabeth fanning her with a palm leaf. Mat sat down at the roll-top desk and stared unseeing at the overflowing pigeonholes. He took the stethoscope from his neck and put it down. David asked, "How bad is it?" and wondered at the loudness of his own voice.

"Not bad," said Mat, "but bad enough . . . what's that thing old Will says—'not as wide as a church door nor as deep as a well but 'twill serve.' Something like that. Heart, David . . . son, don't look like that. If she'll spare herself, she'll live to a ripe old age . . . only . . ."

"I know," said David dully, ". . . only, she *won't*."

But after that attack had passed Elizabeth seemed much better during the rest of the summer. David and Tobias talked to her, pleaded with her, each in his own way. Mat had talked to her too, bluntly, honestly. And she listened and smiled and promised. But when, again, Tobias, with David as his advocate, urged that he resign and that they stay on in the States, she shook her dark, smooth head. She wouldn't, she said quietly, be happy. They were not to worry. They were not to fuss. She would take excellent care of herself during her holiday. When she returned to China, she would be perfectly well, they would see.

Shortly before David went to New Haven to enter medical school, Lizzie, briskly mixing bread dough in the great sunny kitchen, made an attempt to alter Elizabeth's decision. She argued, a little shrilly:

"You've given the best years of your life to them heathen, Elizabeth, and I can't see for the life of me why you want to go back there—murdering dirty place as it is . . . Tobias is willing to settle down. You could make a home for David."

Elizabeth sat in the Boston rocker. The big sleek tortoiseshell cat was in her lap. Its purr was as loud as the kettle singing on the range. The sun came through the windows and shone on the polished brass and copper. It was a pleasant room. Elizabeth rocked, slowly, her feet on a small carpet-covered hassock. She said, finally:

"I don't think you understand, Aunt Lizzie. That is—my home. Over there. China."

"Land sakes," said Aunt Lizzie, disconcerted and offended.

"Don't," said Elizabeth softly. "I didn't mean it that way. But look, all my married life . . . among people, who are my people now. My baby lies there . . . where she lies must always be home, to me."

"David's here," Lizzie reminded her.

Elizabeth's face, thinner, and without much color, was illuminated, and her dark eyes shone. After a moment she said, "Yes, he's here"; and then she said, "But he doesn't need me, Aunt Lizzie."

"Fiddlesticks," said Lizzie Lewis, "as if he hadn't always needed you—"

"Don't say it," said Elizabeth, whiter, and in a whisper. "Don't, please. Don't you suppose that's been the one thing that's nearly killed me . . . needing me perhaps and I not here? But he's a man now, and . . . and he's grown used to being without me—us. Tobias needs me most, he always has."

"Mercy," said Lizzie practically and astonished, "I don't know what's come over you, Elizabeth; of course Tobias needs you. And you've been a good wife to him. But can't you be a good wife to him any place excepting China?" she inquired in bewilderment and some impatience.

The cat purred comfortably, and the kettle sang. Lizzie covered the dough with a cloth and set it aside to rise, and opened her oven door to look at her cake and to test it with a broom straw. Closing the oven door gently, she turned. Elizabeth had not spoken. Sharply her aunt inquired "Well?" on a rising note. She thought, If her mother were here. But Mary Lewis was not and had she been it would have made no difference.

Elizabeth said:

"I was trying to think how I could make you see. He'd give it up for me, of course. I know that. But do you think I'd let him?"

"There's poor folk here, and suffering people," said Lizzie, herself a staunch supporter of the mission and wondering at her own heresy as she spoke, "Tobias can do good at home—"

"It isn't home," repeated Elizabeth stubbornly.

CHAPTER VI

IN THAT year the first term at Yale Medical School opened on
the seventh of October. David, accompanied by his father,
arrived well ahead of time, in order to take his entrance examinations and that his father might satisfy himself as to his
son's lodgings. They found, without difficulty, a private boarding
place already overflowing with students and with one of these,
Herbert Woodruff, of Watertown, David arranged to share his
quarters in order to conserve expenditure.

Woodruff, a rotund and amiable young man, was delighted to
find a companion who knew his part of the country so well. "If
you were not set upon this China business," he lamented frequently during their first year, "we could set up offices together."
Watertown, he declared, was a coming town. The hospital
founded five years before was a growing institution. When he
graduated he would, he said, take over his father's practice and
prosper. He knew Mat Brent well, liked him, scoffed at him a
little. "Good old fogey," he remarked, "but hopelessly behind the
times!"

Tobias, meeting Woodruff, was rather attracted by the youngster's energy and ambition; and satisfied that David, having found
a friend, would be well companioned, left New Haven feeling
that the boy was well established.

David's first letters home were enthusiastic. He could never
have enough of the town, its towering, magnificent elms, the
wide shaded streets, the traditions of the campus. The medical
school was located over a mile from the college, on York Street,
and the clinical courses were given at the New Haven Hospital
where dispensary and clinics were held. The medical library,
part of the university library, was on High Street, and David
wrote his mother cheerfully, "Don't worry about my not getting

sufficient exercise. I must walk leagues in the course of a single day."

He wrote fully of his work, from day to day, quoting freely from textbooks, from Gray's *Anatomy,* and Shafer's *Essentials of Histology,* Wood's *Therapeutics and Materia Medica,* and Mann's *Prescription Writing* and many others. His father laughed over the letters but his eyes were bright with pride. Elizabeth, showing them to Mat Brent, as the early northern winter closed in, said, smiling, "I suppose you feel that he is taking himself very seriously."

"He'll shake down," declared Mat, "he's a good boy." He thought privately, no lad with eyes in his head and a heart in his body could be anything else with such a mother. Aloud he said, "But you're doing him an injustice, Elizabeth, an injustice."

It was an old battle between them; he knew himself defeated before he entered the field. She said, her knitting needles flying, "I do not think so, Mat. We do not possess our children, you know. They belong to God, who lends them to us for a little while. Sometimes for so brief a time." Her eyes were very far away; they were homesick. Mat said, sharply:

"I don't pretend to be much of a Christian, not in your sense. And I can't understand you, Elizabeth. A little resignation is all right . . ." He broke off and clapped his heavy hand on his knee. He said, "This stubbornness of yours is suicide, Elizabeth Lewis."

He never called her by her married name. This amused her faintly. She had ceased to be Elizabeth Lewis so many years ago. She could not project herself back into that distant girlhood. And when she did not reply, Mat added doggedly, "It's your own concern, of course. But in pampering this man of yours—"

"I'm not pampering him, Mat," she denied quietly.

He went on, ignoring her, "You'll be cheating him of a wife, some day. Seems to me that after all, you're not thinking of him —much."

"Dear Mat," said Elizabeth. She put out her too slender hand and touched his knee. She said, "I don't believe you, naturally. I think there are many fruitful years ahead of me . . . but—if what you say were so . . . I wish I could explain it to you, Mat . . . could make you see. Suppose—suppose," she said with a catch in her breath, "that we retire. And that something happens. He'd be lost, here, without me. But, in China—if it happened there, don't you see how it would help him . . . to go on? He's needed there, Mat. You can't know, you haven't seen how they look to him, and love him. How he does battle for them . . ."

Mat growled something. It might have been "damned heathen." It might have been something else. There was no telling, Elizabeth didn't hear, couldn't know that he would have sacrificed every living soul in a country he had never seen, and would never see, to spare her a moment's anxiety, to save her from an instant's pain. He got up heavily. He said, "No use talking to you, my girl. I come over here and neglect my sick and chew at you for hours on end. But it don't avail me anything. Tell that learned young whippersnapper to write me now and then," and stomped off, down the steps.

He himself wrote David, in his illegible scrawl:

"Your mother seems better, she's resting more, taking better care of herself. I tell her she has to if she wants to go to New York at Christmastime."

They had Christmas together, in Carthage, as David's vacation began on the twenty-second of the month. But afterward the Condits went down to the city to pay a visit to the Smith cousins. Permelia and Abigail were getting old and they were tired. After this year they would no longer conduct the boarding house with its double parlors and narrow carpeted stairs, its air of staid respectability, its clattering hired girls and "permanent" paying guests. They would sell the house and retire to Jersey, where they had been born.

During vacation David acquainted himself with the great city hospitals. In two years he would be eligible for an internship. He had talked it over with Mat, at home, and with one or two of his professors at Yale. It seemed to him that in order to prepare himself for the sort of work in which he would presently engage, he must seek as varied an experience as possible and among the poor of a crowded city. Bellevue held him. The old gray buildings, the secret life of the river flowing by, the steps worn with the patient, the hopeful, the desperate feet of frightened people. He told his father—"If I can get an appointment at Bellevue."

But it would be difficult. The competition would be hard. Still, his mind was set upon it. He told himself stubbornly, I must get that appointment.

His university degree would mitigate in his favor. And if his marks were good, if he came recommended?

Elizabeth, when her strength permitted, went shopping, in Grand Street and at Stewart's. She must replenish her household linen and her other goods for the next long stretch of years ahead. She went calling too, on the various of her acquaintances. Mrs. Martin had long since died but there were others. It seemed to her, sitting at tea in their stately houses, her sealskin jacket and muff, Tobias' extravagant Christmas gift, laid aside, that she had nothing in common with these good, pleasant women, so immersed in their household affairs, their children, the social activities of their church. They questioned her and listened with the wide eyes of children to her replies. But she could not make them see, or understand. And sometimes the clothes bothered her. In China one wore one's clothes until they were too shabby to wear any longer. If there was a gown one especially liked, it could be copied by a native tailor. One subscribed to *Godey's* or to *Leslie's Weekly* and so, in a measure, knew how the styles were changing. But that didn't matter. Here, the cut of a sleeve, the cascade of ribbon trimming, the tilt of a bonnet seemed all-important, even to these sober and unfashionable women with whom she came in contact. And she longed often for the comfortable completeness of the Chinese garments she—and Tobias too—had worn with increasing frequency during the last years.

Tobias was occupied, he was asked to preach from a number of city pulpits, and did so with all his old eagerness and vitality. If he could only make people see the reality and importance of his mission!

One night he and David went down on the Bowery together.

There was a rescue mission there in which Tobias was interested. After listening to the service, to the sound of a battered organ and of battered voices lifted in wavering and pitiful praise, in the bare room overheated by its central stove, they walked out upon the streets together, under the gaslights. It had snowed recently, and there was a delicate whiteness which, for a brief space, would overlay filth.

The saloon doors swung, warmth streamed from them, light, the sounds of people shouting and talking. Theaters and dime museums were patronized and the streets were crowded. Here and there were figures in doorways . . . and there were men in the gutter. Women went by . . . or halted briefly.

When they returned to Murray Hill, Elizabeth was already in bed and the two men sat for a little time in the parlor, talking. David, idly turning over the pages of a photograph album, was considering his finances and wondering if he could afford to have a cabinet photograph taken for his mother while he was in the city. That would please her, he knew.

His father was still fulminating on the section they had just seen. He was accustomed to squalor, accustomed but not resigned to vice, yet he had been shocked to the core, as had been De Witt Talmadge, some years before him, walking the same streets.

"Sin," he was saying, "ignorance."

David looked up. He said, after a moment, "I don't think so . . . I dare say I agree with the ignorance but . . ."

His father regarded him, aghast.

David said quickly, "Just the little time I've been in the clinics. The things I've seen—when you think of the children born with the seeds of disease already planted in their pitiful bodies . . . They haven't a chance," he said after a moment, "unless science can bring it to them. And they are innocent."

His father nodded. He said, " . . . 'unto the third and fourth generation' . . ."

David shook his head impatiently. He said, "It isn't fair. . . . A man can't select his forebears. If one could begin by teaching those forebears . . ." He stammered a little in his eagerness. He was very young, the small yet immense world into which he had recently been inducted was new to him, and strange. It was brutal and pitiful and wonderful. There was death in it, and horror. There was also hope, and a lamp shining. He couldn't make his father see. To Tobias the body was of little moment. The life within the body was of little moment. It must be lived so that it reflected the soul to God's glory but it was not the important thing. The important thing was the soul. The soul first . . . then what did the body matter?

But how, asked David of himself, painfully struggling to see beyond the things which had always been so true for him, how could you expect a man to possess a clean soul in a dirty body? How could you expect a man to preserve the health of his mind if the tabernacle was unclean?

He said, gropingly:

"President Lincoln said 'all men are created free and equal' . . ."

His father waited, anxious, quiet. His mind went back to a day of rejoicing, in China . . . when the mission received the word that the long and bitter war was over. And to a day of almost intolerable sorrow, a day of mourning for a *man*.

David asked, "It's a dream, isn't it? Because it can't be true."

His father said sternly, "In God's sight, it is true. The least of these . . . whether the man lying in the gutter or—"

David broke in, twisting his hands together. "I can't believe that. One man is born to poverty and disease, and what you call sin. Can it be sin if he knows no better? If you're hungry, you steal. That's the first law, self-preservation. One man is born to ease and a sound body. He isn't tempted. So remains—good. Perhaps. I don't know that either. It isn't equable," he said again, "and it can't be so always."

Tobias argued:

"If God has seen fit to set each of us in his own station of life—"

"Oh—*God!*" cried David, in despair.

Tobias looked at him, his heart aching. It was perhaps natural that David should go through his youth-time of doubt and questioning. He himself had escaped much of that, perhaps because of the calling to which he had dedicated himself from boyhood. But David's calling, if noble, was different. Science resolved no doubts; rather, it created them. He spoke, and he knew that his son did not listen. As they parted for the night, he said, his hand on the boy's shoulder, "You are but a lad, David. Do not question the wisdom of your Heavenly Father. And pray, every night, every day, for guidance."

Still troubled, he went into the room where Elizabeth slept, the same room, the same bed to which he had brought her as a bride on the eve of their voyage. He stood looking down at her, his hands clasped behind his back beneath the long coat tails. How serenely she slept, how beautiful she was. He had shared everything with her, over a quarter of a century. This he could not share. He dared not. And this was something the boy must go through, alone. Perhaps later he would remember some word of his father's and be comforted. Perhaps not. He was no longer a child accepting everything without question. And he was of a new generation, which doubted.

Tobias knelt by the bed. If he, the child's bodily father, could not help, there was One who could.

When the three weeks' holiday was over David returned to New Haven. The spring recess would be for one week only and he would not then return to Carthage. It would be too expensive a holiday for so brief a time. He had, however, his mother and father with him, during that week. They had found suitable lodgings, and it was pleasant to have Elizabeth beside him walking under the elms, small and erect, in a plaid walking dress, the tight bodice conforming to the lines of her slender waist.

He afterward remembered how gay she was during that time. They had a gala dinner at the New Haven House, and one day Tobias hired a carriage and they went driving. They inspected the university buildings, and Tobias met several of David's instructors. And Elizabeth was in a gale, for the most part, of gentle amusement, particularly at David's elegant new mustache, the first he had persuaded to grow, and much lighter in shade than his hair. It did not, he said ruefully, caressing it with an unaccustomed hand, conform to the fashion of the day, being stubbornly curly! She laughed too at the greatest extravagance of the last term, a blazer, which he had bought for tennis. For pleasurable exercise he must have, his time was short, and his football days behind him. But he had met several very pleasant families in town whose daughters had introduced him to lawn tennis, an entertaining if not particularly strenuous and, he feared, not especially manly game.

When he left them at the railroad depot it was with the assurance that the time would pass very quickly and then they would be together again in Carthage for the summer, before the longer parting.

But before his first year ended, late in June, he received word that his parents were returning to China. Mr. Henderson, long in ill health, was retiring. In the months which had passed since the Condits had taken leave of the mission, the burden of the work had grown. The force had been augmented but the necessity for leadership remained. And so they were sailing.

David went down to New York to see them aboard the train for the long overland journey. Elizabeth, in the dim parlor of the Smith house, held him close in her frail arms, this big man whom she had borne in agony and from whom she must once more take her departure. Each time, she suffered the almost mortal pangs of something closely allied to childbirth. And yet she was happy. Tobias had been restless of late. There was work for him to do, work into which he could plunge himself.

At the station she kissed David again. His father kissed him too, his son, as tall as he, regarding him level eyed. They said the last sad things one says, leaving so much unsaid. They committed him to a wiser care, and they left him.

He cried, as they boarded the train . . . "In another three years . . . !"

In another three years he, too, would board a train, and would return.

"Three years," said his mother. The tears ran unchecked down her pale and slender face, which remained undistorted. Tobias' arm was around her, as it had always been.

It was around her when she died, not many months later. She had stood the train trip well, and the first weeks of their passage. But there had been a bad storm over the Pacific, shortly before the goal was in sight. Tobias had comforted and soothed her. She had apologized . . . "It's stupid of me to be so afraid." But she was remembering, and remembering made her ill, her frail body shaken with the pounding of her heart.

On the mission houseboat, going to Fuhchau, she suffered the second bad attack. And three days after their heralded arrival, three days after her hands had lain in those of her friends, three days . . .

She said, faintly, to Tobias, "You must not grieve." And she implored, "Let me stay here."

He promised. Here she must stay, and here he would stay until the time came for their reunion. He wrote to David, after the first brutal message had been sent, in Mat's care, "You understand that it has always been your mother's wish to be laid to rest in the mission churchyard beside our little Lydia."

David understood that much. But there were other things, other decrees, which he could not understand, and which Mat Brent with his blundering affection, and his own silent sorrow, could not explain to him . . . the justice, the *why*. Nor could his great-aunt enlighten him, walking through the darkened rooms in her frame house, with an abstracted and undirected step. Yet she had, at least, her resignation and her belief. Mat had not; nor, found David, had he.

The year and three months which had passed since his entrance into Medical School had been full of events of national and international importance. Earthquakes in Europe, revolution in Bulgaria, riots and hangings in Chicago, and Dr. McGlynn, in New York, excommunicated for his advocacy of a man named Henry George. But to David the time had brought three things of vital importance: his mother's death; the conclusion of his first year at New Haven; and the awakening of doubt that the social scheme was under Divine conduct.

His letters to his father were stammering attempts at consolation and years later he was to read his father's journal, and especially one page, written in a hand very unlike Tobias Condit's usual firm, fine script.

"*She is gone*. But a few hours ago the dear companion of my earthly journey departed this life, in quietude and peace, as if she slumbered into death. Released from all suffering and care she will sleep sweetly until the sound of rejoicing breaks the silence and heralds the opening of the portals of eternal joy. I have already sent the message to David. What it must mean to him I dare not dwell upon. That I cannot be with him now adds to my burden. But there is One who wept at the tomb of Lazarus, whose heart is full of a divine compassion. I must hold fast to my abiding faith in my Heavenly Father which His word enjoins. I tell myself over and over, this is not the end, it is but the beginning. I know this in the deepest reaches of my nature. But it is bitter to be alone."

Writing to David, at a later date, Tobias told him that if the matter could be arranged he would never return to America. "Let me," he wrote, "live the rest of my life here, and to some good purpose, until it pleases God that I join your mother." He spoke tenderly of David's sorrow and consoled him with the reminder that they would some day be together again, in China. "The three of us," he said, "you *must* believe that, David."

David, returning to New Haven, found believing easier when one did not think about it, pull it to pieces, examine it. Upon dissection, belief became a cadaver. Work, hard and unremitting, was the only salvation; afterward at night one might fall, almost senseless with fatigue, across the hard, narrow bed, and sleep, without dreaming.

His friends were very good to him during the first few weeks, especially Woodruff, in his practical, unverbose way, the Wesleyan classmates who were students with him again and with whom he had renewed his intimacy, and those of the instructors who had come to know him. And as the year went on there were times when he could almost forget that he bore within him a living sorrow. They had been separated so often and for so long, he and Elizabeth Condit. Now and again, this present separation seemed merely another, soon to be concluded. But there were moments, coming suddenly, by day or night, alone or in company, in classroom or lodging, walking the streets or sitting at a desk, when full realization took him by the throat and reunion was, in the ordinary course of events, uncounted years ahead . . . and even then, uncertain.

Work was full, vital, strengthening. There were days when the brain reeled and the stomach turned at the sight of so much waste and so much misery and ignorance. Yet there were others, to offset these, in which the heart was high with hope for the future, and his own two hands seemed strong enough, once they had learned the ways of healing, for the working of miracles. And there was the spring, returning green and sweet, to the elms, when the campus was scented with the recurrent fragrance of the year's wild youth and the blood was hot and strong in his veins and merely to be alive, and learning his craft, was enough.

In this second year he pored over the thumbed books and stood breathless beside the older men while their clever hands probed and listened to the sharp or droning utterances of their voices . . . *"this patient, gentlemen . . ."*

In this year he saw, more fully, pallid death and bloody birth, and in his nostrils were all the odors of humanity; in this year he stood watching the major operations under the flaring gas lights, listening to the step-by-step explanations, to the importance of "antiseptic" surgery. And all through the months, under direction, he worked and struggled and thought and argued and listened and succeeded. At night, in his room, half a dozen classmates would often gather and the air would be filled with the rank blue smoke of the stogies he had first abominated and then learned to embrace. Voices penetrated the smoke, the light would pick out a mouth shaped to laughter, lips set in stubborn disagreement. And always the eager voices went on, with their eternal questing after knowledge, their short memories, their plans. This was a man's world and if women entered into it, it was only at second hand, and by the doors of a young vainglorious boasting, as David, harking spellbound, was soon to learn. As for himself, the only women who at this time came insistently into his intimate knowledge were those whose bodies, patient or impatient, lay stretched upon an operating table or beneath a sheet or upon a slab; or whose hands went out to him at clinic, and whose haggard eyes begged for hope. They were a means to an end, these women, they were lessons to be learned. And he found himself harboring for them a certain rebellious and wounded pity. And not for them only, but for the broken bodies of men and for the lamenting of children. Sometimes he threw down his books and cried aloud that he could not go on, it was too much to demand of a man, that he fight these losing battles with so small, so inexact an equipment of knowledge.

His father had feared he would become hardened. He need not have been concerned. Sometimes David would pray without words that he might form some protective shell, that the blows might become blunted. He was afraid. What if he made irrevocable blunders? That the best men in their time had made them, he knew. How could they go on? Yet, only by blundering could one learn. A life was lost that a hundred other lives might be saved. But could a man bear to think back on that one life?

Woodruff, to whom he sometimes spoke of these things, shook his round head. Intensely practical, lacking imagination, he plodded ahead, highest in the class in theory. He said, warningly:

"You can't afford to look back, David. Can't you take it all more in your stride?"

But David could not.

In the spring before his graduation David took the examinations for Bellevue. He was both fortunate and well equipped. Despite the great competition, his appointment was secure.

CHAPTER VII

DR. BRENT traveled to New Haven for graduation, much to David's delight and amazement; the latter emotion partly induced by the sight of his good friend, arrayed as the lilies of the field never were, in the very latest style of light trousers, darker coat and a spectacular cravat of large proportions.

"Store clothes," Mat explained confidentially, "and I don't mind telling you it's a pretty uncomfortable rig. But if my collar's choking me, how must that young man feel?"

"That young man" was Richard Wright, Esq., of Philadelphia, who had returned from his modern Grand Tour, and his seasons of incarceration behind the walls of European learning, and who was now more or less settled in the banking business with his father. Richard, recently engaged to be married to a handsome and suitable young lady, had, in the interests of friendship, made the trip to New Haven to be present at David's graduation.

Richard was, indeed, the very last word in sartorial perfection and above the high-winged collar his round face beamed at David with pride and affection. But engaged to be married or not, his was still a roving eye as David, with some amusement, noted. There were a number of pretty young ladies and their portly mammas present at the ceremonies.

Their summer garb, enlivened with ruffles, and their small tilted parasols above furbelowed bonnets and ringleted coiffures, struck a frivolous and charming note. Richard was enchanted and expansive. He hadn't, he said, been properly thawed out since the Great Blizzard until this fine June day.

"And now," he announced, when the exercises had been concluded, and he was back in David's lodging, watching the new graduate pack his modest belongings, "now, Dr. Condit, we must arrange to find you a fashionable practice. Among women, naturally. There's nothing like the fair sex to set a man upon the

109

road to success. Of course," he added thoughtfully, "the megrims and swooning spells of our mothers' day have passed. I ascribe it to the new fads of wheeling and tennis. A young woman whose skirt is at her ankles and whose upper proportions are encased in a tight-fitting jersey is too Amazonian a specimen to indulge in pretty by-play. But still—"

Mat, seated on the bed, furiously smoking a cheroot, grunted with irritation. Young Wright infuriated him, with his airs and graces, with the heavy signet ring he wore, the pearl in his cravat, the checked waistcoat and trousers and the foreign affectations he had picked up on the other side. But David grinned affectionately at his one-time classmate. He knew, none better, the fund of sincerity and loyalty, the gift for friendship, housed in the heart which beat beneath the violent checks. Over the period of years since their parting, Richard had not ceased to write to him, absurd, travelogue letters with sketches on their margins. And more than once he had sent him money with a stern command that he was not to return it: "I have not overdrawn my allowance for the past two months. The Pater has rewarded me amply in his astonishment. As we cannot celebrate together, I implore you, David, to toast me in something, be it only water. By the way, I have met here in my hostelry a most engaging young woman. She is somewhat shorter than I, of pleasing plumpness and divinely fair . . . If it were not for that old Gorgon, her mamma—" And so on, *ad infinitum.*

"You forget," said David, while Richard cogitated ways and means, "that I have still to serve in a hospital."

"By Jove," agreed Richard, in the manner which alienated Mat, "so you have. A beastly bore, what?" and he twirled the drooping ends of his chicken-blond mustache and gazed through a single eyeglass at his friend in a fashion which caused Mat Brent to choke in his comfortless collar and to long for a woodshed and a piece of stout lath. "Dude!" said Mat under his breath.

"Talk English," advised David, with a sly, blue eye for Mat's annoyance.

"But I am talking English," countered Richard, aggrieved. "It's all the rage now in the upper crust. None of your crude Americanisms."

Mat slammed his hand down upon his knee. He was purple. David said, shutting a large and battered grip, "Don't mind him, Uncle Mat, he's putting it on to impress us."

Richard twinkled faintly and relapsed into his mother tongue, with only an occasional "I say" to embellish it. He suggested presently, "But while you are in New York, we will see something of each other. I may be able to give you some introductions which will be helpful. Dolly—my betrothed, Miss Clinton, has numerous friends in the city."

"You are still forgetting," David told him, "that at the conclusion of my interneship, I sail for China."

"Still set on it?" asked Richard. He sighed. "I had hoped that you would alter your mind."

"No," said David, "I won't."

Mat sighed too. This was the nearest to a son he had ever had. To be sure, it was perhaps not to be expected that a modern young man would care to bury himself in the little village and live out his life as a country doctor. But Mat had hoped . . .

Young Mr. Wright, with his new eyeglass, his newer side whiskers and his cherished mustache, betook himself home again, and Mat and David traveled back to Carthage. It had been arranged that until his departure for New York David would live with Mat and help him in his practice. "All the practical experience you can get, my boy, will be of great value," the older man had counseled.

From Natural Bridge David wrote his father that he was settled for the time being, and that he was, he feared, of less assistance to Mat than the old man professed. But at least, as in his younger days, he could keep the horses groomed and fed, and the buggy shining clean. He could administer chloroform, hold a basin, assist with a dressing.

One day shortly before David left, they drove out into the country to a rather ramshackle farmhouse set in beautiful trees, deep in rank grass and flanked by shabby lilac bushes long past their bloom. The shingles hung crooked, the steps were out of plumb, and the outbuildings in a state of disrepair. It was rather unusual to find so much neglect in that part of the country and David expressed mild astonishment.

"It's Sim Dexter's place," explained the doctor; "you know him, don't you? He's a shirk, shiftless as all get out. Fine wife, though, and a family. There'll be more family before we leave here, David, I guess, according to the summons I got while you were down in the store. His wife's a nice little woman. I've brought all the young ones into the world. A shame, too," he said, clucking at the old mare. "I declare it grieves me to the heart to have to bring a baby into a house already overcrowded and where there ain't, often, enough to eat. Sim, he's no farmer. His father was a good one, this was quite a place in its day. But Sim—he gets work now and then over to Carthage in the saw-mill, and then drinks up his wages. I'm sorry for his wife. You, Mary," he shouted suddenly, as they pulled up and the mare reared slightly, "look out!"

Mary was between six and seven. She was an undersized and undernourished child, in a faded and tattered calico dress, with bare brown knees and feet, and a ragged sunbonnet swinging from her hand. She had wild, long, mouse-colored hair and gray-green eyes in a pinched face. She grinned at the two men, without shyness and announced, "See . . . ? I lost a tooth," with her mouth stretched to its widest. And then, as David hitched the horse to the post and got out and she saw Dr. Brent's black bag, shabby and bulging, she asked gravely, "Did you bring our baby in that . . . ?"

"Perhaps I did, Mary, perhaps I did," Brent answered, chuckling, and hurried past her, but David stopped a moment to bestow a copper penny upon the child and to ask, "You'll like that, won't you, Mary, a new brother or sister?"

She looked up fearlessly at the tall young man with the bright blue eyes and dark red hair and curling mustache. She shook her head, clutching the penny. "No, I won't," she said clearly, "there's two younger'n me, already. I think we'll have to drown this one the way we did Tabby's kittens."

Smiling, yet a little heartsick, David went on into the house and was presently very busy. Sim, a stooped, lean man, his scraggy whiskers stained with tobacco juice, his teeth broken and discolored, slouched around, with no animation. David boiled water and tore a clean, ragged linen sheet into strips. The dark, untidy kitchen was overrun with children, the two younger than Mary, the three older. David, marshaling his forces, issued orders to the oldest boy and girl, who gaped at him in some astonishment and then went, flat-footed, to do his bidding.

It was a dirty and dismal house. But the woman in the big bed with the sagging mattress was small, pitiful, clean, and she had courage. When it was all over and Brent's big careful hands held the purple, scrawny body of a living man child, she smiled and closed her eyes. Women came into the world to work against odds, to scrub and bake and clean and squeeze the few pennies, to watch the crops sicken, perhaps, and die, to work in the fields, to marry, to lie down at night beside a drunken sot who wasn't worth his salt but for whom one had a strange irritable tenderness. And to bear his children, wondering how they would be fed. It was better that those children be men. Men had the easier lot.

When, later, David and Mat went out to the buggy, Mary was standing by the hitching post chewing thoughtfully on her penny. David took her small, dirty fist from her mouth. "You might swallow it," he told her, "and then Dr. Mat would have to come and cut a big hole in your little belly!"

Mary rubbed the mentioned part of her anatomy thoughtfully. It gave her enough trouble as it was, she couldn't seem to fill it up. She grinned, the missing tooth a startling gap in her freckled face, at the big young man and watched him drive off. She loved Dr. Mat very much. He was good to her. But she had never seen anything so dazzling as the other doctor, the one who had given her a whole penny to hoard or to spend. And she ran off to hide it before her father found it and took it away from her.

"We'll look in to-morrow," said Mat as they drove away under the row of trees and turned into the main road. "They'll do, for now. I told Sim what to do. He won't, of course. But the older girl is sensible enough and there's a good neighbor woman. She would have been there this morning only she had to go take care of her sister in Wilna."

David said thoughtfully:

"The baby—I don't know, of course, but—"

"He'll live," said Mat shortly, "more's the pity. Don't know why they do. Woman hasn't had enough victuals to feed herself on, much less the child. But there's good stock and stubborn blood and he'll grow up—hungry."

David said hesitantly:

"I've something saved . . ."

"Keep it," ordered Mat, "you'll need it, in the city. Don't start out doctoring with the notion that you have to feed and keep your patients as well as cure their bellyaches and bring their young into the world. It's a thankless business."

"How about you?" asked David, smiling, and resolving that, one way or another, he would tide the Dexter family over a bad time. A box of groceries to-morrow, perhaps—

"I'm an old fool," said Mat shortly. "You needn't be. You've got your life before you. You'll marry, raise a family. I have neither chick nor child . . . only these folks hereabouts, who count on me."

"I'm not likely to marry," said David soberly. "I wouldn't ask a woman to go to China with me."

"We'll see," said the doctor. He returned to the Dexter family. "She'll do. Hasn't much strength, but she'll do. I haven't lost a case in a good long while, David. Nothing's worse than when you do. But it's a funny thing now, you'll find a lot more mothers dying in the big city hospitals than you do at home, even in houses like Sim's."

David nodded. By now medical science knew something of what it owed to Ignaz Semmelweis, who had been permitted to die discredited and insane. Yet Dr. Oliver Wendell Holmes had long since arrived at the same conclusion as had Semmelweis, and independently of the latter's findings; and to-day, as David and Matthew Brent drove along the white, dusty country road, Pasteur, the chemist, now professor in the Sorbonne, had demonstrated the truth of the Austrian's theory; and Lister, against terrific odds, had proven his major theory of antisepsis.

In all his practice Matthew Brent had seen few cases of child-bed fever. He said so now, as the noonday sun grew molten over their heads and the mare trotted briskly along. "Look you, David, you've been graduated from a great school and you'll soon be working in an up-to-date hospital. Remember when you get back to China you'll have a hard row to hoe. You won't find things to your liking there. Not from what you've told me about it. You'll break your heart a hundred times over," he said.

"I guess so," David told him slowly, "but it will be worth it, won't it?"

"That depends on you," said the doctor.

They drove into the Brent yard and David took the horse around to the barn. Amelia rang the dinner bell. Her men were always late, but their dinner waited, plentiful, piping hot. After-ward Brent lay down on the sagging sofa in his office, his hands folded on his stomach, the shades drawn and a handkerchief over his eyes. He'd take his cat-nap before office hours began, as usual. While David, in the kitchen, sitting on the end of a table, while Amelia clattered dishes, discussed with her, biting into a doughnut, the needs of the Dexter family. He wasn't much of a housekeeper but if Amelia would give him a list he'd take it to the store. Amelia clucked despondently. "If you ain't the spit of Mat," she declared, "like enough to be his own flesh and blood. Sometimes I declare I can't sleep nights on account of thinking of that man ending up in the poorhouse from giving away everything he has."

But the list was forthcoming, in Amelia's crabbed hand.

At the end of summer, David left for New York and took up lodgings near the hospital, for two weeks before his service be-gan. There he opened his old books and refreshed his memory, smoked too much, drank too much coffee, went, not without a rather pleasant sense of sin, to attend his first theater where from a modest situation he observed, not without emotion, the tragic beauty of Miss Fanny Davenport.

He wrote his father:

"I am aware that you do not approve of playgoing, but I cannot help but feel that the theater has a message to bring and that, rightly presented, it cannot be otherwise than wholesome."

During this period he revisited the places in which he had been with his parents during their holiday weeks, crossed once again the marvelous span of Brooklyn Bridge, attended the Eden Musée and regarded the electric light at the top of its tall pole at Madison Avenue. His only social visits were paid to one or two of his old instructors at the Collegiate School and once he went to New Jersey to see the Smith cousins who were settled in a little house in Orange.

Eventually, his holiday over, he mounted the Bellevue steps with their wrought-iron railing and entered the doors of the gray stone building which was to claim the greater part of his waking—and many of his sleeping—hours for the next two years.

Here it had stood, with the river flowing past, for the past ninety-four years, and not the least change the river had seen had been that from gentleman's estate to hospital. But its roots went back farther into the town of New Amsterdam when from a modest poorhouse, conducted by a church and a little hospital, built by the West India Company, Bellevue had moved, and moved again and grown into the sprawling succession of buildings with the elegant name. From candlelight to lamplight, from lamplight to gas. In the stark never-ending battle with disease and filth and poor equipment, from a building which housed sick and mad, prisoner and pauper, it had grown, and David entering into this new period of knowledge in the oldest hospital in the United States, never passed up or down the many steps without thinking of the feet which had trod upon them, steadily wearing away the stone.

He soon grew to orient himself in the labyrinth of pavilions, the Sturges, the Marquand, the Townsend and others, soon grew to know, as familiarly as his own face in the mirror, the Emergency Hospital which cared for the maternity patients in the old engine house on East Twenty-sixth Street. It seemed to him that, in the course of the hard, long days, he walked for countless weary miles through the corridors. It wasn't the walking that bothered him, it was the question—was he drawing closer, was he, at the end of an occupied day, one step nearer his goal?

As usual, and easily, he made friends. Men liked him, and women smiled at him. There were pretty women among the nurses, the big white aprons spotless, their grayish blue, striped uniforms rustling, stiff with starch, the round cap perched on hair that was brown or black or red. Social intercourse between the young internes and the nurses was not encouraged, but it flourished in secret, as must any sweet and forbidden fruit. Therefore, some of David's gayer colleagues laughed at him for his reluctance, and his professional manner.

But if he had no heroines at the time, he had heroes in plenty. He would follow the doctors on their rounds, listening, watching. He would stand almost breathless, as he had stood at the New Haven Hospital, in the torrid operating room with its odor of carbolic spray, and watch the surgeon moving deftly, with skill and precision. For the time would come when he could not watch but could only pray, in some remote part of his intelligence, for then it would be his hand that held the knife steadily and drew so quick, so sure a line upon the field of operation, and his eyes which, his life concentrated into their blazing blue, would watch and decide and send the message to brain and muscle.

Over the table the gaslight flickered. It was not enough. There were candles taped into bottles to augment the illumination; and it was the duty of one person to see that the fumes of the anæsthetic did not rise and explode in the tapering flames.

The service was rotary: medicine, obstetrics, surgery. During his last six months he would be required to serve courses in erysipelas, obstetrics and acute alcoholism, and would during this time be resident within the hospital instead of, as now, boarding in the district.

The hours were long and tedious. At night the gas-lighted wards were eerie. Wails broke the silence, sobs, the voice of terror, the voice of pain. Oaths, prayers . . .

It was only recently, he learned from a graduate nurse, that the gas was permitted to burn all night. At a not very distant date in the past two candles were permitted each ward per week—other necessary candles must be supplied by the nurses themselves, out of their twelve dollars a month allowance. For the dimly burning gas had been turned off entirely by the captain of the night watch, at five A.M.

Even now in David's day the wards were cheerless and, to a person of imagination, a little terrifying in the darker hours.

Written reports and written orders were comparatively new. David, learning this, marveled how the hospital had ever been conducted, in all its vastness and intricacy, in an earlier day. In a day, too, when even the matter of plumbing had been more difficult and hot water had to be carried in buckets and pails as needed.

His social activities were few, for lack of time and means. When certain of his friends went racketing on their evenings off, he did not join them. They thought none the less of him, liking him for all his seriousness and application to work. His old name of Chinese Condit had followed him here and was presently superseded by Sobersides. Although when, through a classmate of David's at Wesleyan, the tale of the epic shanty battle reached some of the men, they regarded him with more respect. And found it justified in the discovery that of all the internes, David's powers of persuasion with a burly and refractory patient, just coming out of the fog of drunkenness and resenting his surroundings, were far the most able.

Then there had been occasions when, riding the swaying "Bus" behind two wildly galloping horses, he had arrived at the scene of the call and found himself with a street fight on his hands as well as a patient.

There could be, he wrote Tobias Condit and Matthew Brent, no wider, better training. He went from street to hovel and tenement, from dissecting room to operating room. He knelt beside dying men and women while flames roared to the wide heavens and burning buildings fell and the shrieks of the injured rose above the clatter of horses' hoofs and the firemen's shouts. He climbed the steep, rotting stairs of tenements and he stood beside small, quiet cribs in the wards. He invaded saloons and houses of prostitution and, whether an honest workingman's wife gave birth or a harlot died in a stupor, his newly learned skill was called upon. He looked on the skin lesions of men riddled with an intolerable disease, and he saw blind babies come into the world. And there were days when he thought, as he had thought before, *I cannot go on.*

The older, the seasoned men, who had bought their briskness, their impersonality, their measured diagnoses in as hard a school, looked upon him with liking. There were always some who rode roughshod; but there were others who went out of their way to help, to advise, to warn. They liked David Condit because of his eagerness, his inherited vitality, his ceaseless way of asking questions, of wanting to know how the wheels went round. "China," said one of the doctors, scrubbing his hands after an operation, "that's a large order. But no larger than here, my boy. Have you ever thought of that?"

He had thought of it, and increasingly so during the past months of his Bellevue service. But while there was great need here, there were also more men to fill it—if they would; over there, a scant handful.

His word was pledged. And his heart remained loyal. Hengong wrote him from Edinburgh:

"We see great things, science is coming into her own. May the time pass swiftly until we meet again, in our common purpose. Golden Peace to you, Younger Brother."

The expiring breath, the cry of the newborn, the smile or curse which greeted him; the child, sitting confidently on his knee fingering his watch chain, the cadaver on the slab, all its poor physical secrets exposed to the watching eyes; the smell of disinfectant, of illness, of death; these were all in the day's work. And when summer came, with its burden, and the ambulance clanged in and out, answering the calls of the heat-stricken, there was no holiday. Only work . . . and learning.

Early that summer young Mr. Wright, passing through the city on the way to visit friends in Newport, stopped off to see him. He deplored the lodging house, with its odors of dust and boiled cabbage, its clatter of heavily shod, quick feet on the stairs, and its landlady with a chronic cold in her head. "My word," said he disdainfully, "I don't see how you endure it."

David grinned cheerfully. He hadn't, he admitted, much time to think about it. What sleep he got was sound enough, and he had not, as yet, perished from starvation.

"But," insisted Richard, "what about your life? Come, my dear boy, this isn't life at all. Theaters, concerts, dances, young ladies . . . ?"

David shook his head. "Hardly," he replied grimly, "with my resources, or lack of them."

"Still against playgoing and strong drink?" asked Richard. "You don't know what you miss."

"Not exactly," David said, acknowledging that he had gone, occasionally, to the theater and for the life of him saw no harm in it. As for drink—he grinned, remembering Ward Forty. Where's So-and-so? the cry would run about the hospital. "Oh," the reply would come, "he's in Ward Forty."

"Ward Forty" was the saloon around the corner. It was not unfamiliar to David. He went there now and then with the others and sampled a glass or two of beer. He didn't like the harder liquors and said so frankly. They held no temptation for him.

Richard, who had acquired a fine palate for wines and for the headier cocktails, scoffed at him. "Unless," he intoned, "you've been under the influence, you never really know life. After all, when you get to China—"

"There's shamshu," said David with a wicked glint in his eye, "and it's potent."

"Shamshu?" Richard produced a little red book and made a careful note. He must, he declared, include China in his next tour. Shamshu . . . and hadn't there been things printed about the flower boats?

David opined that probably there had been. Personally he didn't advise his friend to journey to the Orient with the purpose of making the close acquaintance of almond-eyed girls sold into slavery.

"This is all beside the point," said his friend. He took out a calling card and wrote upon it. "This," he said, "is a reminder," and stuck the card into the cracked mirror. David read the penciled lines with indifference. A man's name, an address on Fifth Avenue.

Richard explained, gesticulating.

"A delightful family," he said. "Mr. Graham is a man of means and culture, extensively traveled. He and his wife have one daughter, and are distantly related to my intended. There is also an orphaned niece, the daughter of Mr. Graham's deceased brother—a charming bit of femininity. They will not be much in town during the summer. Mr. Graham is building at Newport and the family spends part of the season at Saratoga Springs. But in the autumn I will make it my concern that you meet them because really, David," concluded Mr. Wright with distaste, "I shudder to think what you will become in this atmosphere if you have no avenues of escape."

David thanked him, as gravely as possible. Richard, even at twenty-four, and the pink of fashion, seemed to him like a distracted hen who has hatched one chick in some hobgoblin form. And Richard, divining something of this, flushed a little. He said, "Dammit, David, you waste yourself on your pills and potions. You'll live poor and die poor and work yourself to the bone, to no avail. Give it up and come into the banking business. I tell you, before another generation has passed the bankers will control the world."

David, lighting a cigar, turned from the bureau. The house was very warm and he was in his shirtsleeves. He said, and laughed:

"Funny, isn't it, but I haven't the least ambition to control the world, Dick."

"No," agreed Richard, "that's the trouble," and shortly thereafter took his departure.

The card remained in David's mirror. It grew dusty and flyspecked, and the slatternly maid of all work marked it with a greasy thumb and dog-eared a corner in her curiosity, before replacing it. An address on Fifth Avenue. Dr. Condit didn't look like a swell. But he was affable and pleasant, and hadn't he treated her for nothing the time she had the terrible pains in her side?

But David forgot the card. He went his way through the summer, occupied, almost always tired. Now and then on a free hour he went down to Mott and Pell streets and walked among the dingy houses and flaring shop fronts, and looked for someone with whom he might speak in his own tongue. These were the Chinese whose immediate forebears had settled in the district after the burning of Barnum's great hoax, the "Junk," Hoboken made, in the forties. To his vast delight, he found one elderly merchant from Fuhchau who had come to the country some years before and David often spent an hour or so with him, drinking the ceremonial tea, smoking the ceremonial pipe, talking of China, and playing long, losing games of chess in the spice-smelling, banner-hung back room of the shop. But he feared that the prescription he once wrote for the old gentleman's chest cold had been disregarded and the prayer papers burned instead.

Then came autumn, and the completion of his first year at Bellevue Hospital and his meeting with Adeline Graham.

CHAPTER VIII

RICHARD WRIGHT had been as good as his word. Arriving in New York shortly after the completion of David's first year at Bellevue, he proceeded to pursue his quarry until at last David surrendered and sacrificed a free evening and went, with his friend, to call upon the Grahams. Although why, he couldn't exactly see, and said so. He added, "I haven't the proper clothes, Dick, and I'm no hand at drawing room conversation."

"Clothes," said Dick, "do not make the man." His own correct and elaborate garments belied his statement. However, early in the evening David found himself in a hired brougham, bowling rapidly through the streets, under a dark autumnal sky.

The Grahams lived on Fifth Avenue, on the north side of the Square. The house was large and spacious and had a solid dignity. David, at Richard's heels, was a little overwhelmed, although he would not have admitted it, by the portly placidity of the manservant who opened the door. Waiting a moment in the large hall, beside a marble stand and an antlered hatrack, Dick whispered, "Graham's very fond of the English manner of living. He has resided in London, over long periods."

The heavy draperies at the archway swayed and the butler appeared and ushered them into the drawing room. It was the largest and most luxurious room David had ever seen. He sat down cautiously upon a small gilt chair and looked about him. His youthful idea of elegance had been fashioned by the heavy, carved furniture of the Smith establishment, and this room, as crowded as the Smiths', but in a different manner, seemed much lighter, altogether gayer in mood. It was a medley of damask and satin and gilt. There were candelabra, and crystal chandeliers, and innumerable small tables littered with costly bric-a-brac. The wallpaper was French and colorful in motive, the draperies of a pale rose velvet over glass curtains of Brussels lace and the thick beautiful carpet a moss-green with sprawling pale pink roses. The walls were hung with pictures in massive gold frames, not the family portraits to which David was accustomed, but landscapes, nymphs, laughing girls. Dick strolled about, his eyeglass modishly fixed, and examined works of art. In every corner there were marble shapes, busts staring with their blank eyes, or full-length statues of graciously modeled women with marble draperies and a proper distribution of marble flesh. On the fine mantelpiece there were china figurettes, shepherdesses and shepherds forever molded in their wistfully amorous mood, and a great gilt clock, with cupids at its base.

Mr. Graham came in presently and greeted them. He was a tall man, florid, with an amiable, slightly formal manner. He wore a house jacket of mulberry velvet with wide, braided lapels, over his light trousers. His dark hair receded from a high forehead and David noticed the rather old-fashioned satin stock and the massive watch chain. He welcomed both young men cordially and rang for sherry and biscuits.

Richard did most of the talking, which centered on Newport. Since Rockaway Beach had ceased to be the fashionable summer resort for New Yorkers, gentlemen with families, means and leisure were turning to Bar Harbor and Newport although the distance from town made these places a little undesirable. "However," said Mr. Graham gravely, "the country is beautiful and the cottage life simple and healthful."

He asked David various questions about Bellevue. He was, it appeared, on the Board. David, almost before he knew it, found himself telling what amounted to the story of his life. Mr. Graham remarked, "How interestin'!" at intervals, and his heavy eyebrows were slightly raised when, on asking where David intended to take up the practice of medicine, he was told that it would be China.

"Admirable," decided Mr. Graham, "very admirable."

He added that he was an annual contributor to mission work.

Later, at their host's suggestion, they joined the ladies in the smaller and somewhat less formal library, which adjoined the drawing room. This apartment was, Mr. Graham said, in reality his den. But, he explained with a smile, the entire household took advantage of it.

Mrs. Graham was a small plump woman in a heavy silk gown and a tiny lace cap. Her daughter, Anna, was a tall, dark, decidedly handsome girl with a talent for the piano, which she later exhibited at her father's request, trailing her long skirts into the drawing room, seating herself at the large, inlaid instrument, with its drapery of silk, and running over several of the newer waltzes. Richard, perfectly at home, leaned his well-tailored elbow on the piano and turned the sheet music.

But David heard very little. He was looking at incarnate melody.

Adeline Graham was short and slender. She had a mass of almost flaxen hair, ringleted and fringed and caught in a heavy coil at the nape of a slender neck. Her skin was delicate and fair, her small face oval. She had immense hazel eyes, and her rosy mouth was a perfect cupid's bow. Her ears were flat and shell-pink, weighted with heavy gold and onyx earrings. David, who had never really looked at a woman's dress in his life, could have described in minute detail the semi-evening gown she wore. It was of blue silk, and scalloped, it had a Medici lace collar and gigot sleeves, was full and long in the paneled skirt, and worn over a small bustle. There was a gold and onyx chain about her neck, and a locket of onyx and pearls. He wondered, with a sudden frantic jealousy, whose picture it contained.

Adeline took little part in the conversation. Sitting erect in her chair, her hands busy with some bright woolwork, she listened to David. It seemed to him that he had never before talked as much, and certainly not to any woman. Mrs. Graham, seated nearby with her husband, glanced from time to time at the young people and smiled slightly. Had it been Anna she might have been a little alarmed, for Anna as their only child, must marry well—and carefully. Anna was already besieged by eligible suitors, but she could afford to take her time. Her appearance at the Patriarchs' Ball had been a great success.

Mr. Graham entered into the talk, with heavy cordiality. They spoke of the new safety bicycle and of the new imported game, golf, and the fact that a golf club had actually been organized at St. Andrews. Mr. Graham was not so sure of the game's absurdity. It seemed to him a game essentially suited to the older man. It had dignity, it was less hard on the heart than, say, tennis, which was developing from a game for young ladies to a more active form of amusement. To all this David listened and made the appropriate replies but with the merest fraction of his intelligence.

Adeline dropped her small lace handkerchief. She bent to retrieve it and David bent too. Their heads bumped smartly. There were tears in Adeline's eyes and laughter quivering at the corners of her mouth as David, awkward and suddenly feeling himself all hands and feet, straightened up, smote the small inlaid table beside her a tremendous blow with his elbow and sent it crashing to the ground.

In repairing the damage he became involved with the wool-work and it was a moment or two before the confusion subsided and things were restored to order.

"I'm a clumsy oaf," he apologized ruefully.

The words had a familiar ring in his own ears. Yet to his knowledge he had never before uttered them. He looked at Adeline. The great hazel eyes were alight, intensely curious. He cried out, "Why, of course, you're the little girl—!" just as she spoke. "You're the boy," she accused him, "who ran into me on the Avenue!"

They stared at each other, laughing, excited. Mr. Graham said, "Here, here," indulgently, "what's all this about?" Adeline explained with quick gestures of her little hands.

It was not, after all, so much of a coincidence. Adeline had lived in this section almost all her life and had taken her afternoon walks uptown and back again every day. David, still regarding her with wonder, laughed again. The same little girl with the golden curls, who had worn a velvet coat trimmed in fur and a little bonnet, fur trimmed too, and lined with shell-pink, and had carried a muff, and a doll almost as big as herself. For an instant he was a big homesick boy again, hurrying home from school. And he could smell violets.

"The lady?" he asked, "your companion? I thought her the most beautiful creature I had ever seen."

Adeline's laughter quivered to silence and her eyes filled. "My mother," she replied softly. "She died . . . about a year later."

He was desperately sorry for her. It did not seem just that she should experience pain.

When, after refreshments, he and Richard had left the house and had again entered the waiting carriage, Richard was impressed by his friend's silence. He remarked lightly:

"You seemed rather smitten with the fair Adeline."

David said shortly:

"That is, of course, ridiculous. I cannot afford to be smitten with anyone, Dick."

Dick whistled. He said, "I left you rather a clear field. However, remembering the cordial invitation to come again, and as often as you can, I feel in duty bound to remind you that Anna is the catch of the household. Graham's only child . . . You neglected her shamefully, Davy. The other girl is charming, of course, but an orphan, dependent upon Graham's bounty. Her father, Graham's younger brother, was not as wise or, if you will, as lucky, in his investments. Dying when Adeline was a mere infant, he left nothing but debts, the child and his wife, who soon followed him."

David, he discovered, wasn't even listening. And Richard had the uneasy experience of wondering if he had unwittingly played Cupid. Knowing David—and the Grahams—he wished that he had left well enough alone. But, pshaw! it couldn't matter much. David would find little time to sun himself in Adeline's smile or cool his heels in the drawing room. And he, Dick, had meant well enough.

The elder Grahams, fond of their niece, teased her a little. "Well, Addie," said Mr. Graham, stretching and preparing to go up the stairs to the enormous bedroom which he shared with his wife, "you seem to have made a conquest. A solid young man, I think, and—I pride myself on character reading—clever, as well. A pity he chooses to bury himself in the East, in his missionary and, I believe mistaken, zeal."

Anna, later that evening, came into her cousin's smaller bedroom, which was connected with hers by a narrow long room containing two huge marble washstands and a zinc bathtub. Anna, her dark hair flowing over her shoulders and in dressing gown and slippers, put her hand over the younger girl's.

"I think you liked young Dr. Condit," she said.

"I liked him very much," Adeline told her, turning from the dressing table before which she was brushing and braiding her hair. "He seemed so—sensible. And yet there is something rather exciting about him. Isn't it strange, Anna, to think that we met once, long ago?"

Anna had been at the piano when the discovery had been made. She sat down on the edge of the bed. "Tell me about it," she commanded.

Adeline told her. Turning, her bright face flushed and her eyes smiling, she asked again, "Isn't it strange? Almost like fate."

Anna was a year older, and decades wiser, than her cousin. She shook her head warningly.

"When young girls begin to talk about fate—" she said. She broke off. In a moment she had added, "He seemed very much attracted, Addie. It—I doubt if it would be wise to encourage him. From what Richard told us he is quite without means . . . and . . . a medical missionary, my dear!" She laughed a little. "Can you imagine yourself among pigtails—and lepers . . . ?"

Adeline shuddered. "No, I cannot," she said firmly, and then dropped her brush and turned toward her cousin. Delicate and smooth, her shoulders sloped from her fragile neck to the line of her immature bosom. She said, "But we are being silly. I don't know Dr. Condit, at all. We'll probably never see him again."

Nevertheless, when she had climbed into bed that night, and had nestled down in the feathers, her slenderness making very little impression, she thought, as the autumnal wind beat against the tightly closed windows . . . But if I *should* see him again . . .

She believed she would.

Adeline was very happy with her aunt and uncle and her cousin. She did not remember her father. Her mother's death had brought her her first sharp grief but she was now twenty years old and her sorrow had lost its cutting edge and was blunted to a gentle melancholy and an occasional sense of self-pity for her orphaned state. But Uncle and Aunt were very good to her, and Anna, although acid at times, was a close friend. Her life in the big house suited her perfectly and, indeed, she had known none other, having come there to live when she was so young. The little social amusements—calling, tea, entertaining—sufficed her. Since she had left the fashionable Fifth Avenue school which both she and Anna had attended, and had been permitted to take her place in society, she had found her time well occupied. There were duties devolving on her because of her aunt's church and charity interests. There were the purely pleasurable social duties. There were sleighing and skating in season, balls and parties and theaters. For Mr. Graham, although a devout man and a pillar of the stately edifice wherein he worshiped, was liberal in his views.

The season in New York, the summer in the country, the daily round, contented Adeline. She had never been made to feel a pensioner. Her gowns were quite as many and as elaborate as Anna's, and she was treated in all things as a beloved daughter of the house.

She had had suitors, from the time she was seventeen. Not as many as Anna could boast, but in most cases as eligible. And the summer before last in England there had been the young man of title with the elegant side whiskers and the astonishing clothes, and the fine old place in Surrey. But his ardor had cooled when he discovered that Adeline was not Mr. Graham's heiress. This had cost her her first disillusioned tears although Anna had comforted her sturdily. "He isn't worth it, Addie . . . conceited young jackanapes, you would have thrown yourself away."

Nevertheless, she had suffered a certain romantic yearning which had dwindled into heartache. It would have been pleasant to have been known as Milady, and to have opened bazaars and distributed patronage. The week spent in the deathly cold, echoing, uncomfortable yet beautiful house had enchanted her, the village people pulling at their forelocks or dropping an aproned curtsey as the coach went by . . .

In England she had learned to ride, and ride well. And now for her pleasure there was a smart little mare in the stables and rides, with Anna and the groom, in the Park.

She wondered if Dr. Condit rode.

He had attracted her very much, perhaps because of his difference from the young men she knew; his difference from the one young man with whom she had fancied herself in love. In a flash of honesty she told herself that half his Lordship's charm for her had been tradition and heritage. She was rather pleased with herself for her interest in this sober young physician of no family and no money and, so far as she could see, no prospects. Of course it did not mean anything. To permit herself to believe that a chance meeting could sow the seeds of a serious attachment would be immature and immodest. Still, she had liked the way his dark red, rather untidy hair grew and the flash of his blue eyes, the bluest she had ever seen, and the line of his mouth, under the quite absurd, and not at all fashionable, trim of his mustache. He was a very big young man, too, with a look of restrained strength about him. She liked that, being herself so small and delicate.

There was a legend about that delicacy. As a child she had been far from strong, swaddled and coddled. Later, growing into girlhood, she had been subject to fainting spells of alarming duration. The family doctor had said quite plainly to Mrs. Graham that she would outgrow these attacks. "Her age, my dear lady; when she marries . . . er—ahem . . ." This had not been repeated to Adeline. It could not be talked about. It was not proper.

Mrs. Graham's mother, since deceased, had had no such scruples. She had belonged to an outspoken era. She had panted her way up the stairs to stand at Adeline's bedside, after one such seizure, and had said, her old cool hand on the girl's fresh, pale cheek, "Eh, my dear, we'll hear no more of fainting and swooning when you've your own man and babies."

Aunt had said, "Mother!" in an agitated tone but Adeline had heard and wondered, the color flooding back into her small face.

"Cotton wool!" said the old lady, stamping out. "Fiddlesticks! Stuff and nonsense!"

That had been long ago. Since then Adeline had three times taken a private vow never to marry. The first time when a close school friend, marrying at seventeen, had died in childbirth. The second when an older acquaintance had disgraced and ruined herself socially and forever by divorcing her husband who it appeared had behaved badly with some woman of the theater, and the third more recent pledge had been made since her one romance had withered before flowering. Men, Adeline had decided, were gross; excepting her uncle, of course, and the pastor of their church, and one or two others. But around young men hung an aura of faintly exciting dissipation, one heard rumors of strong drink and weak women, and it seemed to her that the scarcely comprehended intimacy of marriage was something that could not be endured by a modest-minded woman. She had even spoken timidly of this to Mrs. Graham and her aunt, setting her firm lips, had admonished her severely. It was a woman's duty to marry, she had said, and there were certain crosses which women must bear in patience and in silence. When Addie was a wife she would understand.

Doctors, thought Adeline, were wise above most men. Clever, understanding. She thought of the little David Condit had told her of his present work, tempering it, of course, to her youth and sex. Yet, however modified, she had had, this evening, a swift, rather frightening glimpse of poverty and pain. And she told herself that to have been for a time in the quiet library of the big house with its air of security, its many calf-bound volumes, its solidity, and to have talked for a time to gentle, sheltered women must have been a pleasant and welcome change for him in the course of his ruder duties.

She slept tardily and ill; and was, at the breakfast table, heavy eyed and pale. Anna looked at her with some concern, as the sun with difficulty filtered through the heavy draperies, danced on the wall paneling, shone on china and silver, and exhibited as well her cousin's pallor and the blue shadows about her large eyes. Mr. Graham, after grace had been said, glanced at her too and remarked with a heavy jocularity, "Addie isn't looking her best this morning. Perhaps we should call a physician. Dr. Condit for choice."

Adeline flushed, and her long eyelashes quivered against her cheeks.

"Perhaps," said her aunt, with a warning glance at Graham, "he would dine with us some Sunday or, if that is not possible, join us at supper on a free evening."

Anna raised her hand in an impatient gesture. Then dropped it in her lap again. Anna was too independent to please either of her parents. She was interested in all sorts of outlandish things. Women's rights, for one. She read too much, and books which were not always proper. She had even attended, openly, certain freethinking lectures. Her parents feared she was becoming quite unwomanly. Her defense of the friend who had divorced her husband had shocked them deeply. What did a young girl know about such matters? Granted that Howard Porter had conducted his affairs without discretion and less good taste, yet he was Alice's husband, a good provider and the father of her children. Alice had made herself an outcast by the public washing of her soiled marital linen.

Anna thought, watching her mother pour the coffee, Addie's a sweet sentimental little ninny; and that nice young man's an utter idiot. A pair of pretty shoulders . . . a mass of blond curls . . . they're no more suited . . . She thought further, It isn't my affair, and after all I'm being very foolish, one swallow doesn't make a summer . . .

But David, upon invitation, came again to the Graham house.

That was the beginning. The end was inevitable so far as he was concerned. He went about his somber duties as intent, as capable as ever, but one part of his mind remained detached. He was in love for the first time in his life. He endowed Adeline Graham with every virtue known to man or woman. Her fragility brought a tightness to his throat, her gentleness was a pleasurable pain in his heart, her delicacy a trembling fear and a delight. And she was so very pretty and so young and her ready laughter had the sound of silver bells. Lying on his hard narrow bed, after a grueling day's work, he would clasp his hands behind his strong neck and dream. And then he would wake to reality. What had he to offer her, this slim, frail girl . . . a life of hard, unremitting work, of sacrifice, an uncertain climate, danger, difficulty . . . It wasn't to be thought of, he must put it out of his mind, he must stop seeing her now, even now that he realized that she was glad when he came and sorrowful when he left.

That she must know he loved her he did not doubt. He had told her so in a thousand silent ways. They were never, of course, alone. At the house Mrs. Graham always sat with them in the room. On the brief occasions when David's duties permitted him to be with her, they were as closely chaperoned. As winter had come on, cold and bright and exhilarating, there had been several skating parties and sleigh-rides. On these, too, they were not alone. Yet, skating, they could clasp hands and race fleetly away from the others, and David thought that these brief moments were the happiest of his life. The arched sky, black and frozen velvet, the stars shining, the lights on the blue-white pond. Laughter, and the ring of the skates, and Adeline's small face under the fur cap, the collar of her short fur jacket turned up about her rosy cheeks, the graceful fall of her skirt, almost ceasing at the ankles, and the touch of her gloved hand in his own. It had been like a flight, in silence and starry darkness. His body had sung with it, and his mind . . .

But he had nothing to offer her; no right to go to her guardian as suitor for her hand. He could not, even if she were willing, take this sheltered child into the life to which he was dedicated.

His letters to his father at this time were marked with caution. He spoke often of the Grahams. They had been very kind to him, he said. Tobias, reading, wondered and was troubled. It was not hard to read between the lines. "Miss Graham—that is, Miss Adeline . . ." David would write, again and again. Tobias thought, not for the first time, how hard it was at this distance, or at any distance, to ask the right question, to say the right word. If Elizabeth were only here . . . He wondered anxiously and gravely if this unknown girl loved his son, and if so, if she was fitted to bear the burdens which his choice of a profession must place upon her?

Tobias was not the only one who wondered. Anna, in the spring, came into Adeline's room one morning and sat in a low chair watching her dress. Mrs. Graham's obese pug lay panting on the hearthrug, and the windows were open a very little to the spring wind. There were sounds of carriage wheels on the Avenue below, the shout of a driver, and there were children playing in the Square.

On the sill a dove perched and cooed, preening its blue-gray feathers, its coral feet precise.

"This is really serious?" asked Anna. "I mean . . . David Condit?"

Adeline flushed and paled. She leaned closer to the mirror and altered the angle of her flowered hat. She rose and walked to the cheval glass and put a hand on the tight bodice, adjusted the swing of her trailing skirts. She was like, thought Anna, watching, the dove, delicate and preening.

Anna's brows were straight and broad and black. She drew them together until they nearly met. Her dark eyes, tilted at the corners, were watchful and anxious. Her full red mouth was set in a straight line, a slash of color in the pale olive of her face. She counseled sharply, "Don't pretend with me, Addie . . ."

Adeline turned. She ran to her cousin and sank down on the thick carpet. Her step, her graceful fall, made no sound. She put her head on Anna's knees. She said, very low, "I believe I love him, Anna."

Anna looked down, somberly, on the gay little hat, the escaping mass of elaborately dressed fair hair, the curve of cheek and throat, pure in beauty, very innocent. She touched the nape of Adeline's neck. She said, low, "I thought so."

"Why do you sigh?" asked Adeline. She raised her face. It was brilliant, it sparkled. She said quickly as Anna did not speak, "You like him, do you not? You approve?"

"Yes," replied Anna, "I like him." Something moved in her own slim throat. She swallowed convulsively. She continued, a little coldly, "Yet I hardly know him, Adeline. He seems—a pleasant young man. But have you considered what it will mean, Addie, being this man's wife . . . in China . . . ?"

"Oh, but," said Adeline, astonished, "if we should . . . that is . . . if he should speak—and I'm sure," she added demurely, "that he will speak—he won't, of course, go to China."

Anna withdrew the caressing hand. She asked evenly:

"Why not, Addie?"

"I'd die there," said Adeline simply. "I'd hate it. I could never endure it." She was silent, as if listening, her hazel eyes veiled. David had talked to her by the hour of China, of his strange alien friends. She had never been any nearer to China than the occasional curios she had seen in shops, than the swift passing of little laundry places in which yellow-visaged pig-tailed automata in blue cotton slaved, mysterious, sinister. "I couldn't," she said; "he'd understand . . ."

Anna had talked to David too, during the moments when Adeline was not in the room. She had questioned and he had answered, although she knew that his attention was riveted on something else, waiting for the sound of a footfall on the carpet . . .

She said, "All his life has been shaped to this one thing, Adeline. What do you expect him to do with his life?"

"He could practice here," asked Adeline, "could he not? Uncle has connections . . ."

"Get up," said Anna suddenly, "you're ruining your frock."

Adeline rose, and looked down at her crisp ruffles. She smoothed them ruefully. She shook out her skirts and the odor of orris root and violet drifted from them, the same odor which emanated from her hair. She asked, turning to the mirror, "Is there too much rice powder on my cheeks, Anna? Aunt spoke of it the other day."

Anna did not answer. She walked over to the other girl and stood looking at their reflections in the long swinging mirror. Taller than Addie, more robustly built, dark . . . Black as an Indian, she thought bitterly, contrasting her olive skin with the younger girl's dazzling fairness. She hated the heavy brows, and the slant of her eyes. She hated the full, generous crimson of her mouth.

Addie turned to her suddenly and laid her arms about her waist and clung to her. She said, "Oh, Anna, if he should not speak!"

Yet he spoke. It was early summer, just before the Grahams' departure for Newport. Adeline's eyes were heavy with long weeping. When she came back, it would be in the autumn. And David would be gone. To China perhaps, or perhaps to England. He had spoken of a year in England if he could afford it. And now she would never see him again.

They were in the drawing room. In the library Mr. Graham sat and smoked his excellent cigars and read the paper aloud to his wife, who was sewing. Anna sat there too, reading, under the gas lamp. She had grown thinner of late, and the weight of the heavy black hair braided too severely, her mother thought, around the noble young head seemed almost too heavy for it to carry. The draperies between library and drawing room were drawn aside. But the piano, that solid piece of furniture, among all the scattering of gold spindle legs and tiny tables, was at the other end of the long room. Adeline was playing and singing. She had a small, true soprano voice. She was singing the song that David had asked for. "In the Gloaming," it was called. "In the gloaming," sang Adeline, "oh, my darling—"

Her voice faltered and broke. David looked down, and forgot that presently he must turn a page. There were tears on the long lashes. "Adeline," said David, low, his heart in his throat, "Adeline, my dearest girl . . ."

Her hands were quiet on the keys. Mr. Graham in the other room cleared his throat and looked up sharply. His wife's smooth, banded head under the little cap was still bent over her sewing. But she had the look of one who waited. Anna, without raising her eyes, turned over a page of her book. She heard nothing. She saw nothing. The printed words on the page meant nothing to her. She found herself thinking of Patti singing "Linda," at the Metropolitan last April. There was no reason why she should have thought of it, except that on that occasion David had been with them in the box. It had been his first experience of the opera. Anna remembered the blazing blue of his eyes when the curtain had fallen. She remembered the pattering sound of Adeline's white gloved hands. She remembered how David had looked, ill at ease in the well-cut evening clothes which had obviously been borrowed from some more affluent friend, and which did not fit him.

She turned another page.

"Adeline," said David, low, insistent. "Look at me, my darling . . . speak to me."

She looked but did not speak. But the hands on the keys quivered from melody to discord and then once more to silence. She rose, with a look of contemplated flight about her. But heedless of the others in the next room, he caught her hands in his . . . To lose her was intolerable. He could not lose her. She belonged to him. He told her so, in that breathless whisper. Adeline laughed and wept. Then she was swept on David's arm in a moment of pure terror and pure rapture through the length of the great room and into the library. Still holding her, and with no regard for the formalities, David spoke directly to her guardian.

"We love each other, sir," he said. "Has Adeline your permission to become my wife?"

CHAPTER IX

WHEN David left the Graham house that night, he was an engaged man, and he was also, in the terms of the letter which, very late, he wrote to his father, "the happiest man alive." Mr. Graham, who still clung to older custom, had overlooked his untraditional manner of announcing—subject to his permission—the engagement. Mrs. Graham had been motherly and kind; Anna had put her strong, slender hand in his own and, with what he imagined were rare tears in her dark eyes, had wished him well. And he had had, although he did not reveal it to his father, a few, precious moments alone with Adeline in which he had heard that she loved him from her own lips, which in an ecstasy of triumph and a passion of tenderness he had kissed, and kissed again.

There remained, of course, the sober talk with Adeline's guardian which must follow; and which would follow, upon his next free time.

In the days which intervened and during which he did not see her, he was shaken and consumed by chills and fever of impatience. The hours were intolerably long. He wrote her this, snatching a moment any time he could to scrawl a line, in order to assure her of his devotion and his longing. He would be good to her, all his life. He would be on his knees to her, never ceasing in love's service and heart's gratitude, he promised. All his doubts had been dissipated, which was inevitable. He no longer thought of the life he had asked Adeline to share as too difficult a burden. Would he not be there to carry the major part of the load? With the divine vanity of love he told himself that, loving each other, they would accomplish miracles.

For the first time, his work in the wards was not of paramount interest to him. Yet, obliquely, the interest was intensified by his preoccupation with the thought of the girl he loved. Every difficult service he rendered to a suffering woman was in a sense rendered to her. All women, old and young, in pain or released from pain, became infinitely precious to him, because of her. This he tried to tell her, in his letters.

She showed one of the letters to Anna. Anna pushed it aside. She said, "You shouldn't, Addie . . . he wrote it for you."

"Of course," Adeline told her, sparkling with laughter and with happiness, "but—you don't understand him, Anna. You've never come to know him very well. I thought—if you'd read . . . here," she said, and put her pink finger on a paragraph—"and here—"

Anna hesitated. Her lips were set as, finally, she picked up the sheets and read the words Adeline had indicated. As her eyes traveled down the page she seemed to grow very still. Adeline snatched the sheets from her. "Not there!" she said, blushing furiously, "not that part!"

Anna said, after a moment:

"It seems to me that you are marrying an idealist, Adeline. It will have its difficult moments."

Adeline danced about the room. She was dressed for the street, she was about to go shopping. Her little boots pirouetted on the carpet. She said, "I'm marrying *David*—" and ran to Anna to embrace her, to hide her face upon her shoulder.

"You've talked with him about China?" Anna asked her slowly.

"No," admitted Adeline, "I haven't. Not yet. I haven't seen him —since." She added, "I'll see him to-night. He's to speak with Uncle, first."

"You're very sure of yourself," Anna observed.

"Why not?" asked Adeline. She stole a glance at herself in the mirror. "Why not?" she asked, and went gayly from the room.

Anna sat quite still. She wished she could forget a sentence or two that she had read. But she was not likely to forget. She wished she could view this marriage dispassionately and clearly. But she could not. Sitting there, quite immobile, she felt as if she were being slowly pulled apart. She loved Adeline, she had always loved her, since in babyhood the golden curls and the straight dark hair had mingled, since her hand had taken the younger hand and her own stumbling steps had guided the baby steps. And because she loved Adeline, Anna was afraid for her. She thought she knew, dimly, into what she was precipitating herself by this marriage. Drudgery, danger, a strange land, strange people, comparative poverty. She knew that Adeline would and must miss the soft ease of the surroundings to which she had been born. She knew she would be strange, and frightened. She knew, too, that she was not the wife for a medical missionary; Adeline who fainted at the sight of blood, who turned her eyes from suffering and wept for pity, but who could not force herself one step nearer any spectacle which afflicted her, not even to help.

Anna thought, sitting there, that she would hate David Condit if he took Adeline away, into that strange and unsuitable life. Yet she believed that she would hate him more deeply and lastingly if he surrendered and stayed in New York, under her father's benevolent protection, growing, by subtle degrees, into the rather portly, dignified family physician, prospering. Returning from his calls by carriage and team and coachman, to Adeline, the perfect doctor's wife, in a big house somewhere, waiting beside a tea table, the room full of callers, with high light voices and pretty frocks. Shutting her eyes, Anna could see it quite plainly. Adeline had talked enough about it, planned it. She'd even said, laughing, "I wonder . . . do you think we might live in one of the new French flats? Of course, Uncle is terribly opposed to them . . ."

Yes, thought Anna, I will hate him if he takes her away and I will despise him if he stays—

That evening David was alone with Mr. Graham in the library. It was more fitting that this should be so. The decanters with the sherry and port stood on the small round table, the cigars were at his right hand. Mr. Graham looked about the room with satisfaction. The pictures, the chairs, even the books were shrouded in summer coverings, as the family would be leaving soon. But even so the room had an air of solidity and peace. He confided to David that Adeline wanted to turn it into a modern "cozy corner." She had seen one in a friend's house and thought it very beautiful. Moorish draperies, and jeweled lamps, and scimitars on the wall.

But Graham couldn't bring himself to the change. He was, he confessed complacently, very old-fashioned.

They talked a little of such unimportant things and then Mr. Graham cleared his throat:

"Dr. Condit, both Mrs. Graham and I are very much pleased at the attachment between you and Adeline. It seems entirely suitable. I believe you are the man for our little girl whom we have loved—need I tell you?—as a daughter. We have not been blind during these past months. And, although I may say, quite without reproach, that you have hurried things more than was usual in my time, we are quite content. But I feel that we must speak seriously together of your future, as it has now become our intimate concern."

David asked, "Future?" and looked up. The ash on his cigar was long and gray. He knocked it off in a tray. His eyes were very blue. He leaned forward, clasping his hands between his knees.

"Yes. I mean, of course, what do you propose to do?"

David said, eagerly. "If, when I finish at Bellevue, we could be married, sir, and start immediately for the West Coast? My—my marriage has, of course, altered things for me somewhat. I have given up all idea of the postgraduate year in England. I feel it would not be fair to Adeline. It would necessitate a very long engagement. And then she would have to come out and marry me, far from her home and her kinsfolk. So, if we married, say, late next fall, and went directly to China . . ."

Mr. Graham looked at him in sheer astonishment. "You are not seriously proposing to go on with your notion of becoming a medical missionary?"

David looked at him a moment. He could not, he decided, believe the evidence of his ears. Surely the older man was joking. But it was evident that he was not. David said, after a moment:

"I have never contemplated anything else, Mr. Graham."

Graham gestured impatiently with his cigar.

"But you must. This missionary work . . . all very estimable, but out of the question. You cannot, in your senses, propose to take a young, delicately reared girl to that unsettled country and subject her to heaven knows what dangers and discomforts. Adeline has never known anything but ease and shelter, Dr. Condit. It is inconceivable."

"My mother," said David stubbornly, "went out to China when she was twenty. She had never been away from home before. She sailed, with her bridegroom, on a clipper ship . . . it took them many months to get there . . . months of storm, of danger. She never regretted it, Mr. Graham."

"We are not speaking of your mother," Graham reminded him, dismissing Elizabeth Condit. "No doubt she was differently brought up. We are speaking of Adeline and of another era. Adeline is a modern girl. She is fond of gayety, of social activity, of amusements. I cannot even remotely picture her as a missionary's wife."

"Why not?" asked David bluntly.

Mr. Graham, who thought of missionaries' wives as austere, rather overpious, flat-breasted, dowdy women, was considerably at a loss. He could hardly express this opinion to David who had been born of such a woman. He said, after a moment:

"Adeline is a good, and a religious girl. We have reared her carefully, in her duty to herself and to others. Our church is perhaps more liberal than your own but that has seemed a matter of small moment to me. We profess the same creed. However, Adeline's training has not fitted her for—"

David broke in impatiently.

"Surely with her intelligence, she can learn? She is not to be a preacher's wife, sir; merely a doctor's wife. Certain things will, of course, be required of her . . . but they will not be over-difficult."

Mr. Graham extinguished his cigar.

"When I consented to this engagement I thought, of course, that it would effect a perfectly understandable alteration in your plans."

David said, after a moment and very low:

"I love your niece, Mr. Graham, with my entire devotion. But I am pledged to China. This has been my dream since boyhood.

I have lived with it for a great many years. My entire life has been motivated—"

Graham broke in.

"Naturally! But circumstances alter cases. If I had for one moment believed . . ." He stopped briefly, then went on. "Tell me, as a medical missionary what, exactly, will be your recompense?"

David told him. Mr. Graham looked at him a moment in silence. Then he inquired:

"You expect to maintain a wife—and, possibly, a family," he reddened a little, disliking intimacy of conversation with younger men, "on this pittance?"

"Other men have done so," said David hotly. "Living is not costly in China. We will live very simply."

"So I should imagine," remarked Adeline's uncle. "I believe that at one time you mentioned a legacy—"

"That," explained David, "is about at an end." He spoke of the fund mentioned, the sum, and how through that fund his education had been made easier. "Otherwise," he concluded, "it would have taken longer. I would have had to work my way through college and medical school."

"You have no other prospects of inheritance?" asked Graham.

"No, sir, none."

"You were perhaps laboring under the belief that Adeline has some fortune of her own?" inquired her uncle keenly. "If so, I must disillusion you. She has not a penny beyond what I give her. My poor brother died in debt."

David was crimson. He said, not very evenly, but keeping his temper:

"I had not considered that point, Mr. Graham. I was aware, however, that you were Adeline's sole support and I was glad that it would be so, that the support would cease upon our marriage."

Mr. Graham raised his eyebrows. The young man was evidently sincere, and absurdly impractical. He said slowly:

"Anna will have a dowry. I know it is no longer a custom much in usage among Americans. I favor it, however. But I have never contemplated supplying Adeline with a like sum, or one in any way approximating it. I would be willing, however, if you would give up your plan of returning to China, to make her a small allowance, for, you understand, her own use . . . frocks, gew-gaws, the things to which women attach importance—you understand."

David said, after another pause:

"I would rather you did not." Then he smiled, quite suddenly, that clear irradiation of his features which never failed to endear him to any audience. "And in any case," he said quietly, "it wouldn't be necessary to discuss it as I shall not give up my plan."

"And if Adeline does not consent—?"

"Adeline?" cried David, stirred. "But Adeline knows, understands . . . she—"

"Have you discussed it with her?" inquired Adeline's uncle.

"No," answered David in astonishment, "I haven't." It was true. He had not. He had not seen her since the night they became engaged. He had taken it for granted that she . . . Why, he had talked to her by the hour about his childhood, his homesickness, his longing to return, soon to be satisfied!

"Then perhaps you had best do so," advised Mr. Graham, "before we continue with our debate which seems to me, to say the least, fruitless."

He rose and rang the bell for the servant. "Please ask Miss Adeline to come to the library," he instructed the man, on his appearance.

He left them alone. He had no desire to be witness to whatever passed between the young couple, even if it was not strictly conventional that they be left alone. In his wife's upstairs sitting room he paced the floor, back and forth, back and forth. Anna, sitting with one of her eternal books in her hand, regarded him with impatience and some pity. She had never seen her father so agitated. Nor had she seen his will crossed, save in the instances when she herself had crossed it.

Mrs. Graham sat sewing. She was perfectly placid. She was planning the wedding. It would all come out all right, the inevitable happy ending. Love, thought Mrs. Graham, an incurable reader of the romantic fiction which had not been held in very high regard in her girlhood, love conquers all.

But at the end of two hours the great door downstairs slammed and Adeline flew up the stairs to cast herself, disheveled and forlorn, into her aunt's motherly arms, and to announce, between sobs, that she would never see David again, never. He was impossible, selfish, brutal. She had been terribly mistaken.

They got her to bed, at last, with hot water bottles, and spirits of lavender, a cloth to her forehead and Anna to sit beside her bed and hold her hand and supply fresh linen handkerchiefs. It was all over between them, Adeline declared dramatically. David did not love her, had never loved her. He had been positively brutal when she told him that, yes, of course, she had expected him to stay in this country now that he contemplated matrimony; and that naturally she agreed with her uncle that a city practice . . . !

She wept and stormed and sobbed herself into drowsiness and, finally, slumber.

One light burned. Anna sat beside the great old-fashioned bedstead with its canopy, which Adeline deplored as too out of date for words. She sat without moving, watching the shadows from the gaslight flicker on the walls. And when Adeline finally stirred and woke to a realization of her grief and outrage and clung to her again, crying, "Oh, Anna—I'll never see him again, and I can't bear it!" Anna drew her close and kissed her. Salt was on her lips. She brushed the heavy fair hair from the other girl's forehead and said drearily, "He'll come back, Addie."

For she was very much afraid he would.

David, tramping the streets in blind misery, came finally to the hospital, sick with fatigue. In the internes' quarters to which he had come recently for his last six months' service, he flung himself on his narrow bed, fully dressed, and closed his eyes. His head ached intolerably. The walls of the room closed about him, they were musty, a little damp. It seemed to his sharpened senses that they reeked of pain. And that this pain had been made a part of himself.

Prayer shaped itself in his mind. Prayer was as natural to him as breathing. In wretchedness, in weakness he had been taught to draw strength from another strength. He said soundlessly, *Tell me what I must do.* Yet he knew. It needed no sign nor portent.

She had cried in his arms, she had pleaded with him. He had thought he could deny her nothing, and he had denied her everything; had denied himself. And why? Because of a dream and an indomitable purpose; because of a seed sown in unthinking childhood; because of something which had been built into his bones and his blood and from which there was no escape.

Suddenly he hated China as a man may hate his mother in a moment of rebellion and frustration. Always, China had stood between him and single-mindedness. No matter what he loved, he could not love it alone and wholly. China stood between. He could not give his entire heart to his own country, because of the love he bore the misted hills of Fukien and the amber flowing of the river. He could not be happy with the woman he loved, because he owed an older allegiance.

China had given him the heart-catching patriotism which rises in a boy's throat and clouds his eyes and makes tremendous his shout at the sight of his own flag, that dramatized patriotism of the exile; but China had taken away the pure devotion, unthinking and unspectacular, which the child, growing up with his country, knows.

China had taken his mother from him, had robbed him of the companionship of a sister, had withheld the fraternal association, had separated him from his father. China had crept insidiously into his blood. She had given him hunger for her food, and thirst for the sound of her speech. She had colored the speech of his own land, she had set him apart from friend and playmate in his boyhood in his own land. She demanded that whatever loyalties he might find in later years must be divided.

And so, hating her who had robbed him, he was seized by such a desire for the feel of her ancient soil beneath his feet that he was sick with it. He was a child again, longing for the sound of Mi-daik's free step, the very smell of the cotton garments worn on her brown, hill body, the glance of her bright black eyes. To go back would be forgetting—perhaps. But it would be so

long before he could return, and meantime the paved streets of
the city were under his tread and the stone of hospital corridors,
and the thought of Adeline, the oval face, the mouth shaped to
a kiss, the sound of her light voice in his ears, the touch of her
hand . . .

He said, aloud—as others had said before him—*it is too much to
ask* . . .

A few days earlier he had been very sorry for Heng-ong; Heng-
ong who wrote him that, his studies soon completed, he would
return home and be married. Heng-ong had never seen the face
of his bride-to-be. She had been betrothed to him when both
were children. She was the daughter of an old friend of the Sia
family. She had been brought up rigidly, carefully, in the old
ways. She would be deft to attend to the needs of her husband,
and those of his honorable mother. She would be small and dark
and modest.

But Heng-ong had never seen her face. And he had been for
some time in Europe. He would have learned other ways. Could
he, David had questioned himself seriously, be happy with this
girl? How was it possible? Yet she could read and write, her
father having smiled his permission to the teaching of things
not usually allotted to women. It pleased him to have a literary
daughter, one versed in the classics.

Reading and writing; were they enough? Heng-ong was committed, as he himself was committed to a life of serious study.
Even now his letters spoke of research. He wished, beyond the
mere practicing of medicine, to devote himself to the inquiry into
the swift and terrible scourges of disease which are a pestilence in
China.

But whether or not Heng-ong would be happy, he would sub-
mit. The scarlet and gilt bridal chair would stop before the door
of his betrothed, and locked within, the bride would proceed to
her new home. She would wear the marriage crown, gold and
scarlet, set with kingfisher feathers and pearls. Firecrackers would
salute her arrival. A child would greet her, at her bridegroom's
door. There would be the ceremonies at the ancestral tablets . . .

She was not of a Christian family, the little bride-to-be of Sia

Heng-ong. The ancient ceremonies would be observed, in this marriage.

Yes, David had pitied Heng-ong. Now, lying there sleepless, he wondered. The girl would have been chosen with care by the elder Sias. They loved their son, they wished him to be happy. Surely in the clan house David had seen a happy marriage; and in the house of Heng-ong's father. Arranged or not, these marriages endured, and must endure. Yet in Heng-ong's case he was not as bound by tradition as his elders. So David had suffered for him and been anxious.

Now, he did not know.

As for himself, he had fallen in love, of his own free will. He had looked upon the face of the girl he desired, he had been a guest in her home. He had thought, because he loved her, that she was perfectly in accord with him.

"Selfish," she had cried out at him, the tears falling, "self-ish . . . !"

She had said that he did not love her; could not possibly love her.

Yet he did love her, desperately, desirously, purely. But must new love supplant the old, as one nail drives out the other? Could a love he had carried with him for this quarter of a century be dissipated by the love which had been a matter of a few months' short duration?

He remembered that there would be operations scheduled for the morning. His hand must be steady, and his mind clear and undivided. Is one's mind ever clear and undivided? he wondered miserably.

Oh, Adeline, Adeline . . .

The week passed. She had gone, he supposed, to Newport. It had been brief, it had been beautiful, it had been almost painfully rapturous, and now it was over.

He wondered what he would reply to his father's letter when it came.

But at the end of the week another letter reached him. It was from Graham. In it he asked David if he would not come to the house once again. The family had remained in town, Adeline was in no condition to travel. She was, he stated, grieving her heart away. Their doctor feared that she might go into a decline. Would Dr. Condit please—at the first possible moment?

David obtained special permission to be absent from the hospital for part of an afternoon, and went, as fast as horse and carriage could take him, to the Graham house, tortured by possibilities of death, despair. He expected to be taken to Adeline's bedside, to fall on his knees beside her, to beg her forgiveness for everything. He thought, as the thudding hoofs bore him closer . . . if there is no other way—?

He set his lips, and the color drained from his cheeks. There must be some other way. He must make her see, understand. He could not betray his entire life, his father, his people—yes, he thought, *my* people—his mother, his friend. . . .

But if Adeline were ill, and asked it of him?

Anna met him in the drawing room. She was friendly, cool, aloof as she was always, with him. He seized her hands in his own, and she winced a little but did not withdraw them.

"Anna—is she very ill? If you knew what I have suffered since your father's letter . . . I—"

Anna said, and now she took her hands away:

"No, she is not very ill, David." She spoke his name for the first time, but he did not know it. "She is merely—unhappy. She isn't," said Anna gently, and smiling faintly, "much accustomed to having her will crossed, you know. Perhaps we've spoiled her —a little. But—she does love you," Anna told him, flushing very slightly, under the dark skin, "and I think she has realized how much your work means to you."

She asked herself angrily, Why are you telling him this, what does it matter? Not long before she had sat in Adeline's room and listened to her mother's placid and practical speech. Her mother had counseled:

"Come, Addie, pull yourself together. You will ruin your eyes and skin. This young man of yours is very stubborn. It is, I suppose, his training. One must admire him for it. There is just one question to be settled. Do you or do you not want to marry him?"

Fresh weeping had greeted her.

"If you do," continued her aunt calmly, "by all means marry him. Go with him to China. As his wife you will be able to influence him to a much greater degree than now. Especially at first. If you are clever, and if you are patient, you need not remain there very long. Perhaps a short sojourn would not be without its amusement and interest for you. I believe that you will be quite able to point out to your husband the waste of his talents and his life. And that you will come home, again, and see him established in a more suitable situation, before very long."

Anna had left the room then, quietly, shutting the door behind her softly. She thought, walking away from it, that women were despicable. How they passed on the knowledge, from one to the other, the soft woman-ways, the female scheming . . .

Yet knowing all this she told David Condit that Adeline was ready to listen to reason. She did not warn him. She despised herself for it. But she, too, carried with her a divided allegiance and one of her loyalties was forbidden. She thought, watching the light flash back to the brilliant eyes, so long as he's happy . . .

"May I see her now?" asked David impatiently.

"She's coming downstairs," said Anna, "immediately."

So presently Adeline came and was in his arms and they were alone. And she cried and laughed, clinging to him. She had been stupid, she said, and selfish and afraid. But he would teach her not to be. And she would go with him, to the ends of the earth.

To do her justice, she believed it, feeling his arms about her, the thudding of his heart, his kiss upon her mouth.

In the following early winter Adeline Graham and David Condit were married, from her uncle's house, and left almost at once for the West Coast, where they would board a steamer for China.

CHAPTER X

THERE was a hiatus of several weeks between David's marriage and the conclusion of his two years at Bellevue. These were weeks filled with the confusion and disorder of preparation. Adeline and the Grahams had returned in early September from Newport. There was so much to be done, dressmakers to consult, household goods to purchase. David, who had possessed his soul in what patience he could muster during her absence, and fed his hunger on her letters, found that now she was restored to him he saw her very little. Even after his hospital term ended and he had more leisure.

When he did see her she was worn out with fittings and shopping. The Grahams had been most generous. Mr. Graham's wedding gift to his niece included her clothes, "enough for years," and the furnishings she would take with her, and a thousand dollars to her account in the bank. Nothing more had been said of an allowance.

David himself had plenty to do. There were conferences with the Board, certain arrangements to be made. And he went during one week to Carthage to see his great-aunt and Dr. Brent. He had tried to persuade Adeline to go with him, if Mrs. Graham would chaperon them, but Adeline had shrieked with amazement. As if she could leave, for a minute! He must, she declared, be out of his mind!

So he went alone, yet not alone, taking with him the memory of her farewell embrace, her whisper—"Don't be gone long, dearest," the regard of her hazel eyes, shining, tear-wet.

He had several days in the old frame house. The season was sharp with frost and just before dusk the sky would be arched in a cool, tender green, lighted with one enormous star. There was beauty and peace, and David, walking the familiar paths with Brent, their breath smoking on the still air, was aware that

the day would come when he would be homesick for this northern town. He tried to persuade the doctor and Aunt Lizzie that
they must come to New York for the wedding. But they would
not. Lizzie Lewis was not very well, and she had grown from
an alert and active middle-aged woman into a woman definitely
old, and timid. She said to him, sitting after supper in the parlor,
which had not changed since his mother's girlhood:

"I can't see my way to it, Davy. I'd like to know your wife . . ."
She sighed a little. Then she said, quietly, "I'm lonely, David.
It won't be long before I'll never be lonely again—"

"Nonsense," he said briskly yet secretly alarmed. "You're going
to live twenty years and more, Aunt Lizzie."

She shook her head.

"I've left you what I could. You know the house and the
farm goes back to the Watertown branch, to your Uncle Peter's
children, who settled in Vermont. But what I've managed to
save, you will have."

David said gently:

"Don't talk about such things, Aunt Lizzie. When I come back
for my first furlough, I'll bring Adeline right up here to you.
She's lovely," he said simply, "you'll love her."

Of Matthew Brent he asked gravely:

"Do you really believe that Aunt Lizzie is failing?"

"How does she look to you?" the doctor inquired.

"The same. No, not really the same," David contradicted himself, frowning.

"That's it," said Mat. "Nothing you can put your finger on, as
a physician. As a plain man, I'd say she was just opening her
hands and letting go. She's alone, Davy, you know. That isn't
easy, when you get old."

Brent wouldn't come to the wedding either. He disliked wed-
dings, he said clearly. Even for David he wouldn't come. He
looked at Adeline's photograph and nodded. She was very pretty,
he told Adeline's affianced. He added, "If you ever get tired of
those heathen, there's a practice waiting for you here at home."

The wedding, in the Graham house, was attended in the main
by Adeline's friends. Those who had not met David came out of

curiosity. They thought Adeline mad, and sacrificial. They whispered together in the big rooms thrown open and merged for the services. Adeline had desired a home wedding, she had wished it to be simple, she said, because David preferred it. It was not so simple. David, after the ceremony, was a little taken aback at the flutter of young women crowding around him with bright, laughing eyes, and high-pitched words of congratulation. The atmosphere was heavy with their scent and light with their merriment and gentle with their easy tears. There were furs and silks, and the delicate clash of china and the tinkling of crystal. There were young men, very elegant, histrionically regretful and sentimentally reproachful, bending to kiss the bride's smooth cheek.

The young Richard Wrights were there. "You wouldn't come to my wedding," Richard had declared, "but you couldn't keep me away from yours!" He had his wife on his arm, a small round person, dimpled and demure, with jewels at her throat and wrists and a frock that sent Adeline into envious raptures. Adeline had but one attendant at her wedding. This was Anna, tall and dark and stately in a gown of pale pink surah, worn over a bustle so small that it caused the feminine guests to exclaim among themselves, and with a long graceful train. She carried deep pink roses and was as pale as the bride.

The last few days in New York were spent in the red velvet and gilt splendor of the Murray Hill Hotel and finally the last farewells were said, and David half led, half carried his wife into the train for the Coast, worn out with excitement and with the emotion of parting from her people.

They were not alone on the overland trip. The Richard Wrights were with them en route to Coronado Beach which had recently come into prominence as a winter resort for Westerners. Mrs. Wright, whose condition was said to be delicate, had been advised by her physician to seek a warmer climate for the winter. And Richard, well able to afford the time and the expense, had suggested Coronado.

David, fond as he was of his friend, had somewhat resented the idea of the Wrights as traveling companions. But as the long days wore away he was glad they had come. They distracted Adeline from her tremors and her tears and her terror. For she was afraid. Clinging to him as the train swayed through the night and the cinders rattled down overhead, and the whistle wailed through the darkness at the crossings, he could feel her anxiety shake her. He was tender with her, and gentle. She was very young and she had sacrificed everything for him.

She grieved, for the most part for Anna. She did not know how she would get along without Anna, she said. And David had suggested, before they left, "Perhaps Anna will come out to China and visit us," and Adeline had cried out with rapture and put her small hands on her cousin's arm and begged, "You will, won't you, Anna?" But Anna had shaken her dark head. She couldn't, she said, stooping to kiss the younger girl, her parents would need her, more than ever, now.

On the way to San Francisco the ladies were together a great deal; they read, and talked, and yawned delicately, and went, with soft rustlings of their taffeta petticoats, to their meals. Sometimes the Wrights and Adeline played cards, David, who had never learned, sitting by, watching and smiling at Adeline's pleasure when she won and her charming petulance when she lost.

But the trip ended, and their ways parted, and after a few days in San Francisco the young Condits boarded the steamer *China,* and sailed down the Bay and through the Golden Gate, bound for the Orient.

It was a pleasant voyage. Adeline proved a fair sailor and a favorite on board. She loved to dance; David, who had never danced, watched her with pleasure in her pleasure, knowing that the dance must cease and that she would come toward him with her light step and her brilliant smile and put her hand on his arm and they would walk away and stand looking down in the mysterious depths of the strange encompassing element through which the throbbing ship plowed its way, and would be silent, knowing they were together.

He was very careful of her, inordinately gentle, remembering the advice her uncle had given him, shortly before his marriage, and delivered with a good deal of evasion and embarrassment. Adeline, Graham had declared, was sheltered, innocent of life

. . . He trusted that David would deal tenderly with her whom he would shortly make his responsibility. And he had added something else, something enjoined upon him by Mrs. Graham, who considered herself in the place of Adeline's mother . . . He hoped, said Mr. Graham, not too vaguely, that there would be no children . . . for a time at least. Adeline was fragile, and—perhaps it would be well for David to consult their family physician?

David did so. The family physician, a large, elderly gentleman with a dark beard and prominent eyes, was a little more to the point with his young colleague. Dr. Condit, himself a medical man, would understand . . . His bride would go with him into a strange country and a difficult climate . . . at best it would be hard for her. In the interests of her health, therefore, he advised—

The remembrance of this conversation troubled David. As a doctor he realized quite fully the dangers of childbearing when the mother was not robust, in the best of circumstances. But marriage without children was, somehow, makeshift. Loving Adeline, he wished deeply, devoutly, for daughters in her image, for sons in whose veins his blood and hers would be united. Nor could a woman be happy, content or fulfilled, he mused in the innocence of his rearing and tradition, unless she be mother as well as wife.

He did not speak to Adeline of these things. He could not. She would evade him when, blunderingly, gravely, he tried. She would blush or tremble or grow patently irritated. There were things which could not be discussed between man and woman, not if they were married a hundred times over. He learned this on the journey East; learned, too, that, although she might lie, night long, surrendered to his arms, it must be in darkness and in silence. And in, he feared, reluctance.

But he was not always oppressed with trouble, with the sense of his responsibility. There were days of pure enchanted peace, with the blue water sliding away, rippling back. There were strange places and the lift of Diamond Head, and Adeline, curious and enraptured as a child, clapping her hands at new, un-dreamed-of wonders.

David had with him his dictionary, his handbook of the Fuh-chau dialect. Often when they lay side by side in the steamer chairs he tried to teach her a simple phrase. This amused her at first, she would repeat it dutifully, laughing, parroting, but she soon wearied. He argued. "But, Adeline, when we reach home you will have to learn, there will be long hours before you—and me, too, for I have forgotten so much. Anything you learn now will help you."

But she could not be held long. She must disentangle herself from her blankets and beckon to some shipboard acquaintance and go walking on the deck, the light Pacific wind in her fair hair, and the bright color staining her cheeks. Sometimes David, watching her, wondered if her delicacy had not been an error on the part of her guardians and her doctor. She seemed strong, for all her look of fragility, and well. She was tireless, dancing, walk-ing, playing at games. She exhibited no symptoms of the faint-ing spells of which he had been warned. As a doctor he could not believe her other than perfectly healthy, fundamentally strong.

Yet she could weep herself into a blinding and authentic head-ache and after their first trivial quarrel she was prostrated in her cabin, refusing food, growing visibly weaker, even thinner, before his anxious eyes, until he apologized for the fancied wrong and she came, half reluctant and half eager, into his arms again.

She was a little anxious about the meeting with his father. "Do you think he will like me, David?" she often asked, brushing her long fair hair before the mirror. She had so much of it that her husband wondered silently why she must needs supplement it by the puffs and ringlets and coils which lay at night on the small table. When he inquired, she had answered with a smile for his masculine density, "Everyone does, dear; that is, except Anna. She won't. She says she can't bear the idea of wearing someone else's hair. But then dear Anna's always been odd."

To her question David would always reply, sincerely. "He will love you, darling. How could he help it?"

Adeline, regarding herself in the mirror, was inclined to agree with him. She wanted very much to make David happy. She tried, in all the ways known to her. And it would, she knew, make him very happy if she and his father were friends. In her heart she was a little appalled by the thought of the strange old man—she thought of him as ancient—who had been a preacher and a missionary most of his life. That he would be stern and austere she had no doubt. But it was pleasing to play with the fancy of being a daughter to him, softening the austerity, amusing him with her chatter, delighting him with her femininity, as she had her uncle.

She said tenderly, "I must be a dear daughter to him, David," and David took her in his arms with gratitude and adoration. It was so exactly what he wanted, a daughter for Tobias, a wife for himself.

In January, 1891, the Condits reached Fuhchau, after a long journey by sea and by land, and Tobias Condit was waiting there to welcome them home.

Until her actual arrival at the mission the trip had been as charmingly unreal to Adeline Condit as something seen from the stalls of a theater. She had grown accustomed to the smiling faces of the Chinese boys on the boat. Clean, neat, deft, they had amused her. But she had not thought of them actually, as the people among whom she must live. They were on the steamer for her comfort and convenience, they were excellent servants. They talked to her in the quick high pidgin English which entertained her very much. She believed that they admired her, for her unsimilarity to their women, her fair skin and hair. They were like trained, animated toys; one clapped one's hands and there they were.

But on the way from the jetty at Fuhchau to the mission her heart misgave her. She saw misery and filth and disease and she shuddered from it and hid her eyes against David's arm. She saw hostile glances, or so she fancied, and it came to her suddenly that this was after all not a pleasure trip, not a lifetime sailing through blue waters and seeing, at one's pleasure, strange and curious sights. It came to her that her journey was completed and that here, on a hill, in an echoing big house, with its tremendous ceilings and great verandas, surrounded by alien people, she must make her home.

It had been arranged that, for the time being at least, the young people would live with Tobias. To that end the house to which Tobias had brought his bride, and to which David now brought his, had been rearranged into two separate apartments, with, however, a common kitchen and dining room. "Yet you shall have," pledged Tobias, smiling at them, "a little privacy. And I shall be away a great deal, moreover."

David said, looking at his father as if he would never get enough of looking, that of course they had expected to live with him for as long as they were in Fuhchau. They would have to remain for, perhaps, a year, he said. But later—well, later, he had dreams of an outstation where he might establish a small hospital and dispensary.

His father nodded. This had all been discussed between them in letter after letter. But for the first months at least David would find his hands full here; in the Woman's Hospital, across the river in the proposed small dispensary.

Adeline, listening night after night to the discussions, the good, sound talk of a longed-for reunion, felt unhappy and uncomfortable. She could not complain of her father-in-law. He was kindness itself. But there was something about the big, stooped, bearded man which eluded her and which she could not reach, either with her daughterly, caressing ways, or her laughter, her eager questions. Although no word had been said and not the least small gesture made, she felt as if she were an intruder between these two men who had so much to say to each other.

And there were others. There were the mission folk, the townspeople crowding in, welcoming David back. He missed familiar faces, those of the Hendersons and the Jaspers. But there were new faces to greet him. And sometimes, taking Adeline on little trips through the city, climbing the steep stone steps with her, stopping to thrust his head into shop or to knock at the door of what seemed to her a hovel, she thought that he had completely forgotten her, as she picked her disdainful way across running gutters or turned her heel on a rough stone.

Her dainty skirts swept along the streets and David decreed a more sensible length. This wasn't New York. He advised a tailor, one who would alter her frocks under her instruction. And with the shortening of the skirts and their ruffled petticoats, Adeline felt forlorn and uneasy, as if her trailing garments had somehow protected her.

She could not become accustomed to these people, so different from the neat boys of her steamship experience. The beggars in the streets, with their great sores, their fleshless arms, their stumps for legs, sickened and horrified her. The playing children, wadded and padded against the damp chill of the Southern winter, the old people; men with their sparse beards, the sexless women; the noise, the outcries, affronted her.

Even the river frightened her, with its freight of boat people and its constant tumult and noise. And there were nights when she lay beside David in the old double bed beneath the netting and fancied the alien hills closing down on her and shutting her out from all light and all companionship.

David did his best for her. The other women in the mission did their best. But they were busy with their schools and their orphanage; they were occupied, hurrying women with little time for relaxation. And they did not think it at all strange that she would have to sit hour by hour trying to learn a language for which she had no aptitude and which she had no desire to learn.

David studied with her, and under the guidance of Sia Ho-mei, who seemed the same as he had seemed when David had left him so many years ago, a little older, perhaps, and thinner, but with the same high forehead and quick intelligent eyes and the serene philosophy which distinguished the scholar. Sia Ho-mei was patient with Adeline, but he feared, as he told David reluctantly, that her heart was not in it. Nor was it. After several months she gave up entirely. She wept, she cast herself into David's arms. She couldn't learn, she said, it made her head ache, and she loathed the tutor, with his patience and his quiet voice repeating the same difficult, absurd phrase over and over again.

So the books were closed and laid aside and David and his tutor studied alone. David's first tongue had come back to him quickly enough, it was merely a matter of practice. And under Sia Ho-mei's guidance he was using the writing brush again and learning Mandarin, the court language, as a helpful supplement to the dialect.

When the attempts to interest Adeline in the study of Chinese failed, David proposed that she undertake to teach English in one of the lower English classes in the Anglo-Chinese college. This, wishing as much to fill up her time as to be of help, she did endeavor to do for a time. But it was an unfortunate experience.

Her letters home were frequent and full. They were also complaining. Once David found her in tears when, returning tired and disheartened from a day in the dispensary, he called her and his voice echoed through an apparently empty house. His father was away on a preaching trip and Adeline was alone except for the servants, and David hurried through to their bedroom, his heart contracted with fear, his weariness forgotten. But it was merely that Anna had written her sharply. "You made your bed," wrote Anna, "lie in it. You knew what your husband's work would be when you married him. Cannot you see your way to becoming an assistance, rather than a burden to him?"

Adeline showed David the letter. It was so unkind of Anna, she said, and unfair. David sat down on the bed and took her into his arms. He thought privately that Anna had a little overstepped herself. It was not really her concern. "I try so hard," sobbed Adeline. "I want to help you, David, but I'm afraid—"

"Afraid of what?" he asked her gently.

"Everything," replied Adeline, shuddering.

It was true. She tried, but she could not conquer it. She was afraid of the people, whose faces told her nothing, the strange people with their stranger ways; people who shook hands with themselves instead of with each other, whose courtesy was a ritual, whose thoughts you could not guess, who mourned in white and rejoiced in scarlet, who believed in horoscopes, who awaited a "lucky" day for marriage or burial and who worshiped alien gods. She was afraid of the Christian Chinese as well—one couldn't change the color of their skins, could one, or the slant of the unreadable eyes? And she hated the food and the dreadful odors and the dirt and the climate.

David did his best, after an anxious consultation with his father during which the older man said very little save, "She is lonely, David. She is not used to us and our ways. She has been brought up very differently from most of the other women here. We must make friends for her."

So David looked outside for friendships for his wife. There was a larger settlement of foreigners in the business community than there had been in his day. They were a rather cosmopolitan group, English, German, Swedish. And there were certain new recreational facilities which they found time to enjoy, tennis and hockey and their own clubs.

Little by little Adeline found herself more and more a part of this group and less dependent upon the mission. That she was criticized, and sometimes sharply, for the things she did, the harmless dances she attended, the card parties, as well as for her more elegant frocks, her use of powder and perfume and false hair, she knew perfectly well. But she had nothing in common with these other no doubt good and devoted but surely narrow and dowdy women, she told David repeatedly. And by what right did they judge her?

In the spring a new disturbance came into her life with the arrival of Heng-ong from Scotland. She had heard much of Heng-ong in the time she had known David. She had expected to meet someone quite out of the ordinary, a Chinese, of course, but a different Chinese, wearing Western clothes, comporting himself as a Westerner. She met merely another Chinese, in the garb of a Chinese gentleman, with a fine, intelligent face and a perfect command of English. Nevertheless he was no less strange to her, and when David took her to call upon Heng-ong's wife, she did not, as David had hoped, find a friend.

The girl Heng-ong had married was small and slender and vibrant with life, as are the Southern women. She spoke a careful, hesitant English. She lived in the great Sia house in the city, a succession of houses, joined together by courtyards, by gardens. Ai-leng was younger than Adeline by a year or so. She had the dignity of a woman of fifty but the quick laughter of a child. She wore her loveliest brocaded coat over her black satin trousers and her hair was elaborately dressed. It was months now since it had been so dressed, since the fringe which denoted maidenhood had been discarded. Her face was pearl-pale with powder, her eyes dark, elongated with kohl, her mouth heavily painted. She wore jewel jade and gold in her ears and in her hair ornaments. And she served, with the help of her women, innumerable tiny, handleless cups of tea to her other-country guests.

She had married Heng-ong and then had remained waiting in his father's house until his final return from Scotland. Now he was home, and would be with her for the rest of their lives. She did not speak of him to Adeline. She listened incredulously to Adeline's light, running talk of David. She was somewhat amused by Adeline's gown, which cramped her delicate body and molded it into a definite shape. She was also a little shocked, although she tried not to be, and tried also not to feel that Adeline's hair was very ugly indeed, in color and dressing. This woman was the wife of her husband's closest friend. As such she was entitled to every consideration.

Adeline, sitting on carved ebony, drinking tea from a tiny table of old red lacquer, watching Ai-leng totter about on her bound and slippered feet, thought—how can David really care for these people, really ever get to know them?

It was not a success. She was presented, with ceremony, to Heng-ong's mother, who sat and smoked thoughtfully and regarded her, her big feet like those of a boat or hill woman, her absurd habiliments, her dreadful hair, and who asked questions, rapidly, which Ai-leng stumblingly translated. . . . How old was Adeline? Did she have a child? Did she expect a child?

It was quite obvious that Ai-leng expected a child. A man child, she told her caller frankly and hopefully.

Such people, thought Adeline, returning home in her chair, borne by her half-naked bearers, had no decency, no modesty.

She much preferred the society of the business men's wives of the community.

And there were evenings when Heng-ong came to the compound and he and David sat talking until almost dawn, when she could have screamed for sheer boredom and loneliness.

Heng-ong was still interested in research. He had fashioned a small laboratory for himself in a shop rented for this work. David went there when his time permitted and worked with him. They had never enough of talking, these two, and yet when they had met after all these years their greeting had been restrained and quiet. They were grown men now, married, members of the same profession. Any emotion they felt was quickly mastered, David's, the more volatile, because he knew Heng-ong would expect it of him and because he knew that Heng-ong was as deeply moved as he.

Adeline disliked Heng-ong.

At first, even with her fear, the city had interested her, the strange things she saw had fascinated her . . . the sellers of food, the ambulant barbers and dentists, the glimpses of a mandarin of the first class returning to his yamen in his fine sedan with his many bearers, the glimpses perhaps of a Manchu lady returning to the Manchu quarters, a woman beautiful by any standards, taller than the average woman of the Chinese, with a pale oval face, beautiful quiet hands and unbound feet; the trips on which David sometimes found time to take her, upriver or down, or, as the spring wore on to summer, the mountain resort of Kuliang or the curving beach at Sharpe Peak.

But David was going away more and more often. He went with his father on evangelistic trips . . . "Body and soul," he called them, "you to preach and I to medicate"; and he went also to several of the outstations; and was away sometimes for days on end.

In the late spring Mi-daik came down from her home in the hills back of Ku-cheng. It was a distance of over ninety miles on dreadful roads. She had walked. She carried with her her youngest grandchild, a boy. And she said, when she saw David, "Now I can die in peace."

She put the quiet, uncomplaining baby down upon a stiff small sofa against the wall. She put her hands on David. And he took her in his arms and laid his cheek against her own. And Adeline, feeling forlorn, forgotten and a little sick, moved swiftly, not too quietly, from the room.

Mi-daik asked, "It is your wife?"

David said, "Yes." He explained that his wife did not speak the language, that she was still strange.

"She is to give you a son?" asked Mi-daik.

"Not yet," said David, "not yet, I-so."

The old name came easily to his lips. Mi-daik said nothing. He knew what she was thinking. She picked up the quiet child. It had been drugged, a very little, with opium before the long journey started. It lay in her arms and stared placidly at David with dark eyes between lids that were red and raw. "I brought him to you," said Mi-daik.

Trachoma, of course. David did what he could during the little time Mi-daik stayed with them. But his heart was sick within him. On his return the beauty of the country he loved had taken him by the throat and shaken him, the hills, mist-crowned and green, the shapes of the trees, and the rice paddies caught together by the frail silver network of canals; night and the stars over the Min, and in the sunlight the molten gold of the river. But since he had been at work, misery had clouded beauty. The bent form of a burden-bearing coolie, the wet cotton trousers clinging to the sweat-soaked limbs, the fine muscles of the naked brown back had a certain moving grace and strength, but David knew that there were calluses, raw and bleeding. The flush of tuberculosis, the rot of leprosy, the blinding of trachoma, the swift fevers, the sweeping plagues . . . And his were only two hands. So many were needed, so many.

He began to talk with his father of the advisability of going to Ku-cheng, there to establish himself, and to open a one-man hospital and dispensary. He could make trips out from there. There were doctors in the city, not enough, but there were some. There were the English doctors of the community hospital who looked after the foreign community and the Chinese as well, there were the mission doctors. He was needed, he thought, more bitterly in the country.

Adeline cried out in horror. She said, and stamped her foot, that she would not go. Fuhchau was bad enough, but here at least was some companionship and recreation. She would not go, she would not hear of it. Did he intend to shut her away from all decent human intercourse, in some filthy little country town in which she might sicken and die of some dreadful disease he would bring home to her?

Tobias was present at that outburst. He left the room quietly, but his shoulders were more stooped than ever. He did not dislike his son's wife. She had a certain gayety and charm which pleased him. And he was certain that she loved David and tried to make him happy. Tried. But could not. No, he did not dislike her, it was not her fault that she was as shallow as a small clear pool the rain has left on a flat rock. She held the sunshine and reflected it, she mirrored the blue sky, but she would not afford any deep long draft of cool water to parched lips. It was not her fault.

In the end, after more than a year in Fuhchau, the Condits went up to Ku-cheng. David was a stubborn man. He had said quietly and sternly, for once not trying to plead with her to cease to weep, to look at him and smile, "My mind is made up, Adeline. It has taken me a long time. But I have decided that my work lies there, in the outstation. And you will come with me."

She would, of course. Only loose women defied their husbands, if they could not alter their decisions by the usual methods; and then too, what could she do? She could not stay on in this hideous mission, with her father-in-law, with David ninety miles away. She could not return home.

Her surrender was not sullen, however, but sweet. It was better so. The smile through tears, the lips pressed to his own, the "Forgive me, David, I've been very silly."

That way was the best, she knew, remembering her aunt's counsel.

So in the late autumn they went to Ku-cheng. David had sent his wife to Kuliang, in the mountains, for the season of summer heat; and she returned refreshed, and in excellent spirits. There had been quite a colony at Kuliang, and it had had its amusing side.

She was glad, once more in David's arms, that after all they were leaving Fuhchau. She did not admit to herself, then or ever, that she was desperately jealous of the bond between David and his father; and of the bond between him and Heng-ong—nasty, sneaking Chinaman, she told herself in the unconsidered phrasing of her own country. And moreover, if she gave in gracefully to David and went where he took her and made the best of it, perhaps he would cease to talk to her about having a child.

CHAPTER XI

ADELINE CONDIT loathed Ku-cheng. In that walled city, on a branch of the Min, she felt an isolation which terrified and alienated her; which was physical as well as spiritual. In Fuhchau her physical loneliness had been somewhat assuaged by the people she had managed to gather about her, her friends at the consulates and in the business community. Much as she had detested the city itself and the life of the mission compound, there was some escape. Here was none.

She looked at her husband with despairing eyes. He was, she thought, so terribly insensitive. This she could not comprehend. She had seen him, with her own reluctant eyes, caring for some diseased, hardly human being, with hands that were gentleness itself, and had watched him wince from the pain of a dirty, unintelligible stranger . . . yet to her pain he appeared blind.

That Ku-cheng was beautiful, geographically, she could not deny. It was high on a plateau, surrounded by mountains. The small Ku-cheng River bordered the city on the east, where there were six gates giving on the water. On the northerly side there were stone steps leading up a steep ascent and to a temple. The surrounding country was exquisite, fields and gardens, temples, mountain peaks, rivers and streams and the downward plunge of waterfalls.

David had canvassed the city before they moved and rented a house which was large enough for their living accommodations and would also serve as a dispensary. There was even a second building, across the court, which could be made over into a crude hospital. One room, which had light from two sides, would serve as an operating room, and the other as a small ward.

Thus their life began. The buildings had been cleaned and whitewashed. Servants had been engaged. And among curious,

sometimes doubting, but, in the main, friendly people they settled down to a new routine.

David was not without friends in the town. The pastor of the
church established by the Fuhchau mission was an old playmate
of his, one Dang Sing-mi, a slender, shy young man burning
with the uneasy zeal of the convert and unable to take for granted
the new earth and new heaven which his other-country friends
had revealed to him in boyhood. He and David renewed their
friendship gladly. Adeline, who had never been able to discover
within herself the slightest attraction for anything or anyone
Chinese, spent long evenings in her bedroom shut away from the
discussions which went on interminably in the small adjoining
study.

At last, she had thought, she would have David to herself. This
was the one extenuating feature of their removal from the larger
city. But she did not. Although his father rarely came their way—
and generally on an evangelistic trip on which David, if conditions permitted, would accompany him—and although Heng-ong
did not come, being too occupied with his hospital and dispensary work and with his laboratory on free hours, she saw very
little of her husband.

She would have seen more had she been able to help him in the
hospital work. She tried. She listened to his instructions, she endeavored to follow them, at first. Before he trained a Chinese
helper, he had to depend on her. But not for long. She fainted at
the sight of blood, sickened at the revelation of an open wound
or sore, and once ran screaming from the room to which a
Chinese woman in the first stages of a difficult labor had dragged
herself. Lying on her bed, her head in the cushions, Adeline
shuddered and fought against unconsciousness. She had not seen
much but it was enough. If David was so inhuman that he
thought he could persuade her to distort and torture her body
in that shameless, brutal fashion . . .

Never. Never . . .

David said, after a few days of endeavor and failure, "Never
mind, Adeline. I'll train one of the boys . . . they're quick, you

know, and docile. Perhaps later, I'll have help, from **Fuh-chau** . . ."

He was not angry with her. Bitterly disappointed, perhaps. He said nothing. He remembered his mother, and her quiet competence. He remembered the nurses he had known. But it wasn't Adeline's fault. She simply was not built to stand the sight of suffering. She was too sensitive, too emotional.

The hospital was rough enough. A line of beds, and such cleanliness as soap and water and disinfectants could produce. The ward filled, slowly; people came from town and from the outlying hills. They brought with them their own unspeakable bedding and their relatives and friends to nurse them. David worked against terrific odds. If a patient on a liquid diet took a turn for the worse he generally knew what had happened. Some kind neighbor, coming to help, had brought in forbidden food. Not all trusted him . . . perhaps he was starving the sick, who knew? Perhaps he wanted their dead—or what was worse, their living—bodies for experiment, for sacrifice to his unknown gods? . . .

There were medical and surgical patients, there were sufferers from the opium habit, there were women . . .

A stoical race, there was little noise connected with the hospital across the heaven's-well courtyard. But there were sounds of distress and there were odors, drifting out. Adeline, occupying herself as best she could with books and magazines from home, in writing letters and in struggling with the house servants, who regarded her with suave indifference and went for all their important orders to David, was increasingly unhappy.

She loved her husband. She told herself so, over and over. She was as good a wife as she knew how to be. She took care of him, in her way. She tried to rest him with her fleet caresses, her light talk, when the long day was over. But she was stifled and afraid. She lacked the physical desire for him which might have brought its own compensations and which, philosophers to the contrary, rescues so many marriages. If, when the work he loved, and she hated, was over, she could have gone to his arms with a wild, beautiful upleaping of pulse and nerve, and sought therein the magnificent oblivion, she would have been better able to endure her days. But she had not been fashioned for passion. For love, yes, and tenderness, for the little charming gallantries of a valentine. But not for the sometimes austere and sometimes laughing ways of ardor.

Very rarely, David went to Fuhchau to attend a conference. On such occasions he took her with him and she bloomed again, the city having become dear to her by comparison. Now and then someone from the mission came up. Dr. Merriman came once and stayed for three days to assist David on some difficult work he was doing, a series of operations. Poor Merriman, a gray, devoted man, left Ku-cheng a little bewildered. He had his wife, as gray and devoted as himself, and he loved her dearly. He wasn't the sort of man who would look twice at another woman or would expect another woman to look twice at him. But young Mrs. Condit made much of him. She had cooked his favorite dishes on the charcoal range, she had worn her prettiest frock, she had talked to him of home, she had, it appeared, hung on his every word. He returned to the mission incomprehensibly pleased with himself.

In April there were torrential rains which slanted down and beat against the shutters and were a steadily falling gray veil between oneself and the mountains. The gutters of the town were running like rivers, the little river itself swollen to astounding proportions. Day after day Adeline sat in the damp, musty-smelling house while David worked in the ward and the dispensary with the boys he had trained to help him, and wished herself elsewhere. She did not wish herself dead. She had been too well brought up for that. It was a sin to wish oneself out of this life. But she was quite convinced that she was the unhappiest woman in the world; and said so, in her letters home.

Correspondence with Mrs. Richard Wright did not tend to soothe her. Mrs. Wright had given her husband a son and heir. She wrote glowingly of the baby's charm, his eyes "so like his father's," his engaging ways, the gifts showered upon him, the money deposited to his account by his grandfather.

She had little care of him herself, she confessed, as an English nursemaid had been engaged. But now and then she bathed him, in his round tin tub in the nursery, and drew a pretty pen picture of herself, kneeling beside the tub in the big firelighted room, her sleeves rolled back, an apron covering her fashionable frock, flushed and laughing and with Richard in the background, watching, pulling his mustache, the prototype of proud young fatherhood.

Heng-ong's wife had had her son, also. David had gone to Fuhchau to officiate. Heng-ong would have no one else.

If, thought Adeline, if after all I had a baby—?

A letter from her aunt which reached her at this time was frightening and warning. "It is possible," wrote Mrs. Graham, "that if you and David had a child he would see the wisdom of returning home. After all, bringing up a baby in that climate and surroundings must be extremely dangerous . . ."

Perhaps, thought Adeline, she was right. Perhaps if she had a child David would see the wicked selfishness of his ways and take her and the baby back to a Christian, a clean country, in which there was light and laughter and companionship.

But she was desperately afraid.

Mrs. Wright had assured her that the experience was terrible, "My dear—such agony—but well worth it," and she had added, "Richard seems to think ten times as much of me, if that could be possible."

Against her fear, Adeline set the rewards of motherhood. If she had a child she would no longer be lonely; if she had a child she would possess a weapon, a strong weapon. And so, between reluctance and acquiescence, she made up her mind.

David was never as tender toward her, as anxiously adoring as after the day she was able to tell him, between laughter and tears, "I think so, David . . . of course, I'm not sure . . . but I hope so . . ."

It was as if she had given him the world. He went about his work with such a vitality of purpose, such a warmth of unspoken happiness that the poor creatures on their unhappy cots felt it and were comforted, and were upheld by his strength. And when Tobias, coming briefly to visit, was told, the two men looked at

each other with a unity of sentiment in which there was no need
for words. The line would go on, there would be a son to follow
David, a grandson to follow Tobias. Perhaps a grandson, thought
the older man, with Elizabeth Condit's eyes . . .

In June of that year the financial crisis raging in the United
States reached its dismal climax and Cleveland called an extra
session of Congress. In July banks and business houses were sus-
pended; and later in the summer word reached Adeline that the
Grahams were ruined, hopelessly and completely, their fortune
swept away.

She was alone when Anna's letter came. Anna's mother was
too prostrated to write, her father too busy, salvaging what little
he could. Anna said, in conclusion, "I am so happy, dearest Adeline, that you at least are safe, with David to take care of you.
To know this relieves me of what would have been a pressing
anxiety. As for myself, I am going to try to find work. I have
learned to use the typewriter and I think it quite possible that I
may find an office position. Papa will not hear of it, of course,
and mamma falls into hysterics if I mention it. But I must earn a
little something, I cannot be a burden to my people. Richard
Wright, whose people, although they have lost a good deal, are
still in excellent circumstances, will help me I am sure, through
some of his connections. Of course his business is just now at a
standstill. But I have hopes that everything will be resumed
shortly. This house is to be sold. We will take a small rented
place somewhere in a less expensive section—"

David had gone on one of his trips into the hills, as the small
hospital was at the moment almost empty. With one of the boys
he had trained, a few instruments and plenty of drugs, he had set
out, to sleep by night in the bare inns, in rooms already occupied
by half a dozen travelers, to ford streams, to tramp rough roads,
and to visit several of the inland towns.

He would be to-day, she decided, after her first burst of helpless weeping was over, in Mi-daik's town. He had arranged to
send the grandchild to the Parker Hospital at Canton, and he
went now and again to visit Mi-daik and her people. Some of
the sick of her village had reached him at his own hospital.

Others had not. He had promised his old amah to do what he could for them. And he knew that Adeline resented the old woman.

She more than resented her. To realize that David Condit had been nourished at this alien, now withered breast made her physically sick. For days after she had seen Mi-daik for the first time she could not look at David without a shudder of repulsion.

Adeline cast the letter aside and wrung her hands. She finally summoned the cook and in the very few halting words she had had to learn told her what she wanted. The woman's grandson, a strong boy, must go to the hill village and find the doctor and bring him home at once . . . at once, do you understand?

And so David was summoned, some hours later. The boy had found him in the very simple place in which Mi-daik and her sons and her sons' sons and their women had their being. He had spent the day there, giving medicine and advice to all who wished it, and he was at supper with the men of the family when the messenger arrived, panting and shining with sweat, in the close heat of the summer day's end. David was sitting at the table, the "nimble lads" between his fingers, plunging morsels of rice into his mouth and laughing for all his weariness at something Mi-daik's husband said to him. Then he looked around, hearing the commotion at the door, and saw his houseboy.

He went back at once, his supper uneaten, his farewells half said and pushed his way the dozen odd miles over rocky path, through undergrowth, by stream and road and trail to Ku-cheng. A hundred times he asked the boy impatiently—what was wrong? was the lady ill? what had happened? But the boy could only shake his sleek black head. He did not know, he said . . . the lady had wept, very much . . .

"What is it?" cried David, bursting into the house. A lamp was lighted. It burned on the round table. Adeline sat there, her eyes on the cheap American clock. She had no sewing in her hands. She sat quite still and waited.

David came to her and caught her into his arms. He was disheveled, he was not very clean. He needed a shave, his face was rough against her delicate skin. "Are you ill?" he asked her in an agony of anxiety. He had thought, tramping the difficult way home . . . the baby . . . of course . . . a fall, a fright . . . and had planned how, if possible, he would get her by river to Fuh-chau . . . the mountain trail was impossible. Or, if that was out of the question . . . how he could send word to Dr. Merriman to Heng-ong to help them.

He almost shook her. He cried again, "What has happened, Adeline? Are you in pain?"

She put the letter in his hand. "Oh, David," she said sorrow-fully, "read that. Isn't it dreadful—they've lost everything . . . Oh, poor Uncle," she mourned as he read, "poor Aunt—"

David's eyes raced over the closely written pages. He flung the letter on the floor. He said, and shouted it:

"You brought me back for that!"

He was incredulous. He was violently angry. He remembered the trip, his anxiety, a cold hand squeezing the life blood from his heart. He remembered his terror . . . if they lost the baby— if, far more important, he should lose her? . . .

But no, she was here, serene, except for her little weeping, her hands clasped on the silk of her dress, sitting quietly under the oil lamp . . . waiting . . .

"For that?" he repeated.

He walked away from her, and stood over against the wall. His hands shook so that he thrust them into his pockets. He said, at last, evenly, as she looked at him with a terrified appeal:

"I was returning home to-morrow night. Surely it could have waited twenty-four hours, Adeline. There is nothing I can do, after all," he reminded her, with a cool gentleness as one speaks to a stupid child, "nothing that you could do. And I was needed where I was."

"Oh, needed!" she cried out to him. "Needed! By those filthy, disgusting people who probably laugh at you behind your back and go on worshiping their horrid idols. Needed! You never think of me, your wife, whom you brought to this dreadful place; or of the baby either . . . I was mad to think of having a child . . . in this hole, this unspeakable hole . . . with a father who doesn't care whether we live or die, but who would walk fifty miles to sit beside some dirty bed in a shack and—and—"

She wept stormily. Outside the door the houseboy listened with intent gravity. He went later into the kitchen and asked a bowl of rice from his grandmother. Resting, he ate it, under the flickering candles. He said sententiously, "A wife's long tongue is the flight of steps by which misfortune comes."

He did not like Adeline. None of the servants liked her. They were repelled by her yellow hair and her fair skin. Their master should have had a beautiful and obedient wife, one with small feet, not a large-footed woman who might have been a simple peasant from hill or field or a boatwoman. Also, this woman did not like them. They knew. They stole from her with utmost placidity, whenever they could. They were entirely insolent to her, and she did not know it. Yet there was not a member of that household who would not have laid down his or her life for David.

The quarrel continued in the other room.

"I have been patient with you, Adeline. You knew when we married what my life would be—"

"I did not!" she contradicted furiously.

He went on, ignoring her.

"And you agreed to be my wife. I have not demanded much of you. I have given up asking your assistance. I know that by your very nature you cannot help me—in the unpleasant things. But there are many ways in which you can help me very much. Sending a messenger to take me from my duty because your uncle has lost his money is not one of them."

Adeline's eyes were dry now, and bright. Her face, pinched and slightly discolored because of her condition, was a mask of fury. She did not raise her voice. When she spoke it was tonelessly.

"I never should have married you. You are completely selfish. Nothing matters to you except dirty heathen. I don't matter . . ."

She turned, while he stared at her too stricken for speech, and walked steadily into their bedroom. When he followed her she was lying on the bed. She did not speak to him but she shivered incessantly as a sick animal might. She did not speak when he undressed her, with deft, swift hands and put on her nightgown and wrapped her in blankets. Then he went out to the kitchen for hot water. It was a close night, almost stifling. But Adeline lay there with her teeth chattering.

She was dimly aware of David moving about the room; of the glass he held to her lips and bade her drink; of his finger on her pulse. She was not conscious of thinking, merely of lying there in the center of a terrific cold in the very core of which there was fire. After a long time the shivering stopped, and she found herself as weak as a child, and as docile. She wept, presently, without sound, tears running ceaselessly down her cheeks. And after a time, she slept.

David sat beside the bed. The lamp burned on the plain dresser. He sat there with his hands between his knees and looked at his wife. There was more color in her cheeks and lips now. The long lashes rested on the curve of her cheek. She breathed regularly, gently. Under the bed coverings the outline of her small and slender figure, as yet undistorted by her pregnancy, was visible.

He thought, she's right, I have been brutally selfish . . .

And yet, what was selfishness? He was not laboring here in any hope of gain, with any ambition other than the urge to heal, to alleviate. He had not even the excuse that through the relief of pain he might save a soul. He was concerned with bodies, not with souls. Yet back of the practical use to which his hands were dedicated, unrelated to the pure evangelistic fervor, was there not the Messianic dream?

He had fallen in love with Adeline Graham because of the texture of her skin, perhaps, the curve of her lashes, the hazel of her eyes. Because of these trivial things and because of his young, strong body's demand for comfort and ease and companionship. Because, too, of something elusive and urgent in the mind and the spirit, which is divorced from the body, yet complements the body's needs. And, loving her, he had married her and brought her into unhappiness.

He did not doubt that he still loved her. It never occurred to him that perhaps he did not, that love had become a synonym for affection tolerant and sorrowful, and for a heavy sense of responsibility. Because he could no longer tell himself truly, This woman is my world and my ultimate desire, he did not therefore reach the conclusion, I no longer love this woman. They had been man and wife for almost three years. That he had known disappointment in his marriage he did not deny, sitting there soberly, watching her. If she had not met his great vitality and unblunted ardor with the like ardor of which, perhaps, he had dreamed, that was not her fault. Women were like that; good women. If she could not see eye to eye with him in his work, that was not her fault either. He had taken her from a sheltered life and from a familiar country and flung her, with no adequate preparation, into a totally different existence. But he had thought that loving him she would learn in some measure to work with him. She was intelligent, and being a woman, gentle.

She was his wife, and she would be the mother of his child. His heart was soundless a moment within him, dreaming on that child. She had a double claim on him, and he had failed her in many things, being what he was. He sighed heavily, and adjusted the covering about her. Perhaps, he thought, reaching the pitiful, inevitable masculine conclusion, perhaps after the child was born things would be different. She would be happier, absorbed in her baby, in her feminine fulfillment.

In the morning Adeline was quite well again, although she still felt uncommonly weak, pleasantly so. She asked, "What happened . . . I mean . . . ?"

"You had a nervous chill," her husband told her, "but you're all right now."

He had not slept. He was changing his clothes, preparatory to making the rounds among the few convalescent patients in the ward and opening the dispensary. Adeline sat up in bed. Her throat rose like a flower from the frill of lace about her neck. She confessed, half laughing, half crying, "David, I'm sorry . . ."

He came and sat beside her and took her in his arms and laid his cheek against the soft, fair hair. He said, "I'm sorry, too,

Adeline. I'm not much use as a husband . . . neglectful and"—
he swallowed, brought it out—"selfish . . ."

"No." Her arms tightened about his neck. She was rested, she
was better, something had been released in her, a hard knot of
misery and rebellion. This man belonged to her; was all she had.
"Forgive me, David. I do try . . . but it is the loneliness and
always being afraid."

He said, "I've been very stupid, Adeline. Perhaps there is someone—someone you like who would come and stay with you . . .
for a little while—"

Her hazel eyes brightened. She sighed. "If only Anna could
come . . . poor Anna." She was silent contemplating the ap-
palling picture of Anna working in an office, among men, robbed
of her heritage, unprotected. Her clasp tightened. She wondered
aloud—"Miss Nielson?"

Miss Nielson was a pleasant spinster with whom Adeline had
formed something of a friendship in Fuhchau. She had come out
to keep house for her bachelor brother, who was engaged in
trade . . . exports of lacquer and other commodities. But he had
married recently.

"The very thing," agreed David, smiling. He rose, stooped to
kiss her, looked at his watch. "I must go," he said hurriedly.

At the door he turned back to look at her. She was lying back
among the heaped pillows, smiling faintly, waiting for the
woman to bring her breakfast. David's heart contracted. She
looked small and lost and alone. He thought—if the Nielson
girl would come.

Miss Nielson came, gladly enough. She was company for Adeline. She was, on occasion, of assistance to David. She was a big
plain woman with plenty of assurance and a fund of small talk.
She managed the house and the servants. She had not lived ten
years in the East without knowing how. Adeline was enchanted
and grateful and gave herself up to a coddled and semi-invalid-
ism. Sophia Nielson adored her with the burning and unspoken
adoration of a plain woman for a pretty woman; and without
jealousy.

The summer drew to a close. It had been rather pleasant for

Adeline since Sophia's arrival. There were even short excursions to the hills, not too far for fear of bandits. There were long idle conversations in the small garden, gossip, chatter over periodicals from home, over changing fashions and changing times. Sophia was really very entertaining. She could read tea leaves or lay the cards for a fortune. David, returning one afternoon and coming upon them before they saw him, frowned and then smiled. It was all very harmless, and Adeline was laughing as he had not seen her laugh since early in their marriage—until Sophia came.

She expanded and bloomed under Sophia's admiration as a flower blossoms under the warm sun. It was all she had needed, an eye to admire, a voice to substantiate that admiration, hands willing in service.

It had been arranged that they were to go to Fuhchau in the early winter, there to await the birth of the baby. One of the Chinese doctors, working in the dispensary with Heng-ong and, like him, trained under McKenzie at Tientsin, would come to Ku-cheng and take David's place for a time.

But in November, a month before their removal to the larger city, Tobias Condit came up to Ku-cheng. David was to accompany him on an evangelistic trip of a week or more. They would travel on foot for the most part, and sometimes by water. They would sleep at inns and in temples, traveling dispensers of salvation and medicine.

Adeline saw them go, more happily than usual. She would not be alone. Sophia, competent and devoted, would be with her. And a box of books had come from Anna, whose last letter had assured her cousin that she was happy in her new position . . . that of secretary to a merchant in New York. "He imports from China," she wrote; "it brings me a little closer to you, somehow."

It was cold in the mountains, the still, cool days wove a spell of bright sky over the travelers. They stopped to see Mi-daik and then went on, sleeping together in evil-smelling rooms, on bare tables or on the unclean floor. Tobias had, David noticed with concern, a heavy cold. He coughed at intervals and was shaken by it. It was nothing, he said, when David tried to get him to turn back.

They went to small villages where they were not known. In one they were stoned. Hostility did not show itself often but now and then it sprang up, unexpected, disconcerting. Tobias was cut across the forehead and lip. He wiped the blood away and grinned at David. "Not very welcome here, I should gather," he said, as David cleansed the wound and put some sticking plaster over it.

He was not angry at the small bedraggled boy who had thrown the stone. Nor would he leave the hill town and, as he told David, "lose face." He stayed to preach in the open streets, and to pray, quite simply and without self-consciousness. And to find a house, less inhospitable, in which he and David might have supper and sleep. David treated half a dozen rather timid patients that night and the next morning they pushed on to the home of one of the Bible women from the mission, where a welcome was sure to be waiting for them.

They stayed two days at a friendly farm where the Dangs' big clean house stood facing the prosperous fields. Services were held there and David's hands were full. He said, laughing, to his father when they went to their beds that night, "We're working at cross-purposes after all, aren't we? You pray them into heaven but I try to keep them on earth a little longer."

Tobias coughed again. David's remedies had not helped him very much, it seemed. David looked at him with a frown of concern. He said, "I think we'd better give up the rest of the trip and go on back to Ku-cheng and get that cold broken up before you go home to Fuhchau."

"It isn't anything," said his father, "you fuss over me like an old woman." He lay back in bed and watched David who sat smoking on the edge of his own. He asked abruptly:

"Have you been content in Ku-cheng?"

"Yes," said David, his eyes lighting. "It's been an uphill pull, but we're getting somewhere." He laughed a little. "The lack of equipment's pretty much of a handicap, but when you have to fight dirt and relatives as well as disease it's considerable of a battle."

"And Adeline," asked his father, "how is she?"

David looked at him in astonishment.

"You said you thought she was looking very well," he reminded Tobias.

"I did not mean physically," his father said gently.

David looked at the floor. Then he looked up again.

"It hasn't been easy for her . . . to adjust herself . . . She will, I think, after the baby is born."

They were silent for a little. He knew how Tobias felt about the child. He said, after a moment:

"In a way, I suppose I have been selfish."

His father did not reply. He thought, Adeline has told him so, if he comes to believe it, if his purpose becomes clouded . . . David said, out of the brief silence, "I suppose any work which matters intensely to the worker makes him selfish." Then he regarded his father in some astonishment. "Not you," he amended, as if he had received a revelation, "yet your work has meant more to you than anything in the world."

His father said, after a minute:

"Selfish? I don't know. Perhaps I have been, David. I can't tell, you see. But I know that I've been happy."

That was the solution, perhaps. Happy people had not time for selfishness. David nodded, and began pulling off his boots. Once in the night he rose and adjusted the covers about his father. He thought, touching his hand, which was too warm, "I'll make him stay on here, for a day or two."

But in the morning Tobias seemed his unfevered self and they pushed on. They ran into rains, they forded a brook, and Tobias' cough grew worse and racked him intolerably.

David said, "We're going back. No, I won't listen to a word . . . we're going back now. You're a sick man . . ."

They went back, partly by chair and bearer, but much of the way on foot. For the last miles of the foot journey David carried his father, now visibly at the end of his strength. In this fashion, and with terror as a companion, they came once more to Kucheng.

Adeline could do nothing but twist her hands and weep. Sophia Nielson was a rock of strength. David sent word to the mission but he knew that before help could reach them Tobias Condit would be convalescent or at peace.

He blamed himself bitterly. If he had forced him to turn back earlier—if—if—

Tobias said, on that harsh and rattling breath, ". . . not to blame . . . David . . . I'm—as—stubborn—as you—"

The lungs were quite consolidated. There was no hope. He died, and died fighting, as he had lived. He had no message to give, no deathbed oration. He spoke David's name and his wife's. He spoke another Name, and was sustained. And died.

CHAPTER XII

THE Condits returned to Fuhchau earlier than they had expected. There was mourning there, in the compound and in the city; there was mourning in the villages for many miles around; among the people of the hills; and there were those who mourned on the river, the boat people. Something very real had gone from many lives. Tobias Condit had had more friends than even his son had guessed. He had gone into the houses of the gentry and sat upon chairs of carved ebony and drunk tea from delicate cups; he had gone under the thatched roofs of poverty and taken his humble meal at the table with the men of the fields, with the workers. He had brought them friendliness and warmth, a tremendous vitality and a purpose strong to violence. He had been single-hearted, he had been perhaps narrow, but he had possessed a natural nobility to which these people, who were closer to him than his own, had responded. And so they mourned his passing.

David, alone at his father's raw grave under the banyan trees, looked somberly at the small stones marking his sister's and his mother's. Three of them there. He himself, he supposed, in his own time.

He went back to the echoing house in which his father had lived and found Adeline with Sophia. She had been much shaken by her father-in-law's death, not because she had ever felt close to him but because death, of necessity, would shake her. She was gentle with David, and very sweet. Now when he came in she moved to him awkwardly, with her new, clumsy tread, and took his cold hands in her own and tried to warm them. She was terribly sorry for David, she had assured Sophia over and over again. He had been so devoted to his father. In her own heart a tiny, secret spark of triumph burned. It would not have occurred to her to wish for Tobias' death. Such sinful thinking was beyond her. But Tobias had died, and David was now dependent upon her for all intimacy.

She settled down in the mission, with Sophia running in and out, with her other acquaintances coming to call, with Heng-ong's wife coming one day to drink tea and to show her her fat and solemn baby, with his shaven head and bright eyes and padded silk robes, and she waited for her own time to come. She had been desperately afraid but now the inexorable approach of her hour brought its own anesthetic.

After his father's death David talked to her more and more about the child. It was as if, lacking his father, he believed the child must in a measure ease the raw pain. He would come home after working in the dispensary and sit and talk, while she occupied herself with sewing. The child would be a boy, of course, he said, and laughed at her for her practical doubts on the subject. There were so many things he would show him, places he would take him.

They would fly great kites on Black Rock hill. And in the Seventh Month they would see the dragon boat races on the Min. They would go by boat to the Pagoda Anchorage, where the wild coast stretched and the strange fisher folk would be in their little boats, and there would be swimming on the tiny curve of the beach. They would go to Sharpe Peak and to the temple on top of Kushan. There would be pigeons for the little boy, fantails and tumblers and pouters, and he would learn one from the other and he would fasten the thin bamboo whistles under their tails and let them fly, making that silver singing sound. He would have fighting crickets in a cage, and singing birds.

David would buy him the garments of a scholar such as he himself had worn, and he would go sometimes to the Chinese school and listen to the drone of young voices repeating the classics. He would speak Chinese before he spoke English and as he grew older there would be the writing brush set to his little hand.

For him the peach would bloom and the wild white plum and the camphor trees and the candleberries and the dragon's-eye fruit trees. For him the grain springing, the translucent green of the young rice, the silver filigree of the canals, the thick, bowed shape of the water buffalo, the wooden water wheel turning. For him the stars above the mountain, and the beaten silver of the risen moon and the dark clouds drifting . . .

All these things David thought, and some of them he said, as the time grew closer. He said, "He'll find a friend, as I did Heng-ong," and he said, "Sia Ho-mei will be his teacher, God willing," and he said, "When he's old enough he'll climb the steps to the temple at Kushan . . . he'll see the inscriptions carved in the stone, and I'll tell him what they mean . . . and at the top there'll be the waterfall and the fish ponds and the drums beating and the gongs—"

Adeline sewed and listened. She was listening to China take her unborn child from her. She was listening to David weave a spell about the child, her child, who stirred within her, with quick, strong movements, the movements of life. She was listening to China and to David claim the child of her body and of her coming torture. She would be an outsider, as she had always been. First Tobias, now the child, and always China.

She said nothing except to nod or to smile at intervals. David had forgotten her, she was merely an audience. Her first fear had been acute. She had feared childbirth. Then she had wanted it, because of her loneliness and because of David. Again she feared it.

She had thought of the child as a weapon. Now it seemed the weapon must turn against her, in her own hand. But there would be a way. There must be a way. Her mind was made up. Her small red mouth was set, a very little. She went on putting careful stitches in the little shirt. Even, meticulous, exquisite. She knew what she must do. Had not Sophia counseled her in her brusque, practical way. "I don't know what I'll do without you, Adeline, but I mustn't be selfish . . ." Had not her aunt's last plaintive letters inquired, "Surely when your dear little baby comes you will make David bring you home."

There must be a way.

The baby was born early in January, 1894. It was a little girl, small and perfect. Adeline had, as do so many small, unathletic women, a remarkably easy time. Or so the attending physician at the Woman's Hospital congratulated himself, and her and David. Of the two, mother and father, David looked the worse when it was all over.

He had thought that Adeline would be desperately disappointed because the baby was not a boy. He had believed that he would be, but from the first time he held the child in his arms, he knew that he was not. Nor was Adeline. A girl, she thought drowsily, relaxed and at peace, would be more wholly her own.

They had discussed names before the birth of the baby. They had not given much thought to girls' names but Adeline had agreed that Elizabeth for a girl was quite pretty. They could call her Betty, she said.

So Elizabeth Condit was christened in the mission chapel, and she had the dark eyes of that other Elizabeth Condit, and the red-gold hair of her father's babyhood, ringleted about her small and shapely skull.

Adeline was unable to nurse her. She had sufficient milk but the quality was not good, and the baby sickened. David, after consultation with the other doctors, took her from her mother and gave her to a woman who had recently lost a child, who came, stoic in her sorrow, to put to the swollen breast this pale and alien child, in place of the man child who would have comforted her while she lived and honored her when she died.

Adeline had not really wished to nurse her child. There was something repellent to her in the function itself; and then, too, women lost their figures, became shapeless. Yet she fought bitterly against the introduction of the wet nurse, a small woman, with bound feet, who tottered about the household, and crooned tunelessly to the sleeping child or lifted it in her arms and fed it from her full, remembering breast. She fought a dozen almost silent battles with the woman every day, snatching from the child's round throat the charms the amah had placed there, storming against the little porcelain or wooden idols she had set up in the baby's room.

"Why?" asked David when she came to him with bitter tales of the woman's idolatry and superstition. "Why bother about it,

Adeline? It cannot hurt little Elizabeth . . . King-eng believes in it. Believing," said David musingly, "is so important somehow. No matter what you believe."

Adeline did not answer. It was all a conspiracy, and against her. She had recovered her physical strength with fair rapidity after leaving the hospital. She was quite content to remain for a time at home and receive her callers. So many came, those in the mission, those of the business section, Heng-ong, and Heng-ong's wife. There were gifts for the baby, padded silk robes, silver rattles and belled bracelets, lacquered boxes and carved chests . . .

But she made no effort to assert her strength, to go out, to busy herself with the household, to shop, to entertain. She lay day after day, muffled to her eyes on the veranda, or, for choice, within doors, and huddled on the stiff sofa during the colder weather. David, looking at her professionally, believed that nothing was really wrong. When they went back to Ku-cheng, she would be all right.

He said as much. She replied merely, through stiff lips, that she would never return to Ku-cheng.

He let that go as a whim, a fantasy which would pass. She had had a normal delivery but there was always a certain amount of shock. He spoke to Heng-ong guardedly. Heng-ong, for all his European training, was Chinese. He did not talk of his wife to his closest friend nor would he expect David to talk of his, to him. But, professionally, David could consult him impersonally, as if they spoke of a stranger.

Heng-ong answered with an equal caution. He believed that Mrs. Condit was exceedingly high-strung, he said. Time would tell, meantime rest was indicated, care; if possible perhaps a change of scene.

But no change of scene was possible. David was very busy, and it was winter; had it been summer he might have sent her and the baby up to Kuliang.

She grew steadily more withdrawn and at the same time more irritable. This required no effort and no planning on her part. It came naturally, it was part of her. The long brooding before the baby's birth, the physical relaxation afterward, then the retautened nerves. Everything was exaggerated, the loathing for the place, the climate, the people. The mere sight of King-eng made her want to scream. There were days when she would snatch the baby from the woman's arms and look at it deeply, thrusting her face into the little face, holding it so tightly that it would weep shrilly; then she would thrust it back again and leave the room without a word. The amah spoke freely in the kitchen . . . this woman, she said, was possessed of an evil spirit—a kwei . . .

But there were days when Adeline scarcely looked at the baby and when she would receive no callers. These she spent on her bed, looking up through the folds of mosquito netting, at the high ceiling. And there were days when she would not eat because she said the smell of cooking from the servants' quarters sickened her.

She would not, when she did eat, touch Chinese food. Her food had to be prepared for her apart from the others. Sometimes Sophia came up and catered for her, or showed the cook how to make certain delicacies. And when Sophia cooked, Adeline ate heartily.

She became, as spring wore on, subject to fits of crying. She would lie limp on her bed and weep. And when David, finding her thus, would talk with her gently and reasonably, probing, inquiring, she could make him no explanation.

She grew pale, and very thin; she was hot and cold by turns. If Sophia or Mrs. Merriman or some of the other women persuaded her to a small excursion in the city, to shop, perhaps, she would turn back before she had gone very far. The streets frightened her, the people pressing close, the walls of shops and houses leaned, they would fall, she would be crushed . . .

It was not a sudden thing, it was slow and of tenacious growth. The fits of irritability increased. One day David came home to find the house in an uproar. King-eng had departed, the baby wept, unappeased, the servants clustered about their quarters, talking agitatedly among themselves. In the nursery where the baby lay, screaming, red in the face, unfed, unchanged and very uncomfortable, the beautiful little porcelain Kuan-yin which lived on the bureau and which belonged to the amah, lay smashed into a hundred smooth ivory-toned fragments, the smile of compassion shattered, the delicate hand raised in blessing and pity tramped underfoot.

Adeline crouched shivering in the middle of the big bed in their room and held her hands over her ears to shut out the noise of her baby's weeping.

To David, when order had been restored, when King-eng had been found and persuaded to come back to her nursling, she said merely that she could not endure to have her child grow up among grinning idols.

It was after that that the other doctors were consulted, the Englishmen from the Community Hospital, those from the Woman's Hospital, who had been with Adeline at the time of Betty's birth, and others. And the trouble was diagnosed, in a word which had been current for a decade only. "Neurasthenia," they said.

Rest. Rest and a slow building up, a slow healing of the raw blind nerves.

Sophia moved into the mission house to nurse her friend. Adeline tolerated her without any visible pleasure. She would not talk to David, she was not interested in the baby. She lay for the most part in bed while Sophia cared for her, read to her, sat beside her. The only interest she evinced was when the American mails came in. Then she sparkled into life, avid for news. Sophia had to read her the letters over and over.

But David had to answer them. She would not set pen to paper. He wrote painstakingly by every mail, to Mrs. Graham, to Anna. His own correspondence had suffered over the years. Once a month perhaps he sent a line to Mat Brent or to his great-aunt. But he had very little time. Now he took time to reassure Adeline's people that she would be all right, very soon; it was a question of rest and care.

Mrs. Graham wrote him sternly, "It is your duty to bring her home."

He had known this for some time. There would never be any cure for Adeline in the place she hated, surrounded by the people she despised. Sometimes he consulted with himself, sitting by the

baby's cradle. The baby, rosy, pleased with life, amused by sunlight or the shadow of a leaf, looked at him with bright dark
eyes and chuckled. She was perfectly happy. She knew King-eng,
put up her arms to be held, was quiet in the amah's clasp. She
knew David, and the servants. But when Adeline, on very rare
occasions, demanded to see her, she shrank away against King-
eng's shoulder and wept.

"You see," said Adeline bitterly, "they've taught my baby to
be afraid of me!"

It was an accusation.

David, working in the laboratory one night with Heng-ong,
said suddenly, "It is no use. I must take them home."

Heng-ong's eyes were wise and understanding. He inclined his
head rather formally. He said, after a minute, "I know."

"Not for long," David insisted eagerly, "you understand that?
Long enough to put her on her feet again and then we'll come
back."

Heng-ong was silent. David looked at him quickly, looked
away again. The little laboratory was quite still but for the hiss-
ing of flame in a burner. Heng-ong's hands shook, very slightly,
and he dropped a test tube. The glass shattered, it was like a
pistol shot. David said, urgently:

"You don't believe that, do you, Heng-ong . . . that I'll come
back?"

David's hand touched his friend's shoulder for a moment. He
said brokenly, "You damned old pessimist!"

He spoke in English. Heng-ong smiled. He knew. He was not
offended. The strong unspoken affection between them was like
something tangible in the room. Heng-ong said serenely, "The
mission does not countenance profanity."

They laughed together. Men do not weep. Each knew it was
good-by.

But David would not admit it, although he made his plans,
consulted his superiors, made his arrangements. He said to Adeline, when these things were nearly completed, "We are going
back to the States, Adeline."

He was standing beside her bed, looking down. Sophia, with

a catch at her heart, a dull pain, slipped from the room and went out to scold a somnolent houseboy. It was a safety valve. She was necessary no longer. She had not been necessary in her brother's house since his marriage, and then the opportunity had come to her to serve Adeline Condit. That opportunity was departing; had departed. She was, beneath the brusque, plain exterior, a passionately maternal and sentimental woman. Now she upbraided the houseboy with a fluency that compelled his admiration.

She saw no reason why he should neglect his job because she had lost hers.

The tide turned late in the afternoon on the autumn day the Condits left Fuhchau. Their many friends were compelled to say good-by to them at the Customs Jetty where the houseboat waited to take them to Pagoda Anchorage where they would board the Shanghai steamer. Heng-ong only went with them, downriver. He had been called on an urgent case to Hok-chiang, up a small branch of the Min. That night the houseboat anchored on the opposite shore where Heng-ong's sampan also waited the turn of the tide. The farewells had been said. Heng-ong had taken his final leave of Adeline. But to David, after their last handclasp he spoke no further word as he boarded the sampan and was rowed away.

David stood alone watching the dark widening gap of water; and all night Heng-ong kept vigil, his somber eyes on the masthead light of the houseboat, shining, a small star, across the black night on the Min. At last his sleepy boatmen roused, to row the sampan up the tide-swollen creek and he could no longer see the last visible token of David's presence. With this departure something went, never to return.

David's homeward journey was accomplished with ease. A nurse had been procured for the baby, a young woman who had come out with a merchant's family and wished to return to the States. Adeline had no care of the child. She stayed below or lay on deck, the color returning to her pinched face. She felt as if she had died and come to life again; as if an enormous burden had been removed.

They were within sight of the Golden Gate when she spoke clearly and with determination to her husband. Nothing had been said of their future. When he told her they were sailing for home she had wept and that was all. No further discussion had taken place since. Now, she said, quite quietly, standing at the rail, "You know that I'll never go back again, don't you?"

He knew. He had known it for a long time. But somehow he had not dared believe it. He had said farewell in his heart to Heng-ong, to those he had left under the banyan trees in the churchyard. He had promised them all, *I will come back.* He had said that once before, as a little boy; now he pledged it as a grown man. He had kept that first promise.

He had had his hour alone with his father and his mother. He had stood there, in the crowded acre, and had looked down on the graves, on the old headstones and the new. He had said, I will come back . . . deep in his heart.

Yet he knew they were not there. His training, his mind, had been shaped to the knowledge that they were not there; not really. But his later training had taught him other things, sometimes at variance with the knowledge which was bred in his bone and which beat in his blood.

Science and faith. Was it ever possible to reconcile them? It must be possible, he mused, standing hatless beside the graves, otherwise there was no peace.

Adeline asked, still standing there beside him, looking at the Western coast of her country:

"David . . . you're very unhappy?" She touched his sleeve. She had not touched him of her own free will for many months. "But," she told him, "I couldn't help it, David. It has been hell," said Adeline, who did not use strong words lightly.

He covered her hand with his own. He said gently, "In time—"

"No," she interrupted, "never. I'll never go back. David, don't look at me so." She shrank away and her voice rose a little. Other passengers looked at them curiously, going by. "Don't . . . I can't bear it. I will make it up to you, David . . . I promise . . . we'll be happy . . . at home."

She had made that vow to herself. If only I can go home . . . anything, I'll do anything. Anything he wants. I'll settle down, take more interest in his work, force myself to it, I'll have other children . . .

Betty, in some curious way, was not her child. Born in an alien land, suckled by an alien woman, she was not Adeline's. She belonged to David and to China.

In San Francisco the word reached them that Elizabeth Lewis had died, and been buried. Dr. Brent sent the telegram to their hotel. "Peacefully," he wired David, "and without pain."

They boarded their train and traveled East. When they reached New York Anna met them. She looked strange to Adeline, in her trim shirtwaist and skirt, her narrow-brimmed sailor perched on the mass of dark hair. She greeted them with laughter and tears, and looked at David over Adeline's head, bent to her shoulder. David's eyes were steady and reassuring.

Betty was embraced and admired. A cab took them and their belongings to a hotel. The nurse would stay with them for a while, until they were settled.

The Grahams were living in a small rented house. Anna was working, every day. She loved it, she declared. Adeline regarded her and shook her head. She couldn't understand Anna.

New York was hot with Indian summer heat and it had changed. There were electric lights in several of the big private houses now, in many public buildings. There were many more telephones since Adeline Condit had sailed for China. She talked to her aunt through one that very evening and was afraid of it, that great mysterious box on the wall.

They had arrived rather late. No more excitement, no more greetings. Adeline was put to bed in the hotel bedroom. She lay there docile, just touching the sheets with her hands. The room was ugly, square, furnished in walnut and red plush. She loved it. This was home, this was safety.

In the parlor downstairs David talked to Anna.

"She will be all right," he assured her, "it is just a question of time, of nerves."

Anna put out her hand and touched him. Then she drew it back again.

"David, have you given it up?"

He had no need to ask her, "What do you mean?" He knew. He said stubbornly and set his jaw. "No . . . I'll never give it up, Anna. But it may be some time before I can return. Adeline . . ."

"I understand," said Anna quietly.

On the following day Adeline, the nurse and the baby were moved to the one spare room in the Graham house. David settled them there before going to Carthage. He had a long talk with Mr. Graham after dinner. Mr. Graham had grown smaller, more flabby. His face was less florid, and his dark hair more gray. He was making a living. That was about all. He spoke of the recent panic, the following depression. "Terrible," he deplored, "you have no conception—things have been going from bad to worse in this country. I am bitterly disappointed in the administration. It is hard on a man of my age to see the fortune he has made honestly taken from him with no chance of recovery. It is entirely unequitable."

He talked for some time in that strain. Then he spoke of Adeline.

"I was shocked to find her in this condition." He looked at David with some severity. "I warned you, you know," he said.

David said steadily:

"It is simply a matter of time, I think, Mr. Graham."

Graham nodded. He asked briskly, "And now, exactly what do you propose to do?"

David replied, smiling slightly:

"I propose to support myself and my family by the practice of medicine."

"Good," said Mr. Graham unnecessarily. "Thank heaven, I still have a little influence. I have been talking to Fletcher, since your first word reached us. You remember Fletcher? He has a large, fashionable practice and he is not as young as he once was. He would like to take an assistant, someone young, strong, who would take many of the minor burdens from his shoulders. He has several likely young men under consideration. But he has not yet decided. I persuaded him to talk with you first. It would be a great opportunity for you, and the making of you. For, of course, when Fletcher retires you would step at once into his shoes."

David remembered the shoes. Congress gaiters. He remembered the man, all waistcoat and heavy gold seals and prominent eyes and a soothing voice. He said, after a minute:

"That is very kind of you, sir. But I must go North tomorrow. I cannot make up my mind immediately. There are things to which I must attend."

"Oh, naturally," agreed Adeline's uncle. "I quite understand . . . your aunt, of course. My deepest sympathy. Coming so soon after your father's death it must have been a deep shock to you—"

"Yes," said David.

Young Condit hadn't improved with time, thought Graham. He had that untidy look. As if he didn't care how his clothes fitted. His hair needed cutting, his mustache was short, stubbly. Curious that Adeline had not made a change in him. Probably just the type to go native, thought Graham disapprovingly, rather liking the phrase. He had picked it up somewhere, Kipling probably—promising young writer, Mr. Kipling, and he enjoyed the flavor of it.

"If," said David, "you wouldn't say anything to Adeline about Dr. Fletcher's kindness until I have had an opportunity . . . ?"

"Certainly not," agreed Adeline's uncle. "I understand. These things have to be decided by the head of the family. But I am sure you would not find Addie averse to such an arrangement."

He added, sighing, "Anna is a great unhappiness to us. I know she means it all for the best, but not the least of my burdens is the thought of her demeaning herself to office work. It is unsexing," he said firmly.

David went to Carthage. He drove over to Natural Bridge and remained there several days with Matthew Brent. They talked, the two of them, half the nights and all the days. Brent saw him to the station, gripped his hand in farewell. "Remember," he said, standing on the platform, a big, stooped figure in baggy trousers and an old coat, "remember, I'm counting on you, Davy."

On his return David found Adeline much better, brighter, more interested in things than he had seen her in months—or was it years? She had been shopping, she had bought her first new dress since she was married. Her things were outmoded, the fashions changed so quickly. She had even arranged her hair differently, and color was bright in her cheeks. "It will be wonderful," she said, "to live in New York again."

She knew all about Dr. Fletcher. Her aunt had told her. She had talked to Dr. Fletcher today, herself. He was a dear. Everything would be made easy for them.

"We are not going to live in New York," said David. "We are going to live in Natural Bridge. Uncle Mat is retiring and I am taking over his practice."

"David!"

It was a wail of anguish. He saw her lips begin to shake, her hands begin to flutter. He took her hands firmly in his own. He spoke to her without raising his voice.

"Adeline, I gave up the work for which I had prepared all my life, for your sake. You couldn't live in China. So I brought you home. But I was not cut out to be an assistant to a fashionable New York physician. I think more of my training than that. I am going where I am needed. And you are coming with me. You are perfectly well, now that you have had your way. You will come with me to Natural Bridge and you will reconcile yourself to being the wife of a country practitioner or—"

"Or what?" she asked sharply.

"Or I shall go alone," he replied.

There was a white line around his lips. His eyes were a cold and blazing blue. He knew, she thought bitterly, that he would not go alone. She could not be a burden to her people. Nor would they countenance her leaving her husband. Not that it would be leaving him, he would, in reality, desert her. A lasting, an irreparable disgrace! But he had made up his mind.

"Very well, David," she said dully, too beaten, too cast down from the high eminence of her triumph to resort to easy tears.

Maturity

1904–1917

CHAPTER I

ADELINE CONDIT lay in a hammock on the new side veranda of the house which had been Matthew Brent's in Natural Bridge. It was still Doc Brent's house to a good many people, and there were some old folks who regarded David Condit as "that new, young doctor" although he had been resident in Natural Bridge for nearly ten years.

When the Condits had first come upstate, they had rented a small cottage house a block or so away from Brent's solid, four-square frame structure. Mat had wanted them to live with him. "What on earth do you want to go traipsing around looking for a house for," he growled at David, "with me rattling around in this old barn like a lone pea in a pod?"

But David had decided on a separate residence. He knew how miserable Adeline would be at Mat's, and Mat, after a time, came to acknowledge the wisdom of his decision. Toward Adeline he was charming; winning her confidence by degrees, prescribing for her "weak spells" when David would not, and concocting sugar pills for her by the hundred. "Why the ructions, Davy?" he would inquire. "What she don't know won't hurt her!" And Adeline grew sincerely fond of the old man, although his high leather boots, smelling of farmyards, his red flannels and baggy trousers and summertime shirtsleeves affronted her sense of the fastidious.

Brent's "retirement" was gradual. Inordinately pleased at having David with him, he very slowly turned over his practice to the younger man. There were, naturally, patients who would not doctor with anyone but Mat Brent. Mat had been good enough for their mothers and fathers, he was good enough for them. But as the town grew by imperceptible degrees and as farms changed hands or new people bought land, David found that he had plenty to do. The newcomers liked and trusted him, the older ones remembered him as a youngster back from foreign parts, riding with Doc Brent on his rounds.

Brent turned over one horse to him and a buggy; in the winter both men traveled by pung, with Brent's old buffalo robes for warmth, earmuffs and heavy clothing. Sometimes they left the pung on a drifted road and negotiated farmhouse or camp on snowshoes. Occasionally in the spring Brent rode, with ancient saddlebags containing his medicines across the saddle.

This life continued for four years. In those four years Adeline Condit bore three children, Graham and the twins, Matthew and Anna.

She had borne these children, with no more than the normal complaining, because she felt that, after this fashion, she redeemed the pledge she had made to herself as their ship approached the harbor. These were her children, born on American soil. They would be an antidote to the restlessness she dimly sensed in her husband, they would recompense him for his unhappiness at leaving China. He would forget China and all that had gone before, with his family about him, growing, demanding. In order to satisfy their needs and to justify himself, he must put aside the things she felt were childish in him, the dreaming things which still irritated and distressed her. Besides, unless a woman could be head of her house, mother of a family, she would die of boredom in a town which revolved about the life of the family. As a mother she was important. She thought often of Anna, of her single state; and it seemed to her that barrenness, which once she herself had so greatly desired, was a miserable, repudiated condition.

There were, of course, drawbacks; the terror of actual childbirth which never entirely left her, the feeling that physically she gave too much of herself. She loved her children but they exasperated her, with their noise and their demands and their quarreling and disobedience. She told herself, when they are older they will understand what I suffered to bear them.

Yet even her pregnancies had not been without compensation. She accepted them as part of the price she had paid for her passage home, as a vow fulfilled. And during the time before her children were born she seemed content to sink into a sort of pleasant stupor of existence, her mind as loosely corseted as her body.

Anna Graham, after whom the last little girl had been named, came to be with her cousin at the time of Graham's birth, and thereafter spent her summer vacations with the Condits. Mr. Graham died of a stroke a year or so after the Condits' return from China. His widow and her daughter moved from the rented house to a boarding house on Madison Avenue and when Anna was in Natural Bridge, Mrs. Graham visited more affluent relatives, genteel and shrunken, reduced by the loss of fortune and the prestige she thought had vanished with it, to a complaining and martyred old woman living exclusively and sorrowfully in the past.

At the outbreak of the Spanish War, Mat Brent grew restless. He summoned David, who had taken over his office hours, and asked him when he was through to come up to the house. It was shortly before the birth of the twins and Adeline, uncomfortable and fretful, called from the upstairs bedroom to know where he was going at that time of night. It seemed to her, she complained when he told her, that he thought more of Mat Brent than he did of her.

David tramped up to the Brent house in the cool April night with the stars translucent in the dark blue sky. Spring was tardy in the North, but its coming all the sweeter. He went, tired but content, into the Brent house, the doors of which always stood wide open. Amelia scurried past him in the hall. She had, he noted with amazement, been crying.

"Well?" he asked his old friend, in the office, with its shabby roll-top desk and uncomfortable sofa, and its aroma of medicine and long-extinguished cigars.

Brent turned from the desk. He had been working there. The usually untidy pigeonholes were almost bare. He answered, smiling at this timeworn joke:

"As well as can be expected. Look you, Davy, I'm thinking of traveling."

"Traveling?" repeated David in astonishment.

"Why not?" asked Brent. "The States are getting too dangerous to live in any more . . . what with gasoline buggies and
girls in bloomers. Seriously—" He pushed his hand through his
mop of gray hair, frowned and flexed the muscles of his right
arm. "Would you say I was in good condition?" he inquired, "as
good as a man twenty years younger than me, or better?"

"What are you driving at?" David demanded, with some impatience. He had had a difficult day. An emergency operation, a
quinsy sore throat, a possible typhoid—terrifying, this annual of
fatalities from the disease, a delivery which had called for in-
terference. . . .

"Been setting in this mudhole all my life," Mat grunted, "like
to get out and see the world. Always wanted to, never could. Can
now, you're here, got you broken in. Going to the war," announced Mat amazingly, "if they'll have me. Doctors ought to
come in handy, in a war. Maybe I'm not too old to shoulder a
gun, if need be."

David's eyes blazed. He asked, "You—you're joking, aren't
you? You know how much I want to go—and can't."

"I'll go for you," Mat told him. "You've released me, you
know. I can pull out without a responsibility. You can't. You've
Adeline . . . and the children to consider, especially now."

"I know," said David. There was a moment's silence. Then he
said, as Mat's big frame settled down in the creaking old chair,
"Look here, Uncle Mat . . . you don't really mean it, do you?"

"Anything wrong with your hearing?" grumbled the older
man. "I've never meant anything more . . ."

His mind was made up, nothing that David could say would
dissuade him. "Nope, son, I'm going. There'll be a lot of boys
from home hereabouts dying down there without a familiar hand
to ease 'em over the hard place. When I come back, I'll retire
in good shape. I'll set down by the stove in the grocery store and
tell the boys how I helped lick Spain. You'll carry on now—and
afterwards."

He did not come back. He got no farther than Jacksonville
where, after heroic efforts among the sick, he died of fever. His
last letter, smelling to high heaven of spilled Jamaica ginger,

said that he had run into Richard Wright—"Captain Wright, if you please, and a smart lad. Seems to have shed his dude ways along the road."

Others came back, to shiver, in the heat of a late summer, to hug a fire when the sun blazed high, with the creeping evil of malaria in their blood, to expel tobacco juice in a straight brown line at the stove and to talk of San Juan Hill and Teddy, the Rough Rider. But Mat Brent did not return.

He left David Condit his practice, and his house and the little money he had managed to save in a lifetime of blunt, forthright sacrifice. He made one request. "Take care," he counseled, "of Amelia."

And so, six years after the Spanish War and almost ten years since their return from China, the Condits lived in the old Brent house and David carried on.

Today, in the warmth of the July sun, Adeline looked around the new porch with its high-backed green rocking chairs and strip of matting and thought complacently of the changes she had made in the house. The old carved furniture had been banished to the barn and the attic, and the parlor was done over with light wallpaper and net curtains and a three-piece suite, upholstered in green. Last Christmas David had given her the ingrain carpet and the bird's-eye maple for their bedroom; and the year before the golden oak dining room suite. The furniture had come from New York, and Anna had sent things from time to time, the Maxfield Parrish pictures which were on the nursery walls, the black and white Gibson drawings which were in the parlor, with the Remington prints David had bought over the bookcases with their glass doors and their bright-backed novels which Anna sent up from the city.

One was in Adeline's hand now. She called Amelia and after an appreciable length of time the old woman came out to the new porch in her heelless slippers. Adeline regarded her without unkindness but with no affection. She would have dismissed Amelia long ago, but for David's edict. "Amelia has a home with us as long as she lives," he said; "get someone else in to help her if you think she's not competent."

There was little love lost between the two women. Amelia had long since ceased to eat at the family table. Those days had passed, declared Adeline and set herself to persuading David of it, by well-worn means. But Amelia herself decided to forsake the dining room for the kitchen, where she ate no more than would keep a bird alive, in company with the youngest Dexter boy who helped around the yard, cut the grass, groomed the horses and otherwise made himself useful.

"Where are the children?" asked Adeline.

Amelia folded her hands in her apron. She could not endure David's wife. She looked at Adeline a moment, a still young, still comparatively slender woman, with high-piled fair hair, and a white dress covered with eyelet embroidery, the skirts of which swept the floor as she lay in the hammock, her finger marking a place in her book. A box of chocolates was beside her and a paper fan. Amelia thought, novel reading, and yet young ones running wild . . .

"Mat and Anna's over in the Perkins' back yard," she answered shrilly, "and I dunno where Betty is. She went off with the Reed girl, down the road, about two-thirty, when you was lying down. Graham's gone with Harry, to deliver some medicine down the road apiece, like David told Harry to."

Adeline's brows drew together. She was only thirty-five and her face was smooth and unlined except for her habit of frowning which had left a triangular mark between her eyebrows. Her mouth was pinched. She disliked intensely Amelia's use of David's Christian name. She said, sharply, and with emphasis:

"I expect the doctor will be late to dinner, Amelia. He has gone to Watertown, to the hospital."

Amelia nodded. She knew perfectly well where David had gone. The trip, ten miles to Carthage, eighteen miles to Watertown, took the better part of a day. If you went by train it took even longer. She said tonelessly, "I'll hold supper over."

Dinner! thought Amelia, departing. Luncheon, midday, dinner, at night! Newfangled, downright ridiculous. She didn't see any difference in the table she set, only David's wife had to put new names to it.

Adeline called after her. "Be sure and see that Miss Graham's room is ready, Amelia, she'll be here to-morrow."

Amelia knew that too. She had known for weeks when Anna Graham was expected for her two weeks' vacation. Amelia liked Anna. She wasn't too proud to come out into the kitchen and beat up the batter for a cake or to sit down in the rocker, with the cat in her lap and ask all sorts of questions about the town and its people and what had happened since she left. She had funny ways, of course. Wore her hair plainer and her skirts shorter than most young women, worked in an office for her living and was always talking about these crazy suffragettes, of whose activities Amelia had never heard except in magazine and newspaper cartoons until Anna came to visit them. "You'll see, Amelia," she'd tell the old woman, "we'll get the vote some day."

"What'll we do with it when we get it?" was Amelia's stock answer.

"Why, use it, of course, you old goose," Anna would answer gayly.

"It ain't been much use to the men," Amelia's verdict would run invariably. And the sunny kitchen, with its great range, would echo to Anna's laughter.

Adeline lay swinging in the hammock. The copy of *Lady Rose's Daughter* dropped from her hand. She frowned again thinking of Graham off with Harry Dexter, going heaven knows where, picking up heaven knew what dreadful diseases. She disliked the friendship between her son and the hired boy, some eight years his senior. She disliked the Dexter family anyway. She tried to discourage Graham from loitering around the barn, coaxing Harry to go fishing or berrying with him. She had argued with David, time and time again. Graham would have a position to maintain. He was no longer a baby, he was eight years old. There were plenty of children in the town with whom he could play safely and nicely; and in Carthage. Every so often she dressed him in the lace-collared suit at which his soul rebelled, and drove over there in the surrey, with Harry in his proper place behind the reins and took her son calling . . . at the parsonage, and other houses. It distressed her beyond words to believe that the boy would grow up an uncouth country child. She had great things planned for him, college, the banking business. But he was hard to manage, reading dime novels half the night, no matter how often she confiscated them, refusing to have anything to do with *Little Lord Fauntleroy* and *Little Men.* "Girls' trash," he said disdainfully when he found his sister Betty weeping over Mrs. Burnett or Miss Alcott or Elsie Dinsmore, as her mother had done before her.

That she loved Graham best of her children, Adeline Condit would not admit, even to herself. He was headstrong, stubborn, handsome, fair as she was, with his father's bright blue eyes. Betty was an exceptionally pretty child, at ten she had the grace and dignity of a girl several years her senior. But Betty was all Condit. The twins were rosy and fat and graceless and engaging. Adeline had suffered intensely at their birth and had never felt very strong since. Sometimes she resented them, remembering.

Her thoughts returned to the Dexter family. They had been an incubus on David ever since his return to the North. Simply because he had helped Mat Brent bring Harry, last of the shiftless Dexters, into the world, he thought the family had a claim on him. Dexter had long since shuffled himself into the grave and his wife, with the help of the older children, ran the farm. There was always sickness there, and Adeline knew perfectly well that David never made a cent from the family. Indeed, his hand was always in his pocket when word came to him that one of the Dexters was down again with something. And it had been too absurd, encouraging the girl, Mary, to go to the city and train as a nurse.

Mary Dexter had been Adeline's first servant problem. David had engaged her to help with little Betty their first summer in Natural Bridge. Mary had been twelve, going on thirteen, at the time and, Adeline admitted, extraordinarily helpful for a child of her size. But then she was accustomed to babies. She had tended Betty carefully but had spoiled her beyond hope, and Adeline was relieved when school opened and an older nursemaid was found. But Mary had been in and out of the rented house and later the Brent house, on all her vacations, helping with the children and in the kitchen.

She was a great favorite of David's. Adeline could remember the first time she saw the child, her pigtails of mouse-brown hair so tightly plaited that her little freckled face was strained, holding out her grubby palm with a copper penny in it . . . "I didn't spend it," she declared, and while Adeline looked on, amazed, David had lifted the child to his knee with a great roar of laughter. "Here's a dime to match it," he had told her.

He'd been giving her money ever since. Adeline dimly suspected that he had financed the girl's going to New York three years before, and had helped her through her training in his old hospital. When she had said something about it he had silenced her briefly.

"Mary will make a fine nurse," he declared, "she's a splendid girl. She deserves to be trained in a good profession. And heaven knows we could do with a nurse around here," he had added, "neighbor women are all very well and they have done wonders in their day. Don't know what the country would have done without them. But times are changing."

Mary, thought Adeline idly, would be back in Natural Bridge soon; and to practice, she supposed, her profession, with the usual airs and graces. Adeline had a wholesome fear of trained nurses. High and mighty, thinking they knew it all. She had only come in contact with one at the time of her uncle's illness when she had gone to New York. Dreadful woman, stiff and starched and intolerably bossy. As for Mary Dexter, who in Natural Bridge could afford to pay her thirty-five dollars a week? People who didn't always pay the doctor, as Adeline knew to her displeasure.

To be sure, David was not wholly dependent on his income as a physician. There was the inheritance from his great-aunt, another, smaller, from his father, and the money Mat Brent had left him. For the most part this inconsiderable fortune lay in a savings bank. It was to provide education for the children and some protection against old age.

The shadows lengthened. The dust rose white under horses' hoofs on the road. The trees on the lawn drooped, silent. There was a distant sound of thunder. The day might end in a shower, badly needed. Mrs. Condit picked up her novel again.

The buggy clattered into the yard. She sat up in the hammock and looked out. Of course Harry was letting Graham drive, for all she had said about it. Her lips compressed, she lay back. A few minutes later Graham came stomping into the side porch. His square-toed, copper-bound shoes were gray with dust and muddy into the bargain.

"Graham, wipe your feet."

"Yes, ma'am," he said obediently; and then, "Look what I got!"

He was well grown for his age, his fair hair curled damply on his forehead. He had an extraordinarily square jaw for a child. He put his hand in bulging pocket and drew forth his trophy. It was a large frog and it was very dead.

His mother shrieked faintly and clapped her hands together smartly.

"Graham! Throw that disgusting thing away this minute!" she ordered.

"Aw, ma," expostulated Graham. "I need it—look, I'll take it to the barn."

"Throw it away," she commanded, "and at once. Then wash your hands and come back here."

He went sullenly from the porch, scraping his feet along the bare boards with a sulky pleasure in the shattering noise he made. Presently he came back and exhibited brown, clean paws to his mother's gaze. "Did you throw it away?" she demanded.

"Yes'm," replied Graham and looked her straight in the eyes. She knew that he lied.

But to prove it she would have to leave the hammock and go out across the yard and search and poke into all sorts of odd unsavory corners. She lay back against the cushions. She asked:

"Why on earth did you want a dead frog?"

"To dissect," said the boy eagerly, his eyes lighting, "out in the barn. The other kids would come to see and I'd charge 'em a cent apiece . . . !"

"To dissect?" repeated Adeline with distaste.

"Sure," said Graham, and dove for the candy box despite her faint protest. "No, Graham, not before supper." He stuffed a chocolate cream into his mouth and talked through it. "Some day I'm going to get me a dead cat and—"

"Stop this instant," said Adeline, feeling ill, but Graham looked at her reproachfully.

"How'm I ever going to be a doctor," he inquired, "if I don't know what's inside of things?"

"But you aren't going to be a doctor," denied his mother, with a sudden spirit.

"Betcher life I am," said Graham and departed whistling, "I'm a Yankee Doodle Dandy," shrilly and off key.

It was not the first time he had threatened to follow in his father's footsteps. David merely laughed when Adeline expostulated. He asked, "Why fret? He'll change his mind a dozen times, he'll want to be a constable or to run an electric trolley car."

"You encourage him," she accused him.

"Why not?" asked David. "I'd be proud of a son who wanted to be a doctor—a better one than I am."

Lying there as the whistle died away in the direction of the barn, Adeline thought, When he's older I can make him see the hard work, the dreadful hours, the being at everyone's beck and call, and the poverty. David will always be a poor man . . .

She'd make him see. She had set her heart upon Graham's entering the dignified banking profession. Richard Wright's boy would be a banker, some day. He was already registered at an expensive preparatory school and at Harvard. It consumed her with fury and impatience to feel that her son would lack any advantage.

David treated the boy with a mixture of good fellowship and sternness. He did not believe in sparing the rod. That was what a woodshed was for, he said. And Graham was headstrong, big for his years, old for his age, a brilliant if superficial scholar and something of a ringleader. He was in every brew of mischief in town . . . At Halloween David threatened to lock him up, and had done so last year, but Graham had climbed from his window to a branch of an oak tree and slid down it to safety, escape and devilment.

But despite thrashings and a discipline far more effective than her own, Graham's worship was turned toward his father. Adeline, knowing this, suffered intensely. The child loved her, was affectionate in unguarded moments, looked for her to tuck him in at night and hear his prayers, but it was his father he tried to ape, walking with David's tread in miniature, even swearing now and then, to Adeline's horror, as David sometimes did, smoking, and nearly dying thereof, one of David's black cigars, at the age of six . . .

Yet he was utterly unlike his father. At eight he displayed an interest in money which David at forty lacked. His father disliked this trait in him; he seemed to carry the boyhood trade and barter spirit a little too far. Occasionally he cheated. "You're right," his father would say on such occasions when Graham after a sound thrashing had cried himself to sleep; "you're right, Adeline, he'd make a better banker than doctor!"

Betty came in through the side door, quietly. Adeline looked at her with cool approval. Betty, at ten, was meticulous about her person. Her long red-gold curls were in place, a ribbon bound them back from her brow. She had the creamy thick skin which neither freckled nor tanned, and her very dark eyes were a startling note in her small face. She carried her sunbonnet swung by its bands from her hand, and her white dimity dress was spotless. She was a good child, exceedingly conscientious.

"Where have you been?" her mother wanted to know.

She had been, she reported, to the Reeds', making dolls' dresses with Fanny. Fanny had hers almost done, but she had shut herself up and sewed on Sunday, reported Betty, wide-eyed with horror.

She was intensely religious with the fervor of childhood. Her father had found her, earlier in the summer, attending a camp meeting conducted by an itinerant evangelist, and had dragged her out, literally by the hair of her head. He did not encourage her preoccupation with Bible, church and Sunday school. Too much was too much, he said. Yet he was very gentle with her, although extremely matter-of-fact when she came to him sobbing that she had sinned in some dreadful, unspeakable way. It usually turned out to be that she had envied Fanny Reed's doll carriage, or had listened to a bad word, or had told a lie.

"She'll get over it," Adeline told him, impatient with them both. "I can't see why you worry so—the way you were brought up."

"That's different," said David. "After all, religion was part of us, then, like the air we breathed, like the skin on our bodies. It had certain terrors, of course. Hell-fire, that sort of thing. But we accepted it, it was natural. This phase of Betty's is superimposed. She is too emotional and too conscientious. I don't like it. I don't like her reading goody-goody books. I want her out in the air more, I want her to romp and play—"

"A tomboy?" suggested his wife scornfully.

"Why not?" demanded David, "it's healthier."

Theirs was not a pious household in the sense of the word understood by the older Condits. Grace was said at meals, but family prayer was omitted. Twice a week, if his duties permitted, David attended church, on Sundays and at prayer meeting. He was a member of the council. Adeline belonged to the Ladies' Aid Society and, not without distaste, the Foreign Mission Society. Once a month the ladies met in her house, to sew and to drink tea. Her own religion was secure enough and perfectly formal. David's, she often thought, was rather less than conventional.

Yet it was his excuse for a number of things. For, for instance, his championship of the out-of-town girl who had established herself and her alleged husband in a house a little out of the village, loud-talking, painted, her clothes tawdry and ill chosen. And when the "husband" had decamped and the woman became ill, and it was discovered that she was nothing more than a common prostitute, the townspeople had convened in order to decide how they should get rid of her. David had created the sensation of the meeting with his unorthodox talk and his sacrilegious quoting "let him . . . cast the first stone."

There had been considerable turmoil. The woman had supported herself after her man's departure by means of her trade.

There were men in the meeting who turned brick-red and looked away . . . and shuffled their feet on the floor.

David had seen to it that the girl wasn't ridden out of town on a rail. He had taken care of her in her illness, and Mary Dexter, home on a brief vacation, had helped him, without shame. And when the woman had recovered and left town, her ticket had been provided. Mary Dexter had been with David that day, in his office, when the woman came to say good-by.

"If I said 'Go and sin no more,' " said David, "you wouldn't understand me . . . and you wouldn't pay any attention." He was talking to himself rather than to the woman or to Mary, standing quietly beside her. "You aren't to blame," he said, "there's something rotten in the social system which condemns you—and makes a place for you. I wish you could stay here, Rosa, and earn a decent living. But the good people of the town would see to it that you didn't. So, good-by, and God help you."

She had kissed his hand. "Now why in time did she do that?" he mused aloud, watching her trudge off toward the station. She had refused to let him take her.

"I can't imagine," Mary answered, smiling.

She had often wanted to do so herself.

David awoke with a start to the realization that Mary was there. He said helplessly:

"I forgot all about you, Mary. And look here, I ought to beg your pardon for dragging you into this. There'll be plenty of people who'll look at you cross-eyed, spending your holiday nursing a street woman—"

Mary said, "I've had plenty of experience, Dr. David. Don't you worry."

Fine girl, Mary Dexter.

But it was not of Mary David was thinking when he came home late that evening to his dinner. He'd had a good day in Watertown. Herbert Woodruff, fussy, rotund and very professional and, as he had prophesied, inheritor of his father's practice, had spent the morning with him at the hospital, where he had performed two charity major operations. Hard to get his own people into the hospital, David had complained to his colleague, too far to go, with trains as they were. Had to be hit-and-miss on a kitchen table with a terrified relative to hold a lamp or boil the instruments, if it was an emergency.

"You would bury yourself!" his old classmate reminded him. They'd gone to Woodruff's for midday dinner. Nice house, nice grounds, neat little wife. They'd talked a lot. Of Gorgas and of Reed, and the work on yellow jack. Of Charles Stiles, who had been a freshman at Wesleyan when David was a senior, and who had discovered hookworm a couple of years ago and had been, in consequence, the butt of cartoonists and poets and editors for some time thereafter; of the old days at medical; of Roosevelt's certain renomination and reelection. "The world's getting no easier to live in," said Dr. Woodruff, over a glass of homemade wine. "Look at the disasters in the past year . . . The Chicago theater fire, the Baltimore fire, and last month the *General Slocum* . . ."

They spoke briefly of the Russo-Japanese War, Woodruff without much interest. "Too far away," he said, "not our concern, trouble enough on our own hands."

David disagreed with him. Nothing was too far away, he argued, no nation could live by itself in a sort of superb isolation.

"Forgot you were still interested in the Orient," said Woodruff, yawning. "Ever hear from China nowadays?"

Yes, David heard. He had a friend doing research in tropical diseases. He spoke of the Boxer affair, four years earlier. "A disgrace," he declared, thumping his fist on the table.

Then, they went back to the hospital.

Driving the new runabout into the yard and shouting for Harry, David climbed out and stretched himself, his face smiling at the lanky boy in the long golden dusk. He'd have to hurry and eat and get ready for office hours to-night. He was tired but stimulated by Woodruff's talk. Too bad he didn't get to see him oftener, he reflected. Adeline and Herbert's wife hit it off well enough.

He went toward the house. He had grown heavier with the years. At forty, he stood almost six feet tall and weighed close to two hundred pounds. His hair was still unruly, still dark red, untouched by gray. He had shaved his mustache during the past year at Adeline's insistence. It was cleaner, she insisted, and more fashionable. Besides, she hated his mustache and always had. She had been delighted at his appearance without it, he looked younger, she declared, by ten years.

He went into the house, the children flung themselves at him, the twins clinging to his knees, Graham hanging on one arm, Betty on the other. He lifted little Anna to his shoulder while Matthew howled "Me too, me too!" Graham said, "Hey, Doc . . ." That was a new one, this Doc business. It was a little smart-Aleck.

At dinner Amelia waited on them, with the help of the grand-niece who assisted her in the kitchen and minded the twins. Presently, after telling Adeline of his day, a recountal interrupted by her sharp, painstaking attention to the children's table manners, he pushed back his chair and went into the office to smoke and rest a bit, until the patients started coming. He knew most of them beforehand. Mrs. Finney, with her chronic indigestion, young Billings with his carbuncle, Mary Dexter's sister Daisy, bringing the baby for him to look over.

The office had not been changed. He had said to Adeline, "Do what you want with the house, but leave the office." It was as Brent had left it, with the desk, the case of instruments, the washstand in the corner, the rocker and the revolving chair, the horsehair sofa and the steel engravings. There were the same bookcases with Uncle Mat's old medical books and his own newer ones. But there was one alteration since Brent's time. His own.

On the walls, between the engravings, hung the painted scrolls, the red banner with the happiness character upon it, and the photographs of the compound. On his desk a photograph of Heng-ong, the eyes smiling into his own, the mouth composed. On top of the desk, the fat kitchen god, the small Kuan-yin, in porcelain, a duplicate of the one Adeline had broken. A pair of chopsticks crossed behind a picture, a carving in ebony, a rubbing from stone, a red lacquer box which held the things for tea. Upstairs in his closet was a chest with clothes in it, a mandarin coat which had belonged to his mother, the tiny two-inch shoes from the feet of a woman no longer living, the garments which had been his as a child and which he had once thought a son of his might wear.

Adeline never disturbed that chest. And she hated his office. She never entered it if she could avoid it.

David sat down before the desk. His account book lay open before him. He looked absently at certain items. They didn't matter. Some day the accounts would be paid—or crossed off.

His hand went out and he picked up a round ivory ball, dependent with a slender string from a pointed ivory stick, and played with it absently. His eyes went to Kuan-yin, smiling at him from his desk top, compassionate, merciful, the Goddess of Women . . .

Heng-ong's last letter was in the desk drawer. He was coming, he wrote, very slowly to a conclusion. Too early yet to tell. The letter was written in Chinese but in Romanized letters to make things easier for his friend. Heng-ong sometimes wrote English, but David had asked him not to. "I don't want to lose it all," he wrote.

Heng-ong was a busy man, between practice and research. He had several children. His oldest child was a little older than Betty.

Ten years. In a way it had been a lifetime. In a way David felt that he was the projection of Mat Brent, blunt, forthright, hard-working. Adeline was contented, if only reasonably. Their relations were now settled. Since the birth of the twins . . .

It didn't matter, he thought, he was too old perhaps to care. It wasn't even much of a blow to his pride.

And if sometimes you found you weren't too old and that blood ran hot and swift in your astonished veins in a blue April dusk, you could plod along and work like a dog and tire yourself out and forget it.

Rosa, the woman from away. There'd been a time when Mary Dexter hadn't been present and Rosa had wept and clung to him and kissed, not his hand, but his mouth . . .

He was sorry for the Rosas of the world. But they had nothing to offer him.

He set the ivory ball aside. Someone tramped up the steps and knocked at the side door, which led directly into the office through a short hall. David rose, in his shirtsleeves held back with rubber bands, to answer. The first of the patients.

As he went to the door he remembered Anna was coming the following day. His step lightened. He was always glad to see Anna. The children adored her, she was company for Adeline.

He opened the door.

"Hello, Pete," he said, "come on in, what's wrong, neuritis bothering you again? Seems like we wouldn't get that rainstorm after all."

CHAPTER II

Anna came the next evening. Adeline drove over to meet her in the runabout, handling the reins smartly. The two women embraced and exclaimed and, Anna's luggage having been taken care of, drove back through the village.

Adeline thought, aloud, that her cousin looked very well, if a little pale. That was the city heat, she supposed. She thought, silently, regarding the other woman's clear, dark, strong profile, Anna has aged, working the way she does, she's only a year older than I am, one would take her for much older.

Anna said, breathing deeply:

"If you knew what this air does to city lungs; it's like a shock of cold water to a tired body."

Adeline tightened the rein, saluted a passing buggy and its driver with her whip. She sat very erect, holding her head high, with its big flower-laden hat, and coils and puffs of fair hair.

"You always liked cold water," she said with a shiver, "even cold baths. You'll be able to have plenty here, half the time something goes wrong with the boiler!"

Anna smiled. She said, "You haven't said how you are . . . or the children . . . and David? He's working hard, of course?"

"I'm fairly well," Adeline told her, "I still have those palpitations. Anna, sometimes I am certain that I have a weak heart. David naturally thinks nothing of it. He contends it is due to nerves and lack of exercise. Dear old Uncle Mat wasn't as sure. He used to give me medicine. Oh, well, a doctor's wife and family are the last people he thinks of; we have to stand aside for his patients."

Anna asked hastily, "You didn't answer me—about the children, I mean."

"They are all right," replied Adeline, turning the corner, "the twins had measles last winter as I wrote you. We can expect such things with David in and out of sick rooms, I suppose. Graham has been splendid, ever since he broke his arm last fall. Betty's never ill, thank goodness. Will you wait a minute, Anna, here's the post office. The mail won't be in yet, but I forgot to mail a letter on my way to the station."

She climbed out in a swirl of pale blue skirts and a glimpse of a lace-trimmed petticoat. Anna watched her enter the post office. She sat there waiting, holding the reins. People passed by, one or two acquaintances stopped to greet her. The street stretched in front of her, tree-bordered, the old houses set back. A boy drove a cow down the very middle of it, taking it, perhaps, to a new owner. He whistled as he came. He was barefoot. The clear dusk lay like a blessing on the town and a cool wind whispered from the mountains. Anna thought, it is the same, it does not change; we will go picnicking in the big woods and sit beside the trout stream and everything will be the same. She thought, I should not have come but I am so terribly weak.

Adeline came down the post office steps. She held her skirts in one hand. She stopped to speak to a passer-by and hurried on to the runabout. She complained to her cousin, "One would think I was a messenger! Half a dozen people have requested me to convey their symptoms to David."

She took the reins and they drove away. When they reached the house Harry was in the yard. He came up, grinning, to greet Anna. The doctor had just come in, he said.

David came striding across the yard toward them. He helped the two women down, shook Anna's hand. He said heartily, "You're a sight for sore eyes, Anna. I hope you've brought all the latest news of the fashion world with you. Adeline is perishing to know if sleeves will be larger this autumn!"

They all laughed, standing there. Adeline argued defiantly. "Well, it's true enough and who can blame me? I declare if it weren't for the magazines and patterns I'd think that everyone went around in calico wrappers and shoulder shawls, the way things are here. David, do bring Anna's bags up to the house. You're standing there looking at her as if you had never seen her before."

David took the bags without a word. At the front steps the children came tumbling down to meet them, to be kissed. "What have you brought us?" shrieked Graham over the other voices. David laid a hand on the boy's shoulder. "Gently," he admonished him, "can't you welcome Aunt Anna for herself?"

In the house Anna laid her things aside in the room allotted to her. It was next to Adeline and David's. She looked around it, the dimity curtains, the dotted Swiss canopy over the small four-poster bed, the plain cherry-wood bureau and washstand, the windows looking out over the yard. It was a cool room, homely and sweet. She was familiar with it; too familiar.

Before dinner was on the table she had to go to the kitchen to speak to Amelia whose face, like a withered apple, beamed at her. "You spoil the old woman," Adeline complained later, after Anna had given Amelia the handkerchiefs she had brought to her, "she's getting insufferable, Anna. Forgetful and, yes, insolent."

"She's old," Anna excused her. "This has been her home for so many years, you know."

At the table they talked of the city, of Mrs. Graham's health, which was not good, of the changes Adeline had made in the house since Anna had been there before. "If only," sighed Adeline, "we could have a telephone, and electric light! But I suppose we never shall. Doing over the bathroom is about the only convenience we've managed. I assure you, Anna, people come from miles around to see the tub!"

"Isn't the runabout new?" Adeline asked.

"Yes, David bought it for me, although I get very little use of it," Adeline told her, helping her to vegetables.

"Come," said David, "it stands idle most of the time. We've quite a stable now," he informed Anna, laughing, "the runabout, the buggy, the surrey and three spanking good horses. And, of course, the cutter and the pung."

Adeline said, "I wish you'd get rid of the buggy, David. It looks a thousand years old!"

"Some day you won't be using horses, David, you'll be driving around in an automobile. Richard Wright's wife has an electric. She drives it herself," Anna told them.

"It wouldn't be feasible here," David reminded her, "they have to be recharged from stations, don't they? No, I'm afraid that's just a dream, Anna, even if practical automobiles could be made —look at our roads! Can you imagine them in winter? I think I'll stick to the buggy and the pung."

"I," announced Graham, "am going to have an automobile when I grow up. A red one with a big horn like the one we saw over to Watertown one day."

"Trip tire you, Anna?" asked David. "You aren't eating, and Amelia's heart will be broken. She's baked twice this week . . . and she's set out her best crab apple jelly and spiced pears."

Anna said, smiling at him, "I am a little tired, I think. And the city has been intolerably warm."

"You don't look up to snuff," he told her, "better let me go over you, in a day or so. You're too thin, we'll have to feed you up, make you drink lots of milk."

"Always drumming up trade," Anna accused him. But her dark eyes, glancing at him swiftly and as swiftly away, were frightened.

A day or so later Anna looked in at the half-open door of David's office. He was lying on the old couch, sleeping. This was a trick he had picked up from Mat Brent. "Worth a fortune to you, boy, that little cat nap after midday dinner, if you can manage it. Don't need to last more'n twenty minutes, but it does the work. Better than all the medicine we dish out."

Anna watched him a moment. He slept quietly, the lips compressed, the brow smooth. There was something strange about his face. Oh, of course, he had shaved his mustache. Her heart constricted, watching him. One big hand hung lax, almost to the floor. He looked immeasurably helpless, his strength in leash, his guard down.

She was turning away when he opened his eyes and saw her, without shock or astonishment, and smiled at her without moving. "Come in," he invited, "I was going to get up and go look for you in a minute . . ."

Anna went in. David swung his legs to the floor, sat up and ran his hand through his hair. "Where's Adeline?" he asked.

"She took the runabout and Graham and went to Carthage," Anna told him.

"Why didn't you go along?"

"I had some letters to write—"

"Want to come out with me? I've half a dozen calls to make, won't take us very long."

"I'd love to," she said.

"We'll take your letters along," he told her. He stood up and approached her. He put his hands on her shoulders and drew her to the window. "Stand still," he ordered.

She was a tall woman but she had to look up to meet his regard. He put a finger on her lower eyelid, drew it down gently. He said, "I thought so. Anæmic. What on earth do you live on, Anna? You've no business getting run down. I'll have to give you a tonic."

"Oh, no, David," she protested, laughing, "I can't bear tonics."

"You'll do as I say," he told her.

He took her pulse. He listened to lungs and heart through the stethoscope, his face grave, remote, his eyes intent. Anna sat beside the desk, her shirt waist off, and looked straight over his down-bent head. Just a patient, she told herself, like any patient.

Her petticoat was trim about her round waist. Her shoulders rose smooth as dark ivory from the white lace of her corset cover, run with rosy ribbons. She sat perfectly motionless.

"Heart's a little fast," said David, removing the stethoscope from his ears. He leaned back in his chair and regarded her. "What's that about, eh?"

She shook her head, laughing, flushed.

"Nothing. Just nervousness, David. I'm not used to being poked at and prodded. You've looked down my throat and into my ears and—"

"All in the day's work. Look here, except for a slight anæmia you seem perfectly sound," he said. "Tired, I suppose. But—still, I'm not satisfied. Sleep well?"

He shot it at her. Anna started. She said, after a moment, "Not very, David. Not always."

"I see. Something on your mind? Your mother . . . this position of yours . . . what is it . . . ?"

"Nothing," she repeated, with spirit, "why should there be?"

"Wouldn't lie to me, would you, Anna?" he asked her.

No, she wouldn't lie. She bent her dark head after a moment. He looked at it, smooth, shining, heavy braids wrapped about the skull. When she looked up again there was a rosy spot of color in each cheek. She admitted, "Yes, there is something . . . but I'll have to work it out myself."

"Nonsense," said David briskly, "two heads are better than one, even a red head like mine. Put your waist on, Anna." He looked at his watch, snapped it shut and returned it to his pocket. "Come along with me, we can talk while we drive."

Presently they drove away, leaving the twins forlornly weeping and Anna promising them peppermint sticks and bull's-eyes on their return, yes, and toffee too, if they demanded it.

David said, "Nice sort of aunt, you are. Have me sitting up all night with a couple of youngsters with bellyache."

"I know," she said, "I do spoil them terribly. Adeline always says that they are completely out of hand by the time I go away. But I can't help it, David. They're so sweet, all four of them. Besides, I hate to disappoint children, it hurts them so much."

"They soon recover," David reminded her.

"I know. But it's like rain on the day you've planned a picnic," she said, "you think you've forgotten next day, because the sun shines and there's always another picnic, yet you haven't."

She thought, he doesn't remember . . . I won't have to tell him. Yet I must tell him . . . and Adeline. They'd feel dreadful if I didn't.

David made his calls. Two in the village, two at farms, and then one which took them through a narrow lane, rutted, grass springing in the ruts, with trees leaning across to weave a thick network of branches through which the sunshine fell in slanted golden rays. There was a busy stream, and a mill and further along, another farmhouse set back from the road. Dogs ran out barking and jumped at David, tails wagging, very friendly.

Anna sat still, horse hitched to the post, watching him go up the overgrown path to the house. A child ran out and caught his hand in her own, and the dogs followed him.

He was laughing, talking to the child, to the dogs impartially. The sunlight fell on his bare head. He carried his coat over one arm. At the doorstep a woman came to meet him; she wore a bedraggled blue apron over an equally bedraggled dress. Her iron-gray hair was twisted into a knot high on her head. Her face was gray with strain. She said, and Anna heard her, "Oh, doctor, I'm so glad you've come."

The door shut behind them. The little yard was quiet. The apples were green on laden trees, the graceful gnarled apple trees, with their wide arms and special personalities.

The dogs and the child had followed David in.

Anna said to herself, I'm a fool, I should never have come. I thought . . . Oh, I don't know what I thought. Perhaps that if it hurt enough I could go back and make up my mind more easily.

She waited for half an hour and then David came out, the woman following. Anna heard her say, "I don't know how we can . . ." and David's clearer reply, "That's all right, send me a bushel of apples in the fall," and paused to stoop and pinch the small child's cheek. He was halfway down the path when the child, who had vanished around the corner of the house, came running after him.

She reached up, he bent down. Something was put into his arms. The little girl said, "He's the best of the litter. I want you should have him."

"Well," announced David, beside the runabout, "another addition to the family!"

He was carrying a Newfoundland puppy, big and sprawling, with clumsy paws and gentle eyes and a fine coat. Anna exclaimed and held out her hands. "Give him here, David, I'll hold him in my lap."

"You'll muss your skirt," he warned her, "and . . . well, I wouldn't be too sure about his habits."

"Never mind, he's darling," said Anna. "Are you going to keep him?"

"I'd be doing them a favor if I did," said David, "these pups would eat the door off a barn." He rubbed his hand roughly, caressingly over the puppy's head. He said, "The youngsters will love him. We haven't had a dog since the red setter died and they're always clamoring for one. Kids without a dog don't seem right, somehow. Sure you can hang on to him, Anna?"

They turned, in the yard, and drove off, through the shattered gate and down the lane. They had gone perhaps half a mile when David suggested suddenly, "Let's turn off here . . . It's early still, and I have no more calls to make. We can spare half an hour. Bring the pup along, Anna, he'll be the better for a run, he won't go away."

A much overgrown road led to the stream. There was a clearing here, and David loosed the reins and let the horse stand free to crop the sweet long grass. Near the stream a big tree leaned, bent almost double by some freak of wind or storm. David tossed his coat beside it. "Sit down," he said; "let the pup go . . ."

The puppy cantered off on his rather unsteady legs and rolled in the grass and sniffed at the horse's slender ankles. The horse turned his head and looked at the small animal with wise, dark eyes. David asked, lying full length on his back in the grass, "Now, Anna, what's the trouble?"

"There isn't any trouble," she began. Her heart tightened. He had remembered.

"Yes. I knew it as soon as I saw you. I haven't known you all these years without learning to read your face, a little. You aren't ill. Just tired, run down. It isn't all physical, Anna. Tell me, my dear; sometimes an outsider can help."

"Outsider!" she said with sudden, still fury.

David looked up at her. The sunlight searched for red lights in her hair, found none, was defeated. She had taken off her hat, it lay in her lap. From the round collar of her shirt waist her throat rose, firm and classic in its line. David said, suddenly, giving her time, "You know, I'm mighty glad women have stopped wearing those high collars. Always looked choked to death . . . reminded me of those poor devils in China, heads through boards . . ."

"You think often of China, don't you, David?"

"Yes," he said simply; and then, "Stop trying to put me off. What is it, Anna? Is it money? You know I've laid by something. You're welcome to it—"

Her eyes filled. "It isn't money, David. Thank you just the same, that's like you."

"Then, what . . . ?"

She didn't answer. He said, "You know—this reminds me . . . once long ago, before I entered medical school, my father and I sat beside the trout stream, not far from here. We had been fishing. We talked about a lot of things. He gave me—some excellent advice. I told him then I would never marry." He laughed shortly. "That's how much we know," he said, "at twenty-two . . ."

"That's what I'm wondering about," Anna told him.

"Marriage?" asked David. "A man, then. I might have guessed." His laughter was stilled, his lips lost their smiling lines. "I hope he's a fine man, Anna. You deserve the best."

She said:

"He is. He's older than I am, David. Fifty. A widower. He has two children. Money, position, culture. All the things which seem to matter. I'm not a girl any longer. I'm thirty-six. An old maid. Poor mamma, she's never recovered from her astonishment that her daughter should be an old maid."

"Tell me more about him," demanded David. "What's his name?"

"John Gregory. I met him in the office. Oh, quite properly. He asked if he might call. Mamma likes him. He could do so much for her, David."

"I see," said David; "but what can he do for you, Anna?"

She looked at him briefly. He was sitting up now, cross-legged, facing her. The puppy came and thrust its head under his arm. He put his hand out absently, caressed it. Anna answered:

"He'd make things safe for me . . . for us . . . He—he's a dear, really, David. Very progressive, very forward-looking. He is in perfect agreement with many of the things which matter to me."

"Do you love him?" David asked after a minute.

"I—admire him," Anna told him with an unusual hesitancy, "and I—I'm really very fond of him, David."

"That means you don't love him," decided David, frowning.

"Oh, I don't know," said Anna helplessly, "perhaps, in a way. Does that matter so much, David, when one is thirty-six and almost alone? I—I'll be entirely alone one day," she added and her voice shook slightly, "and if I marry John . . ."

David was silent. She looked at him, with an appeal which widened her eyes to their fullest capacity. She said, "I had hoped, coming here, that I'd see things more clearly. Being with you and Adeline, in a home . . . a happy home."

David said, "You'll have to decide for yourself. If you do marry him, we'll miss you, Anna."

"Oh," she cried, "you won't lose me, how can you?"

She thought, but you must, you must, otherwise what good would it all be?

She put out her hand to the little dog, running between them. David's hand met hers, held it a moment. He said, "Better be sure, Anna . . . it won't be as easy as you think, perhaps . . . unless you are."

Anna said:

"You're thinking of romance, and a girl's daydreaming. That's over for me, long ago—"

David asked abruptly:

"Then, there was someone—?"

"Yes," said Anna, and looked toward the clear stream, tumbling among rocks, mirroring the trees in its still places, laughing its way to the river.

"I see . . . but what happened?"

"He didn't love me, David," she said. "This . . . this sometimes seems to me the sensible, the practical thing to do. Adeline," she added, "would think me mad to throw away such an opportunity."

"You haven't told Adeline?" he asked her, wondering who the idiot had been who might have had Anna for the asking.

"Not yet," said Anna, "I shall later. Not perhaps until I've made up my mind. I don't know why I told you," she said, trying to laugh, "unless it's because you've such a sure hand with the probe."

He got to his feet, helped her to hers, picked up the reluctant puppy. "We'd better get on back," he said.

They were silent most of the way home or else concerned with the wrigglings of their new charge. Adeline shrieked when she saw him. He galloped up to her and put his none too clean paws on her skirt and barked and capered. The children were wild with delight. Anna had not forgotten to stop and buy the candies at the corner store but the sweets were as nothing beside the puppy. Matthew, especially, took him to his heart. He raced with him on the lawn, was knocked over, clambered upon and suffered it with screams of delight. Adeline said resignedly, "Well, I suppose I can be glad that you didn't bring home a calf, David. I hope you'll keep him in his place, out in the barn and yard. I can't abide a dog in the house."

"Newfoundlands are very good watchdogs," announced Graham with his air of knowing everything, and Amelia supplemented the remark with, "And they eat you out of house and home into the bargain."

That night lying beside Adeline, who was sleeping soundly and audibly, David crossed his hands behind his head and considered, staring at the open windows. He thought . . . if the fellow isn't good enough for her—

Funny, how you took Anna for granted until you realized someone else didn't. He had always liked her, very much. Since his return to the States he thought of her as one of the family, someone always there if you needed her. He looked forward to her visits and experienced a sense of loss when they ended. On their rare trips to New York Anna was there, waiting.

She was a marvelous woman, he thought, quiet, but with plenty of giddap and git to her, no cowardice or flabbiness. She would be a wonderful wife and mother.

He'd like to meet Gregory, to size him up, for himself. Men were less easily fooled by other men than women were. If Anna was considering marriage because she was lonely, because she wanted security for her mother, because she was tired of working, why, then he must because of the affection he bore her dissuade her. She would never be happy. Women of a former generation might have found happiness and contentment in a suitable, sober, middle-aged match. But not Anna. She was too modern, too sensitive.

He must warn her of this. Yet he knew, in his heart, that she would not lightly pledge her word. And that once pledged, she would never break it, no matter if she realized her error, no matter how much she deplored it. A promise to marry was a sacred thing. All her notions about the new woman, suffrage and the rest of it hadn't changed certain fundamental beliefs in her; and never would.

He was tired and he could not sleep. A dozen things plagued his mind. He was deeply concerned with Anna's problem, but it was not, he told himself, his problem, nor could he advise her and solve it for her. Yet he had given considered grave advice to hundreds of patients on their emotional problems; and had been disappointed when in some instances they had disregarded him. He found himself a little dubious, looking back. By what right had he undertaken the regulating of life, other than the life of the body, in disease? He told himself, lying there and watching a patch of moonlight widen on the floor, that doctors knew too much, and too little; took too much upon themselves; set themselves up as confessors, judges, juries; and especially in small towns in which their positions were unique.

He could not tell Anna what to do, or what not to do, although she was very close to him. She was as a sister to Adeline, and therefore to himself.

He wrenched his mind away from the moving appeal of her speaking eyes on his, as they had sat there together under the bending tree. She was not a child, she was a grown woman, she had earned her living these many years, had become protector instead of protected in her relationship to her mother.

Now, he thought of some of his patients; of, particularly, the diabetic child he had seen in the morning; of the woman dying very slowly, not ten minutes from the house in which he lay, of cancer. What could he do for her? Nothing but smile at her, sit beside her bed, drug her into some measure of relief, and lie to her. It appeared to him that such a lie was justified. There was in his profession a time for truth and a time for falsehood.

The case he had lost last week. Could that have been prevented, how deeply did the fault lie with him? Half of this business was guesswork. Sometimes you guessed right; sometimes you guessed wrong; sometimes anybody's guess was as good as yours; and often you were outguessed by the dark power with which, every day, by humble means, you battled.

Living here as he did, he lost touch. He tried to keep abreast of the new discoveries of science. He bought the new books, he read the medical journals, he talked with other men. But he was not where discoveries first became known. He lacked contact with a great hospital, with brilliant minds, with the research workers. There was so much to learn; so much that was new since his graduation from medical school. He must remember to read again that recent article on the Roentgen rays, he had meant to talk of them to Herbert Woodruff—this discovery, less than a decade old, had infinite possibilities; the accurate position of a bullet or other foreign body could be determined, there need be no more fumbling and guesswork there.

He turned, sighed, kicked off a cover. The walls of the house were not thin yet it seemed to him that he could hear a stifled sound from Anna's room, next door, as if she moaned in her sleep or, waking, wept. Across the hall Betty slept, and next to her the twins, with Amelia's grandniece. In the finished attic above, with its dormer windows, Graham had his room, across from the storeroom and Amelia. It must be warm up there, thought David, but Graham loved it, the space, the slanting roof, the privacy. He would complain when, Anna gone, he would be brought down to occupy the spare room in the summer heat.

David thought of his children. Curious how little you knew about them, although they sprang from your body and grew up under your eyes. Betty, for whom he felt an especial tenderness, was a good child. Too good. But she would regain her balance, and once past the troubling greensick years of her early teens, would be a poised and beautiful girl. The twins gave no concern save in the ordinary way of mischief, although their father did not quite like small Anna's soft way of giving in too readily. Matthew rode roughshod over her. He had but to open his mouth and bawl, and the coveted toy, or place in the carriage, or selection of their game, was his. Adeline spoke of Anna as sweet and sacrificial. David was not quite as sure. Sometimes it seemed to him that Anna surrendered because it was the easier way, and because she basked like a kitten in the admiration of her elders, cooing their complimentary approval.

Graham? He frowned a little at the moonlight. Of course, Graham was a child, scarcely out of babyhood, and yet there was in him something fixed and headstrong which troubled his father.

Adeline sighed in her sleep, flung out a hand and touched him. He drew closer to her, listening to her breathing. She slept and he was alone. She might have been a million miles removed from him. Sometimes when she was awake, and speaking with him, moving about his house, she was still remote. Was there, he wondered, one human being who really knew another? He thought of his father and mother and believed his question answered. If ever two people had moved and breathed with a unity of thought and purpose, each complementing the other, it had been these two. But such a marriage was rarely achieved.

Anna's husband would be a fortunate man, he thought. David knew Anna well enough to guess at her fund of sweetness which was not cloying, but sound and wholesome, a little tart even, like the juice of a fine flawless apple. In the curve of her mouth and the lift of her deep breast there was a suggestion of ardor, of a passion which expressed itself in her mothering attitude toward Adeline, toward, even, her own mother, and in her spirited embracing of abstractions and of causes. Yes, the man would be most fortunate who would awaken her capacity for emotion and center it upon himself, transmute it, to his own needs.

If she loved him.

David said, "Adeline?" under his breath. He no longer wanted to be alone. He wanted to talk, to speak of trivial things, to know himself companioned. If Adeline would wake and speak to him . . . scold him a little, sleepily, be sorry because he could not sleep.

Adeline murmured something, turned away from him and buried her face in the pillow. She shrugged her shoulders as if something irritated her. He thought, two old married people, used to each other. Yet their marriage was not elderly.

He heard a whimper and whine from below stairs. It was the new pup, of course, not, as Adeline had decreed, in the stables, but probably in the kitchen where Amelia had smuggled him. If the creature started to howl, in its infinite loneliness and strange surroundings, it would arouse the house and Adeline would have good cause for anger. He rose quietly and fumbled for his slippers and a dressing gown, and left the room. The moonlight patch widened. Adeline did not wake.

He went, sure-footed in the dark, down the stairs and along the familiar way. In the kitchen the pup flung itself at him in an ecstasy of greeting and relief, nuzzled his bare ankles wetly, whimpered, barked with excitement. "Will you shut up," David demanded severely, "do you want to disgrace us both?"

He lit a kitchen lamp, found milk in the ice box, heated it on the back of the red-glowing stove and watched the Newfoundland push his eager nose into the saucer. Then, picking him up, he took him into the office and put him on the sofa under a disreputable old working coat. He lit the lamp and sat down at his desk. He might write Heng-ong, he thought. He had not answered his last letter.

The dog slept, sprawled, comfortable and fed. The little flame burned clear yellow in the brightly polished lamp chimney. David wrote slowly, asking a dozen questions, answering as many more. He thought of Heng-ong working in his augmented laboratory through the long, torrid nights. But it was not night in China now. He wrote, "I would give so much to work with you—"

Inadequate words. What had a doctor in an upstate Northern village to do with research into tropical diseases?

"Oh—" exclaimed Anna, at the doorway.

He turned and saw her, very tall and straight in her white nightgown, with some sort of a wide shawl caught about her, her hair in two thick braids swinging over her shoulders, to her waist. She said, before he could speak:

"I'm sorry, David. I was wakeful, I thought I heard someone stirring. Then the little dog cried and I wondered, and after a while I got up and came down to see."

"If it had been robbers," he asked, smiling, "you would still have come?"

"I suppose so." She looked at him clearly, directly in the lamp-light and then turned. "As long as it's just you . . ." she murmured.

"Wait a moment," he said. He left the dog where it was, asleep, turned down the wick, extinguished the little flame. "Stand quite still," he bade her, "we'll find the way together."

They went through the sleeping house and up the front stairs, without speaking. At the landing she whispered, "Couldn't you sleep either, David?" and he answered, "No. But I shall now. I was restless, it is very warm to-night."

"Good night," he said, at the door of her room, hardly above his breath. His hand touched, for a moment, her round shoulder, and stroked the light stuff of the shawl.

The door closed after her. David went back, in the darkness, to his own room.

CHAPTER III

O N THE following day David, just finishing his midday meal, became aware of the shrill sounding of the door-bell, an astonishing departure from the informal ways of the household. Millie, Amelia's grandniece, answered the summons and returned with the information that it was "someone to see the doctor."

David pushed aside his plate. "Who is it, Millie?" he inquired, but Millie shook her tow head. "Never set eyes on her before," she announced. "Seems like she's all of a dither. Crying too."

Adeline sighed, "You can't even eat a meal in peace," and then turned her attention to Graham, who had wriggled down from his chair without so much as a by-your-leave. Matthew upset a glass of milk and roared with premonitory terror. Anna, helping him to wipe it up, glanced at David. She was very pale this morning, she looked as if she had not slept. David, inserting his napkin through a silver ring, murmured, "It's all right, Addie, I was about through anyway," and left the table. Adeline stared after him, perturbed by the general confusion. She slapped Matthew's hand, called after Graham to no avail, and wiped a rim of milk from small Anna's rosy mouth. She complained helplessly to her cousin, "It's always like this, Anna . . . a perfect uproar."

David went toward his office, with some curiosity. He knew the people of his section, in the village and the neighboring villages, along the star routes. It wasn't likely anyone from Carthage, he thought; they had their own doctors. It might be someone from the hotel . . . an emergency of some kind, in that case.

Entering the office, his regard was brief and inclusive. The girl, waiting for him with obvious nervousness, was a complete stranger. She sat bolt upright on the end of the sofa, her rather grimy handkerchief a wet wad in one hand, her face swollen and blotched from weeping. David said, "Good afternoon, I'm Dr. Condit . . . what can I do for you?" and, sitting down in his swivel chair, turned to face her, putting out a hand to draw a straight chair up to the desk.

Encouraged by his matter-of-fact tone, his quiet regard, the girl suppressed a sob, and stammered something unintelligible. He asked, "Won't you come nearer? . . . this chair here, beside me."

She came, with reluctance. She was tall, moderately robust, dressed plainly, but not cheaply. She had magnificent hair, somewhat disheveled, under a big hat. Her skin was fine despite the ravages of tears, and she had a weak mouth held, apparently at normal, half open; either, David decided, from adenoids or habit.

She stated abruptly, with no preliminaries and in a hoarse, not unattractive voice which may, or may not, have been natural to her, and held no trace of the slight upstate accent, "You've got to help me out, doctor."

His heart contracted. There seemed to be no need for further elucidation. The sunlight poured in through the shutters, touched briefly on the glass framing David's license, lingered a moment on the outstretched exquisite hand of Kuan-yin, slanted across the girl's frightened face. She turned aside, wincing. David said gently, "Suppose you tell me about it?"

She had not intended to tell anyone about it . . . that is, not more than was necessary; just to make her demand and await the answer. But now, leaning forward, she replied slowly at first and then with a torrential rush of words.

David listened. The story was perfectly familiar to him, he had heard it often enough before, in one guise or another. Uncomplicated, sordid. When she had finished, gasping a little, her distended eyes riveted on his own, he said:

"You've been to other doctors, you say, and they've refused you. So you know that there's nothing I can do—"

"You must," she said, "you must!"

"I cannot. This man—you say he won't marry you?"

"He can't," she said sullenly, "he's married. I thought I told you that. He gave me money . . ." She began with the haste of desperation to fumble in her pocketbook, pulling out bills, a number of them, dirty, sticky, and leaned forward to press them into David's hand. "Here," she said, "it's a hundred dollars. I'll give it all to you, every cent."

He folded the bills, and put them in her lap. He said gently, "It's no use. You don't understand—"

His voice went on, trying to explain, to make her see. She said, finally, "All right. I'll go. But you make me sick, you doctors, setting yourself up as judges. What do you know about things? Afraid of your own skin, don't care about mine . . . you and your ethics." She made a wry face as if the word were sour on her tongue. "What about me?" she demanded. "No chance to earn my living, no chance to have any life of my own now, to get married some day, if there's a decent man anywhere around."

David said, "Quite apart from the laws of my profession, I cannot destroy life. . . . You're a strong girl, you might even be a brave one. This much I will do for you. When your time comes if you want to come back here, I will put you into a hospital and take care of you. I will try to find your baby a good home. I know that it would be impossible for you to keep it . . . as things are," he said, half to himself, and repeated, *"as things are."*

He looked at her with a certain hopeful eagerness and then imperceptibly shook his head. No, she would not go through with it.

The girl got to her feet. She said:

"Thanks—for nothing. I'll go somewhere else. To the city, I guess. There must be doctors in the city who'll do what I want and no questions asked . . . What do I owe you?"

"Nothing," said David. He rose, halted beside her. He said urgently, "I beg of you to reconsider. . . . Do you realize that you will be risking your life?"

She asked him, over her shoulder:

"What's it worth to me now, anyway? If I'd had any spunk I'd have got shut of it weeks ago—when I first knew what was going to happen to me."

The door closed behind her. The sunlight still fell in patches on the floor, patterned from the half-closed shutters. David stood still in the middle of the room. She would find someone, and no questions asked, he thought bitterly. He recalled the man he had known, some years ago, who had refused a similar appeal, and who, when the girl dragged herself back to his office, having "found someone" in the meantime, had taken her in and performed an emergency operation in order to save her life. He had succeeded; and her family reported him to the police. He was now behind bars, somewhere, a ruined and a broken man.

David shuddered. He turned back to the office and stretched out on the sofa. There was a thin, unpleasant reek of perfume with a musk base. He closed his eyes and tried to banish the girl from his mind. From whence had she come and toward what new hideousness was she going?

Sleep was impossible. He rose presently, hearing the children race by his door. He washed his face and hands in clear, cold water and put on his coat, and went out of the house. Adeline was nowhere to be seen. Anna was playing croquet with Betty on the side lawn. Betty threw down her mallet and ran up to him and flung her arms about him. He thought, holding her, what if it should be Betty, some day?—and felt sick to his very soul.

Under his feet was the green springing grass and beneath that the good soil, over his head the arched summer sky and the clouds drifting and the moving wind. So much beauty, and yet wherever you turned so much ugliness.

Anna asked, coming up to him, moving with her slow, sure grace, "Going out on your rounds, David?"

He said that he was. "Want to come along?" he asked. Anna hesitated, looking from him to Betty. She said, finally, "No, I don't think so, not this afternoon. Betty and I must finish our game, and I've promised Graham to go exploring with him—"

"Exploring—?"

"He has a shack in the woods, somewhere, back of the mill," she explained, smiling, "and before supper the twins and I are to have a high tea for Matthew's soldiers and Anna's dolls. The only way we could persuade him to play host was to invite his regiment."

"I see," said David. He lingered there a moment irresolute. It was all very still and peaceful, the shuttered, sturdy house, Amelia's high voice raised in a hymn from the kitchen porch, Betty with her curls bright in the sunshine, the trees stirring to the wind. And Anna . . .

Looking at Anna, the clear, dark face, with the intelligent eyes and fine modeling, was an antidote. He would have liked to lie down in the grass and watch her playing the game with Betty, intent on the ball and the wicket. But he couldn't. He couldn't lie there and watch her and drowse a little in the sunlight. He had to get into the buggy and drive from one house to another in pursuit of his enemy, pursuing this stratagem, planning that campaign. He had to spend the summer afternoon sitting in close rooms, with their odors of illness and medicine, advising, counseling, and engaging in a ceaseless battle. He must be back in time for the citizens' meeting he had called. There should be some way to combat epidemics which took the town and its surroundings at intervals—the last outbreak of measles had cost several lives. But people still persisted in deliberately exposing their children. "But it's better for them to get it now than later, doctor," and when one child came down with a contagious disease the other three or four in the family would, as like as not, be put to bed with it . . . including, perhaps, a delicate infant. There must be some way to educate people to open windows and let in the sunlight—

A small boy galloped up on a patient horse who appeared astonished at his own speed. The child rode without a saddle, bare heels gripping the animal's sides. He shouted and waved, out of breath. David hurried to the picket fence which surrounded the front yard. "What's wrong, Johnny?" he asked.

The boy said, gasping, "It's Pop, Doc. He's took awful bad. Ran a rusty nail in his foot, yesterday. It's swollen up something fierce!"

"I'll be right along," promised David, and went off to the barn where Harry waited with the buggy.

He drove out of the yard. Anna waved to him, and called something, Betty waved. Turning out of the gate, he drove down the road. He was in a savage, angry mood. The girl who had come to his office—he didn't even know her name—could not be dismissed from his mind. She stuck there like a thorn, she drew blood, she infected all his thinking.

When he returned late in the afternoon, the sun was westering, and the shadows long. There were pleasant sounds from the side veranda where Anna and Matthew were holding their festivities with cambric tea in a doll's china set. Adeline lay in the hammock reading, and Graham with the puppy at his heels ran across the yard to meet him. David took his firm, sunburned little hand and went up to the house. He had to wash and get on to the meeting.

"May be late for supper," he called back as ten minutes later he left the house again, on foot.

Adeline laid her book aside. She said, "He generally is," and sighed. She looked down at the tiny table set with the miniature china, painted with roses. She said, "Run along to Millie, children. Aunt Anna's played with you long enough."

The twins departed reluctantly. Anna rose from the small chair on which she had been crouched and sat down in a rocker. She commented, "They're darlings," and watched them trot off together.

Adeline was complacent. She said:

"They're nice children, I think. I try to have them so. Of course, they run as wild as Indians, all summer. I'll be glad when school opens, for Betty and Graham. Anna and Matthew won't be going for a year yet. It isn't easy, Anna, to bring them up properly. David's no help. He says as long as they're healthy and reasonably obedient, that's all we can expect of them."

Anna laughed. "Well, isn't he right?"

"You always take his part," her cousin accused her fretfully. "I assure you he isn't easy to live with. Half the time he doesn't even hear me when I speak, his excuse is that he's thinking of something else. He carries this town on his shoulders. If it could end with a prescription or an operation . . . but it never does. No wonder we're poor," she added.

Anna said quietly, "I don't think you're poor, Adeline."

Adeline shrugged her shoulders.

"I suppose you wouldn't. I can't understand you, Anna. You care so little for money, position. . . . You had a dozen splendid chances to marry, before the crash. Now, of course, you won't have any that can matter . . . working in an office, with a lot of coarse men, wearing yourself to a frazzle, dropping your old friends."

"Some of them dropped me," Anna reminded gayly, "and very good riddance!"

"Oh, you'd put a good face on it," Adeline declared. She turned in the hammock. "You and David are a lot alike," she declared, as if astonished, "neither of you has any real ambition. When I think of the name he might have made for himself as Dr. Fletcher's assistant and later with a practice, all ready-made, I could scream. It's perfectly maddening!"

"David wouldn't have been happy in New York," reminded Anna.

"What about me?" demanded Adeline. "Couldn't he have thought of *my* happiness and the advantage to the children? He's selfish to the bone, Anna."

Anna said, with spirit, "You've a strange idea of selfishness, Addie."

"You'll never see things my way," Adeline told her without rancor, "so there's no use arguing. I just have to reconcile myself to spending the rest of my life in this place, with hardly a soul nearby who interests me or with whom I have anything in common. Never going anywhere . . . there are so many places I want to go. But David can't get away, and I can't go alone, even if we could afford it. I had my heart set on the Exposition at Buffalo. We had planned to go too, but at the last minute there was a patient he couldn't leave. It's always that way. . . ."

"David loves you," said Anna, "he would cut off his right hand for you." Sudden color flared in her cheeks, and she looked away from her cousin. "He's a good husband," she added firmly.

"Of course," cried Adeline, "that's just it! He would cut off his right hand for me, but—he can't take me on a trip! He can't move away from here to a city where he'd have more opportunity. He's a good doctor, everyone says so. Herbert Woodruff has been trying for years to get him to go to Watertown. He offered him a partnership. But David won't hear of it. He says he's needed here."

Anna was silent. Adeline went on, forgetting that there were things of which one did not speak to an unmarried woman.

"He's a good husband, we have a roof over our heads, we don't starve. He doesn't quarrel with me, or beat me, if that's what you mean. But what sort of a life is this, Anna, anyway? . . . it's simply existing, it isn't living, not really. And we've grown so far apart. I suppose because—since a while or so ago . . . I wouldn't . . . that is, I suppose all men are alike, they think only of their own pleasure, they don't consider a woman and how she feels, or her health. . . ."

She stopped, and then said hurriedly, "Never mind that. . . . I forgot you weren't married."

Anna said sharply, "I'm not exactly a child, Adeline. I'm thirty-six years old. I suppose," she went on steadily, "you're trying to tell me that you and David aren't living together any more?"

Adeline said uncomfortably:

"Yes, if you must put it crudely. I mean, no, we aren't. Ever since the twins were born . . . I've been wretched. I'm not at all well, although David insists there's nothing really wrong. A lot he knows. I wake up at night with the most dreadful palpitations and simply wringing with perspiration. And I won't have any more children. I'm not equal to it. And there's only one safe way—"

"It seems to me you're not being very fair to David," Anna said.

"You're always talking about women's rights. I should think you'd realize that perhaps a woman has some rights—in this matter," Adeline told her.

Anna looked away, across the yard. She could see the main street, almost empty except for some playing children. Graham was coming slowly toward the house; he was still far down the road. She argued:

"Still, it isn't fair. You aren't really ill, Adeline. You're bored

and nervous, that's all. David's a young man, in the prime of
life and strength. You made certain vows—"

Adeline broke in, her small face earnest and plaintive:

"I've been a good wife, Anna. I went with him to that terrible
country and suffered . . . I can't tell you what I suffered." Her
features grew pinched as she was briefly silent, remembering.
"Then, we came home. I promised myself that if we could come
home I'd make it up to him. When he decided to practice here
instead of in New York I came with him without a complaint—
that is," she amended honestly, "after I saw his mind was made
up, I didn't argue with him any longer. I made a home for him,
I gave him children. I've tried to further him every way I could.
I've seen to it that he has as pleasant a home and as well brought-
up a family as possible. I've done my duty toward David, Anna,
and you can't deny it."

"I do deny it," Anna contradicted her clearly.

Adeline looked at her sharply. She said, without the slightest
trace of humor:

"You shock me very much, Anna, an unmarried woman . . .
pray what on earth can you know about these things? You've
had no experience, you can't possibly judge. . . ."

Anna moved her shoulders impatiently.

"I'm not exactly an idiot, Adeline. David was terribly in love
when you married. So were you. He hasn't changed, that I can
see."

Adeline laughed thinly. She said:

"I must say, along with your modern ideas you've stayed very
romantic—like a schoolgirl. You don't understand, you can't,
possibly. That side of marriage . . . it becomes a habit, after a
while . . . for the man, I mean. I've always—hated it," admitted
Adeline, low. "At first, of course, when, as you say, one is terribly in love, it's different. But later. . . . It certainly isn't an important part of marriage, Anna, whatever you may say. The
family, the home, the settled things . . . after twelve years it
becomes inevitable, my dear."

She was superior, a little aloof, and she put Anna, the spinster, properly in her place. In the brief silence they saw Graham turn in at the gate. His mother called to him.

"Come into the house," she ordered, "and get washed for your dinner. And leave that dog outside, he's filthy, simply covered with mud. I won't have him tracking up the carpet."

Anna rose and went in, ahead of Graham, and upstairs. She sat for a long time in her bedroom, balancing a writing pad on her lap. She had told John Gregory . . . "Before I return, I shall have made up my mind. I will write you."

She had not written.

The pad remained blank. She put it and her pen aside and lay down on her bed, her eyes closed.

She could not understand herself, or rather, she could and did not wish to do so. Had she not loved Adeline all her life? Why, then, did she suddenly despise her? And why had her heart lifted on a great wave of happiness, relief, even, when Adeline had told her—

She knew why. She fought it, lying there. What difference could it make to her, possibly? None whatever. She was angry at Adeline and indignant, for David's sake, and she was immeasurably happy.

She told herself, her arms crossed behind her head, her broad lids covering her eyes, you're—you're a dog in the manger, Anna Graham. . . .

She heard David come in. His footsteps, light unless he was particularly tired, were unusually heavy to-night. He slammed a door twice, as if he derived some pleasure from it. Something, thought Anna swiftly, had gone very wrong.

At the table that evening he was without appetite and obviously irritable. People, he stated, were fools. Blind. Couldn't see things right under their nose. He had argued himself hoarse advocating certain health reforms and he had got nowhere. That stagnant little pond on the town's outskirts was a magnificent place for breeding disease. Do you think he could get it drained? He could not. Not unless he did it himself, with his own hands, or paid to have it done. Children bathed in the pond, cattle drank from it, brooks which ran back of the privies of half a dozen farms emptied into it. . . .

Adeline said sharply, "I wish you'd remember you're at the table, David." She indicated her disgust by a gesture, pushing back her plate and her eyes dwelt mutely on the interested faces of the children. Graham, of course, had a question to ask, an unthinkable and honest question at which Adeline shuddered, and which David answered absently.

Adeline said, rising:

"Well, as you've spoiled my dinner anyway—and it's late . . . I must get ready for church."

It was the midweek prayer meeting. David said, "I'm not coming. I'm in no humor. You and Anna go along."

Anna said, "If I could beg off—? I've a headache. . . ."

"Never mind. Harry can drive me, I will take Graham and Betty," Adeline told her with resignation.

Graham protested, squirming, "Aw, ma—!" but Adeline paid no attention. "Go to Millie," she said, "and put on your best suit and do see that your ears are clean," she ordered.

The children left the table presently and David and Anna were alone. David, drinking his coffee, said:

"I suppose my absence in church will be commented upon. Nevertheless, I'm not going. I'll give you something for that headache, Anna—"

"No," she told him, "it will pass. I just couldn't bear being cooped up in the heat and with a lot of people to-night, somehow."

David looked at his watch.

"I doubt if anyone comes to the office after eight. We might take the buggy and drive for a little—or walk, if you'd rather . . . if you think it would do your head good?"

There were very few office patients that night. Shortly after Adeline and the children left for church, and the twins had been put to bed, David and Anna walked down the road, away from the village, with Pete, the Newfoundland, at their heels. It was a quiet night, very still. David said, looking at the dusty white on trees and bushes in the clear dusk, "We certainly need rain—"

Anna did not reply, walking along beside him, and David said, after a moment, "I've been in a bad humor all day. No mood for churchgoing. Everything's at sixes and sevens . . . ever since that girl came to the office. . . ."

"What girl?" asked Anna.

"It doesn't matter, just a girl. . . . I couldn't help her. I doubt if anyone can, really. Then this afternoon, that stubborn fool, Hastings. . . . I may be able to save his leg, I doubt it; I'll know for sure to-morrow . . . if he'd called me before. But he didn't. . . . And the meeting . . . everything went wrong there. They think I'm a crank. That pond's been there since time immemorial; besides, they argue, it's on the outskirts, it's as much up to the other town, as to us, more, they say. Moreover, they don't believe me." He turned and looked at her walking quietly beside him and said, "Forgive me, Anna, blowing off steam this way."

Anna said, "Do, it will do you good."

He didn't hear her. Frowning, he went on. "Thought I'd got a grip on my temper long ago. Hadn't, apparently. Crops up every so often. Looks as if at forty I ought to have better sense than to shout at people and pound on things with my fist. Never get anywhere that way. Ever occur to you, Anna, that we don't really grow up, as the children say? I mean, we take on certain protective devices to prove to the world we're adult, but underneath we're just the same. Oh, we work, have responsibilities and all that, of course, and we don't follow our impulses as readily perhaps, there's a deterrent to them, probably artificial enough. But underneath we're the same. Forty! I can't believe it. I feel the same . . . inside—no wiser than at eighteen, no stronger, no less helpless. . . . The only difference is that at eighteen I had moments when I thought I could lick the world. I know I can't, now. And I don't know as much as I did at eighteen either. I've had my education, I've practiced as a physician for a good many years . . . but . . ."

Anna said, "I know. . . ."

"I believe you do." He whistled to the pup, running ahead of them. "Come back here," he called.

The pup ran on unheeding, wild with the delight of freedom and the dusty road and the good smells . . . the exciting scents he might follow to their sources if only a little time were allowed him. But a runabout turned out of a hidden road and came toward them, the horse galloping, breaking from his even trot, the whip laid freely over his sides. The light wagon swayed in the ruts, and the driver leaned forward, urging the animal on.

"Look out!" shouted David. But it was too late. And Pete had not been quick enough.

The runabout came on, at break-neck pace. David shouted again, standing in the middle of the road. Anna, white, cried, "Don't, David, the horse is running away . . . you'll—"

The horse was not running away. The driver pulled up suddenly and the horse, checked cruelly, nearly sat back on his haunches. His owner leaned out of the carriage, a thickset man, far gone in drink. "Get out of my way," he told David, and added a string of senseless profanity.

David was very white. He said, "*You* get out—now."

Anna was running down the road. She bent over the dog and then picked him up and came back, carrying him. He was not dead. David heard him whimpering shrilly.

He took the man by the back of the collar and jerked him out of the carriage. Holding him, as he struggled and swore, he picked up the long black whip. He asked, "How'd you like to have a taste of this yourself?" . . . and lashed him over the shoulders. "That's for my dog—and that's for your horse . . ." he said.

The man was screaming. "I'll have the law on you for this," he threatened. "You can't do that to me—"

"Can't I?" asked David, with satisfaction.

Anna had come up, the dog in her arms. She said, "Pete's leg is broken, I think, David . . . if we can take him back to the house . . ."

He had a split second in which to marvel at her. Her fine eyes rested, briefly, almost indifferently on the man, reduced to terror and blubbering in David's clasp.

The runabout stood a few paces away, the horse standing still and quivering.

David let the man go. He said, "Get back in your rig and go on. If I ever see you beating a horse again—"

The man muttered something, sullenly. He climbed into the runabout and twitched at the reins. David looked down at his hand. He still held the whip. He called, "You can get along without it, I'll keep it to remember you by."

The runabout moved off, in the dust.

David said:

"Anna—if you'd forgive me . . . I took it all out on him, the whole day, I guess."

She said, "Let's get back to the house, David."

He took the dog from her gently. "Looks like . . . yes, I think the leg's broken, we'll set it and get it into a splint. . . ." They went back along the way they had come, Pete, except for his grieved whimpering, lying still in David's arms. They reached the house and went into the office. David, deft, quick, gentle, put the dog down on the sofa. "If you could hold him?" he asked Anna.

She held him quietly and strongly. David said, as if he spoke to a child, "I'll have to hurt you a little, old man."

The pup's tail wagged feebly, and he licked David's hands with his rough, warm tongue.

When it was over, David sat back in his chair. He said:

"Look here, Anna, I made an exhibition of myself. . . . The fellow was drunk—I hadn't any right—"

She asked, "Who was he . . . ?"

"I don't know," said David, "never saw him before. . . . But I had no business . . . Anna, why didn't you stop me? You could have, you know."

She said, a little unsteadily:

"Yes, I suppose so. . . . Yet I didn't want to, David. I hate cruelty. . . . I—I wanted you to thrash him."

David rose and stood looking down at the dog. It was quiet in the house. There was no clatter from the kitchen. Two lamps burned in the office. Amelia must have lighted them before they came in. Anna was on her feet too. She bent to stroke the little dog and touched David's hand. He said, suddenly, "Ah—*Anna*—"

She was in his arms. How, she never knew. But she was there. Held tightly, and without words, his cheek against her hair. She lifted her mouth to his in a wild, unreasoning rapture, and closed her eyes. She thought, this once, just this once and I won't ask for more—not ever.

They stood there embraced and embracing for a long and mindless moment. Somewhere a door slammed, and there were voices. They had not heard the surrey drive into the yard. "Anna—" called Adeline, "David—"

Anna wrenched herself from David's arms and ran from the office. He could hear her mounting the steps to her room. He stood quite still but the hand he put out to touch the dog was unsteady. He said aloud, "Pete, old fellow, what are we going to do—?"

CHAPTER IV

David did not see Anna again that evening. Adeline found him standing in his office, his hands in his pockets, looking down at the restless little animal on the sofa. She stripped off her silk gloves and laid her hat aside. She asked, "What's the matter . . . ? Where's Anna?"

David did not turn. He replied carefully:

"She has gone to her room, I think. We were walking . . . a drunken man came careering down the road in a runabout . . . and this happened." He indicated Pete's leg, stiff in its small splint. Pete rolled his eyes expectantly toward Adeline. She paid him very little attention as a rule; he felt that she disliked him, but he did not dislike her. She possessed a pleasant odor, and trailing, swishy skirts which he longed to chase and seize and roll upon.

Adeline put her cool hand on the dog's head. She said, "Poor Pete—how did it happen?"

David told her. She paled slightly and exclaimed, "You didn't really whip him?" she asked. "Oh, David, that was very wrong of you, very foolish." She looked at him with exasperation. "How on earth can Graham be expected to control his temper if you set him so bad an example?" she demanded.

David admitted that he did not know. Adeline said impatiently, "You might better have gone to church. Do come out of here, it's so close and stuffy. Isn't Anna coming down again?"

"I have no idea," David answered shortly and stood aside to let his wife sweep out ahead of him. Graham was in the hall clamoring with anguish, "Must I go to bed . . . *must* I?" Betty, with a docility infuriating to her brother, kissed their parents and mounted the stairs primly, her crisp small skirt and ruffled petticoat immaculate. Graham looked after her with a fleet fraternal hatred, submitted to the pressure of his mother's small

248

mouth upon his cheek, jerked his head at his father and followed his sister, stubbing his toes on every step.

Adeline rolled her gloves up neatly. She said, "Anna spoke of a headache at dinner. Have you given her something for it, David?"

He said that he had not, and suppressed an ugly ironic merriment. Adeline started up the stairs. "I'll see how she is," she said. "You don't have to go out to-night again, do you, David? If not, I'll come down and join you on the porch. I believe the Gateses expect to stop by."

David said heavily:

"I want to go down the street and see Ellen Taylor. I'll be back directly."

Mrs. Taylor lived a few houses away. David turned back to the office, picked up his bag, and went out of the house. He stayed half an hour with the old woman, talked to her daughter on the porch afterwards, said the soothing, empty things which, every day, he was forced to say, and left. The daughter stood looking after him. He was, she thought, the kindest man in the world. Then she shut the front door and went back to her mother.

David stood irresolute on the street. Three people went by and hailed him and received no reply for their pains. A man driving slowly past in a runabout halted suddenly and informed his companion, "That's him, now."

David went back to the house. He told himself, I've got to think this thing out. But he couldn't. He could not discipline his mind to anything resembling clarity of thought. He tramped up the steps and greeted the Gates family, father, mother, daughter, who were sitting talking with Adeline. Amelia had brought a pitcher of lemonade and some cookies. David found himself entering into an argument with Hank Gates. He grew excited, waved his arms, raised his voice. Adeline looked at him, frowning. She knew him well enough to know that his mind was not on what he was saying. What on earth was wrong with him?

"I hear Mary Dexter will be home this fall. I wonder if she

will find any work?" said Mrs. Gates, tactfully changing the subject.

David said, "There'll be plenty of opportunity. People need a trained nurse around here. I'll find work for her. If I could persuade the town to employ her as a district nurse, half our battles would be won."

No one had ever heard of a district nurse. David said stubbornly:

"Cities have heard of them. They do a wonderful work. Not alone in nursing but in prevention. It's time we made a little progress along these lines."

Gates opined that it sounded like a lot of unnecessary expense and nonsense to him. What were women for, wives and daughters, sisters and mothers, if not to care for their own sick? His wife reminded him tartly, "Well, I'll be frank to say I'd like to hand you over to some woman you can't abuse and nag at when you're sick, Hank—you're perfectly impossible."

They all heard the wagon wheels at the gate, with someone speaking loudly from the darkness, and ordering, "You come right along with me, and do your duty—"

"Who in the world—" wondered Adeline mildly.

"It's Hi Jones," said Mr. Gates a moment later when the law of the town as exemplified in Mr. Jones, the constable, appeared, sheepish and uncomfortable, in the doorway, followed by a man whom David recognized if no one else did.

"Evening, Dave," said Mr. Jones, "evening, Hank . . . evening, ladies." He shuffled from one foot to the other. "This is Dr. Condit," he explained to his sullen companion, "and this is Mr.—Mr.—"

"Perkins, Lemuel T. Perkins, from New York City."

"Come in," said David, "and suppose we discuss this matter in my office. . . ."

Adeline exclaimed and shrank back in her chair. The Gates family sat forward, curious and interested. Mr. Perkins, of New York City, who had sobered considerably since David's encounter with him, expanded before an audience and began to press charges in a loud and domineering voice. He wished David arrested and jailed, for assault and battery, he demanded damages, he had been half murdered, set upon and beaten. He had come to town for the purpose of buying some property. He was an important person. He wouldn't stand for it, by this and that.

The ladies winced, affronted. Gates cleared his throat. David took Mr. Perkins deftly by one arm and his friend Mr. Jones by the other. "Come on in the house," he suggested, "and talk things over a little more quietly."

In David's office Mr. Perkins became somewhat calmer. He even said, rising to turn the porcelain representation of Kuan-yin over in his thick, short-fingered hands, "Been to China, eh? . . . my father went there once, in a sailing ship—"

David said, "Look here, Perkins, I admit that I thrashed you. I'm perfectly willing to go to jail for it, if you like. But I won't admit that you didn't deserve it. You were driving recklessly, you were intoxicated. You ran over my dog and broke his leg. I think perhaps the shoe's on the other foot unless you would rather call things square. What about it, Hi?"

Hi Jones liked dogs. Pete licked his hand and spoke to him confidentially, and Hi said belligerently to the out-of-town visitor, "Drunk and disorderly, were you, and risking the lives of townsfolk and their property? I've a good mind to lock you up instead!"

Mr. Perkins wished himself back in a town where justice was justice, provided you knew the right people. Hi continued, fixing him with a stern regard, "Time you folks learned you can't come into a peaceful town and raise ructions. Dr. Condit here is our most respected citizen. If he thrashed you, you probably deserved it, just as he says."

David said, "Look here, Hi—I've a suggestion to make. If Mr. Perkins wants satisfaction, suppose I give it to him. We'll go out quietly, the three of us, behind the barn. You can hold a lantern and referee. Mr. Perkins is in slightly better condition than he was earlier this evening. My thrashing seems to have knocked some sense into him. He's not as tall as I but he's heavier and, I should judge, younger. How about it?"

"Well," said Hi admiringly, "if you don't beat all, David." He plucked the insignia of his office from his chest and put it in his pocket. He then said, briefly, "Come on, then."

Mr. Perkins was not interested. He muttered something, glared impartially at David and Mr. Jones, vowed, picturesquely, that he'd be drawn and quartered before he ever set foot on this particular soil again and with Hi, laughing and a little disappointed, at his heels, withdrew the charges and himself, by the side door.

Dave presently went back to the porch. Conversation ceased upon his entrance and was then resumed. David explained lightly, "Just a little difference of opinion. . . . I made a diagnosis and wrote a prescription and the patient didn't like it."

The Gateses left after a time. Adeline said, rising, "Well, it will be all over town, David. I suppose you know that."

He knew it, he said shortly, and didn't care. Was she or was she not coming to bed?

Later, lying beside her in the dark, he reflected that he had been as disappointed as Hi when the gentleman in the runabout had refused to meet him—back of the barn. There would have been release in that encounter, in the use of muscles and the deadening of all other thought. He had been grateful to the Gateses for appearing that evening, just as he had been grateful to Mrs. Taylor for her need of him. He had been grateful for the diversion created by Mr. Perkins and his unwilling constable. But now he could no longer refuse to face realities.

Adeline, her fair hair in crimpers, and a hint of cold cream on her small nose, was already sleeping soundly. He thought . . . Anna—Anna had been like a sister to Adeline. . . .

When had he fallen in love with her? Asked, he might have replied that he had always loved her, in a sober, unthinking, brotherly way, ever since his marriage, and particularly since his return to America. But loving wasn't falling in love.

Had it been when he saw her after long absence, this summer, when, regarding her professionally, he had decided that she was not looking well, and had felt pity for her and a certain dim, not quite realized fear? Or had it been in his office that day when he had listened to her heart quicken under his touch. Remembering that, his thoughts faltered. Yes, it *had* quickened under his touch, and what explanation had she given . . . nervous, she'd told him, that's all. . . .

Or had it been when she told him about John Gregory and when, manlike, he had looked at her with new eyes, with the realization that another man loved and desired her? Or had it been just tonight . . . with the puppy in her arms, and her quiet voice speaking and her dark eyes resting indifferently on the absurd figure of Perkins. . . .

He did not know, he would never know. Nor did it greatly matter.

He asked himself, the pillow hot beneath his restless head, in what way could I have prevented it?

In no way. He might have stood beside her in the office, he might have held his arms to his sides, he might have let her go from him, unembraced, yet the damage would have been done, he would still have known that he loved her.

No, the damage would not have been done. She would not have known, she, at least, would have gone free.

He did not ask himself, does she love me? He knew. Her mouth had told him, mutely, under his own, the ravished, startled lips forgetting their astonishment, blossoming into warmth, answering, responding; her body had told him, molded to his own; and her eyes, as she wrenched herself away, and opened them, her eyes which had not spoken to him of anger, or of shame, but of a pure, unthinking rapture.

She had loved a man, she once told him, and that man had not loved her. It had been long ago.

Myself? he asked himself gravely and without vanity . . . *myself?*

There was no understanding in this, no reason, no logic. He had been desperately in love with Adeline, he had married her, he had continued to love her. If she had faults, who had not? If he had been bitterly disappointed, had not she also been disappointed? She lay beside him, the woman who had been his young wife, the woman who had borne his children. What did he feel for her? He had not asked himself this question for a number of years. Even now, he could not answer it. If it was not love it was something which in his ignorance, or his wisdom, he believed supplanted romantic love, or passed for it in the majority of marriages. Affection, sometimes exasperated, but deep-rooted, a curious gratitude, an impatience, responsibility, loyalty—

Loyalty!

Their relationship had not troubled him for some time; and, never, since the beginning, overmuch. He had accepted it, he had accepted his own attitude toward it. Had he been desperately in love with Adeline still, had he been in love with her at all, would he have suffered this alteration, would he have remained virtually undisturbed?

He had not, as the uncomfortable phrase has it, enforced his rights, because, he had told himself, Adeline had her rights as well, the right of denial, if she so pleased. He would and could not use her as his property simply because, legally, she belonged to him. He had told himself that, now and again in the last year. But had that been the real reason? It reeked now of a conscious nobility. Was not the real reason that, as Adeline no longer attracted him, as he no longer desired her, his pride would not permit him to employ her to fulfill some temporary, purely physical demand, devoid of emotional urgency?

Adeline stirred. She complained drowsily, "Do stop turning and tossing, David . . . what's the matter . . . have you indigestion?"

He caught himself back from laughter. He felt much more like weeping. He said, "No, Addie, I'm all right. Turn over and go to sleep. I'm sorry I disturbed you."

She said something unintelligible about the spare room. On occasions when, if Adeline was ill or restless, or David came home late from a hard case, he slept in the spare room. She spoke now out of dreams. She had forgotten that the spare room was occupied.

"Addie—" he said.

But she was asleep again. He had an impulse to take her shoulder in his hand, to awaken her suddenly, roughly, to make her sit up and talk to him. He wanted to ask her, What has happened to us . . . was it all an illusion, that once we had something valuable and beautiful? I don't mean the dark intimacy of our bodies, Adeline, that can't be valuable in itself. But wasn't there something—something young and hopeful, some quick meeting of minds, some dual dream? Or was it only my dream? Yet it must have been yours too. You loved me, you could not endure to let me go, you followed me to China, you hated it, yet you stayed with me. Where has it gone, Adeline, why must I lie here tormented by the thought of another woman? Could you not have kept me, my dear, or is the fault entirely in myself?

What would she reply if he woke her to shout, I am unfaithful to you, Adeline. . . . Oh, not in the way you'd think and which would affront you, and that's curious too, because you don't want me, after all, so why should it matter to you, yet I know how much it would matter—

Adeline slept, without dreams.

In the morning David came late to the breakfast table. Anna was there before him. He had awakened early, watching the sun slant in at the windows, and listening for the sound of her footsteps. But he had felt in that brief moment before full consciousness returned that something had happened, that things were altered, that he was almost unendurably happy. Then he had remembered, and listening for Anna in the next room, had been miserable beyond words.

In the dining room Anna was busy with the children. Small Anna was her especial charge, at the table. She was apt to be a little careless and given to wide, disastrous gestures of her predatory hands. She was not a pretty child but she had arresting eyes and a fair, exquisite skin. She called to David and said, proudly, "I gave my oatmeal to Matthew."

"But you don't like oatmeal," her father reminded her.

Anna looked at him a moment and then away. They had greeted each other mechanically. But now their eyes met briefly. The night had left no scar upon Anna's features. They were pale, perhaps, and her full sweet mouth was slightly compressed. Her overwide, very black brows were drawn, but she spoke gently to the children and with laughter.

Adeline came in, in a loose, becoming wrapper. She said, with a yawn, "What a night. . . . I hardly slept a wink. I think, David, if you didn't drink coffee at dinner you wouldn't be so restless."

She was carrying a book in her hand. She put it down on the rocker near the window. She said, too low for the chattering children to hear, "I wish you wouldn't leave that book around. It was in the sitting room. Betty had it, yesterday. Please lock it up in your office if you must have it."

It was a copy of *Leaves of Grass*. Adeline had ruffled the pages years before and then flung it aside. "Coarse, indecent, horrible old man," she had declared, "call that poetry? . . . it doesn't even rhyme, it doesn't make sense and where it does make sense— I prefer not to understand it."

David, when breakfast was over, put the book in his pocket and took it back to the office. Sitting down, he turned a page here and there. Whitman knew. This book was as if you held the living, vital flesh of the man between your hands.

Adeline was dressing to leave the house. There was to be a church social in August and she must go up to the Gateses' and conduct the committee meeting. Anna would go with her, would she not?

Anna, standing in the side hall a moment, alone, felt a brief touch on her arm. David said quietly, "We—we have to talk, Anna—"

She nodded gravely, her eyes intent on his own. Then suddenly she shook her head. She asked, with weary impatience, "What good will it do?"

"I don't know," he admitted, "but I must talk to you, Anna."

"Not now."

"No, not now. Later."

They were speaking quietly, warily, almost as enemies might speak. Adeline's heels clicked on the stairs. Graham shouted, running past them. Pete, loathing his durance, barked. David said suddenly, wretchedly, "Oh, my dear!" and turned and left her standing there, leaning against the wall, one hand pressed in the natural, unconsciously dramatic gesture, to the beating of her heart beneath her full, deep breast.

From the front hall her cousin called, "Anna, are you ready?" and Anna answered, "Yes, in a minute, Adeline." She discovered that she was panting as a runner might and she waited a moment until her composure should return. Walking out to meet Adeline, she thought how long the rest of her holiday must be . . . and how bitterly brief. She decided, I'll go back to the city, I'll make some excuse, I'll say mamma is coming home unexpectedly and needs me.

But she knew that she would stay; she knew that she could not rob herself of one moment, one hour; no matter how unspeakably the moment tortured or the hour wounded. She told herself, sitting quiet and erect on the big veranda of the Gates house while the women all about her planned and exclaimed, argued and chattered, fell into idle gossip and were recalled to themselves briskly by their chairman, I'm vile . . . horrible—I loathe myself—he will loathe me, too, after a while.

She could not bear to look at Adeline, fresh and immaculate in her white frock, her fair hair deftly in place, a little glow of color in her cheeks.

They had played the same games, shared the same food, the same bed; it had been to her that Adeline had confessed her love for David Condit, just as it had been in her arms that Adeline had sobbed out her earlier disillusionment and youthful heartbreak; it had been Anna's hand that had held Adeline's securely through their mutual childhood, girlhood . . .

She said again, silently, *How I despise myself.*

Perhaps, she thought, walking home through the sunny streets, perhaps if I am careful not to be alone with him, perhaps if we never speak of this again? . . .

Yes, that was the better way. The coward's way but the better. Ignore that brief moment, forget it, if you could. Next summer she would not return and surely David would cease to remember.

The days of her stay ran past fleetly. It was easy to plan and to make it appear as if she had not planned . . . she was sorry, she could not drive with David on his rounds, she had promised Graham. No, she could not walk downstreet, she must help Adeline with her sewing. No, to-day she was taking all the children on a picnic to Lake Bonaparte, would it be all right to use the surrey?

Two days before she left he spoke to her, finding her alone on the kitchen porch, hanging out dish towels for Amelia.

"You're coming with me to-day."

"No, David—"

"Yes," he said stubbornly, "you must come. Unless—unless you can tell me honestly that it meant nothing to you. If you can tell me that . . ."

She regarded him, tried to shape her mouth to the words which would set her free; and could not. His eyes were very blue, blazing into her own. She surrendered finally. "Very well, David, I'll come."

It was a perfectly usual thing for her to drive with him on his rounds. She had done so over and over again during earlier visits. This would occasion no remark. Adeline, who had felt the heat of the past few days, lay reading in the hammock and waved to them as they drove out, looking up from her book, returning to it again, before the sound of wheels had passed.

David said, "There are three calls . . . and then—"

He made the calls, and she waited for him in the buggy. When the last was completed he came out to her again, climbed in and took the reins. He turned the horse toward the road they had taken once before, toward the place where they had sat that day and she had told him about John Gregory.

It was like reliving something one has dreamed. The horse set free, the coat folded there by the tree trunk, the stream running by, chuckling wisely to itself, slipping over the worn, brown stones, sliding into still shadows to hold the mirrored image of a bending tree. Insects hummed, a drowsy bee blundered past, drunk with summer. Flowers starred the rank grass.

David said, as she sat there, waiting, very still, as if she held herself by an effort:

"I—I don't know what to say, Anna. It was something outside myself, almost without my own volition. I hadn't known until then, I suppose, that I love you—"

Color flooded her face and neck, and receded slowly. She said, and the knuckles were white on her clasped and tightened hands, "You don't, David, not really. It was everything. . . . That man in the road, and the little dog. You were excited, perhaps, a little insane—"

"And you—?" he asked her.

She said nothing. He put his hand out toward her, and then drew back. He said, looking at her intently:

"Both of us, perhaps. You don't think I could kiss you and let you go without a word? I don't know if it makes it better or worse to tell you that I love you, Anna—"

She said, on the merest whisper, "I don't know either. I hoped not—for all our sakes—"

"Oh, Anna," he cried out, despairingly, "sitting here, trying to talk about it, as if it didn't matter, as if it were something you could dispel with a word!"

He pulled her into his arms, setting his back against the rough, round trunk of the tree, and holding her across his breast, her face in the hollow of his shoulder. He said, "Let me hold you, this way, Anna, once more, and kiss you again—like this. . . ."

After a long while, he lifted his head. She was so white that he was afraid for a moment. Her clear olive skin was gray, and even her mouth had lost its color. Her eyelashes were heavy against her cheeks. She raised them and looked at him, the intent, eager, demanding face close to her own. She made no effort to escape. She lay there quietly, acquiescent, and she said, "It was not kind, David. . . ."

"No," he admitted with a stifled, despairing sound.

She sat up then, moved a little from him and put her hand on his sleeve. She said, "We're being—"

"Don't say it," he implored her. "I know. . . ."

Then he asked her simply, "What are we to do?"

"Nothing. What can we do?" Anna asked him.

"Adeline—" he said with a puzzled gravity. "No, don't wince like that, Anna, we must speak of her. Adeline's my wife. I loved her and I married her. We have children. I owe her fidelity and affection. She no longer loves me very much, perhaps, but I am part of her. She depends on me. She would be lost without me.

She is not as strong as you are, Anna. I am her whole world. She may not care deeply for that world, she may sometimes regret that it is not quite different. But the fact remains."

Anna said, "I know—"

He went on, looking at her:

"I am forty years old. No headstrong boy, ready to smash up an existing world for the sake of another more desirable. You are thirty-six, Anna, no longer a child or a girl. We are reasonable people. Neither of us would wittingly hurt Adeline. You have loved her even longer than I. There are certain things impossible to us, because, for good or evil, we are what we are. That is why I asked you what are we going to do."

She said stiffly, because it hurt to speak, "I have loved you a long time, David. Since that first evening, I think, when you came to call, since I played the piano and Dick Wright turned the pages for me."

"I'm not worth it," he told her with humility. "I have not merited your love. I think now—I want to think—that even though I was unconscious of it, it has sustained me all this time."

"It should have done so," she said tonelessly, "it reached out to you always across the miles and the years . . ."

"Was that what I felt," he asked softly and in wonder, "sometimes, watching an evening sky or the sun rise, watching the light dance on water, seeing a tree sway in the wind and the grass tremble? Was that why my heart lifted and I forgot so much, remembering only that I was alive and the world so sweet to live in, Anna?"

"David—" she besought him, her throat closing on a sob.

His hand went out, groping for hers, closed hard over it and held it fast. He said, as if astonished, and not as irrelevantly as she might have thought, "You would have loved China, Anna. If you had been there, with me—"

She cried out, between laughter and tears:

"But I *was,* David . . . truly, I was. Your letters—you wrote so seldom—I had them to read, to reread. I read every book on China I could lay my hands on. I went to hear missionaries speak; some were so dull, David, and some were so fine. I talked to

people I knew had been there, on a trip or to live. And I dreamed
—oh, you'll think it so foolish of me, I dreamed, after you left,
of studying medicine, of coming over one day to work with
you—"

"Dear Anna—"

"You're not laughing at me?" she asked anxiously. "I wanted
to, so much. But I knew that my father and mother would never
permit it. Then when the crash came it was out of the question."

"You would have done this—for me?" he asked slowly.

"Yes, for you. I don't believe," she answered a little sadly,
"that I was ever noble or devoted or sacrificial enough to have
wanted to do it just for the doing. But you were there, working.
I did speak of it at home. They laughed at me, and were horrified
as well. Women doctors were dreadful creatures, unsexed, a little
ridiculous. Had I any idea of the long hard time of preparation,
the things I would encounter? Few medical schools were open to
women. . . . It was all a dream, David, the sort of dream a girl
dreams, now and again."

"Dreams—" he repeated, echoing her.

"This, too," she reminded him, "and we're wide awake."

They regarded each other, intently. Their hands were close in
one another's. They looked as if it were the last time, as if they
could not look enough. After a while Anna spoke.

"This morning," she said, "I despised myself. I don't know,
somehow. I keep telling myself that I'm not taking anything
from Adeline. Yet that isn't so."

It was the first time she had spoken her cousin's name. She
barely faltered over it.

"You aren't taking anything from her, Anna." David's lips
closed to a straight line, and he was silent. Anna thought, will
he tell me—what she has told me? Yet she knew he would not.
If he had complained of Adeline, if he had spoken of misery,
of loneliness, of lack of understanding, she would have hated it
in him—and taken it to her breast for cold comfort. But he did
not.

She said dully, "I don't know. We'll never know—"

"This doesn't belong to her, Anna, and never has," he told her.

Anna said, half whispering:

"There's John . . . but I never deluded myself that I could give him what is yours."

"John? Gregory?" He looked at her with a sudden cold blaze of anger. "You—you're going to marry him, Anna?"

"Why not?" she asked. "I won't be cheating him any more now, simply because this has happened. If you'd never spoken, if I'd gone all my days believing that you didn't know I existed —as I believed up until now—it would be just the same."

"But you can't, now," he said, and the sudden sweat sprang out and drenched his forehead and the palms of his hands.

"David," she asked gently, "must I go all the rest of my days alone? I've told him that I can't give him—romantic love or passion, but only a deep affection and companionship. He knows, he says he will be content."

"No man in his senses would be content with that, from you," said David, looking at her with eyes made keener by love and frustration, reading the controlled ardor of her mouth, the deep sweetness in her dark eyes, the lines of the fine, mature body molded for the surrender to delight and the joyous sacrifice.

Anna said, after a moment:

"I want to forget you, David. Oh, not forget you, actually, but to forget this. And the years before. I think I may, after a while, if I marry John Gregory."

"I haven't any right . . . to lift my hand to stop you, Anna," he said.

He rose. He told her, lifting her to her feet, "Come, we must go home now," so gently, so tenderly, that she was back in the dream again and clung to him a moment, without speech.

Presently the little clearing was quite empty of humanity. The flowers spoke among themselves, the stream murmured its ceaseless and limpid secrets, and the clouds drifted, white, above the bird-haunted trees. There were no voices to break the silence, other than the voices of wind and water, and of feathered throats and of growing, green things, the summer choral.

CHAPTER V

THAT evening when the last patient had left the office, David sat for a long time at his desk. Heng-ong's letter was on the blotter. He took it up, and read it again. "If you were only here," wrote Heng-ong, "working with me. I feel that I am on the track of something important. If we could find it together, Younger Brother. . . ."

He found himself speaking aloud, as if Heng-ong were in the room. The words which formed themselves on his lips were not English words. Yet he had not spoken Chinese for years, save now and then to utter a phrase to amuse the children. Adeline always disliked him to do that. When Betty was small he had tried to teach her the Lord's Prayer in Chinese and had found it sweet and touching to listen to her valiant efforts. Adeline had not encouraged her nor him.

David laid Heng-ong's letter aside and took his head in his hands. He shook it savagely as if he could shake that kaleidoscope of thought, dream, misery, indecision into something which might remotely resemble a clear pattern.

Anna was lost to him. If he had kept silent, if he had neither moved nor spoken he might have held her, in a sense. He might have had the ecstatic misery of seeing her occasionally, of touching her hand in friendship, of listening to her low voice and her laughter. Now, it was impossible.

She would marry John Gregory and cut herself off from him, a clean surgical operation. But, he told himself ironically, the severing of heart and spirit and emotion could not be accomplished after the aseptic fashion of a good surgeon dissevering tissue, muscle and nerve. There would be infection and this was a wound which would not heal by first intention. When it did heal there would be the scar.

That she contemplated marrying John Gregory for his, David's, sake as well as her own was perfectly apparent. He jerked his mind from the thought of her marriage. He had always had too much imagination. Perhaps that's why I'm not a better doctor, he thought, staring blindly at the letter beside him.

Such a sacrifice was unthinkable. He believed that he was not misled by her arguments, her reasonable explanations. It was a sacrifice. There must be some other way.

There was, of course, one way. It led to uncomfortable and unpleasant places, it was a mean street, furtively peopled, insufficiently lighted. It was not his way, and it was not Anna's way. He thought, I suppose we were both of us born with a sense of sin; I wonder if people who lack it are happier?

When he finally went upstairs Adeline had been in bed for a long time; Anna's room was dark, no light showed beneath her door and there was no sound. He knew. He stopped there a moment in the hall and listened.

Adeline was reading in bed. She was immersed in last year's great success, *The Little Shepherd of Kingdom Come*. She looked up as he entered. "I thought you were never coming," she said.

She looked very pretty, he thought. His visualization of her was dulled by familiarity but to-night it was as if he had new eyes. Her fair hair, evenly crimped, lay over her shoulders, bound back by a gay pink ribbon. Her dressing sacque was pink, featherstitched in blue. She had color in her cheeks, she looked well, younger than her years. While she read, and he undressed, she absently pinched the thin skin between her eyebrows with her thumb and forefinger. The frown lines were getting so deep, she thought, in the middle of a sentence, she must do something about them. White of egg . . . ?

Her mind continued to wander from Mr. Fox's story. Men in nightshirts looked ridiculous, she decided. Amelia and Millie made David's by hand, of fine linen. They made his shirts too, an old-fashioned absurdity when one could buy garments so much more cheaply nowadays.

David went out to the bathroom and presently returned. He had put on his dressing gown, the one she had given him for Christmas, and the slippers Betty had needleworked. Adeline laid her book aside. He could, she suggested, open the other window. It was really very warm.

He made no move to or to come to bed. Instead, he left the lamp burning on the bureau and drew up the low slipper chair beside her. He said, "Adeline, I want to talk to you a moment."

She was comfortable, not too drowsy; her day had gone well; the children had irritated her very little, she had had pleasant callers in the afternoon. The Wrights had written that they might come and pay a short visit in the fall, in their new automobile. It would take them days, a week or more, to get there. But Mrs. Wright was anxious for Adeline to see the car, of imported make, the very last word in motor cars. . . .

Her mind occupied, wondering how in the world she might entertain their friends suitably, she smiled absently at David and asked, "Well?" considering ways and means, her short, rosy upper lip pressed down on the thin line of its fellow.

"I've been considering," David began carefully, clearing his throat. "We—we have been here a long time, Adeline. I suspect that you aren't altogether happy—that you missed the city and your friends a good deal. I cannot alter that, as things stand, but I am wondering. . . . If I could get someone to take over my practice here, and I am sure that I could, Woodruff knows a very sound young man—would you be willing to return to China with me?"

"China!" Adeline forgot the Wrights. She stared at her husband, hazel eyes immense and dilated. "Are you out of your mind?" she demanded.

"I don't believe so," David answered with a sudden smile. "Look here, Addie, I came home to please you. I left everything that mattered to me—"

"I suppose I didn't matter—or Betty?" she interrupted, her voice rising.

"You know what I mean. Don't be willful, Adeline," he entreated. "I left the work that was vital to me, the people, and—yes, the country, if you want to put it that way. Once we had been settled there for a number of years and new men came out to take my place, I had planned to do more and more research.

Along Heng-ong's lines. I could go back there now, there would be some way in which I could make myself useful. . . ."

She commented bitterly, "I thought you'd forgotten. I see I was mistaken."

"I'm afraid so, Adeline." He rose from the chair and tramped restlessly about the room, fingering her silver toilet articles on the bureau, stopping to straighten a picture on the wall, absently, meticulously. She could have screamed, watching him. He said, from across the room:

"This is my second home. I am fond of it, of the people who rely upon me . . . but—Adeline, in a sense, I stagnate here, it is as if I were working with only a part of me involved, as if my right arm were buried, over there. You must understand. Thirty years of my life were centered on China. Ten years cannot undo thirty. If you would go back with me—? It wouldn't be as difficult, my dear. The children are older. They would love it, they would not be so hard to transplant. There would be new people, to amuse you and to keep you occupied. . . ."

She said, "If you want to get away from here, why don't you consider another city? . . . if you are so set against New York, there are still other cities where you would find opportunity. You know how gladly I'd consent to such a move. . . ."

"No," said David, as if to himself, "that wouldn't help—"

"Wouldn't—what are you mumbling about?" she asked impatiently. "I declare, David, I don't understand you at all."

"Perhaps not," he admitted. He thought, it's of no use, of course; it was insanity to suggest it. He felt older than his forty years and defeated. His shoulders sagged. He had been childish; a hurt and frightened child who seeks to run to his mother's breast to derive comfort and a sense of security once again.

"I can't believe that you are serious about going back to China," Adeline told him.

He said soberly, "I am quite serious, Adeline. Don't brush it aside to-night. Think it over. There are fine schools there, now, better than when we lived there. The children will be taken care of . . . you and they will go out of the city during the summer heat and rains. You will make friends, you have," he added persuasively, sickening at his methods, "a gift for making friends. You will have ample opportunity to exercise your talent for the executive. There is a great deal you can do there, Adeline. You are older, in better health, no longer a frightened girl. Surely you might be happy there. . . ."

Adeline said violently, "Never. If you make up your mind to this, David, I shall be forced to go with you. What else can I do? I have no other means of support, and I could not, in my duty as a wife, permit you to go alone. But I shall die. I know it," she repeated. "I shall die. . . . I loathe China, I despise it . . . the stupid mission people, the natives, everything about it . . . the food, the climate. And I would be separated from my children."

"You're talking wildly," he said gently, "what do you mean, separated from your children?"

"If you think I'd expose them to disease and dirt and the vileness of those surroundings!" she said. "I have plans for them. You never give their future a thought. Betty is a beautiful child, she must have every advantage . . . even here there are some I can give her . . . music, and later, drawing. . . . I want her to marry and marry well. Graham is to go to college and into the banking business."

"Graham," her husband reminded her, "wishes to become a doctor."

Adeline set her lips. "That is pure childishness," she declared, "hero-worship. He will get over it."

David asked, "This is your last word then; that you will go if I force you to; and that, if you do, you'll leave the children at home?"

She answered evenly, "Yes."

"Very well," said David. He moved toward the bureau, extinguished the lamp. "Very well," he said, speaking slowly out of the darkness which encompassed him, "we'll not discuss it again."

When he came to bed he was aware that she was crying. She cried less readily nowadays than formerly. He put his arm under her shoulder, drew her more closely to him. His heart was much heavier than her light weight against him. He asked wearily, "What is it, Adeline?"

"Oh," she sobbed, "it's *you*, David! You despise me, you think me hysterical, unkind, entirely out of sympathy with you—I can't make you see. We're different. Two different people. If—if I could, I'd go since your heart's set on it. But I *can't!*" Her voice rose in a sheer wail of terror. "I only said that about the children because I knew that you—I can't go, David, I can't. Just thinking about it makes me ill. I did not know you were unhappy here . . . if you'd told me before, if we could have talked it over. David, why won't you go to New York . . . or to Syracuse . . . any place away from here where you will have more opportunity?"

He said, "Stop crying. You're shaking all over. I'll never mention it again. It was just—a dream, I guess. No, we'll stay here, Adeline. A city practice, a fashionable practice—that's not in my line. And I am not unhappy here," he assured her. He added, once more as if to himself, "It is simply the pull . . . sometimes I hardly notice it, I am busy, I forget. But it always comes again . . . like a man torn apart, bloodlessly, on a rack."

But she was not listening to him. She had thought, perhaps if I implore him now, if I promise to be kind to him again, if I let him know that I am willing?

It would be of no use. If he could not go to China, he would not take the shorter journey, the one for which she longed. She turned away from him silently, and lay on her side. She thought, I'll see Graham dead at my feet before he comes to this—a country doctor plodding his rounds in a little, half-alive town.

David, lying there quietly told himself, you thought you could straighten things out, didn't you? . . . you thought that you could save Anna and yourself. You knew what might save you, it was the surer, the easier way for you.

He wondered briefly if it were not the coward's way, thousands of miles between them, no likelihood of seeing her again, with the work he loved, and the deep, mothering land taking him in her arms again, claiming all his thoughts, his time, his emotion.

Prayer was as much a part of him as breathing. He did not often pray consciously; yet prayer was the sustenance upon which from childhood he had been nourished. Sometimes it was a wordless petition which went up from him, sitting silent beside a deathbed, or a bed beyond which Death waited; Death, whom, if humanly possible, he must cheat of victory for a little span of years. Prayer, in any time of doubt or dismay, was a weapon which hung invisibly at his side. His mother, his father had forged that weapon, had placed it in his hands. If, sometimes, it rusted, it was always there; if sometimes he lost faith in its unfailing efficacy, he had never laid it away in some attic limbo of the consciousness to which grown men relegate many things of their childhood.

You couldn't, he reflected, pray yourself out of the morass into which you had wandered because you yourself had made your path obscure. It wasn't as simple as that. But there was a guidance which would show you how, in terror and pain, you might by your own efforts find your road again.

The night bell pealed sharply. David sat bolt upright. Adeline sighed and moved her body impatiently. David got out of bed and went to the window. "Who's there?" he called.

"Lem, Dave . . . it's Alice . . ."

David turned back from the window. In the darkness he got into his clothes, swiftly, without fumbling. Adeline asked sleepily, "Who is it, David, it must be after midnight."

"Alice Gilbert," David told her, lacing his shoes, "and a good two weeks before her time."

He went downstairs and to the porch where Gilbert waited for him, nervously. Gilbert's horse and buggy were hitched outside. "Don't wait to hitch up," Gilbert implored him, "I'll drive you back again."

On the way to the farmhouse, David said, "Here, better let me drive . . ."

"I know," said Gilbert guiltily, "but it's her first, Dave, and if anything happens to her—!"

"Nothing's going to happen," David assured him, "unless she surprises you with twins."

"Twins!"

Sufficiently distracted from his anxiety, Gilbert clucked to the horse. They reached the farmyard and turned in. Lights blazed in the windows. Alice Gilbert's mother, a sane and practical person, was waiting. She said, "I've the water boiled, David, and 'bout everything you'll need right to hand."

"You're a marvel," David complimented her, tramping up the stairs. "How's Alice?"

"Scared. But she's got grit . . . It was just about an hour ago," began Mrs. Morse, going into details—

Alice was little and pretty and very white, in the big bed. There was sweat on her forehead but she smiled at David. The pains, she said, were pretty bad, and were getting closer—

David, sitting beside her, holding her cold, wet hand in his warm clasp thought, I never get used to it, the suffering and courage. Most always they have courage . . . No . . . and never get used to wondering if I'm not helping to bring into this world somebody who'll make it better for his or her coming . . .

He had felt that way in China. He had said to Heng-ong more than once, "Who knows but this is the man child for whom all China has been waiting?"

Alice screamed; and then set her lips. David pushed the damp hair from her forehead. "I'm so ashamed," she murmured.

"You needn't be," he said cheerfully. "I'd like to meet the man who'd go through this."

He left her there with her mother and went downstairs. Lem was pacing about, gnawing his underlip. He was a faint, sickly green. David said, "Here, I can't have another patient on my hands."

"Will it be long, Dave?"

"Long enough," David answered, "no matter how short it is."

"I can't stand to hear her scream."

"She knows that, she's trying not to—for your sake."

"I know . . . Excuse me," apologized Lem, suddenly formal, "I think . . . maybe . . . I'm going to be sick . . ."

He departed with a conscious dignity. David, watching, laughed a little; then ceased to laugh. He went into the kitchen. Lem joined him later, very shamefaced. "Is there anything I can do?" he asked.

"No. How do you feel?"

"All right, now. But I swear, Dave, this will be the last time . . ."

"Don't say it," warned David hastily, "you'll repent some day."

He went back upstairs again.

Dunno, thought Lem, what we'd do without him. He's a lot like old Doc Mat, some ways . . .

The sun was high and the birds sang, the cattle cropped in the sweet green pastures and the wagons and carts and rigs were driving smartly into town before David left the farmhouse. Alice was asleep, smiling. Mrs. Morse had the youngster tucked in his cradle; she had bathed and oiled and wrapped him in blankets. Lem, trotting along by David's side to the rig, was red with pride and excitement.

"Finest boy you ever seen, isn't it?" he demanded.

"Just about, Lem."

"Weighs ten pounds if an ounce . . . !"

"Shouldn't wonder," agreed David; "better for Alice if he'd weighed a little less."

But Lem wasn't paying much attention. He drove David into town at full speed. "Whoa!" cautioned David, "don't want to have you break your neck before you get back again."

Lem grinned at him. "There's folks I want to tell," he explained, "and I bet a round or two that it 'ud be a boy—"

Smiling, David went into his house. The breakfast hour had long since passed, but Amelia had his for him, in the kitchen. She had set a pot of fresh coffee on the stove when she heard him drive up. He told her, sitting on the corner of the table, "It's a boy, up to Lem Gilbert's."

Millie squealed with the warm, intimate interest of the country girl in birth or death. Amelia nodded. "Knowed it would be."

"How?" asked David, sitting down at the kitchen table.

"Way she carried it," Amelia answered.

"Oh," said David respectfully, "wish you'd tell me beforehand, it might collect me some bets—remember the time Jo Hicks bet me a bushel of pears against a new hat? I lost!"

"I don't hold with betting," Amelia reproved him sharply. But she turned from the smoking skillet to smile at him. "Just the same," she added, "there's a lot an old woman like me knows, for all your book learning."

Adeline looked in, briefly. She said, "So you're back." David admitted it, told her the news. She nodded without interest, commenting merely, "It's like Alice Gilbert to have her baby in the middle of the night; she always liked attention and excitement."

"She didn't have it until this morning," David told her mildly.

Adeline turned to Amelia.

"Miss Anna won't be home for luncheon to-day, Amelia, she's gone over to Carthage to pay a visit," she said.

David pushed his coffee from him. It had become suddenly tasteless. Adeline complained: "I don't know what she wanted to go for, it's her last day with us. But she said she'd promised the Freemans. They've got someone up from New York visiting them . . . one of those suffrage women," explained Adeline disdainfully.

Anna returned in time for the evening meal. She avoided speaking directly to David either at the table or while they were all together on the front porch after his office patients had left. At ten he was called out to go some distance away, to the logging camp where, according to the excited messenger who had come to town on horseback, there had been a shooting. "Accidental or on purpose?" inquired David, following him out to the yard and shouting for Harry to saddle the mare. "Some says one thing and some another," replied the messenger cautiously, "but we figured it was more important to fetch you than the sheriff."

The small logging camp was reached by a corduroy road. There were acres of beautiful standing timber, and a sawmill, up beyond two fine farms.

David, urging his horse ahead through the difficult byways, was little concerned with beauty and a moon at its full.

Reaching the place, there was not much he could do. An operation was out of the question. He could ease the wrench of dying, that was all. Few details were to be had. An accident, explained the men, tight-lipped. Cleaning his gun, he was . . .

But the hunting season was still many long weeks away.

David rode back to town. There would be an inquiry, of course, there was the business of the death certificate. Deadly tired, he reached his house shortly before one in the morning and went to the office to set down his bag. The lamp burned there. Pete, inordinately proud of his ability to limp with considerable speed and manipulate his splint-fast leg, stumbled out from beneath the desk chair. A voice said, "Be quiet, Pete," and Anna rose from the sofa. She was fully dressed. She had been lying down, one cheek was crumpled and marked from the hard corner of an uncomfortable pillow.

"Anna!" exclaimed David, in astonishment.

He closed the office door. The house slept. Pete, composed now that his idol was at home, again reconciled himself to dreams in which all four legs were hale and tireless. Anna said, slowly:

"I go to-morrow, David . . . I hadn't meant to do this. But I couldn't sleep . . . I knew you'd be back before morning . . . I came down to wait for you . . . to say good-by, I suppose . . ."

He had never before seen her weep. He had seen tears standing in her eyes, clear black eyes, tear-bright, on long past occasions. But this passion of weeping frightened him, shook him as if each separate, scarcely heard sob wrung his heart physically. He drew her to the sofa and took her in his arms.

She said, very low, "I thought I might have this much . . . just hold me, David, quite quietly, for a little while."

The lamp burned lower and the dog stirred in his sleep, barked in the excitement of dreams, following some delectable, impossible scent. David sat without speaking, holding in his arms the living, breathing, treasurable body of the woman he loved. They did not talk, there were no words. Good-by can be said in so many ways; in none more deeply than in silence. It is a forlorn word until one stops to recall its meaning.

Once she stirred and said, "I want you to know I cannot regret it. I have tried. I have told myself that I must. But I cannot, David. It's part of me, it's been so long."

And later, as dawn, pale and as yet unwarmed by gold or the rosy drifting of clouds, grew gray beyond the window panes she spoke again. "If there were a way—but there is none, David, not for us."

The eastern sky brightened, and from some hidden nest in the trees beyond the open windows, a bird woke to song.

Anna had been asleep for perhaps a dozen brief minutes. Sleeping he held her and looked down into her face; on closed curving lips, generous and red with the vital blood; on the lashes, dark on her cheeks and the modeling of cheek bones, the firm jaw line, the small, straight nose, the weight of black hair above a wide forehead, the close-set, small ears. Here, on his heart, this image, forever and forever.

From the desk Kuan-yin smiled her ivory-tinted benison and her lifted, merciful hand was beauty in miniature. David thought, this much out of all the rest of my life. He was a strong man. He would live thirty years perhaps, perhaps more. Thirty years . . .

"Anna," he said, very low, "Anna—?"

She opened her eyes without astonishment. Why should she be astonished, who had so often dreamed of waking to meet his regard? She said, "It's day, is it not?" without resentment, and moved from him a little. She took his face in her two strong and slender hands and kissed his mouth. Her eyes which had been quiet and dry when they opened to his, were so no longer. He knew the taste of her tears on his mouth, and felt them on his hands. She held his hands to her cheek, she mourned over them. It was as if she were saying good-by to a dead and beloved child.

Now, she had risen, was moving toward the door. David woke from a stupor of pure misery which had held him softly yet inexorably, and moved to bar her way. "Anna?"

She shook her head. She smiled at him very faintly. The door closed behind her.

David went and stood at the window. Day was new, bright as a fresh-minted coin. He found himself saying mechanically and gravely, "We need rain badly." His own voice woke him, shook him back to an approximate sanity.

There were voices in the kitchen. Amelia must have come downstairs. The day had begun.

He went out, demanded coffee. "I won't be at breakfast," he said, "I've a patient to see."

When Adeline came down with the children and when, later, Anna joined them, David was not in the house. Amelia explained tonelessly, "He's drunk his coffee and driven out," she said.

"But!" exclaimed Adeline. She turned to Anna with a gesture of despair and apology. "He never came in at all last night," she said. "And now, to go off again like this . . . Perhaps he's forgotten your train. You may not see him again, Anna."

Anna answered, thinking, I've never lied to Adeline before in our lives. "I did see him, Addie. When—when he came in. I went downstairs to get a book I'd forgotten to pack. I said goodby to him then, in case—"

It was a lie; and yet not a lie. She thought, and clasped her cold hands in her lap, if she asks me any more—

But Adeline was not especially interested. She said, "You must eat, dear . . . you've a long trip ahead of you." Little Anna, her face working, set up a loud wail. It was contagious, and Matthew joined his twin in clamorous weeping. Even Graham's lips were set against unmanly tears and Betty's eyes overflowed. "Goodness," cried Anna, seeking to comfort, yet glad of the diversion, "one would think you were never going to see me again!"

Some weeks later as summer, full-bosomed, lavish, reached her maturity and turned with resignation toward the early, briefly magnificent beauty of autumn, David, returning home at midday, found Adeline supine on a couch in the sitting room, with Millie, awkwardly sympathetic, and Amelia, tight-lipped but practical, hovering over her. The children were nowhere to be seen. David's heart stood still. Adeline had been crying, she was in a state bordering on collapse. He asked sharply, "One of the children?" and saw, at the same moment the letter lying on the floor. Adeline rose and flung herself into his arms. She cried, "David, it's Anna—"

"Anna?" he said slowly. "*Anna?*"

Amelia beckoned Millie from the room and closed the door. "Anna?" asked David again and shook his wife slightly.

"After all these years—close as we've been—to treat me this way—" Adeline said.

Anna was alive. The blood flowed back to his heart. He sat down, drew Adeline down beside him. "Come," he ordered, "stop crying, Adeline. What is it, what has happened?"

"You may well ask," she said, anger flaring; "she's married . . . that's what's happened!"

"Married?" said David. He thought, I'm like a parrot, I sit here and echo the things she says. It doesn't make sense.

"Some man," said Adeline. "Here—here's the letter." She stooped for it and put it in his hand. "A widower, with two children . . . and I suppose," added Adeline practically, her first shock passed, "plenty of money. But not to tell me, to marry him 'quietly' she says, no one present save her mother and the pastor's wife as witnesses! And . . . look . . . David, why don't you read it? She says her husband's business will keep him in England at least nine months out of the year."

He caught himself back from saying—England? Anna had not told him that. He read the letter, forcing his eyes to follow the even, small black letters, the curiously personal handwriting, with its lack of ornamentation, its firm greek E's . . .

"I'll never get over it," declared Adeline, "we've been like sisters. She must have known him while she was with us this summer. She never said a word. Now that I think of it, I thought her changed, secretive. I wouldn't have believed it of Anna, she's always been so open with me."

She began to cry again. David put his arm about her automatically. The letter was crumpled in the fist clenched on his knee. He forced himself to consoling, practical speech.

"Hush," he said, "don't take on so, Addie. She didn't mean to wound you, you know that."

"Yes," mourned Adeline, "I know. But don't you see, David, we've lost her!"

CHAPTER VI

SUMMER was a memory. Autumn burned brightly, a running flame through the mountains, a torch flung to the trees. Round and sweet, the apples reddened on the freighted boughs, and skies held a deeper, bluer clarity. Sometimes very early in the morning there rose a delicate haze, as elusive as happiness, as kind as illusion; and always there was an odor, sharp and stimulating, of burning brush.

On an autumn day Mary Dexter came home from New York. She stepped from train to platform, a little tired from her journey, her pale clear skin faintly overlaid with dust. Her youngest brother, Harry, met her, grinning widely. He had borrowed the Condit runabout, having explained to David that the Dexter farm wagon, being springless, might "shake her up a bit." Their greeting was entirely unemotional. He said, "Hello, Mary," in reply to her greeting, and busied himself with her luggage. When he had arranged to call for the trunk, later, he helped her in and drove off. There was certain news, and he gave it, without embellishment. Yes, the farm was all right, they'd had a fair crop. No, ma wasn't so well, seemed like she got tired pretty easy, and complained now and then of a stitch in her side. They'd had plenty of firewood, Perkins had butchered and sent them pork, one of the cows had died, ma had had good luck all summer with her setting hens and butter.

Mary asked, "How is Dr. David?" Harry gave her his slow, lopsided grin. "He's all right," he declared, and was silent. He said, after a moment, "Working too hard, though. Never saw such a man for driving himself. He wants to see you, soon as you can."

Mary nodded, looking about her with a deep sense of homecoming. Here, nothing changed, or so imperceptibly that one could scarcely distinguish alteration, even after absence.

She was a tall, slender girl, with the mouse-colored hair of her childhood, braided around her head. Few hats became her because of the quantity and straight, fine quality of that hair. She was pleasantly plain, for the most part. When her normal, wholesome color flooded her cheeks and brightened her eyes, she was almost pretty. She looked best of all in the uniform of her hospital. Her eyes were nearer green than gray, and not large. But they had a noble directness of gaze, an invincible honesty. Her best features were her teeth and her hands. She was never overgiven to speech and she looked, as she was, friendly, competent and intelligent.

Driving toward the farm, she wondered, without, at the moment, very much concern, what her home-coming would mean. When David Condit had helped and advised her to train for her profession, it had been with the idea that she would in the nature of things remain in the city and earn her living. But her mother was not well; although she demanded nothing of her, Mary's duty, as she herself saw it, was to return home for as long as her mother needed her. She did not doubt but that she could obtain work, at home; not steady employment perhaps, but sufficient to keep her, and to help out with expenses. She knew intuitively that the restrained joy she was experiencing in looking once more upon familiar things and anticipating familiar faces and ways, would become blunted and would pass. She would miss the city and the small world of hospital, the precision of her duties, the support and decision of those older and wiser than herself. She would miss her friends, the excitement, the gossip, the undercurrents moving beneath the routine. But not yet, she thought, taking a deep breath of air as sweet, as faintly frosty as clear vintage wine.

They turned in at their gate. Since Dexter's death his wife and children had labored from dawn to dark to keep their acres. They had smartened things up appreciably. There had been new lumber, paint, nails, hinges, employed in a slow retrieval of the trim neatness Dexter's slackness had permitted to lapse into a partial decay.

In the evening she walked to town, to the Condit house. It

was a long way, but she enjoyed it, in the clear bright darkness. Now and then someone passed, offered her a lift, recognized her and stopped to chat. She walked on, afterward, wishing to be alone, turning over in her mind the things she must ask David about her mother, wondering if in her sharp overanxiety her mother's condition appeared more alarming than it was. Hard work, childbearing, and a none too strong constitution to begin with had worn Sim Dexter's wife to a brittle, premature old age. Mary thought, setting her pleasant mouth firmly, I could turn to, of course, and take most of it from her shoulders. But it would be a waste of my training. Better if I went to work and earned enough to get a woman in to help her.

Turning in at the Condits' she ran her hand a moment along the picket fence, the wood cool and hard to her touch. She thought, going up the path, how much she owed David Condit. As a small child, hoarding a bright copper penny, she thought him a younger and more amenable edition of Santa Claus, in whom at six she had ceased to believe. She had not seen him again until she was twelve and he returned to Natural Bridge to live. For seven years he had been as close to her as her own family, closer in a way; closer certainly than the father who had died long before, or than her brothers. It was David Condit who persuaded her to continue her schooling, who kept her at it long after the majority of girls, situated as she was, had left and returned to the farms or tried to find clerking positions in the stores. Because of him she had struggled through snowdrifts, or trudged under a blazing sun, and had managed to enter and finish high school in Carthage, stopping with a family known to her, helping with housework and children to pay for an uncomfortable bed and her board.

He'd said, "You want to make something of yourself, Mary. You can. You're bright, you've plenty of spunk. Don't let them tell you that education isn't important for a woman. Sometimes I think it's almost more important than for a man. A man can get there, somehow, fighting his way. If he doesn't intend to enter the professions in which book learning is essential, he still has plenty of opportunity, in business, as a good dirt farmer. But women need all the help they can lay hands on. You keep on with your schooling, and I'll see that you get a chance. Is it a bargain?"

It hadn't been easy. She had been homesick in Carthage, although it was only ten miles from her village. She couldn't get home often. She had little pocket money for railway fares. She could not impose on David. He gave her money for clothes, for schoolbooks. She saved a little, although it meant going without many things and being a little shabbier than her classmates. The housework was hard, though she was tall for her age and wiry. She had to get up early, she went late to bed, after the dishes were washed, the chores done and the children tucked in. There were nights when she walked the floor with a fretful baby, hushing the child, a book open on the bureau in order that, as she passed, she might read a sentence and commit it to memory.

There were voices on the Condits' front porch. She recognized Adeline's. Mrs. Condit had never liked her much, she reflected; perhaps she resented Dr. David's helping her. Not that Mrs. Condit hadn't always been pleasant to her when, infrequently, they met.

Mary went up the side steps to the office. The door was shut, but beyond it she knew there would be a hall, wide enough for a few straight chairs in which patients might wait if the doctor was busy, and beyond that the office, and still farther, the small room in which David made up his simple drugs as Mat Brent had done before him. There was no one in the hall to-night, no woman sitting patiently, with a child in her arms or beneath her apron, or both; no man turning a cap over in his hands, staring at the toes of scuffed shoes. Mary knocked at the office door.

"Come in," said David.

He was standing beside the desk. The window was open, but there was a faint odor of tobacco. David turned. The lamplight fell upon him and Mary thought, regarding him with the eyes of old affection, that his face was thinner, that his eyes had receded a little under their heavy brows. The head was as high as ever, and the dark red hair very slightly gray, on one patch, over the temples. He had shaved his mustache, she saw next, and in a way it made him look younger.

"Hello," David greeted her with delight. "I thought you'd be along pretty soon. Come here and let me get a look at you."

He took her by the shoulders, shook her slightly. Pete stirred from his cave under the chair and ventured out, barking. David spoke to him. "Be quiet," he said, "and get used to her, we're going to see a lot of her around these parts."

Pete limped cautiously toward Mary. He exaggerated his limp a little. He had learned that it earned him extra pats on the head, and a forbidden lump of sugar now and then. Mary stooped to caress him. "Nice puppy," she murmured soothingly, and Pete, sniffing at her skirts and ankles, decided that he liked her, that she was not a menace, and returned to his cave at a word from his master.

"Sit down," said David. "You're pretty thin, and you haven't any color. I see you still have freckles."

Smiling, she sat down by the desk, and folded her hands in her lap. "Well," commented David, from the revolving chair, "so you're back. How's your mother?"

"Not very well. I wish you'd come out and see her some time, Dr. David."

"I shall. I'll drop in for a cup of tea or some apples. But she won't have anything to do with me professionally. Still, I've kept an eye on her, Mary. You mustn't fret. With you back, able to help a little, she'll be fine."

Mary tilted her round chin.

"You needn't beat around the bush with me, Dr. David. I know too much—or too little, I suppose. But enough, at all events, to realize that she'll never be fine again."

"No," agreed David, "perhaps not, yet she'll live her time. We can prolong that, if she'll let us. More rest, less anxiety . . . a lot of ways. But I expect that she won't let us, Mary. I don't believe there's anything seriously wrong with her, anything acute. I do believe she's worn out, her strength shaved down to a narrow margin, her heart beating a little faster, all her organs weakened, under long strain, much more than they should be at her age. But she has years before her, my dear, if we take due care."

Mary said bitterly, "Living's so hard on most women that I don't wonder a lot of them find dying easier."

"We're not going to let your mother die, yet a while," said David.

"No." She was silent a moment, looking around the office. She said, smiling, "This is as much like coming home as the farm, somehow. I've never thanked you, Dr. David, not properly. I've tried to, in my letters. But I can't."

"Forget it," he said, embarrassed. He cleared his throat. "What do you expect to do, now?"

"Nurse, if I can get work," she said. "It's out of the question for me to go back to the city and nurse there, now. I'd like to be around if Mom's going to need me. I'll take what cases I can get. I'd always be close at hand and, in between, I could go home."

David nodded.

"There'll be work. In the village, and outside of it. There are plenty who can afford to pay for nursing care, once we educate them to it. I'll see that Doc Kimball and Doc Madison, in Carthage, know that you're available. You could work there, it's near enough," he suggested.

"If you would—that would be fine. I'd like to work with you, though," she told him.

"You shall," he promised, well pleased. "There'll be times when you're not on a case and resting up on the farm when I'll drag you out by the nape of the neck and get you to help me. There won't be any pay and there'll be plenty of responsibility. You'll do all sorts of odd jobs, you'll give an anesthetic and you'll scrub for a home operation and you'll even tie off sutures, if I can persuade you to it. There'll be times when I'll leave you to watch a pretty sick case for me, and it won't be easy. But it will be experience."

She smiled and said, "That's just what I hoped you'd say."

David rose.

"I'm going out on a call, drop you off on my way, Mary, or did someone drive you up?" he said.

"No, I walked."

"Come on, then—we'll stop by and speak to Mrs. Condit . . ."

"She has company," Mary reminded him quickly, "I'll come up and see her to-morrow perhaps—"

"Nonsense," said David, "what's got into you? She'll be glad to see you, no one's out there except some of the sewing circle, figuring up how much they made from the social." He laughed. "Come along," he said.

Light from the front hall streamed back of them as they came out on the porch. David's arm was around the girl's shoulder. "Here's Mary Dexter, folks," he announced.

Women rose and took her hands, Adeline spoke to her from her hammock, there was a confusion of voices . . . "Hello, Mrs. Gates . . ." and "How are the children, Mrs. Condit?" . . . "Thank you, I'm very well . . ." After a few minutes David grew restive. "I've got to get going," he told them.

Mary went down the front steps with him, and out to the yard where Harry waited with the buggy. Harry greeted her with exaggerated courtesy, "Oh, so it's you, Miss Dexter. Haven't had the pleasure in some time. Be careful of the step," and he laughed as they drove off, racked with his exquisite comedy. Mary said, "Harry's grown. Is he any mortal use to you, Dr. David?"

"Harry's a good lad," reported his employer. "Wish he'd wanted to keep on at school instead of working. But he was dead against it. He earns his keep, Mary. I wanted him to go home, nights, he wouldn't hear of it, sleeps up in the barn, you know, made himself a comfortable little cell there. Adeline's scared to death sometimes for fear he'll start a fire. Likes to read in bed—Wild West stories, mostly."

He asked her some questions about the hospital, the city. He said, "Don't get down as often as I'd like—always meant to keep up, make a trip two, three times a year. Can't get around to it, somehow."

"Have you had any visitors this summer?" Mary asked.

"You should have been here last week. Our friends the Wrights were over from Philadelphia. Came in a big Panhard car. Must have driven twenty miles an hour over the dirt roads. They looked dead-beat when they got here, been stopping off all along the way. Frightened Matthew almost to death, in their goggles. We kept the car in a place fixed for it in the barn for three days and about everyone within ten miles came over to see it. Quite a lot of excitement. No, no one else has been up except," he added very carefully, "Mrs. Condit's cousin, Anna Graham."

"Oh," said Mary, "I remember her. She was here often before I went away. She was lovely," said Mary sincerely. "I always wanted to see her again."

"She got married," said David, "just a few weeks ago, and has gone to England to live for a while."

He slapped the reins against the horse's back and was silent. Mary spoke twice and he did not answer. She thought, did I say anything? . . .

"Dr. David—"

"Eh?" He woke from some secret abstraction. "Were you talking to me, Mary? You must excuse me. I get these spells now and then, thinking of something else—getting old, I guess."

He left her at the Dexter gate. "Tell your mother I'll come around to-morrow and see how you're getting on," he said. "Good night, Mary, I'm glad you're home again." He added, as she stood beside the buggy looking up at him, her face a white blur in the starlight, "I'm proud of you, you know that, don't you?"

He reached home early enough and found Adeline sewing in the parlor. She said, as he came in, "You spoil that girl, David."

"What girl?" he asked vaguely, his mind still on the case he had left. Chicken pox? Of course, chicken pox; a virulent case. If it wasn't chicken pox—

"Mary Dexter. And dragging her out on the porch, with your arm around her!"

"Why shouldn't I put my arm around her?" he inquired mildly. "I've known her since she was no bigger than the twins."

"Oh, I know," said Adeline impatiently, "but you know how women are. And if Ethel Gates saw a man run a splinter in his foot, she'd run around town and say she watched his leg being amputated."

"That's nonsense," said David shortly, and did not mean Mrs. Gates.

"Just the same," declared Adeline, rising and putting aside her work, "Mary Dexter isn't a child any longer. She's twenty-two, if she's a day."

"Why, so she is," exclaimed David, astonished. He started toward his office, his voice trailing off—"Beats all," he was saying, "seems like yesterday."

But yesterday becomes today and today is quickly tomorrow. The years between the autumn of 1904 and that of 1909 were like streams flowing imperceptibly one into the other, on their way to the eternal sea. There were shallows and depths, fleet reflections and sudden storms, the waters darkening, the hard, silver hammering of rain.

For these people, as for all people, time was counted by events rather than by hours or weeks or months. David, looking back over the years, would remember certain things. He would remember the day in 1905 when St. Joachim's Hospital burned in Watertown and when the new hospital was planned. He would remember the birth of Anna's child, a boy, in that same year, in England. He would remember Adeline weeping and laughing over the letter. . . "But she was so old to have a baby, I worried so about her, wasn't it sweet of her, David, to name him for you?" He would remember Graham, at eleven, standing scarlet and tense at the wash basin while Adeline washed out his mouth with soap, "He used a horrid, disgusting word, David, I heard him!" He would remember taking the boy into his office and talking to him gravely, frankly, "So, you see, Graham . . . putting nasty names to these things doesn't alter them. They're important, and they can be very beautiful. They can be ugly too, or even comic. It all depends on how you look at them, son." And Graham, shuffling his feet, and turning his head aside and finally blurting out, "Well, I thought—that is—I've been on farms enough . . . and seen animals . . . it *is* like animals, isn't it, Pop?" And he would always remember his own reply, "Just like animals, I suppose, Graham, if you want to see it that way. I don't, that's all."

Another milestone was Betty, at fourteen, grown terribly prim yet given to giggles, and wholly given over to the throes of first love, for one Alex Gates, who had gone away to college and was going to be a lawyer, and some day certainly governor and probably president. Betty, mooning at meals, her spoon advancing to her curving mouth, halting there, her dark eyes dreaming, her copper curls tied back with a bow. Betty, pleading to stay up an hour later, to go alone to a barn dance, to pin her hair up high . . .

He would remember the day when he realized that Anna and Matthew had shot from babyhood into thin, slightly awkward, heart-catching little boy and girlhood, with certain teeth missing and sudden tempests and an aversion to soap and water. He would remember the dog, Pete's, death in 1907, of the poison which had been put out for rats. He would remember special cases, one lost here and another saved there; and perhaps that one night, taking Mary Dexter home, when he had said to her, "I don't know how I got along without you, Mary, till you came back, you've been a rock of strength."

Five years. His hair was a little grayer, but his weight remained the same, he hadn't had a sick day, unless one counted that abscessed tooth which had raised Cain with him until he'd had it out. Probably Adeline would remember the occasion more sharply than he.

But most of all he would look back and see how by imperceptible degrees the agony of Anna's loss, the frustration, the long nights of wakefulness and useless longing, had abated into something very like resignation. Not forgetting, never forgetting. But where there had been pain there was, slowly, less pain, and then peace. And where there had been desire, there remained only sweetness.

Anna was happy, she wrote Adeline, over and over again. She had returned to America once a year since her marriage. She had not come upstate. Her husband was so occupied, the little time they had here, her mother, who lived with them, was old, she could not leave her long alone in England. But twice Adeline had gone down to New York to be with her cousin briefly and had returned with glowing reports. Anna was a fortunate woman, John Gregory was the best of husbands, devoted, considerate, lavish; and the baby engaging, if delicate. Anna had the most fashionable clothes, John would load her with jewelry if she would permit it. Her hair was definitely gray, said Adeline,— "Strange, and I haven't a gray hair in my head,"—but very handsome. She had put on weight.

David could not spend five years mourning what he might have had and what he would never have. There was no purpose in it nor sanity. There were days, even weeks, when he didn't think of Anna at all. Then something would recall her to him . . . he would turn past the clearing where, upon two occasions, they had been together; he would come late, alone, into his office and it would seem to him suddenly, although she had not been in his mind all day until that moment, that she would rise from the old couch there and speak to him. Or driving along a road in spring, listening to the bells on the harness in winter, watching a flight of swallows swift and dark, writing their graceful secret language against a sunset sky, he would find that his mind was full of her; and his heart.

In the outside world a war between Russia and Japan was concluded; the Cape to Cairo bridge had been completed; cholera became epidemic in Germany; and the Wright brothers flew twenty-four and one-fiftieth miles in their airplane in thirty-eight minutes. The Chinese and the French fought at Tonquin; and Peary made a new record, reaching latitude $87° 68'$ North. There was an earthquake and San Francisco lay in smoking ruins, rising to face this new disaster and to create a new city. Plague in Paris; race war in Texas; and President Roosevelt coming out for simplified spelling and against nature fakers. Paris watched a balloon race; and America, in the person of Lieutenant Lahn, U.S.N., won the Gordon Bennett cup. There were floods in Ohio; and in London women demanded attention to the Female Suffrage Bill. There were earthquakes and fires, fighting and riots all over the face of the patient globe, and Manchuria returned to Chinese rule. The first commercial wireless dispatch was sent across the Atlantic; kings died and rich men died, and there was a financial panic. Courts-martial, assassinations, murders were part of the international procession. Congress passed an act providing for remission to China of part of the Boxer indemnity and it no longer cost five cents to send a letter from America to Great Britain. President Roosevelt, having refused a third term, departed from the White House and William H. Taft moved in. Lieutenant Shackleton reported having reached within one hundred eleven miles of the South Pole and electricity crept from city to countryside and people who had laughed at the telephone a few years before consented to party lines and spent their spare time listening in on their neighbors.

The Senate adopted an Income Tax amendment to the Constitution, and both Dr. Cook and Commander Peary announced their discoveries of the North Pole.

But David, looking back, would recall few of these things. For few were important to him. He read his newspapers with the eyes of the average, occupied man in a small community, part of the outside world and yet sufficient unto itself. There might be fighting in Turkey, but meantime a neighbor broke his leg or a homestead was foreclosed. A school might burn in the West, but last night you yourself went out and fought to save the barns and stock of a friend.

He was more closely in touch with China than with events in his own country. Heng-ong, toiling on his research, having given up the practice of medicine in order to devote himself to it entirely, wrote him of developments there. But Heng-ong, too, was more concerned with his immediate personal labors than with the taking of a Japanese steamer by his countrymen.

The newspaper reader knows horror at distant disaster, and sympathy with suffering, but these are impersonal emotions. Sometimes the really important item is buried on a back page, or listed under Vital Statistics and has no headlines. A death, a birth, a stock falling or rising, and the headlines are forgotten, they do not concern you; but this does. Therefore this is important.

Adeline's memories of those five years were confused and drab, they ran along the routine lines. Here and there something became fixed and memorable. The visits to Anna, who didn't know her luck, perhaps; the increasing dislike of Mary Dexter. "You'll get yourself talked about, David, up all hours of the night with that girl"; the change in fashions, the peekaboo waist, the sheath gown, the dotted veils which became her fair skin so well, the huge Merry Widow hats. Memorable, too, the day she discovered the slight sagging under the delicate line of her jawbone and wept, a little and alone, for the passing of youth, which has to pass before one becomes conscious of its loss. Then, her arguments with Graham, curiously violent, like quarrels, started in his eleventh year and continued until his thirteenth. "Graham, you don't want to live in a small town all your life . . . Look at your father, giving his waking and most of his sleeping hours to his practice, worn to a thread all of the time, getting little thanks for it. . . . Uncle Richard Wright has promised there'll be a place for you with him some day, if you study hard and graduate from college with honors. You—your father wastes his life, you mustn't . . ."

On such occasions she always forgot that she was talking to a little boy. Graham's chin set each time, and his blue eyes darkened. "I won't be like Pop," he said once, "but I'm going to be a doctor, see? A surgeon. A great surgeon . . ."

Why wouldn't Anna come to visit them when she was home, and bring her son and her likable, estimable John? Why wouldn't David go to New York to see them with Adeline? Surely he could take a day or two off?

There was Amelia's death. "Poor old Amelia, but it's better for her, after all," and the installation of Millie in her place. It was hard to train Millie to more desirable, formal ways. There was the disgrace of someone's daughter and the dishonor to someone else's son. "If my children behaved like that, I'd never hold up my head again." There was the beginning of the Reading Club which she proposed and of which she was president. There were the books of Robert Chambers which held her fascinated, portraying deftly and delicately a life for which she had always longed and which she would never have.

Five years passed slowly, yet too quickly for Adeline Condit, and little remained to mark their going, but the loss of a pound or two of flesh, the sagging of a muscle and an added line at the corner of the eyes.

For Mary Dexter these five years were crowded with incident, with excitement. Her first case, upon which she ventured anxiously, almost timorously and then with increasing confidence, actually learning, as time went on, to sleep for part of her twenty-four hour duty; and the cases, in between, with Dr. David were worth remembering. The boy on the far farm, who had gone to the city and had spent three days in riotous living and who would pay for it, perhaps, with his sight, who might never again see the rising sun, or a cloud heavy with rain, the laughter in a girl's regard, or the dew shining on a flower. Mary would remember David's voice saying, "You can't lie down on this job . . . not for a minute. I'll be back in the morning, Mary," and the clasp of his hand on her own. She would remember the long hours, fighting sleep, the big boy restless and moaning on the bed, the stuffy room with its locked door, the irrigations every fifteen minutes, the voice of the relentless woman who had borne that son outside the locked door. For she sat there as the day wore on, inexorably reading her Bible aloud . . . the words fell like hammer blows on Mary's brain . . . "strange women . . . whose feet take hold on hell." And the words were colored by the laughter of a drunken man in the kitchen, father to the boy, husband to the woman.

There were other cases; operations; the old woman with pneumonia with whom she'd been three days alone. David hadn't been able to get through, the drifts were so high . . . not by sleigh nor on snowshoes. She'd been alone with the patient in the isolated house, stoking the wood stove in the parlor, getting the meals, returning to the bedroom, working, never even taking her clothes off. Then it had ceased to snow and the wind broke and David had shoveled a path to the door. She would remember that case because she had cried, seeing him, from sheer relief and weariness, clinging to him, and he'd said, "Poor youngster . . . but you've pulled her through, Mary . . . all by yourself."

Other cases; birth and death. And at home a sister married, a brother buried—sunstroke it was, and the shout from the hayfield bringing her out to him, on flying feet. Her mother, growing better . . .

In the autumn of 1909 her brother Harry rode into the Dexter yard in the doctor's new buggy. It was early morning and Mary, home for four or five days since her last case, was spreading linen on the lawn to bleach. Her sleeves were rolled up from her brown arms, and her braids were loose over her shoulders. She looked quickly as Harry drove in. "What's the matter?" she called.

"Doc wants you to come back to the house with me, quick," said Harry, "it's Mis' Condit, she's took sick. I'll wait while you get your things."

"**F**OLLICULAR tonsilitis," David told Mary briefly, meeting her at the door, "she's pretty sick."

He added, leading the way up the stairs, "I've urged her repeatedly to have her tonsils out. She wouldn't hear of it—I remember the struggle I had with her over Graham—"

He stopped speaking, led the way to the bedroom door. He opened it and stood aside. He said cheerfully, "Here's Mary, Addie, she's come to look after you."

Adeline Condit was acutely and uncomfortably ill. She ached, she could not swallow without severe pain, her sudden, high temperature made her flighty, given to snatches of delirium. It was a difficult case, Mary reflected a few days later. The routine was familiar to her, the easing of the racked joints, the rubs and sponges, the throat irrigations and medication. She had stripped the room of all but essentials, and with a small cot brought in and placed beside the bed she isolated herself with her patient. The adjoining spare room served for a dressing room, and in there, with the door open between, she ate her meals, brought up and left outside the door on a tray.

The children had been parceled out to the neighbors, and the house was very quiet. David came in and out, wearing a ragged old bathrobe over his clothes, and sleeping across the hall in Betty's room. There seemed to be an epidemic of streptococcus throats in the neighborhood and he was exceptionally busy. Most of the cases were comparatively mild but several, Adeline's among them, were severe.

Madison came over from Carthage to see her, and later Herbert Woodruff was called from Watertown in consultation. Herbert, reading Mary's neat charts, looked at her with approval. "Nice little girl," he told David on the way downstairs, "seems uncommonly competent."

David agreed absently. "Yes, very. She's devoted to Adeline," he said.

Woodruff made no comment. It had seemed to him that Adeline was not devoted to her nurse. She had been sharp with her, demanding, petulant, the few times she had spoken to her during the time Woodruff was present. He said, leaving the house, "Well, I think you have no cause for worry now. Everything's clearing up nicely . . . provided we have no complications."

Adeline was a difficult patient. She wanted a dozen things at once. She would get out of bed. She fretted about the children, she demanded David's constant attention, which he could not give her. Nor were complications lacking . . . first, a severe bout of rheumatic fever, and finally the dreaded development of endocarditis.

Woodruff came again, and looked grave. He pulled thoughtfully at the small Vandyke beard which, with its professional air, lent dignity to his rotund countenance. Pain over the cardiac region, rapid pulse, the murmur distinct to the listening ear.

Adeline, lying in bed with an ice bag over her heart, watched Mary moving softly about the room. She said, "I wish you'd pull down that shade, it isn't even with the other, it makes me nervous."

She resented Mary Dexter. She had never liked her. She thought her forward, grasping, taking David's kindness to her for granted. She gives herself airs, thought Adeline, submitting to Mary's careful, sure hands, thinks she's a cut above the rest of her people—

They couldn't, she reflected, keep her condition from her. She knew that she had a serious heart ailment. She knew that she would die of it. A small creeping triumph pounded in her breast. She had always told David that she had a weak heart. She reminded him of this that evening, as he sat beside her and Mary waited within call in the spare room.

"But your heart was not weak," David said gently, sitting beside her, his hands clasped loosely, his shoulders sagging. "This has all come about from the bad throat and the rheumatic fever . . ."

Adeline shook her head. She thought she knew better. Her fair hair, brushed and braided, hung over her shoulders. She looked very small in the big bed. She was silent a moment, drowsy with the drugs given for relief of her pain. David, watching, looked sharply at her face, pinched, a bluish cast about the lips. She murmured, her breath short and hurried, "I'd like to see Anna—"

Almost immediately she drowsed. David went into the spare room to speak with Mary. He gave her her orders, the stimulant for the failing heart action. He said, frowning, "She's somewhat cyanosed—"

They spoke low, almost under their breaths. David said, looking at her keenly, "You're all in, Mary, you're not getting any sleep. I'll get a night nurse. Herbert will send me someone from Watertown."

"I can manage," Mary told him. She hesitated a moment. She added finally on a long breath of resolution, "But I wonder . . . it isn't that the case is too hard, Dr. David. But Mrs. Condit doesn't like me. I—I have a feeling that she resents me. In her condition—perhaps it would be wiser if you found someone else and I left—"

"That's absurd," he said, his voice rising a little, "you're imagining things. You know sick people, and how irritable cardiac cases become. You get a good night's sleep, Mary, I'll sit up with her. I don't expect to be called out."

Adeline's voice reached them faintly. They both turned and hurried to her. She had propped herself against the pillows, her cheeks flushed with fever. She was gasping, definitely. She demanded, "What are you whispering about? I heard you . . . behind my back. Oh, don't look at me like that—you're just waiting for me to die, Mary Dexter, so you can marry him yourself . . . I won't . . . I'll get well . . . you'll never set foot in this house again—"

David, taking her thin wrist in his hand said, "You're talking nonsense, Adeline . . ." He looked at his watch. Adeline's faintly blue lips were closed. She looked at him with a spark of triumph which, directed toward Mary Dexter, was definitely malicious.

Mary, her hands shaking slightly, was measuring the digitalis into the little glass.

Later, when Adeline slept, Mary spoke to David in the hall. She said, regarding him directly, the bright color flooding her face, "You see how it is, Dr. David. I'll stay on, of course, until you get someone else."

"She's half delirious," he told her, "and many cases of this kind are abnormally suspicious. Mary—you've been a tower of strength, you wouldn't fail us now?" He put his hand on her shoulder gently. "This is a phase . . . I realize how unpleasant it is for you—it will pass—"

"Very well," said Mary; and returned to her patient.

During the time she sat there or busied herself with her routine duties she was aware of Adeline's speaking, dilated eyes upon her, watching her sharply. But she said nothing except to move restively under the younger woman's touch. When David came in to take up his vigil she was asleep and Mary reported, very low, "It's of no use, Dr. David, I irritate her and upset her. You must try, for her sake, to get someone else in the morning."

After a moment he nodded. "Go to sleep now, I'll call you if it is necessary."

Mary went back to the spare room. She took off her uniform, put on a cotton kimono and lay down on the bed. She was desperately tired and she could not sleep. Humiliation shook her to wakefulness every time she found herself sliding into a coveted drowsiness. She was not given to tears, so she did not weep. But her temper rose steadily. She had always had difficulty with it; it was tinder to a spark. She had learned to control it, she had had to control it, but long-suffering patience was not one of her virtues. She had been for weeks in the Condit household, fighting silently not alone disease and the complications of disease, but her patient's palpable dislike of her. If David had not agreed to release her, she did not see how she could go on. At the best, Adeline's convalescence would be long and difficult. And although her heart might compensate, might become normal again, able to bear the strain of ordinary living, Mary did not believe that, with a return to health, Adeline Condit would forget her rancor and her suspicions.

The unfortunate part of it all was that one short sentence of Adeline's could be like a wedge deftly inserted beneath the entire structure of Mary Dexter's feeling for David Condit, prying, loosening, threatening to destroy forever the unthinking, grateful regard in which she held him, a regard which was part filial and part fraternal and informed by something closely resembling worship. This structure had been built up, piece by piece, since her childhood, and cemented with an unaltering affection. But she had never thought of him as a man, with arms to embrace, with lips to read the lover's litany. With this word of Adeline's between them she felt that she could never again meet him in the old companionship, the partnership which had developed in the past five years.

She tried to think, clearly and sanely. She asked herself, as countless women have asked before her and will ask again, have I been in love with him all these years, not knowing it but betraying it to—*her* by some manner unknown to me? . . . Is that why other men . . . ?

She was twenty-seven years old. There had been "other men" briefly, not seriously. She would have been unique had she passed through her training without an occasional accelerated heartbeat. There had been one carefree interne, a charming lazy youngster from the South, who had a way with women; and there'd been an older man, on the staff, to whom she had looked with the voiceless adoration of youth. Hero-worship, ephemeral love affairs bloomed and died so inevitably in the hospital atmosphere.

But neither of these encounters had put forth roots. The interne kissed lightly, and as lightly went on his way. More than a kiss, and that taken and not given, he knew he would not obtain from Mary Dexter. The older man had not known that she existed except as a competent and intelligent automaton; could not dream that twice she had wept, in her cell-like room, at a reprimand and that the days on which he was scheduled to operate were red starred on her mental calendar.

Twice in her three years in New York Mary had had proposals

of marriage. One had come from a patient who, convalescent, dreamed of the luxury of a life of service, and who moreover fancied himself deeply in love with her; and the other from the brother of a classmate.

She had considered neither.

Since her return to her home, two of the lads she had grown up with had exhibited an interest in her which they had not felt when she was little and freckled-faced and a target for snow-balls. She liked them both; loved neither.

She thought, if she should be right? . . . if I've always had my heart fixed on him . . . without knowing it, so that it spoiled other men for me? . . .

That, she assured herself, was absurd. She had no right to attach any deep meaning to a sick woman's utterance; to permit it to disturb her in this fashion. To-morrow perhaps, in a day or two at the latest, David would find a nurse to relieve her and she could go on back home, and pray for a long hard case to occupy her mind, one of Dr. Madison's perhaps, and then before much time had passed, she would find herself smiling at the self-searching and humiliation of this night.

She turned on her side, pulled a quilt over her, to her shoulders, and slept lightly, a sleep shot through with fleeting dreams, and the uneasy consciousness that, at any minute, she might be called.

In the next room David sat in a big Morris chair drawn up beside the bed. He relaxed his muscles and rested, as he had learned to do, without abating his watchfulness. If Adeline stirred, he knew, he was there, ready to do what was needed. The lamp was shaded from her closed eyes, there were menacing shadows in the big room. Beyond the windows was a black sky shot with stars, and a heavy frost. Wagon wheels rang in the hard, frozen ruts. Winter was nearly upon them, it would be early, the trees were already bare of leaves, and the winds from the mountains cut to the bone. There had been snow flurries, and there would be storms. There would be snow and high drifts and on clear nights the magic pattern of the Northern Lights, weaving, unweaving, clear, brilliant white, strange reds and greens, shooting upward, dying down . . .

He thought, lying back in the chair, that it might be a difficult season. He had attended three scattered cases of diphtheria already. He must see if he could procure some more antitoxin. It was not perfected, as yet, nor sure, but its usefulness had been proved.

Adeline spoke, on her labored breath. She complained,

"I don't want to die, David—"

He moved closer to her, took her hand in his own. "You're not going to die, my dear," he said.

"I'm frightened—"

"You are dreaming. Try to sleep. You must rest, be quiet, give yourself every opportunity."

She said, "I've been a good wife to you, David, as good as I knew how . . ."

"Addie—"

But now she slept again. He stared at her, his eyes aching. He saw her as he had first seen her, in the silken gown—blue, was it not?—with the gold and onyx earrings weighting her delicate ears, and the small, rosy mouth shaped to a smile. He remembered her singing the night he had told her that he loved her, seeing her tears. He could hear her voice . . . It was the same voice which he had heard for years, beside him, in speech or song, lifted, at his side, at church to the pumping of the old organ, or in a snatch of melody about the house.

Yet not the same.

He remembered her on shipboard on the way to the East, looking at him with an arch tenderness over the shoulder of some fortunate man who held her in his arms as they danced. He remembered her tempests and tears in the mission compound, in the house in Ku-cheng. He remembered the day their daughter was born. And all the days after, in a swift marching procession.

Wherein had he failed her? Why had he failed her? He had loved her, desired her, married her. And love had burned to the ashes of familiar affection, a little resigned, and a little intolerant.

He had been unfaithful to her by word of mouth, and in his heart and in the urgency of his desires.

He shook himself physically, with a sick impatience. Why was he thinking . . . remembering, as if Adeline were dead, of a heart ailment? There were many years before her. She would get well, these things took time.

She woke again. He leaned to her, his finger on her pulse. She said, as if wandering, "It's been such a *queer* sort of life, David, not at all what I planned, not what I wanted."

"Adeline, my dear—"

"That girl," she said, not at all as if she wandered, "she'd make you a better wife, I suppose . . . I dislike her very much, David . . . not that it matters. No, it does matter . . . Promise me, David . . . promise me—"

She was struggling to sit upright. He laid her back against the pillows again, gently. She implored, holding him, "Promise me you won't marry her, David. I couldn't bear it, in my house, using my things, mother to my children—"

He answered gently, consolingly as one speaks to a child, "Of course, I promise, Adeline."

She was silent a moment longer. She began to pick restlessly at the counterpane with her thin, her wasted hands. He caught them in his, covered them with his own. She smiled faintly. She said:

"Anna . . . Anna would have suited you better, I expect, than I did. Do you know, it's very funny, David, but I used to think, before we were married, that she was in love with you, too. Of course, that was silly of me, I suppose. But it pleased me to think it. I'd show her your letters, sometimes, and watch her face . . ."

His heart contracted sharply. He said quietly:

"Don't talk, dear. Try to sleep."

"I don't want to sleep," she said wildly, "I'll have to sleep such a long time . . . in the cold and the dark and alone." A shudder took her, convulsed her. "David," she asked, and put her arms up to him, "why must I die, like this? You've saved so many other people, David, can't you save me—don't you *want* to?" she cried out to him.

He held her close, there were tears in his eyes, sharp tears, they cut, they wounded; they were wrung from pity for her, for himself, for humanity. She murmured, as if to herself, "That's it, you don't want to . . . because of that girl . . ."

"Adeline—"

"I wish Father Condit were here," she said strangely. "I was afraid of him, I never liked him, David, you were such friends, the two of you—I've always been jealous of your friends—Hengong, Uncle Mat, Father Condit—but if he were here . . . Why don't you pray?" she demanded suddenly. "You were taught to pray."

It was time for her medicine. He gave it, deftly. Presently she slept, without speaking. He sat there in the Morris chair and watched her face in sleep, sharpened, somehow, shadows around the nose and mouth. On the surface this was a happy marriage, a suitable marriage. Young and in love they had taken certain vows, had hoped with high hearts, had believed, and yet it had been a failure. Speaking to him, out of drugged dreams, she had told him so.

Toward dawn, when human life falters in its sleep, when houses are quiet and an enemy waits, stalking the shadows, an enemy—or a friend, who knows—toward dawn, before the full strong tide flowed back into mortal veins again David aroused Mary Dexter from her sleep.

They worked together, without the muddle of hurry, yet in a sharp restrained haste. Not many words passed between them, merely the quick orders, the questions, the replies. There was sweat on David Condit's forehead and his mouth was set in the hard line of the soldier who does unremitting battle and who knows himself defeated.

Toward dawn, in the forty-first year of her age, her heart action having failed, Adeline Condit died.

CHAPTER VIII

SNOW, in large flakes, of intricate and delicate patterns, fell, unhurried and in silence, from a hushed and leaden sky. There was no wind. On the cheeks of the people huddled together in the churchyard the snowflakes fell softly, less salt than tears. The harnessed horses, with blankets flung over their haunches, shivered, waiting. The ropes creaked, the words of comfort and hope were spoken; women wept and the faces of men were grave and a little terrified, because all were witnessing a ceremony, beautiful and barbaric, one at which one day they would be the chief celebrants, each in his own time; yet would not hear the prayers, nor witness the flung earth, being dead.

Mary Dexter lifted her compassionate eyes and looked at David Condit. Snow, evanescent as beauty, lay upon the collar and shoulders of his greatcoat, and powdered his bare head. Matthew and Anna, small, and wondering and afraid, stood beside him, with Ethel Gates; Betty, her pretty face swollen with tears, was in the curve of his arm, and Graham, his blunt childish features composed to an older mask of rebellious grief, had his arm about his older sister's waist.

Presently it was over. Flowers and the strewn branches of pine and cedar hid a scar in the earth. The carriages received their freight, the horses, stamping with impatience to be off, were released from waiting.

The snow ceased, and the sky darkened; the churchyard was empty of people.

Neighbors had taken charge of David and his house. There was warmth and food and the subdued talk of people, who, motivated by kindness, are nevertheless sustained by a curious, inner excitement and by the magnificent knowledge that their limbs are free, their veins run healthy blood, their hearts still beat to love and laughter, fear and distress; and by the knowledge that this grief is not their grief. They spoke of David among themselves, he was "taking it very well," they said; they spoke of the children, "poor little motherless creatures!" and of Adeline, whom some had liked and some had not liked but all had known. The ways of God were beyond questioning, they said, for she was a young woman and the mother of a family.

The children had returned home to a house that was very strange to them. Mary Dexter was with them, as Anna and Matthew, especially fond of her, had clamored to have her there. She put them to bed, worn out with a scarcely realized and little comprehended sorrow, set Millie to watch over them and went downstairs. The neighbors had gone, each to his lighted home. David was sitting in his office looking blankly at the familiar walls. Millie had cleared the dining table of the abundant supper which had been served to all who came, and Mary went into the kitchen alone. After a time she brought coffee and some thin bread and butter sandwiches to David. She said, setting the tray down on the desk, "You must eat something, Dr. David."

He nodded, and put out his hand for the cup. Black, unsugared, strong, the coffee was heartening. He drank it, and ate the sandwiches. He was, he discovered suddenly, ravenously hungry. But at supper he could not have eaten.

He was thinking of Adeline, but more of the children. Anna and Matthew were very young, they would adjust themselves. Betty's grief was deep and dutiful, but she, too, would adjust herself. He was more troubled about his older son. Graham had been Adeline's favorite, he had been closer to her than the others. They had quarreled bitterly and been peculiarly at odds with each other, but beneath the nervous tension which stretched like a fine, thin, singing wire between mother and son there had been a profound affection. Graham had said, when David told him of his mother's death, "But—but I thought you were the best doctor in the world!"

"No, Graham, I am not. But even if I had been I could not have saved your mother. Everything possible was done for her, my boy."

Graham, before tears overtook him, had muttered, "Then I

don't want to be a doctor—if you can't—she never wanted me to be—"

David thought, sitting at his desk, I left the children pretty much to Adeline. Now, what? Mother and father in one. No easy task . . .

Mary spoke gently, at his elbow. "If you no longer need me . . . ?"

He said, "Run along," without turning. "Harry driving you home? That's right. Thanks, Mary, you've been a great help to us all."

She went out softly, her eyes stinging, and left him alone. He sat there without moving. The important thing, the thing which hurt him most was that he could not grieve more, in honesty. He could not put his head down on his arms, and weep, solitary and without shame. He was compelled to sit there and think of the practical things, of the children's future, of certain conventions . . .

Millie was too young, she could not stay alone in the house with him; he must find an older woman to look after his comfort and the children. It was fantastic, but so it was and nothing could change it.

Betty came down the stairs. She wore slippers on her bare slender feet but she was shivering in the flimsy protection of her white nightgown. She murmured, "I couldn't sleep," and David held out his arms to her. "You'll catch cold," he warned her, without reproach. He put out his hand and took his old office coat from the back of the chair and wrapped it around the child. She was tall and slender with the awkward grace of her adolescence. He held her quietly, while she sobbed against his shoulder. He thought of the day of her birth and of all that the intervening years had brought them all. Betty stirred and spoke sleepily. "Did you hear from Aunt Anna?" she asked.

The cable replying to his message lay on the desk. He answered, "Yes, she cabled us, Betty, she sent her dear love to us all—"

Betty said drowsily:

"I wish Aunt Anna would come and live with us now."

David held his breath. The child's eyelids closed, and she slept, suddenly and deeply as young people sleep. After a long time he rose carefully from the old chair and carried her up the stairs and put her in her small, narrow bed, and drew the covers over her. The windows were open. He stood at them a moment, marking that the snow had ceased to fall and that the sky was brilliant with stars.

He went downstairs and put out the lights and came up once more in the dark and to his room. It had been restored to its old appearance, Adeline's trinkets and silver brushes and cut glass bottles stoppered in silver were on the bureau. The pictures were back on the walls. Everything was as it had been.

David went to bed. There was a long period during which he did not sleep, thinking back, searching his mind and heart. In neither dwelt any passionate profundity of grief, raw and bleeding, from spirit and body, leaving each incomplete in its separate way he knew, and humbly. Yet there was sorrow. The woman he had loved and with whom he had lived for the better part of twenty years had died and with her something of himself had also died, something which had belonged exclusively to her, and to her time, and which no lessening of love and no failure of desire had killed, something which could perish only with her; and had so perished.

Sleeping fitfully, he woke twice to speak her name and to put out his hand, encountering emptiness, and to remember. Sleeping or waking, it was a night of vigil from which he must rise to face the empty sense of loss and strangeness, a new day and a quite different life.

In the morning Betty was in her mother's place at the table, and Graham looked at her resentfully. The twins ate cheerfully and with good appetites. They had loved their mother, they would miss her, they had scalded their bright eyes with tears, but they were hungry and Millie's hot biscuits were fragrant and fresh. They were, after all, charming young savages, eleven years old, and death was to them a name and a strangeness which would increase and then lessen. Meantime the sun shone, they were hungry, they had been for a little while the center of attention, and they need not for a short space go back to school, which they detested.

David had wanted them to return at once, but Ethel Gates had advised against it. She had done bitter battle for mourning but there David had overridden her. "What will people say?" she demanded, aghast. "I don't care what they say," he retorted, "I won't have those youngsters going around in black . . . it would be too depressing for them, it isn't natural or right." But on the matter of school he had finally given in. "Do you want people to feel that the children lack respect for their poor dear mother?" she asked him, her prominent eyes snapping. After all, she had been Adeline Condit's closest friend in the village and as such had some rights.

So Anna and Matthew were withdrawn for a week from the school in the town and Graham and Betty, who were attending high school in Carthage, were kept at home also.

After breakfast, which was interrupted by Betty's leaving the table, setting down the coffeepot with a shaking hand and running from the room, David went out to talk to Millie. Millie was resigned, she had expected dismissal, but she was to be married to the blacksmith's son and the loss of her position did not bother her overmuch. She knew just the woman, she declared, who would come in and take things over. Mrs. Carter, from over near Wilna, a widow of over fifty, respectable, hard-working, fond of children, clean, and a good cook. She'd already spoken to her, said Millie.

As he returned to his office the telephone spoke shrilly. It was a comparatively new part of their daily life, and Millie was still frightened out of her wits by it. It hung on the wall, a solid square box, and made unexpected noises. David unhooked the receiver. Somebody was calling him. "I thought," shouted the man, over the buzzing wire, "If you'd step over . . . ? or—if you'd rather not, I'll send to Carthage."

"I'll be there in twenty minutes," David promised him. He sensed, hanging up the receiver, that the husband of his patient seemed almost shocked at his alacrity to obey a summons.

He went out on the kitchen porch in the cold, bright air and called to Harry to bring the horse and buggy around. There had not been much snow, he would experience no difficulty.

Life went on.

The seasons swung, the hills were green and the apple trees bloomed with a rosy snow in the orchards. The children were like colts with the return of life to the earth. Betty was tremulous with excitement. Any day might bring another letter from Alex Gates, and summer vacation was not far off. The twins and Graham under the rather carefree guidance of the capable Mrs. Carter were thriving, coming in from school or during holidays to eat large slices of fresh baked bread and brown sugar in the kitchen and listen to the housekeeper's entrancing tales of her youth, of the peddler with his red cart and his pins and needles, pots and pans, with whom she had eloped from her parents' farm, of the itinerant shoemaker who came to the house and made shoes while you waited. If he didn't come, you went barefoot . . .

In the early summer Anna Gregory and her husband returned to America. She had written David, following her cable. She had written with grief and sincerity. Reading her letter, he put aside the thought that she had forgotten the years between, remembering only the small girl with whom she had grown up and whom she loved. He pushed the thought from him because there was in it a certain amount of resentment, wholly selfish. Why should he resent it that Anna wrote gravely and sorrowfully of the death of a woman who had been as a loved younger sister to her, and ignored certain other ties between them? How else could she write?

He did not hear from her again for a long time. Then in the spring she wrote that she was coming home and leaving her boy with his grandmother in England as the trip would be brief. "John has decided to retire," she wrote, "and we have bought a pleasant place in Surrey. We will not be in New York very long, just long enough for John to settle his affairs. I doubt if we come back again, David . . . I wish you would come down and see us while we are there, as it will be impossible for John to get away long enough to pay you a visit. I want to see you so much; and the children, if it can be arranged."

He would not go, he thought, putting the letter aside. What was the use? He had said good-by to her once and with a finality from which there was no departure, and—

But he spoke injudiciously to Betty, and Betty was round-eyed with pleading. "You'll go, won't you," she begged him, "and take us? We've never been in New York, that is, I was a baby when you brought me home from China and the other children," Betty reminded him reproachfully, "haven't been any farther than Watertown in all their lives!"

He said, "We'll see, Betty, I can't promise."

Anna wrote again before she sailed. "I am counting on seeing you, David . . . and so is John. We've taken rooms at the Waldorf, and want you and the children to be our guests for as long as you can stay," she said.

In the end, he went. He might have known he would, he thought, as he sat in the train and watched the speechless excitement of the children, their noses against the grubby panes. Anna was car sick and Matthew was cross, but Betty managed them with a deftness and understanding beyond her years. She was only sixteen but she had matured definitely during the last few months. Graham, assuming a boredom and dignity very amusing to his father, was not above wishing himself in the cab with the engineer.

New York had changed very much, thought David, ushering his small fry into a snarling motor cab at the depot. He had not been in the city for several years and the taxicabs, imported from Paris, which had created such a sensation some years before, were now accepted as part of the daily life of the New Yorker. The traffic was heavier than he remembered it, the lights dazzling and to the children supremely fascinating. They went direct to the hotel where the Gregorys waited to receive them.

The great hotel, just at the dinner hour, was to the children an authentic glimpse of fairyland. Women in bright, soft frocks, with light wraps about their shoulders, men in high hats and evening clothes, the sound of music playing, the scent of food and flowers. Matthew said, "It must be just like heaven," as, a little frightened, he found himself in an elevator for the first time. But Graham, his nose in the air, said sharply, "You're silly, Mat, it's just a hotel," but Graham's eyes were bright. He thought, sometime I'll live in a place just like this, see if I don't.

Betty, who had seen several girls of approximately her own age, was silent. Perhaps she shouldn't have let Mrs. Carter supervise her clothes for the visit, perhaps she might have persuaded the dressmaker to follow the patterns in the magazines. . . .

David thought only, I shouldn't have come.

He knocked on the door of the Gregory suite. Anna said, opening it, "I've been watching the clock—your train was late, David."

As simple as that. Yet not so simple. She had not changed, save to grow somewhat heavier. It became her, as did her gray hair. Her husband was standing behind her, smiling. He was a substantial man, with a pleasant dignity. He had honest eyes and a good determined mouth. He shook David's hand, was charming with the children, putting them instantly at ease.

"We've ordered dinner up here," he said, "we thought the little people would be tired from the trip."

Anna showed them the rooms she had taken for them, a big one for David and Graham, an even bigger one for Betty and the twins. A bath connected them. "Do you think they'll be all right?" she asked David anxiously, "I thought they'd rather be together. I've a young woman coming in the morning to take charge of them all, and look after them for you. She helped me with David the last time we were over. She is very capable. She will take them to the Park and the Eden Musée and amuse them generally. That will give you freedom, David, if you want to visit the hospitals, call on people. John is occupied all day . . . but we thought while you were here we could go perhaps to a concert or two, take a motor car drive perhaps . . . The Wrights are coming over Thursday to be with us—"

David said, looking at her across the big room, "That's very kind of you, Anna . . . I hadn't planned to be away so long. I can't, really, afford the time. I arranged to have my practice

looked after while I was away but I had expected a few days at
the most—"

She stood quite straight, with her hands at her side. She said,
after a moment, "I see . . . But, I had hoped . . . you see, it's
been a long time, David, and I don't think I'll be back again . . ."

She wore a dark velvet dress, with a little train. She had pearls
in her ears and on the front of her frock she had pinned a miniature set in pearls and diamonds. David moved across to stand beside her. He asked, "Is that your boy?"

"Yes," she said, "that's David."

A nice youngster, thought David, looking at the painted ivory,
not much like Anna; more like Gregory . . .

Anna said, as they stood there close, without speaking, "I—I
think John would like me to order dinner; that must be the
waiter, at the door now . . ."

Leaving the room she said, turning, "Ah, stay, David—"

He stayed, nearly a week. The children were beside themselves
with delight. The companion Anna had engaged for them proved
to be a pleasant girl, with a lively sense of fun and excellent discipline. She came after breakfast and stayed until after supper,
which they ate upstairs in the living room or, as a rare treat, down
in the big dining room. She took them driving and sightseeing, to
the Aquarium, the Zoo, the Statue of Liberty, and they loved every
minute of it. And she took them shopping also, as Anna bade her.
When David protested, Anna said gayly, "But there's so little I
can do for them, David, so far away."

Betty had her first real party frock, Graham a new suit, Anna
and Matthew were provided for, lavishly. David hated it. Gregory's money, spent on his children. Yet he couldn't hate Gregory.
Gregory was likable, one respected him immediately. And that
he was a good husband would have been apparent to the most
impersonal and indifferent eyes. David's eyes were neither.

The Wrights came over from Philadelphia to see them all.
Richard pinched Graham's ear. He asked, "So this is the young
man who is going into the banking business with me some day?"
Graham shook his head. "I'm going to be a doctor," he said stubbornly. David looked at the boy keenly. Then he'd forgotten what

he said the day of his mother's death. His son's eyes met his own with a flash of defiance. "A surgeon," he added, "the best surgeon in the world!"

"That's a large order," said Wright, laughing.

They spoke of Adeline in the subdued voices people affect on such occasions. Who would have dreamed that they would never see her again, she had seemed so gay and so well during the happy time of their visit to Natural Bridge . . .

The Wrights were in town for two days, and then returned to Philadelphia. David, during the days of his visit, went to see the men he had known at Bellevue, to various hospitals to watch operations and through charity wards. He saw many places he had known and was amazed and saddened at their change. He went to Chinatown, spruced and smartened and rather American in character and looked for his old friend with whom he had once played chess on his free hours. But the old man had returned to his forefathers long since, had ascended the Dragon and was no more, his remains doubtless having been sent back to China to bring peace and honor to his dust. . . .

David was not alone with Anna until the night before he left for home. Returning from a trip to Brooklyn where he had witnessed a long and especially interesting operation, he found the children at supper with Anna in attendance. She explained that her husband had been detained. "He will dine downtown," she declared, "and we—will dine here. Shall we have dinner upstairs instead of going to the dining room, David?"

When the children were in bed, they had their dinner. The doors were open through the suite and connecting rooms so that they might hear the least stir. The helpful young woman had gone home, for the last time. Anna said, when the waiter had left them, "John thought . . . perhaps I would like to see you alone, David, and talk a little . . . he's very good, he understands . . ."

"What do you mean?" David asked her.

She said, "After all, we've been friends for so long; and Adeline was—" She broke off. She said, pouring his coffee, "We haven't talked much of Adeline."

"There is nothing to say," he told her heavily, "other than what I wrote you, Anna. I did what I could."

"I know," she told him.

They were silent a moment. Then he asked, leaning forward, "I may not see you again, Anna, while we two live. Will you tell me something, honestly?"

The lace at her breast stirred with her quickened breathing. Her eyes were direct, looking into his, very dark under the soft braids of gray hair wrapped, in her own fashion, about her shapely head. Her heavy eyebrows had not become gray. They were black, and drawn together now in a frown of concentration. She answered, "I'll try, David."

"It's just—are you happy?" he asked her, "really happy, Anna?"

She smiled faintly and regarded him. She put her hand up and touched the miniature among the laces at her throat. She said, "I am happy, David. Or, shall we say contented? Or, is it the same? I have my boy, I have John. He is very good to me, my dear."

David said, "I had not meant to speak of this. I made up my mind not to speak of it—I have reproached myself, very bitterly . . . for over five years. If—if I caused you to sacrifice yourself . . . I would never be easy—or happy—"

She said, the color bright in her cheeks, "All this time you've thought that . . . ? My poor David . . . !" She looked at him unsmilingly. "Perhaps," she said, low, "it was . . . at first—a sacrifice. Perhaps I just thought so . . . I had wounds . . . they bled, rather freely, for a time . . . It wasn't easy . . . But after a while . . . No, David, I'm happy, contented, call it what you will. It was the better way, after all. If it had been anybody else but John it wouldn't have been . . . But it was John, thank God," she added.

He despised himself for the stab of pain which took him, and straightened his mouth to a set line and hid his eyes from hers, quickly . . . not perhaps quickly enough, for she caught her breath in something very like a sigh. He had never wished Adeline dead; nor had she; but if he thought . . . had she waited . . . ? and if she thought . . . had I waited . . . ? they would have been less than human.

Neither spoke their thoughts.

"David," she said anxiously, "I've been so troubled about you—alone . . ."

He assured her gravely, "I'm not really alone, Anna . . . Does it seem disloyal of me to say not much more alone than for some time? I suppose it does. There's my work, not the work I wanted most perhaps, but it suffices; and the children. I'll muddle through for them, somehow, and perhaps I'll be given the wisdom to see that they get through without muddling. I don't know. There isn't much you can do for them, is there, aside from food for their bodies and a shelter for their heads and the best education you can afford? Not much, except telling them certain rules . . . you wouldn't turn a child out on city streets without cautioning him to watch the crossings. Yes, that's all you can do, Anna, look after their bodies, direct their minds as much as possible, which isn't very much, give them certain warnings and set certain standards . . . And make them feel that you're always there, so that they can come to you . . . if you're lucky enough to have their confidence. I don't worry much about Betty, she's a good little thing, still overconscientious, and emotional. I don't worry at all about Matthew. He has something sturdy in him, something undefeated. Graham's going to be a problem and Anna troubles me at times. But I'll do the best I can," he said, as if he made her—or someone—a promise.

"I know you will," she said.

Gregory came in. "Finished your dinner?" he asked, disposing of his hat and stick. "Fresh coffee there, Anna? Good. I'll have a cup with you." He smiled at David and at his wife. The eyes she raised to his own were clear. David thought, watching, he loves her very much. I think she loves him.

It was all right then, or right enough at any rate. He had seen her, and she was happy. He had seen her, gentle and serene, with her own especial fund of strength, sheltered, cared for, and still beautiful. He could go back undisturbed by any questioning thoughts of her life with Gregory. She was taken care of, she would be safe, always. And if his pulse had been shaken, holding her hand in his again, watching her move with grace and dignity across the room, that was because the pulse forgets last of all, if it has been denied. It was madness to remind yourself that —had she waited . . .

He thought, saying good-by to her on the following day, surprising the bright withheld tears in her dark eyes, as she bent to kiss the children, as she reached up, quite simply to kiss his cheek, I'll always love her I suppose . . . in a way . . .

When he had gone, the children with him, and John Gregory and his wife left the station to which they had taken their guests and were driven back to the hotel, Gregory laid his hand over his wife's. "Is everything all right, Anna?" he asked with a restrained anxiety.

He guessed; ever since he married Anna Graham he had known where her heart had severed a long allegiance, for if she had not brought him passionate love she had brought him a passionate and enduring honesty. She said, holding his hand tightly in hers, "It's all right, John, of course, you must know that. Only I am so sorry for David sometimes . . . I can't tell you why, I hardly know myself . . . it's as if he'd never found himself, as if he were always being pulled to pieces . . . John, how soon can we get away, and go home? . . . I'm so lonely for my baby."

CHAPTER IX

IN THE summer of 1911 Mary Dexter and a grave, attractive young man who was employed in the bank at Carthage, sat on the porch of the Dexter house, talking. It was early evening, and the dusk was golden and green and Mary's small garden breathed out the exquisite odors of nicotiana, heliotrope and roses.

Mary had gone to high school with Henry Turner, but although she remembered him from those days, he did not recall her, a shabby, intense child who had sometimes watched him playing football, an ancient and respected senior, president of his class and son of one of the best known men in the town. It distressed Henry Turner now that he could not remember that vanished Mary, he resented that there should have been any time in his life when he had not been aware of her, for he had been very much in love with her for over a year, since, in fact, the day he had gone to call upon a friend of his father's who was ill, and had found Mary in charge, trim in her uniform, sparing of her pleasant smile, but friendly.

Since that time he had seen her often, and drove several times a month to Natural Bridge, staying with relatives there, in order to have an evening with her, if she were free; and to ask her, during the last six months, to marry him.

He had asked her again, this evening. He argued with her that there was no reason why she couldn't, she had often said that she liked him . . . Given to understatements, as Mary was, could not "liking" be construed as something warmer and deeper? Absurd to argue that her mother needed her. Since the married daughter had come home to live, and her husband had taken over the farm, Mrs. Dexter had far less to do, could take things easy. The other boys were working, there was not the pressing urgency of the money Mary earned. As his wife Mary would never have to lift her hand again. He was not dependent on his salary at the bank. He had a comfortable amount of money, and a pleasant old house, the homestead which had belonged to the Lewis family at one time.

He was still arguing with her when David Condit drove into the yard. Mary's brother-in-law came out from the back of the house, and David called, "Can't stay a minute . . . I just want to speak to Mary," and climbed out to hitch the horse and come toward the porch. Mary watched him walk through the golden twilight. He had changed, she thought, since Adeline's death, yet in such an intangible way she could not put her finger on it. It was as if he had suddenly—or was it slowly?—become resigned . . . to something. She did not know what. His stormy encounters with those of the village board who could not see with his eyes, who blocked the changes he considered progress, were as sharp and aggressive as ever. He fought as hard for a case, or for the cause of a friend. But something had gone out of him, something young and forward-looking, a restlessness, a rebellion. When they were together, which was often, he spoke less of China, of the past, and less of the future. He appeared to live, and without complaining, from day to day. Mary believed that Adeline's death had accomplished this, and was sorry. She could not know that another chapter had closed, and that in seeing Anna Gregory for the last time he had said good-by to something passionate and sad which belonged to his maturity, just as in bidding farewell to Adeline, much of his youth had gone. Not that he had ever dreamed of some immeasurably lovely and unhoped-for union with Anna. But Anna, content in her marriage, identified with her husband's interests and with her child, had shut a door in his heart. Beyond that door he would not look again. The dust of the years would drift and collect and lie like a soft gray pall, the hinges would grow rusty, and there would come a time when he would no longer be able to open it, even if he would.

"Thought you might like to make rounds with me," David said, greeting Mary and her guest, "but I see you've company. . . . How are you, Henry?"

"Need me, Dr. David?" Mary asked him.

"No, I don't need you. Just thought, as it was a pleasant evening—" He sat down on the step, his voice trailed off, he took a deep breath. "Lovely here," he murmured, "quiet—what smells so sweet, Mary?"

"The garden," she replied. She turned over her hands and exhibited several calluses on the palms, with considerable pride. "See those?" she asked, laughing. "I'm not as good with rakes and shovels and hoes as I thought. And I have to carry the water. I've asked Jack to pipe it out for me and maybe he'll get around to it some time."

"Heard from Harry lately?" asked David idly.

Harry had given up his position as the Condit factotum and had gone to seek his fortune in Syracuse. Another youngster had groomed the doctor's horses and cut the grass in the yard for the past year.

Mary answered, smiling, "Oh, yes, he's making out all right, I'm glad to say."

Turner cleared his throat. He wanted to know what David thought of the Standard Oil case and the new currency system plan which President Taft had endorsed and which Representative Lindbergh had attacked before Congress. David shook his head. "I leave those things to bankers like yourself, Henry, and my friend Richard Wright, who is growing old and fat and addled worrying over money—but it's his job to worry."

"Do you mean *the* Wright," asked Turner, a little awed, "of Philadelphia and New York?"

"The same," David told him, "but as to 'the' Wright . . . !" He laughed a little. "Funny," he added slowly, "to see your old friends step out and become important. They are never more important to you than they always were . . . a different sort of importance. I was in college with Dick."

Presently he rose. "I must be getting along. I've some people to see. Jenny Howell has had one of her attacks again, saw her earlier in the day. May have a case for you to-morrow, can't tell. Well, I'll be going, I have to get back home. I left Betty crying over some sentimental novel or other and powdering her nose because Alex was coming to call." He sighed, and then laughed. "Beats all," he said, "the way they grow up, can't get used to it somehow. Graham's beginning to talk already about 'when I'm a Yale man.'"

Mary and Turner rose and walked to the buggy with him. Turner asked, his hand on the wheel, "When are you going to get yourself a car, Doc?" and David grinned. "Some day," he promised, "when I've got the youngsters through school. Meantime, this rig suits me well enough. Doesn't go very fast, but gets there just the same, doesn't need gas, runs on water and a little hay." He ran his hand caressingly over the arched neck of the old horse, satin to the touch. "Don't have to change tires, either," he said, climbing in, "and that's some comfort."

"We're thinking of buying a car," Turner told him, "that is, I'm trying to persuade my mother to it."

"You'll have to come over and take Betty riding," David assured him. "Alex Gates is completely loony on the subject . . . He's decided that he won't be a lawyer after all, he'll be an automobile manufacturer or something. His father is nearly distracted with him."

He said good evening and drove off, turned out and down the road. Mary and Turner walked slowly back to the house. Turner remarked carelessly, "Doc Condit's getting pretty old and set in his ways . . ."

"Old!" said Mary indignantly. "He's not old—he can't be more than forty-seven."

Henry Turner was in his early thirties. He shrugged adequately broad shoulders. "Nevertheless, he's pretty much of a stick-in-the-mud. Can't blame him, year in and year out in this place. He's clever, too," he went on, "I've heard people talk about him although, of course, we have Madison, ourselves, or Woodruff in Watertown. Can't understand why a man with Condit's education would want to mew himself up in a place like this."

"Someone has to," Mary reminded him.

"I suppose so. My mother said last time she met him that he was getting more and more like old Mat Brent . . . Not in medicine, I suppose, for I've heard my father tell how Doc Brent used to take a penknife out of his pocket and wipe it on his pants' leg and lance a boil with it," said Turner, laughing.

Mary laughed with him; then she said soberly, "But at that he didn't lose many cases."

"Dumb luck," Turner decided. "Let's sit down here—it's growing dark, isn't it?"

"Not luck, perhaps," Mary told him thoughtfully. "I think because people trusted him, looked to him, didn't worry or inquire—" She broke off, thinking of Mat Brent, who had brought her and all her brothers and sisters into the world; and of the first time she had seen David Condit. Her long-fingered, competent hand went up and fingered a fine silver chain she wore about her throat. It was a nervous habit, one she hadn't realized had grown upon her.

"But Condit," said Turner idly, "he's a queer old duck just the same. . . . Told him once he should come over and have a look at the old house, it's been changed some since father bought it, you know. And he said, 'No, thanks, I'd rather not. I've driven past it times without number since I came back here to live, but somehow I have the notion I'd rather remember it as it used to be.' That's his trouble, I guess . . . wanting to remember things as they used to be. But never mind him now, Mary, when are you going to get over being so stubborn and tell me you'll marry me?"

He leaned closer to her. She could see the square outline of his smooth-shaven jaw, his pleasant brown eyes. A likable young man, Henry Turner, substantial, well thought of in his circle, hard-working, progressive. Since his father's death he had neither squandered nor lost his inheritance. His mother was a delightful elderly woman, completely surrendered to her son's wishes, living a pleasant life, full of small things and small excitements, in the old Lewis house.

Now Henry took Mary's hand from her throat and held it in his own. He asked, "What's on the end of that chain . . . a locket . . . someone's picture in it—someone you knew in New York?"

"No," answered Mary. She colored so faintly that he could not see it in the gathering dusk. "No—"

"If you marry me, you'll have gold chains," he pledged, as seriously as a child playing London Bridge, "and a diamond ring—"

"I don't care about gold chains and diamond rings," she told him, laughing; "are you trying to bribe me, Henry?"

"No, I'm not. I'm just being clumsy and trying to tell you how much I love you. You must care for me, Mary—a little? You let me kiss you, last time—"

Mary said honestly, "I wanted you to kiss me, Henry—I liked it."

His arm went about her. There was no one within sight. They could hear a clatter of dishes from the kitchen and a thump which was Jack pulling off his boots, and a snatch of melody which was Jack's wife, Estelle, singing. Electricity had not traveled down this road. The lamp on the center table in the parlor had a brave red shade of china, painted with flowers. It cast a rosy glow on the drawn curtains.

"If you liked it," said Henry, low, "if you wanted me to, why then . . . ?" He kissed her, held her close, kissed her again. Her mouth was cool and sweet under his own. She made no attempt to release herself. He asked, after a minute, boyishly puzzled and disappointed, "Why don't you kiss me back, Mary?"

She shook her head and drew away slightly. She didn't know. She did not know why it was pleasant to be made much of, to be embraced, and yet not desire to embrace in her turn. Henry said, as she drew a little away from him, "I can't understand you —leading me on like this—making me think—"

She interrupted. "I haven't meant to, Henry. I've—I've liked having you with me, and I've wanted to love you." Her voice broke a little.

"Is there anyone else?" he asked instantly. "It isn't like you, Mary, to let me kiss you and then . . . You're not like a lot of girls around here."

She said, "There isn't anyone else, of course. Please, Henry . . . no, not again . . . I've been very foolish, I haven't meant

to hurt you, I thought perhaps if I let you kiss me, I'd know.
I should have known better. After all, I'm not a child, I'm
nearly thirty years old, an old maid," she told him, trying to
laugh.

"I wouldn't be such a fool as to think it was Condit," he told
her soberly. "He's old enough to be your father—and even if
people do say—"

"What do they say?" she asked quickly.

Henry grew uncomfortable. His seniority fell from him, he
was like a squirming small boy hauled up on the carpet before
a teacher.

"Oh, nothing," he stammered, "all foolish talk, you know
what small towns are like . . ."

"Just because I do know, I'd like to hear what you've heard,"
she told him steadily, "I have a right to know—"

"It isn't anything, really. They've nothing better to do than
talk . . . you know how people are. They just said that he
helped you through training—"

"Well, he did," said Mary with spirit, "and I've told it myself, why shouldn't I? I'm not ashamed of it, I'm proud that he
thought me worth helping, worth having my chance. If it
hadn't been for him I would have grown up on this farm, ignorant and miserable and overworked, married perhaps when
I was eighteen or so and had a flock of kids and more hard
work by now."

"It isn't that," Henry assured her hastily. He had known for
some time that Mary Dexter had a nice little temper of her own,
he did not wish to run foul of it. "It's that—oh, they say that
his wife didn't like it, that she thought you—you were after
him," went on Henry, getting it out quickly, and over with as
soon as possible, "and that she asked him before she died not
to marry you."

"That's ridiculous," said Mary shortly, "very stupid and unkind. Oh," she said, lower, "I hope he hasn't heard any of this
. . . And moreover, it couldn't be true. Where did you hear it?
You've got to tell me, Henry. You can't tell this much—and not
tell me more!" She added scornfully, "As if anyone in their

right senses would believe that. There was no one with Mrs. Condit when she died except Dr. David and me."

"It came from Mrs. Gates," said Henry reluctantly, "she told someone and someone told—"

"Of course—and it wouldn't lose in the telling!"

"Someone told Cousin Helen," he went on doggedly, "that the last time she—Mrs. Gates—came to see Mrs. Condit before she—Mrs. Condit—died—they were alone and Mrs. Condit told her she was going to make the doctor promise—"

Mary was silent. She remembered the last time Mrs. Gates had been there, three days before Adeline's death. Mary had gone out and left them alone. "You look pale," Mrs. Gates had told her kindly, "why don't you go out in the yard and get some air? I'll stay for a while and call you if you're needed—"

So Mary had gone out, not however for more than fifteen minutes. Her patient could not entertain longer than that. Doctor's orders.

Henry said, "You're angry. But you made me . . . and, well if you must have it, there is talk, Mary. You go off with him so much, out into the country, to the logging camps, to the mine even . . . and you're together all hours—"

Mary said stonily, "The last time we were together 'all hours' we were together all night! He performed an operation. On a kitchen table. I boiled his instruments and scrubbed for him. I gave an anesthetic. And because the patient's condition was critical . . . he'd shot himself in the abdomen—we stayed there together, all night. And then Dr. David went away for a while, and I stayed on. I suppose we had a lot of opportunity for love-making," she ended bitterly.

"Oh, I don't believe a word of it," Henry assured her magnanimously, "I know you wouldn't look at him twice . . . but I was just telling you how people twist things. . . ."

"You've told me plenty," said Mary ungratefully, "too much. And now, if you don't mind, I'll go in and fix mother up. Her back's been bothering her, I want to give her a rub and put her to bed."

"But," argued Henry, "it's early yet . . . why, supper hasn't been over much more than an hour!"

He was aghast at the cruelty, the unreasonableness, the mendacity of women. Mary had begged him to tell her the gossip; he had told her; and now he was dismissed, and cursorily. It wasn't fair. He said so, hotly.

Mary had risen and he rose too, and stood beside her, arguing his case. "Look here, you wanted me to tell you. And isn't it enough for you that I don't believe—?"

"I don't give a damn what you believe!" cried Mary.

Henry's breath caught. He had known women who swore. They weren't the women he wanted to marry. He had heard of other women who did, one read about them in books. They belonged to a different stratum of society. He said, absurdly, sulkily, "You needn't be profane about it!"

Her anger was dissolved in laughter. "I'm sorry, Henry, I forgot you hadn't much sense of—well, say humor," she apologized.

Henry, who enjoyed a joke as well as the next man, even the sort of joke he wouldn't repeat to Mary, well, not until they were man and wife anyway, was outraged. Mary said soothingly, before he could speak, "And do run along, I promised mother, really I did."

"When will I see you again?" he asked after a minute.

"I don't know." She stood on the step above him. She had on a plain little dress, checked gingham, trimmed with rickrack braid. She put her hands in its pockets. She said, "Not for a while . . . I've been thinking . . . I hadn't meant to—lead you on, Henry. Perhaps it would be better if you didn't come any more."

He pulled her down to stand beside him, his hand closed over her wrist. "You mean," he asked, "you don't want to see me any more . . . that you won't marry me, after all?"

She shook her head. She answered, after a moment, "Yes, Henry, I guess that's just what I do mean."

"Was it because of what I told you?" he began angrily, and

then he added, "Oh, I see. If it was, that means that you and Condit, after all—"

She interrupted. "Don't be a complete fool, Henry. No, it wasn't what you told me. At least I don't think it was . . . that just made me see—a lot of things. Maybe now that my mother's all right and has people to look after her, I'll leave this fall and go back to the city. Yes, perhaps that's what I'll do."

She was no longer thinking of him. Henry said something which sounded suspiciously like "You'll be sorry," and went off down the path, to tramp up the road to the village and his Cousin Helen's house. He'd stop for a drink in the town to brace himself in order to meet Helen's bright and curious eyes. She expected him, each time he came visiting, to go home engaged. Well, he wasn't. He kicked at a loose stone in the road and swore, more fluently and picturesquely than Mary had. His mother would ask him, when he got home . . . He was a little comforted, knowing beforehand his mother's indignation. "She can't be in her right mind!" she'd tell him.

But it was cold consolation. He loved Mary. She wasn't as pretty as a dozen girls he knew, nor as witty. She didn't care about cards, or social gatherings, or dancing; not that she was very religious, it wasn't that. She was all wrapped up in her work which, privately, he thought a trifle messy. She wasn't, even, very young. But there was something about her . . .

"Oh, *hell!*" said Henry brokenly, to a green-eyed, dusty-backed toad which hopped into the road ahead of him and sat squatly, regarding him gravely.

There were other girls. He'd get over it, he told himself, but without the conviction he would muster a few months hence.

David, passing by, halted and hailed him. "Want a lift?" he cried. "I'm going back to town."

"Thanks," said Henry shortly, "I'd rather walk."

David drove on. He hadn't thought of Henry Turner since he left the Dexter farmyard. He'd been too busy. Jenny Howell was all right. Indigestion. She was set on it that it was heart. He'd been bothered about her, wondering a little himself. Easy to make a mistake in diagnosis sometimes . . . And to-morrow he supposed there'd be a new baby in the Peters' household. And if old lady Hopkins wasn't better in the morning he'd make 'em put Mary on the case.

Mary and young Turner had looked sort of—comfortable, sitting there together when he drove in. It was all over town that he was courting her. Helen Sterling, Turner's cousin, had had considerable to say about it the past few months, every time David stopped in to see how her rheumatism was getting on. "A wonderful match for Mary Dexter," she'd say, "who's never had anything in her life before." He'd been pretty sore about that, he remembered, and had told Helen just what he thought Mary had had and how lucky Turner would be to get her, "the shoe's on the other foot!" he had declared, and he remembered now how Helen's malicious eyes had twinkled, "Speaking of shoes," she'd asked in her shrill voice, "I haven't stepped on your corns, have I, David?"

What in tarnation had she meant by that anyway?

Two hours later he turned in at his own yard, and presently came up on the porch where Betty and Alex Gates were sitting. Alex had a mandolin and was yowling like a tomcat, as David mutely and unkindly observed. Alex had a year more of college. He was a very attractive young man, eager and amiable, but with strength in his handclasp and the set of his jaw. David dropped down on the step beside his daughter and put his arm around her. She had done up her hair and he wished she wouldn't. What was this fearful thing women wore in their hair nowadays? A rat, wasn't it? What a name! As if Betty didn't have hair, and to spare!

"Youngsters asleep?" asked David, yawning.

Betty made her report. Graham wasn't in bed, neither she nor Mrs. Carter had been able to persuade him to go. He was up in the attic room adjoining his own, which he had fitted up as a sort of laboratory. It was crowded with beetles, butterflies, cocoons, rocks, stamp collections, tattered books, test tubes and a few strange-smelling, apt-to-explode chemicals. Here Graham labored and sometimes did dissections until the result drove them all out of the house and his father put a temporary stop to it.

Anna and Matthew had gone protestingly to bed. Anna had given Matthew her share of the chocolate creams Alex had brought them. Matthew had been sick.

David looked at his watch in the flare of a match he set to his cigar. Alex was asking permission to smoke and produced a pipe. It was ten o'clock. David said, "Time for you to be getting home, my boy," and Alex nodded and rose. He hesitated a moment. Betty gave him a little push. She said, low, "Run along, do, leave it to me." David, hearing, his mind on other things, wondered. He rose and went into the house and up to the attic to rout Graham out. Graham was fifteen, a big boy, not easy to handle.

When the struggle was over, David came downstairs again. He looked into his office. Nobody had been there during the evening, no memorandum in Betty's or Mrs. Carter's handwriting was on the slate he had hung by the telephone.

He sat down at his desk and opened his case book. Funny how hard it was as the years went by to make yourself keep records. But he had done so. Now and then there was a case which merited more than the usual terse report. The Mittner case, for instance. He looked at his notes and expanded them in his mind. He might write it up, get it typed and send it to the medical journal. Mary would help him, she had an eye for clear, concise writing.

He thought, if she marries Turner I'll miss her, I've grown to depend on her.

Betty came in. Her high-piled hair with its unseen additions made her serious face seem very small. She had, he thought, the darkest eyes he had ever seen since his mother's had closed forever. Her fair skin was faintly, becomingly tanned. She wore, he noticed, her second-best frock, one made for the last school dance. She asked, "Are you busy, father?"

"No, my dear." Father. It had a settled sound. It was heavier and at the same time less docile somehow than the Papa of his childhood and Betty's. Things changed, even forms of address. He looked at a letter on his desk, stamped and sealed, directed to Heng-ong. Fuhchau had gone through a series of alterations, first Fuchau—as the post office still had it—and now Foochow—well, it had never been even Fuhchau to the Chinese.

Betty sat down on the sofa. It was a rather new one, spruce and smart. She had insisted upon it, the other was a sight, she had declared, disgraceful!

"What is it?" David wanted to know, smiling at her. She seemed so very mature, and what went on in back of her smooth little forehead he, for one, couldn't fathom. You couldn't expect to, could you? These lives given briefly into your care, they grew suddenly so self-contained, so self-sufficient. They loved you, but they left you very far behind. As it should be.

"It's Alex . . ."

"Well?" He was still smiling. David liked Alex Gates. He liked him as well as he did his father, a good, dependable man, better perhaps, and much better than he did Mrs. Gates . . .

"He wants me to marry him."

David regarded his daughter in amazement. No blush, no stammering, a cool statement of fact. He said, gently:

"But, Betty, you are only seventeen and a bit!"

"I shan't always be seventeen," she told him with a flash of amusement, "and of course Alex must finish college."

"But the law?" asked David uneasily; "his father's heart is set on it."

"I know," said Betty, "still, it's Alex's life, isn't it? And his heart's set against it. He'd hate it, he'd be unhappy. It would mean years more and nothing at the end of it. Not even a very good lawyer," she argued, and smiled. "I can always get the best of him in an argument."

"That hasn't much to do with his legal capabilities," David told her, smiling. Sobering, he went on, "But I didn't think it was serious . . . you're so young, Betty, so very young . . ."

"I'll be eighteen next winter," she reminded him, "and Alex thought, if we could be married next summer?"

"And then what?"

"He has a position promised," she answered eagerly, "a classmate of his, his father is in the automobile business . . . it's just what Alex wants to do."

"His people won't be happy about this, Betty," David reminded her; and he added, "I don't know that I am, altogether."

Betty rose and came over to him and sat down on his knee. She was a tall girl, well made. The bodice of her pretty, frilly dress was strained across the small, apple-round, apple-firm breasts. She put her arm about his neck. She said, as if absently, "You do need a haircut—!"

"Possibly," David agreed. "But let's not talk of that. I—I can't give you any money, Betty, or much of a wedding. I have to think of college, for the boys. And if Graham persists in studying medicine—"

"I know. You're sweet." She tightened her clasp until he protested. "Alex will come talk to you. We want to be engaged. Perhaps not now, I mean, publicly, but you and his father and mother would know . . . and then, next summer . . ."

He said, after a moment, "I have nothing against Alex, Betty, he seems to me a very fine young man. But—at your age! My dear, you've been nowhere, seen nothing, you've no experience. Marrying at eighteen . . ."

"Eighteen and a half."

"At twenty, even . . . I can't reconcile myself to it."

"But you'll let me, father?"

"And if I don't . . . ?" he asked her.

"I'll be awfully sorry, we'd both be." Her eyes filled, unexpectedly. "I'd hate it, but I'd marry Alex anyway," she ended firmly.

Times had changed. David sighed a little; he said, slowly, "I would not stand in your way, Betty. But I must talk this over with Alex and his parents . . ."

A loud wail drifted down the stairs. Betty jumped up. She cried, "Oh, dear, that's Matthew, being sick again . . . ! I begged Anna not to give him the chocolates . . ."

She flew up the stairs and David followed her, feeling at once very old and very young; old because of the cumulative wisdom his nearly fifty years had brought him; and young because Betty's generation seemed so wise, without experience.

CHAPTER X

THE Gates family, if united in sighing over the youth of the protagonists, made no opposition to the engagement. Alex's father was disconsolate because of his son's decision not to study law. He had dreamed of Alex becoming a lawyer, and perhaps one day a judge, since the boy's childhood. However, "It can't be helped," he told David philosophically, over a glass of wine in his untidy "den" at the Gates house, "and if we oppose them, they might elope and you know what people say when young folks do that!"

David nodded, knowing very well. In the autumn after Alex's return to college, with Betty mooning about the house like a lost soul and only coming to life when she had letters to read or to write, he wondered how he could talk to Betty about her approaching marriage. Girls, he supposed in this day and age, didn't remain entirely ignorant. Other children saw to that, and occasionally he questioned if it was such a bad way, after all? Shocking it might be, and crude, but, coming from one's contemporaries, one could discard much and maintain a sort of balance. He was a physician and Betty's father, yet he doubted his ability to advise her, although there had been other girls to whom he had talked, gravely and clearly. But they were not his daughters. The bond of blood between him and Betty made it doubly difficult. He wished he might ask Mary to talk to her; he knew of no one with a saner outlook. But Mary was unmarried and Betty might take it amiss, which was very silly; because, after all, the realization that Mary spoke academically and not from personal experience should make it easier!

Betty, competent to run his home, to oversee Mrs. Carter and the younger children and to adapt herself to the role of hostess for her father, seemed mature; yet she was still such a child. She grew as excited as Anna, for instance, over a parade, a Chautauqua, a circus in town, or some social meeting of the school or church. She took her Sunday school teaching with the gravity and dignity of a person twice her age, but she flew into a tempest if Graham teased her, she smacked Matthew soundly if he annoyed her, she wept bitterly over "The Rosary," she wrote poetry in the silence of the night, when she and Alex quarreled, as they did frequently, the course of their true love not running smoothly at all.

During that early autumn she spent much time in the kitchen learning to cook and bake. She had always had a light hand for the housewifely things but now she made a business of it, made scrapbooks filled with recipes from women's magazines and nearly drove Mrs. Carter distracted with her new notions and ideas. She had to fill up her time somehow. She was out of school. She was soon to be married. She sewed industriously. She wanted a hope chest. Couldn't she have this? she asked her father eagerly. "Have what?" he inquired. "The cute old chest upstairs. Come and see . . . !"

He stood by while she opened it. The Chinese clothes came forth from their wrappings. Betty had never seen them. She exclaimed and admired, she tried on this and that and laughed to see herself in the mirror, quaint and arresting. "May I have the chest?" she demanded. She had to ask twice. David was standing staring down. The scent of the garments reached out and held him. Nothing so stirs the memory as odors. The fragrance was musty yet spicy, it transported him thousands of miles and a great many years. The clouds sailed high about the dragon's-eye fruit trees, and the sails of the boats were brown against a sunset sky, and the Min ran golden blood. There were shouts in his ears, and there was speech on his lips . . . "What did you say?" Betty asked him impatiently.

"Nothing," he said. He added, "You may have the chest, Betty. Put the things out on the bed in my room, will you?"

She inquired reproachfully, "Have you had them all this time? Look, that's not too little for Mat, is it? When he comes in, I'll have to try it on him . . ."

The younger children were amused with the Chinese garments

for a day or so. Graham was scornful. "Kids' things, for silly dressing up," he commented. They made him uncomfortable. The last year of his mother's life she had talked to him a great deal about China . . . how she hated it, what it had done to her . . . "I've never been really well, since." He thought now, looking at the strange costumes in which Anna and Mat postured for his benefit, maybe she wouldn't have died, if his father had never taken her there?

He was a curious boy, and torn, as his father had been before him, if differently and at an earlier age, between two loyalties; his mother's love for him, her possessive, confiding, probing love, and his own love for his father. He could derive no comfort of the latter. It drove him to saying, to doing the wrong thing.

After a little while David and Betty put the things away in David's closet. The chest was dusted and aired and into it went the fine white handmade underwear, the nightgowns, the table and bed linen which Betty collected and laid away, in lavender sachets. Later, she would buy some silk stockings out of her allowance. Would they keep, she wondered, would they rot? She had possessed few pairs in her lifetime. She thought it would be heaven to have, say, half a dozen pairs altogether, heavy, clinging black, a little daring.

One evening in October she looked into her father's office. He was not busy, he sat tilted back in his chair and was reading the medical journal. Smoke ascended in blue wreaths about his head, which was beginning to be of the pepper-and salt variety—red pepper, silver salt. Betty, with a trivial question to ask, came in and stood beside him. David laid aside the magazine. "Sit down," he bade her, "I want to talk to you."

She sat, obediently, on the sofa and folded her hands. Her eyes danced. He looked at one and the same time portentous and awkward. But his first sentences were neither, they were grave and tender and straightforward.

Betty, listening, flushed to her eyes. But she said bravely:

"Yes—I know—I mean, I've known a long time. I mean, you needn't bother."

David said, smiling, "I want to bother. If there's anything that isn't straight in your mind? If your mother had lived this would have been her job—and—well, I'm afraid I've left you to Mrs. Carter for a long time."

Betty said surprisingly:

"There were some things . . . Aunt Anna, the time we visited her . . . she talked to me. It was all right then."

"Aunt Anna?" There was a stab, unexpected and hurting, at the thought of Anna and his child. Betty nodded. She said, "I've known, oh, you know—all the things one isn't supposed to know, since I was knee-high. Then when you talked to Graham he told me, of course. It was just that things were a little confused until I saw Aunt Anna." She added, "Not any longer. You forget, I'm eighteen, nearly." She smiled at him, almost patronizingly. "Alex says we mustn't have children for a while," she told him.

"I see," said David. He added gently, "It's your life and Alex's. I dare say he's justified. You're both very young. Yet, I'm not so sure."

After a minute he said:

"This brings your marriage pretty close. I'll be lonely, Betty, I'll miss you."

He thought, you old fool, making yourself out the martyred parent, King Lear, beard-waving! Of course I'll miss her but that won't be unendurable, we're father and daughter, but we're a generation apart.

Betty came and perched on the end of the desk. She asked, after a minute, "Is it true that Mary's going to the city?"

"To visit?" asked David. "Well, it's likely, though I don't remember her doing it before."

"No, to live." Betty looked at him, and then away. She said, "I heard it to-day—someone told me. . . . Father, is it true that you promised our mother before she died that you wouldn't—wouldn't marry Mary?"

David went a slow painful scarlet. He asked, almost with violence, "Who—who told you that?" and his eyes were so hostile and affronted that Betty shrank a little.

She answered truthfully, "Alex did."

"And where did he hear it, if you please?"

"I think," Betty almost whispered, "from his mother. . . . She said . . . she had seen . . . mother—just before she died . . . and that mother had told her then . . . she was afraid. . . ."

David answered slowly, regarding her steadily.

"With all due respect to Alex, his mother is an interfering woman. If a word of this should reach Mary Dexter!" He was fascinated by the sight of his own hand opening and shutting, as if without his volition, on the desk blotter— "If a word . . ." He broke off. Betty's eyes were brimming. He added mildly, "Well, it isn't your fault. . . . Your mother, my dear, was not completely herself before she died. She didn't know what she was saying."

Betty cried out, "Then you did promise!" And to his great amazement she added, "I wish you hadn't, oh, I wish you hadn't!"

"Please, don't be absurd, Betty. You don't know what you're talking about," David told her sharply.

"I do know. You'll be so lonely when I'm married. I've been thinking about that a lot. And the children, there should be someone to look after them. We love Mary, all of us," Betty said.

"Mary, my dear, is eighteen years younger than I. I've always thought of her as a sort of daughter—an elder sister to you all." No, he thought, that's not true, I have never thought of her that way . . . in what way then, after she came back here to live? As a comrade, I suppose, friend. . . . Fools, people who say there can't be friendships between men and women, I suppose if I were nearer her age I wouldn't think so either. . . .

"I shouldn't have said anything!" Betty, penitent, slipped off the desk and bent to kiss his cheek.

"Run off, go to bed or sit up half the night writing to that young man of yours," he told her.

"You're not mad at me?"

"No, in heaven's name, why should I be?"

But she lingered at the door. She said, "I mightn't have said anything, only people—they do talk, you know. They have."

"Come back here. What do you mean?"

"About you and Mary—"

"Oh, I see." He nodded, after a moment. "I suppose that was to be expected," he said half to himself. His face was very dark. Betty had never seen him as angry and as silent in anger. She went slowly to the door. David said, before she reached it, "Don't be stupid, I'm not glaring at you!"

So that was it! He sat there heavily, thinking. Ethel Gates! She was to be Betty's mother-in-law and he had to be decent to her. But, he thought, she'll make a mother-in-law and a half, my poor little girl! Ethel Gates and Adeline . . . he could imagine Adeline's eyes sliding around at her friend after Mary had left the room, he could hear Adeline's voice. The promise he had made her, to quiet her, if it would make things easier for her . . . the night he knew she must die . . . he had forgotten it, it had completely left his mind after the first few days.

Now it returned again, and troubled him lest Mary Dexter hear of it. Was she really leaving the village? If so, why?

He rose and left his office. He shouted upstairs to Betty, "Going out a while. Take any calls, I'll be back presently."

The yard boy was nowhere to be seen. David harnessed up and drove out. He went straight to the Dexter house. Mary was sure to be at home, he knew she had left a case not two days before. He hitched the horse and went up the steps and knocked, and Mary opened the door. Behind her he saw the lamplit confusion of the living room, sewing strewn about, a satchel half packed on the couch, the red lamp glowing.

"Come in," Mary told him, holding the door open. "Mother's gone to bed, Estelle and Jack went down the road to make a call, the children are around somewhere. What's the matter?" she asked, looking at him anxiously.

"Nothing," he told her, following her into the room and dropping into an old high-backed rocker. "Only I just heard you're planning to desert us. I couldn't believe it, but this looks like it—" He waved his hand around, at the room.

Mary said slowly, "Yes, I was going to tell you tomorrow—"

"I see." He was definitely angry at her. His voice betrayed it, as did his eyes. "It seemed queer, sort of, hearing it from someone else. Look here, how'll I get along without you?"

She said quickly, "Oh, but you will—you'll make out alone."

They were silent, briefly. It seemed to each of them, according to his separate understanding, that an epitaph had been pronounced. Mary heard it with an aching sorrow that was purely emotional and David with an astonishment of acceptance that was purely intellectual. Mary went on quickly, "There's some talk of Watertown's hiring a district nurse. It hasn't gone through yet. She wouldn't cover this territory I suppose, but it's a step in the right direction."

"Never mind that now. Why do you want to go, Mary?"

"Mother's all right," she told him, leaning back against the worn upholstery of her chair, the light on her brown hair, her gray-green eyes avoiding his own. "Estelle will look after her. They no longer need me much. Harry hopes to move on and get a better job in Rochester with the Eastman company. He's sending money home. The others help. I—I can't begin to tell you how grateful I am for all you've done, the trust you've shown in me, the experience you've given me. . . . But, I'm growing stale here, in a way. I want to go back to duty in the hospital, private cases, or a floor job, for a while. You understand that, don't you? I've lost touch."

"Yes," he agreed slowly, "I understand perfectly. I wouldn't try to hold you back." He hesitated. He must say to her, is it because of anything anyone has said—of you and me? But he could not. Her eyes were clear, she looked at him now with frankness. If she had heard nothing it wouldn't be mending matters to tell her. Perhaps this was the providential way out, for her. He thought, gossip is a disease, undermining, sapping, there's no immunity and no cure, that I can see.

He rose after a moment or so and held out his hand to her, and when she took it, he pulled her to her feet. He did not let her hand go. He stood there holding it gravely. He said, looking down from his great height, "It will do you good to get away. I'm a selfish old idiot. I hope you'll be happy, in New York. You'll write me, won't you? And you'll have to get back for Betty's wedding."

"Betty's wedding!" she repeated.

"Next summer. It isn't—what's the word?—announced yet. But it will be."

"She's only a baby!" said Mary indignantly.

"That's what we think," he told her, smiling, "but I suspect she's pretty nearly a woman. Old enough to fall in love at any rate. And Alex isn't the type of youngster she can keep dangling. There's something funny about our social—or is it biological?—system," he said half to himself, "which sees to it that young people are old enough to mate before they're old enough for the responsibilities of marriage."

Mary went with him to the door. In the little, badly lighted hall they stood close together for a moment, without speaking, as if in some way each derived comfort from that contact. David asked, "You'll let me know when you're going?" and she answered, "It won't be for a week or so, I've a lot of things to attend to." He nodded, and they stood there a little longer, still in silence. Then he jerked his head at her and said, "Well, good night, I'll be going along," and left. The door closed. She heard his footsteps on the wood boards of porch and steps, she heard him speak to someone or something, on his way through the yard, and, after a moment, the sound of horse's hoofs.

Mary went back into the house and stood by the center table in the quiet living room, and looked blindly about her. She told herself over and over again since that evening with Henry Turner, when she had decided between one breath and the next to go away, that she was going because of the gossip and the harm it might do David Condit, the pain and astonishment it might bring him if he heard it. Yet that wasn't the truth. I'm not so noble, she thought, taking herself and her sewing upstairs to her bedroom, I'd stay on regardless, just to be with him.

She was going because she was exceedingly unhappy. Whether she had always been in love with him or not she didn't know; or whether she had just grown to love him by degrees, with an emotion quite divorced from the established affection she'd always had for him. She had asked herself before this, if her feeling for him, whatever it was, had created a sort of emotional immunity. She hadn't been able to answer that. Then Henry had come along, the first of the men she'd known since her return to stir her pulse, if faintly, and to set her wondering if she hadn't been feeble-minded for years, deliberately refusing and discarding the warmth and glow, the misery and responsibility of a full life, if she had not been living vicariously for longer than she cared to count?

Wanting Henry to kiss her wasn't wanting to marry him, not by a good deal. She'd found that out. She'd asked herself angrily, what in the world's the matter with me, am I emotionally deficient? She knew that wasn't true. And the fact remained that she had not consciously thought of David Condit as a lover until Adeline Condit—

The old story of the children and the beans.

She laughed with merriment at herself, sitting on the edge of her bed, listening to her mother's quiet breathing through the open door which connected their rooms. She thought of what Henry Turner had told her, the promise David had made Adeline. She couldn't believe it, and yet, it would have been like Adeline Condit. She was afraid of me, Mary thought, with a spark of triumph, a spark quickly quenched. In the blackness which followed its brief life and death she thought bitterly, she flattered me, I guess.

Mrs. Dexter woke and spoke her name. Mary went through into her room. "I'm here," she said, bending over the bed. The older woman turned on her side. "That's all right then," she murmured, and slept.

Mary stood there waiting for something, she didn't know what, a word, a sign. Her mother would miss her greatly but she would make no complaint. Mary thought, what if I should wake her, talk to her, ask her advice? But she knew she would not. She would not know how to begin. Mrs. Dexter had borne children and had worked for them. She loved them and they her. She neither invited nor demanded their confidence. She made no attempt to counsel them. When they were small she punished them impartially, when it was necessary. She rarely praised. It was not her way. She had been all her life too harried and tired to make friends of her children. She would not have desired their friendship had she given it any thought. She wanted merely their mute affection and, in her old age, a little peace and a modicum of comfort.

Mary turned and went back to her own room. She undressed and put away her things neatly in the fashion now second nature to her and went to bed. She thought, he's had a hard life, I'll not make it any harder for him if I can help it.

She did not see him again until shortly before she left. She came up on a Sunday afternoon to say good-by to the children. Anna wept frankly and loudly, clinging to her, and Matthew sniffled, drawing his coat sleeve across his treacherous eyes and snub nose. Graham gave her a hard handshake. He was a big, handsome boy, with his mother's fair skin and hair. He said gravely, in his new, deepening voice, "When I'm a surgeon, Mary, you'll come take care of all my cases." Mary smiled up at him, as she knelt there on the floor of Anna's little bedroom and embraced the disconsolate child. "By then," she reminded him cheerfully, "I'll be so old that you'll have to get a nurse to look after me!"

Betty came in, and presently David tramped up the stairs and regarded them silently. He asked after a moment, "We'll miss her, won't we?" and they chorused that they would. Betty looked at him sidelong and then away again. Presently Mary rose to her feet.

"I'll send postcards," she volunteered.

"A cannon," asked Matthew, bloodthirsty as usual, "to shoot my soldiers?"

"If you want," she promised, smiling, "but I thought that a good officer kept his soldiers from being shot, didn't you?"

She went downstairs with David, and stopped a moment in his office, looking around it as if she might never see it again. Yet she knew it by heart. He said, standing beside her, "Come back to us, Mary, if things don't turn out the way you think they will."

He was alarmed to find her close to tears. He touched her smooth hair gently, as if she were Betty. He asked, "And what about Henry—doesn't he expect you to come back?"

"I don't think so, Dr. David," she answered, "I hope not."

After her going things were not easy. David missed her at every hand's turn; missed her on his cases, missed talking to her, missed the safety valve she had provided. He could let off steam to Mary, he could come away from welfare meetings hopping mad and take it out on her. She always listened, often in silence, or agreement, but sometimes she argued with him. It didn't matter. His mind struck bright sparks from her mind and that mattered, very much.

Winter closed down, there was an epidemic or two, he was kept occupied. Mary wrote at intervals, and a letter came from Anna. Her mother was ill, there was very little hope, it was a question of weeks, months at the most. "When she goes," Anna wrote, "I shall bring her back. She loved England, but only as a guest. She wants to come home."

Anna, to whom he had said good-by forever! Well, he wouldn't see her when she came. Or, would he not, would it not be only right that he help her if she needed him, that he be with her when her mother was laid to sleep in her own soil? But that was, of course, absurd. Gregory would be there.

Early in April Anna Gregory traveled to New York with the body of her mother. Her husband was not with her, he had been obliged to remain in England. David, to whom she had cabled, met her on a day faintly chilly but brilliant with a blue sky and sunshine like daffodils. He had made the arrangements she had asked of him, he went with her to Greenwood, his arm was about her when the last words were said and the last things done. She told him, as he went back with her to the hotel, that she would stay no longer than necessary, she must get back to her husband and her boy.

He thought, it's queer, it's as if her mother's death snapped a link between us, as if I and her mother—and Adeline, belonged to the past. Yet they had once belonged to the present also, together with John Gregory.

It was nothing she said by word or gesture. She had been grateful to him for coming. One could not have said that she clung to him, for such was not her nature. But she was glad to have him with her. It was not that there was something between them, a barrier; it was rather as if that which had existed between them, which had been a barrier, had gone. Its departure brought them no closer, but set them further apart.

He had planned to stay only until the services were over. Anna asked him if he could not stay on, and dine with her the following evening, quietly. She wanted to ask him so much, especially about Betty. "Her letters are charming; she seems terribly in love. But surely, David, she is very young . . . what in the world are you thinking of?" He admitted that what he thought did not matter. "I would like you to meet Alex, he's all right," he declared, "but as for staying . . ." He frowned. "I'd like to, but, Anna, if I do there is a friend here I must see."

"Who is it?" Anna wished to know. She was pale and clearcut in her heavy mourning, standing at the window of the living room in her suite. "Someone I know?"

It was Mary Dexter, he told her.

Anna's face lighted with pleasure. She remembered Mary very well. She had liked her, so much. Wouldn't it be possible to bring her to dinner then, tomorrow evening, if he felt he shouldn't return without seeing her?

She looked at him with an appealing affection. He thought, I might be anybody she's just fond of—curious! Yet it wasn't curious, after all. He missed in her, he decided, weighing his answer, the stormy thrilling flash of the spirit, emotional, lovely. That had gone. No, it had not gone. A moment before she had spoken of her boy, and he had seen it then, in her eyes, heard it in her voice. It was not for him; it had once been his for a long time and he had not known it. His awareness of it had been very brief. Now she had transferred it, and that was as it should be.

He'd try, he agreed presently, to get hold of Mary and bring her to the hotel.

He reached Mary at the hospital by telephone. Her voice over the humming wire was startled, and a little anxious. What was he doing in New York? Was anything wrong at home? She had not heard from her mother or anyone for several days. Everything was all right, he assured her, telling her of Anna's invitation. Mary's hesitation was slight. She said she was leaving her case that evening. She might be called again tomorrow. But, of course, she decided she would be glad to come.

David went the following evening to the address she gave him, a registry where a number of nurses lived. He waited in the staid and not very comfortable little parlor until Mary came downstairs. She looked, he thought at once, thinner. But her frock under the heavy coat was becoming and her eyes were bright. She gave him her hands, smiling. "The very last person I expected to see!" she exclaimed.

At the hotel, Mary apologized to Anna for her lack of more formal dress. "I don't go out much," she explained. Anna put her arm about her and beside her mature majesty of presence the younger woman looked very slight, very small. "You are just right," she declared. "I'm so glad to see you. Perhaps you will give me more news of David than I'm able to discover from him."

After dinner they went back to her suite. They talked as old friends talk, of the children, of the town. And when Mary left, early, David went with her. Anna said, giving Mary her hand, "Stop by on your way to bed, David. I probably won't see you in the morning, as you're leaving so early."

Out in the street, whipped by the winds which swirled dust and papers in patterns in the gutter, Mary lifted her face to the stars. "She's lovelier than I remembered her," she said.

"Yes," agreed David gravely.

On the steps of the registry he held her hand a moment. He said, "I wish I hadn't seen you, Mary. You make me impatient with my lot, I hadn't realized I missed you so much."

"You're going back tomorrow?" she asked.

"I must," he said. "Well, good-by then . . . you'll let me hear from you?"

"Of course. And you'll tell Mrs. Gregory how much I enjoyed being with her?" She was opening the door with her key. She added, over her shoulder, "And you know how nice it was—seeing you. It made me homesick."

David went back to the hotel. When he knocked at Anna's door to admit himself he found her writing at the desk. She

said, "You weren't long. Take off your things. Sit down—you've
cigars with you?"

"You wouldn't, I suppose, want to visit us before you leave,
and see the children. They would be wild with delight. I would
have brought them down except for the circumstances."

Anna said regretfully, "I can't." She added, "There are things
I must attend to here, for John. And then I'll get back as soon
as I can. David's in school now, you know, I hadn't a minute to
run up and see him before I left—"

"In school?" asked David, aghast. "Boarding school, you
mean?—at his age!"

"They send them away from one early over there," she answered. She faced him, leaning forward slightly. She asked suddenly, and in his opinion brutally, "David, why don't you marry
Mary Dexter? She'd make you very happy."

He felt helpless, as if he were the victim of a conspiracy. He
answered, "Are you out of your mind, Anna? I don't want to
marry anyone . . . let alone a girl almost twenty years my
junior!"

"She doesn't think of you as twenty years her elder; she's very
much in love with you, David."

"Anna!" He felt himself flush, the childish trick, the curse of
the red-haired. "You simply don't know what you're talking
about!"

"Oh, but I do," she disagreed. "None better. You wouldn't be
making a mistake, David, always presuming you're fond of her."

"Of course I'm fond of her," he said angrily, "who wouldn't
be? I've known her since she was six years old . . . but you—"
he looked at her with reproach—"you, of all people, Anna!"

Anna said serenely, "Perhaps that's why." She rose and came
over to the fragile love seat on which he sat, bulking large against
its delicate satin upholstery, and sat down beside him. She put her
hand on his sleeve. "David, I thought that last time . . . it was
good-by. I was glad. It wasn't; we can't arrange these things.
This time it will be. I—oh, please don't think I've believed that
after all these years you'd shut yourself out of life because of me.
If I went into life with some reluctance, for both our sakes, I've

been amply rewarded. I realize that more as the years go on. I'm very happy. I want you to be. You would be, with Mary Dexter . . . but you simply won't let yourself see it."

He said, and did not know that he spoke aloud, "Adeline disliked Mary."

"Yes," said Anna, "no doubt."

She rose and looked down at him. She said, "I had no right to say anything. Women are meddlesome, David."

"Never mind," he said and smiled at her, "not meddlesome, just matchmakers. I'll jog along somehow. I'm getting too old to change. In a rut. I couldn't take on a new responsibility, make my life over again."

"You could," she denied, "any one of us can. Haven't you learned that?"

David looked at his watch. He said, "I'll have to go now. I wish you'd come to Natural Bridge, Anna. . . ."

"No," she told him, "I can't. And I'm sailing very soon." Her eyes lighted. She went with him to the door. Standing there, she put her hands on his shoulders, reached up and kissed his cheek. "Good-by, dear David," she said.

CHAPTER XI

SHORTLY after her return to England, Anna Gregory, driving alone to the station to meet her husband and her little boy, who was returning home for a brief vacation, was thrown from her carriage and killed. The horses, new and nervous, had shied in the Surrey lane at the loud, terrifying approach of a red, shining motor car. Anna had not been able to handle them; they had run away. When the alarmed motorists, neighbors of the Gregorys', found her, Anna was dead. The shattered carriage was overturned at the side of the road; the horses stood still in their broken traces, and shivered incessantly.

This was the word that awaited Gregory as he alighted from the train, his hand in that of the small boy walking sturdily beside him, their eager eyes searching the small crowd assembled at the station. And this was the word that, by cable, reached David Condit.

Before Anna died David had believed his severance from her final. Now, staring at the sheet of paper on which he must set down empty, uncomforting words addressed to her husband, he realized that death alone is final, an end to wayward thought, the hoping against hope.

No, not final. Her son lived, in him she possessed a lien on immortality of the flesh. Others lived who loved her, and while they did so, there, too, was immortality. After they died, after there were none left to speak her name, she yet survived, as all of us must survive, the miserable and the generous in spirit, the struggling and the conquered. Else there was no sense in it. David had heard his colleagues argue, "if the practice of medicine teaches you anything, it teaches you that six feet of earth and a decent dissolution are all one can hope for." It hadn't taught him that. He had sat by a great many deathbeds and he had watched people who died sleeping and did not know they died; and those

343

who died in full consciousness; some in pain and some without pain. And, though he had battled death with the full strength of his mortal skill and knowledge, he had known, in defeat, the complete conviction that he had witnessed the release of an immortal soul. He couldn't argue it, he could produce no proofs. It was a knowledge as close to his veins as his blood, something built into him, with which he came equipped into the world.

Anna's death, the manner of it, brought shock and horror and a vast rebellion battering itself to weariness. Why? It had been so unnecessary and so peculiarly cruel. It was the manner of her passing that wrung him intolerably. Her death in her own bed he might have borne. Not this.

Yet he would bear it, he had no right not to, he thought. Suddenly he was aware that he could mourn her with no passion other than that of grief.

Betty, unconsciously sensitive to his suffering, and herself grieved beyond measure, came to ask him if she should postpone her wedding. David said, "No," with some impatience, and then at the sight of her swollen eyes, was gentle with her. "She would not want you to," he assured her, "she loved you, she wished you to be happy."

Mary wrote him, "I saw a notice of her death in a New York newspaper. It is too incredible. . . . I can't believe it. . . . I almost wish I hadn't seen her that evening, she was so kind, and so wonderfully alive."

The thought of Mary was a sore place in his brain. The last conversation he had had with Anna had concerned Mary Dexter. He thought, we wasted our time. . . .

Yet he had not, even then, expected to see her again.

Anna's death occurred in May, 1912; and in July, Betty's marriage. David, uncomfortable in the formal garments into which he had been persuaded, gave his daughter away and felt, as his only emotion at the moment, the discomfort of the high collar sawing his neck. Ethel Gates behaved as mothers do, only, he reflected grimly, more so. There was a reception for friends at his house, which Mrs. Gates had, competently, almost belligerently, arranged. Matthew ate too much, and Anna was discovered under the table after the young people had departed amid a shower of rice for Niagara Falls, befuddled and sleeping, having drunk all the dregs in the glasses of homemade wine. It was, altogether, a highly explosive occasion, David thought, helping the reproachful Mrs. Carter with his children, and feeling inclined to thrash Graham soundly for no reason other than the poor one that he, at least, had behaved himself. If Betty were at home! But she wasn't, and it was because she wasn't that all this had happened. He was almost relieved when elderly, obese Mrs. Spencer took it upon herself to have a stroke. He had warned her for years that she ate too much. He reflected grimly, not stopping to change his clothes, that Betty's wedding and Mrs. Gates' catering had at least brought him a patient.

After leaving the Spencer house he found himself reluctant to return home. The younger children, purged and purified, were doubtless asleep. Graham would be reading in bed against orders. Mrs. Carter would be worn out with the festivities. It was a hot night, too warm for easy slumber. He drove around to the parsonage, and seeing a light in the study, knocked and was admitted.

He and his clergyman, James Miller, were old friends. They were sometimes in agreement, sometimes not, but always companionable. Miller was perhaps ten years older than David, a thin, brisk man, kind, opinionated, loyal.

"Thought you'd be around," he commented when they were together in the study. "Marrying a daughter's a sorry sort of business. I've married three."

"You married mine too," said David, without enthusiasm.

"Yes, in that sense. Sit back, take off your coat. You look as trussed up as a chicken on its way to the block."

David took off his coat and vest. In his shirtsleeves he felt better. He sat back. He said, "Mind if I smoke?" and lighted a cigar without waiting for permission. His pastor eyed him mildly. "You probably smoke too much, isn't there such a thing as tobacco heart?"

"Probably, but I haven't got it. I'll live a hundred years yet," said David, "I'm as strong as an ox—"

"And as stubborn," commented Mr. Miller amiably.

"Maybe so. Just been to Spencers'. . . . Letitia's had a stroke."

"Dear me," exclaimed Mr. Miller, distressed, "is that a fact? I'm very sorry. Perhaps I should go around . . . not that Letitia and I always get on."

"Don't go, not to-night. She won't know you. She'll come out of it, though, in time," said David gloomily, "and be a nuisance to herself and everyone else. She's got a marvelous constitution, as she may find to her sorrow."

"I don't like to hear you talk like that."

"I know. I won't. I'm pretty much at odds with myself, that's all." He got up and walked about the study. He said, over his shoulder, "For two pins, I'd chuck it all up and go off somewhere, start over."

"What's got into you, David? Betty's marriage? There are the other children."

"I'd take them along," declared David.

"You can't," his friend reminded him, "they won't stand transplanting at this time. You have to see Graham through, especially. You'll be proud of him some day."

"I suppose so." David prowled back to the shabby chair and sat down again. He said abruptly, "In a little while, I'll be fifty years old. How much longer have I? Not the hundred I pledged myself a while back. Twenty perhaps. What'll I do in them?"

"Good, as you've been doing; and you'll live in your children."

"Must I?" asked David, tilting his head against the chair. His very blue eyes, still extraordinarily bright, were half closed, glinting color between the lids. "Must I? Suppose I don't want to? Suppose I've a notion to live them for myself?"

"You've heard from China again!" said Mr. Miller shrewdly.

"Yes. Heng-ong, of course. A Commission is being formed to study pneumonic plague in Manchuria. He wants me with him."

"You can't go," the clergyman told him mildly.

"Why not?" David shot upright, opened his eyes widely, glared at him. Then he sank back again against the chair and his shoulders sagged. "I guess I can't. Research puts no sons through college and medical school," he agreed dully.

Mr. Miller observed presently:

"I never told you that I wanted to be a missionary, did I? Yes . . . in Africa. China never drew me somehow. Africa did. I can't tell you how or why. . . . I was almost thirty before I heard the call to the ministry and gave up my business to study. Thirty. . . . How long have I been here, David? . . . a little longer than you, isn't it? I wouldn't have been here at all except for my mother. She made me promise not to offer myself to the mission service."

"Why?" asked David.

"Oh, she was afraid, like a great many women. She wanted me to marry, settle down, be safe. And she was dying, she was leaving me, so I promised."

"You believe in deathbed promises?" asked David. "I mean, that they should be kept?"

"I can't conceive of any other course," his friend told him, astonished.

David shook his head angrily. "I can . . . a dying man or woman—they don't see things as a whole, you know . . . they're being selfish, binding you, trading on your grief, your weakness; their own weakness. Afterward, when they see more clearly and with more than mortal eyes, surely they must regret? There must be a constant sound of weeping in heaven," he said slowly, "the weeping of self-reproach. . . ."

Mr. Miller asked, "You would break such a promise, then? I don't believe you've ever broken a promise to the living, David. Then why to the dead?"

"No," said David, "perhaps I haven't. I may have, I don't know. I might make a promise and find it impossible or unjust to keep it. Can't tell. As far as a pledge to the dead is concerned—" He stopped, abruptly. He thought, I'd forgotten!

He had forgotten. He had been arguing without personal compulsion. His friend was regarding him with something deeper than ordinary interest. David thought, so he's heard?

He considered, that's it, of course. He thinks I have been

speaking for myself. Well, he admitted to himself, rising and stretching his arms above his head, perhaps subconsciously I have.

Later, leaving the house and driving home, his thoughts were with Anna again . . . the last thing Anna had said to him, almost the last. She'd been mistaken, of course. Women were like that.

But Mary was once more in his mind and now he found he could think of her without the sensation of putting one's finger on a bruise.

With Betty gone, to spend her short honeymoon and then to travel to the Middle West to an unfamiliar city where her young husband's position waited for him, the house seemed empty and the other children uncommonly out of hand. The summer was long and intolerably hot. Toward the end of it he was called to the Dexter house. Mrs. Dexter had fallen from a stepladder. "Took a dizzy spell," Estelle explained, "putting things away on the high shelf in the closet."

She had a broken arm, fractured in two places. David reduced the fracture, and made her as comfortable as possible. Watching her stoic acceptance of pain sent him back across the years, remembering another occasion on which she had suffered without outcry. Estelle drew him aside when the opiate he had given relaxed her mother's worn face and she slept. She said hesitantly, "She doesn't want you should send for Mary."

"I shall, just the same," he informed her cheerfully; "she really does want her, you know, only she won't admit it. And Mary would never forgive us."

He went back home and put in the long distance call. Waiting an interminable time he thought, "I want her too."

It was a different sort of longing from the one he had cherished for Adeline and which he but dimly remembered, which had been young and eager and, in essence, selfish; different from the longing for Anna which he had known from the first must be denied and which had possessed the added sharpness of an acknowledged frustration, the added depth of awareness of what fulfillment could mean. It was different, it was selfish also, and it was compulsory. He had not needed Anna to tell him that Mary

Dexter would make him happy. He had known that, yet had not admitted it to himself, the day she said good-by to him in his office.

Her voice, after a long time, sounded in his ears. He said gently, trying not to frighten her, "It's David Condit. . . ."

"Mother . . ."

"Just a broken arm . . . we'll look after her until you can get off your case and come—"

"What did you say?"

He repeated it, shouting. She asked, and suddenly the connection was better and he could hear plainly, "Should I put on a substitute?"

She did not ask, "Are you telling me the truth?" She knew that he was. He replied, "No, it's not necessary. She'll do, till you come. How long will that be?"

"The end of the week," she told him.

So at the end of the week she came. Her mother scolded her weakly, "I'm all right, so much fuss about a broken arm, I told Estelle I didn't want—"

"Now that I'm here, you can't discharge me," Mary informed her gayly. She looked at her mother as if she were a beloved enemy . . . bringing her back. . . .

David came often to see them, more often than the case warranted. If they hadn't known that his bills were infrequent and never covered the amount of time he spent with them, Estelle and her husband might have been alarmed. Even Mrs. Dexter grew faintly querulous. "What in time's wrong with the man?" she demanded. "I'm up and around, ain't I, and as good as new except cutting up my meat and fixing my hair, and he can't do that for me!"

On Thanksgiving Day David and the children were asked to take dinner with the Gateses and their relatives. Alex and Betty settled, rapturously from their letters, in the West, could not come but it was plain that the Condit connection was now the Gates connection. Groaning, David went. Graham was delighted to go. He was at the age when food, plenty of it, was important. "See that you don't eat too much and disgrace us," he hissed at

Matthew, walking over, "and you," he ordered the lanky and sensitive Anna, "see that you don't go and get drunk!"

Anna burst into tears and David had his hands full. He arrived exhausted at the Gates door and resigned himself to the almost interminable four o'clock dinner, heavy and lavish, with its enormous turkeys and trimmings, its pies and cakes and vegetables, soups and side dishes.

There were Gates cousins present and to spare. The room grew steadily hotter. Gentlemen stealthily loosened their belts and ladies thought longingly of the bedrooms upstairs and the relaxing of corset strings.

After dinner the guests composed themselves in the parlor for light conversation. The host fell asleep. Three of the cousins argued politics. The children were sent out in the yard to play, sedately, if possible, and Ethel Gates drew David aside, past a beaded curtain, relic of an earlier era, and into the room where she grew her plants.

"I wanted a word with you," she said, "after all now that we're connected I feel I can speak freely."

David, stifled with food and in the oppressive air of the small conservatory, murmured something. She took it for assent. She said, "Now that Mary Dexter's back again—and a slim excuse too, her mother's only broken her arm and no one dies of that—people are beginning to talk again."

"What about?" asked David. He plucked at a rubber plant rather harshly, and Ethel winced. She went on, performing her duty as she saw it, a thoroughly good, intolerant woman, motivated by the unconscious desire to cause misery, and an authentic loyalty to her dead friend. "About you and Mary Dexter, of course. You can't be so blind that you don't know there's been a good deal of gossip, even if you are a man."

In Mrs. Gates' experience men were slow in perceiving undercurrents, it was all a part of their large, comfortable stupidity.

"No," said David, thinking, if I lose my temper? . . . but I must not lose my temper, this woman is Betty's mother-in-law, "I'm not entirely blind. I've heard rumors, from time to time.

I can imagine where they started." He looked at her sharply and her high bosom swelled with indignation.

"If you're inferring that I—" she began.

"I implied nothing," David replied with a wicked emphasis, "yet it's possible I infer a good deal!" His light, sharp tone became deeper; he added, "This is nonsense, my dear woman, not worth wasting your breath."

Ethel Gates disliked being my-dear-womaned; she disliked being caught up in a slight misusage of the language. She explained, "I don't believe it, David, Adeline—poor girl—must have had some grounds for what she told me. . . . She cried, and clung to my hands. . . ."

She dabbed at dry eyes. David regarded her with loathing. He said quietly, "Yes, I've heard that Adeline told you she intended to ask me to promise her that, after her death, I would not marry Mary Dexter."

"Oh!" said his hostess, her dramatic moment spoiled, and much taken aback. She rallied, and fixed him with a glittering eye. "I don't accuse you of planning to break your sacred promise but you've been seen far too much with the girl, now and in the past," she stated.

"There is," David said carelessly, "nothing sacred about a promise of that type."

Ethel Gates grew very red, which was alarming, as her complexion was naturally sanguine. She gasped, "Do you mean to tell me, David Condit, that you are going to marry Mary Dexter . . . after all?"

"After all what?" he inquired. "No, I'm not telling you anything. I doubt if she'd have me, in the first place."

"Doubt! She'd jump at the chance," she argued scornfully; "everyone knows that, why did she go away and train if—?"

"I think she trained because she couldn't become a qualified nurse without training," said David, amusing himself. Amusement was a little flickering flame at the core of the ice which was his anger.

He turned a little in the wicker chair which creaked under

his weight and looked musingly at a pot of begonias. He said, "This discussion is to no purpose. . . ."

"My duty to Adeline. . . ."

"Fiddlesticks," said David rudely and rose. He looked at his watch. "I'll have to get along," he said, "it's about time that I began to get the first Thanksgiving patients."

But she halted him before he reached the beaded curtain. She lowered her voice. "David, if you marry that girl people will say that you have been—she's been—that is—you've had relations for years," she ended bravely, "since before Adeline died, even."

David was white. His nostrils flared slightly and he thrust his hands abruptly into his pockets. He announced, "I'd be glad if you'd mind your own business," and everyone in the parlor heard him and started from their semi-stupor. He went through without speaking, and out to the front door. Ethel was now purple. Her husband started up from his nap and looked anxiously at her encarmined countenance and at David's back. He asked, "What's the matter?" as the door slammed. David went around in the yard and collected his children. Even the twins knew better than to question him. They were silent all the way home. On arrival their father said brusquely, "Find something to do, will you? Get out and run . . . it will do you good—"

He went to his office. Graham sauntered out on the porch and breathed the frosty air. He asked, aloud, of no one in particular, "What's the matter with the old man?" and when Matthew echoed him, turned on him harshly and boxed his ears for disrespect.

Alone in the office which was his refuge as well as that of many people who came there, David sat down, thrusting his legs out straight before him and stared at the littered pigeonholes. It was growing dark, the green-shaded light stood where he could switch it on with a jerk of his hand. He thought idly of the old lamps which Millie, and Amelia before her, had kept shining and polished for him in bygone days. He glanced at the telephone and recalled the first telephones in town, one in Hart's Hotel, one in the drug store, and how one couldn't call the other without making its connection through Carthage first.

He thought of these things, bygone and trivial, because he did not want to think of Thanksgiving dinner at the Gateses'.

He said to himself finally, that's it, of course. I was right. That's why Mary went away when she did. Well, she's not going away again if I can help it.

Sitting there, he pondered on the curious fact that in his lifetime he had loved three women, all well, all differently: Adeline, Anna, and now Mary. He was dimly astonished to realize this. Surely, when he had first fallen in love with Adeline Graham it had seemed to him that this love was eternal. Perhaps, after its fashion, within its limits, it was. Anna . . . he still loved Anna, did he not?

His father had loved a woman and married her and had had no thought of any other until he died. That had seemed natural and right to Tobias Condit's son. It was the ideal that was part of his tradition. He knew and none better of the men who loved not one but many times and, he had always presumed, in some intolerance, lightly . . . had presumed in fact that such was not love at all but the carnal compulsion masking under love's name. Now he wasn't so sure—how could he judge—he who had not kept his heart faithful to the one woman?

It had not needed gossip to point his way to Mary. He had been completely aware of her for a long time. When this awareness had reached him, he could not have said, any more than he knew when the alteration in his affection for Anna woke him to his love for her.

He was an average man, he believed, trying to find himself in this maze of remembering and uncomprehension. He was not bound solely to the flesh nor patient with the lechery of men. He had loved no woman solely for the delight and ease her body might afford him.

He shook his head impatiently, trying to clear it. He stared at a calendar and reminded himself that he must see Dr. Metzger, the new health officer appointed during the spring from Carthage, next week. There were matters he wished to discuss with him.

The children came back into the house and started the phonograph upstairs. Graham's dog, Buster Brown, a mongrel with dignity and intelligence, scratched at the office door, and Mrs. Carter came to knock a moment later and inquire about supper— if any. "Bread and milk for the children," David told her, "nothing for me."

No patients came. Evidently they would save their ailments until a later hour. He wondered vaguely how many appendices were rushed to hospitals or removed suddenly at home, after feast-day dinners. He rose, looked for his overcoat and a soft hat and left the office, calling kitchenward to Mrs. Carter, "I'm going out for a walk. Write down any messages on the slate. I won't be long."

The night was clear and cold. Frost was a delicate tracery of silver on the bushes. The stars were brilliant. David thought, walking along, perhaps it would be wise to buy a car in the spring . . . one of those Model T's. They've held up since they first came out, five years ago. They say Ford intends to sell seventy-five thousand of them this year. It's a pretty large order—

Queer, how you could think with the surface of your mind and underneath the other thoughts went on all the time.

He walked fast, setting himself a brisk pace. His blood warmed, he swung his arms and thought, I ought to do this oftener, I'm putting on fat around the waist. But I'm as sound in wind and limb as ever, can't feel old somehow. Another couple of years and I'll be fifty. Fifty . . .

He stood at the Dexter gate and looked toward the house. There was the red glow from the windows. He thought, I didn't mean to come here—or did I?

He went in, banging the gate behind him; it swung to with the sound of wood on wood, the creak of hinges. Presently he knocked and Mrs. Dexter opened the door. Her arm was still in a sling, and he asked, patting her good shoulder gently, "How goes it—not too much trouble? It's a slow process, bones knitting."

She replied that if she could ever lift her hand to her head again she would be all right. "Mary," she called down the hall, "here's the doctor." Mary appeared from the kitchen. She wore a voluminous apron, her soft hair was disheveled and her face bright from the warmth of the stove. "Had your dinner?" he wanted to know.

They'd had it and cleared away, she replied. She came toward him wiping her hands on the apron. David asked, "Busy now? Like to go for a walk? I'm trying to walk off my turkey. Come along, Mary, do you good, you don't get out enough when there's no garden to dig in—"

They heard Jack come up on the porch whistling "Everybody's Doing it Now." David went out and stood there talking until Mary came toward them in a trim tailor-made suit, just to her ankles, and a toque. "You'll be cold," said David, eyeing her, "can't you put on a coat over that outfit?"

She wouldn't be cold, she declared, the jacket was lined.

They walked down the road and presently struck off through a side lane, just wide enough for two side by side. Trees bordered their way, bare and skyward-reaching, stark under the stars. In summer their branches were laced together in an intricate green pattern, with sunshine filtering through. Mary spoke of her mother's arm, it ached so she said at night, but heat helped. David nodded, and told her presently about a curious case he had attended lately, a man from the line works. Then there was a silence. Mary broke it. "You had dinner with the Gateses?" she asked.

David said, "Yes," shortly. "Far too much. The kids came home like pouter pigeons." He added, "I can't stand that woman!"

"Mrs. Gates?" Mary laughed a little, and David added hastily, "I shouldn't have said that. It's all in the family now. However, Betty married into it, I didn't. I like Alex. He's all right, so's his father—"

Mary said practically, "Mrs. Gates isn't so bad. She's just used to running things, that's all."

"I suppose so," agreed David. Suddenly he stopped, and took her by the elbows. "Wait a minute," he said.

The stars looked down, the trees were still. They might have been quite alone in the world. Then they heard a car pass slowly on the main road, and the sound of wagon wheels. Something stirred in the underbrush, a cottontail ran by them fleetly, its heart thick with terror.

Mary asked, "Going hunting this season?"

"I suppose so. Some of the men want me to take a few days off and go up into the mountains. Maybe I shall, I don't know."

She waited, not apprehensive, wondering and subtly excited. Why had he brought her here, what did he wish to say to her?

He asked, "Look here, Mary, you—do you care for me, at all?"

Her heart gave a great sickening leap. She answered evenly, "You know I do, Dr. David."

"I mean, enough to marry me?" He stood away from her, not touching her, and went on rapidly. "Not offering you much. I'm a lot older. I've a daughter married, suppose I'll be a grandfather by this time next year, and there's the three others to give me plenty of trouble, growing up. Haven't got much either, except what I can earn and that's little enough. Have to see Graham through college; Matthew too, I expect. Not much to ask you to take. Selfish, too, thinking more of myself than of you. But I need you, that's all. I've known it a long time, Mary—"

She asked him clearly, "You'll never regret that you'll break a promise—if you marry me?"

"So you did hear about it?" he said. He was silent. Then he answered, "No, I shan't regret it. Understand me, it meant nothing at the time. I made it because Adeline was dying—anything to help her that night. It seemed pretty silly, Mary. I didn't think of you that way, at all then. You're a nurse, you've seen people die, you know the things they say—would you feel bound, if you were me?" he asked her.

She was silent a moment. Then she answered, "No, I wouldn't." She put her hands on his arms. "If you need me—"

"Wait a minute. You're not going to sacrifice yourself because an old blunderer like me needs you. It's more than that. I suppose I wouldn't need you if I didn't love you, not really. And I won't take you unless—or are you just sorry for me, Mary?"

"I've always loved you," she said. "For a long time I didn't know it. Later, I suspected it, and always I've fought it, pretty hard. See here . . ." She released her hand, pulled at the silver chain. Warm from her clean flesh, the drilled copper penny swung in the starlight. David asked, peering, "What's that?"

"The penny you gave me," she said; "a penny for my thoughts, I guess, all of them, always."

He put out his big arms and took her in them. She said, breathless, "Have you considered? People will talk . . . so many know, I suppose . . . they'll say—"

"Do you care?"

"No, David."

"It's all right, then," he told her. "Yet I'm doing you an injustice, I expect. There'll be times when it will worry me. It doesn't now."

He bent his head and laid his cold, eager mouth on her own. He said, after a while, "I'm a lucky man"; and then, practically, as if she were his child as well as his lover, "Come along now, you'll catch your death of cold in that flimsy outfit. Beats me, the vanity of women!"

CHAPTER XII

THE first year of David's marriage to Mary Dexter was, in all respects, an illuminating experience. The disparity in their ages might have prompted him to believe that he could mold her to an echo, a feminine semblance of himself, and all the more easily because of the pseudo-guardianship he had maintained over her for so many years. It was just as well that he harbored no such ambition, for he learned more about his young wife in these first twelve months than in the quarter of a century preceding them. For one thing, he had apparently committed bigamy; for, if he had certainly married the child to whom he'd once given a copper penny, the girl that child became and the mature woman who had been his working partner, he had, as certainly, married someone else, who was quite unfamiliar to him.

He had always known that Mary possessed spirit. He hadn't known that her temper was often of the hair-trigger variety. She suffered neither fools, bigots nor stupidity gladly; she was given to snap judgments; she held very decided opinions; and she possessed, to a greater degree than any woman he had known intimately, a sense of humor, or was it merely a sense of proportion?

The practical details of the arrangements for their wedding lay with him. Mary had wished to go away quietly, to another city, and there be married. David had demurred, with some heat. "You'll be married in your own home," he told her, "with all the trimmings. As simply as you please, of course, but by our friend Miller and with as many of the neighbors present as care to come."

He persuaded her, not easily, but eventually. She had not cared for herself; she had cared for his sake. She knew well enough the sort of whispering and embroidering of rumor their marriage would occasion. But she knew, as well, how stubborn David Condit could be, and so yielded, with sufficient grace and a little helpless laughter.

After the ceremony they went away, for a short time, to a camp in the Adirondacks loaned them by Watertown friends. It was winter, and it snowed; they were shut in together by a driving, white storm. When it cleared they dug themselves out, and found the sun round in the heavens, a pale yellow disk, as brittle and transparent seeming as a seashell. The branches of the deciduous trees were blinding, their nakedness sheathed in the cold glitter of ice; while the evergreens were candles burning upward in dark green flame, their roots in snow and frozen earth, their aspiring tapers lifted toward the pale, pure blue of the sky.

Near the camp there was a small, ice-bound lake. David and Mary took brooms and cleared a space of snow, and skated, holding hands, as entertained as children by the exercise, the occasional spills, the clarity of the dry air. This reminded David of something, dimly; and when, trudging back to the cabin one morning, he remembered, he put the memory from him without rancor or regret, with merely a faint sadness. No earthly experience could ever be repeated, line for line, color for color, enchantment for enchantment. There were always variations to make each different; and comparisons were fashioned from disloyalty, to those who lived and to those who lived no longer.

The night before they returned home David lay wakeful, as Mary slept. The stove was a scarlet glow in the one big room, he heard the twigs snap in the still, bitter cold, and the sliding, soft weight of snow falling from roof to ground. His wife's slender arm lay, relaxed, across his chest and he touched her hand lightly, thinking with sorrow that he had cheated her, bringing her neither the lyric wonder of his love for Adeline nor the deep magic of his unhappy passion for Anna. Yet these thoughts he put from him also, for he had already learned dimly, and was to realize with an increasing certainty, that what he had to give Mary was, at the very least, uniquely her own. And included, woven into the pattern of their long comradeship, the healthy ardor of a vital man whose senses were not blunted, but sharpened, by control, the tolerant tenderness which stemmed from his long knowledge of her, and a devout gratitude which certainly he had not experienced, in such measure, for any woman before her.

To his maturity his wife seemed very young but she had, in love, both wit and wisdom, and to love she gave the quick, unterrified response. From the first he could feel, almost tangibly, her watchful and protective devotion, warm as a cloak but less confining. It left him perfectly free.

The younger children were enormously pleased with her coming. She told them, after her return home, taking them, scraggy, healthy youngsters, in her arms, "You're still to call me Mary, you know—you'd rather, wouldn't you?" and they were enchanted by her intuition and her light, practical touch. But Graham held back for a time, dubious, markedly resentful, much as he liked her. He was now sixteen, a tall boy, broadening out, oppressively conscious of his adolescence, feeling immeasurably older and superior to the twins. He was ridiculously, almost insolently formal with his stepmother. David raged over him. "I won't stand it!" he announced some six weeks after his marriage. "I'll give that young man what for!"

Mary was brisk and decisive. "Leave him alone," she cautioned. "I'll never forgive you if you don't. He'll come out of it all right, provided you don't goad him into believing he must maintain his attitude as a matter of pride. He was closer to his mother than the others, David. He's at a difficult age and I . . . I *forbid* you to say anything to him!" she ended firmly.

"Forbid!" David regarded her in amazement. Forbid—this chit whom he'd bought with a copper penny! Then he laughed. "All right," he said meekly, pulling a long face, "you're the boss!"

She approached him, laughing, and put her arm about his shoulder. She was quick in all her movements, but not hurried; she possessed no fluttering and girlish graces, and as yet no deliberate dignity. She said, mockingly, "Poor David—you should have known better than to marry me. I'm certain to henpeck you."

He thought not, smiling a little to himself. In a sense, he found himself thinking later, women had ruled him, up to a certain point . . . his mother, Adeline, Anna, and now Mary. But there was within himself something solitary and self-contained which was untouched by any woman. This was possibly true of every man, even the most notoriously uxorious. And in his own case, those who had had the strongest influence upon him had been men . . . his father, Matthew Brent, Heng-ong. . . .

In the spring David committed an extravagance and bought a Ford. Shining and new, it created a sensation in the family. Graham forgot his aloofness to make abortive and forbidden attempts to drive it, and Matthew spent long hours swarming under and over it when it was static in the portion of the barn allotted to it. "Do you think Pop'll ever let me drive it?" he demanded of Mary, and she said, "No doubt, when you're a little older."

She was perfectly rational with the children and neither Anna nor Matthew felt any change in her relationship to them simply because she had come to live with them. Nor, after a while, did Graham. In time he forgot his resentment and was completely enslaved by her, possibly because she made no effort to enslave him. He thought that she had grown much prettier, there was more color in her clear pallor, and her gray-green eyes laughed so often. She was gay in her quiet way, and amusing and, because of her profession, perfectly intelligent along the lines which most interested him. So he fell in love with her, a little, in a shy, wholly unconscious way, and did not know why, when she told him she would have a child—"Think the house big enough for another, Graham?"—he flushed and stammered his answer, and, escaping to his attic room, found himself close to unhappy tears.

This, too, passed and he was able to be disdainful of young Toby Condit, who, born in the fall of 1913, was a red and lusty baby with a voice like the Bull of Bashan.

There were people in the village slower to be won than Graham, and Mrs. Gates was never wholly won. From one or two quarters a veiled malice operated and Mary, sensing it, was irritated. "We haven't done anything wrong?" she argued, less saddened than angry.

"So long as we know that, why worry about people who don't matter?" David told her, not in the least troubled. His entire concern had been for Betty, for Betty alone of Adeline's children knew the legend of his promise. She had not answered his letter announcing his intention to marry Mary Dexter, but after his marriage she had written him. She said, "At first I was pretty much upset . . . not that I don't love Mary dearly, I do—but I worried somehow. I've gotten over that, I can't tell you how or why, it just suddenly seemed to me to be so absolutely right. I understand better than I would have done last year. I hope you'll both be awfully happy."

Betty's son, named for her father, was born several months before Mary's boy. David stood the inevitable comments bravely. He announced that, yes, he liked being a grandfather, but added privately to his wife, "That doesn't make you a grandmother, Mary, remember that!"

Betty, her baby and Alex were home for two weeks at the time of Tobias' birth. The old Brent house could not stretch to include them, so they stopped with the Gateses and during this visit Betty and her mother-in-law came to grips. Mrs. Gates could divorce herself from admiration of her grandson long enough to unburden herself to her daughter-in-law, but Betty, shortening her baby's long, heavily embroidered christening robe, to his grandmother's disapproval, said finally and firmly, "I'm sorry, Mother Gates, but I won't listen to criticism of my father or of Mary." She was a little frightened at her mother-in-law's reception of this ultimatum but she stood her ground and told Alex afterward, "I suppose I was awfully rude . . . but I had plenty of justification."

Alex for the first, if not the last, time was forced to make a decision between his wife and his mother. He did so, secretly alarmed, for he had always felt his mother's domination strongly. But he did not regret it. After all, he, and not his mother, was the head of his house.

The young Gates family returned West and Mary was up and around, ordering her household. Mrs. Carter no longer ruled the Condit kitchen, for she had resigned on David's marriage.

She had been in command a number of years and did not relish the thought of another woman. Mary found a strong, competent girl and set herself to train her. Tobias throve, his mother cared for him, nursed him, weaned him, saw him and the twins through whooping cough, which he took early and the older children late, and made such alterations to the house as appeared necessary to her. In addition she oversaw David's diet, his rest periods and his bills. She bought a typewriter, edited and typed the occasional articles she prevailed upon him to write. To her vast delight more than one of these found its way into medical publications. She said, in the second summer of their marriage:

"Some day you ought to write a book."

"Have you gone crazy . . . a sort of medical *Daddy Long-Legs?* . . ."

"No, not a novel. . . . By the way, Anna found an old copy of *Three Weeks* somewhere and I took it away from her, gave her something else instead. Not that I believe in forbidding things, only she's apt to be pretty emotional and she takes everything so seriously. . . . No—I mean essays, David. You always like those David Grayson writes. I mean, that sort of thing. . . . Thoughts of a country doctor—"

"Wonderful! If I set most of them down in black and white I'd be sued for libel."

"You could omit those," Mary suggested. "You know, David, you can write, barring the fact you can't spell and will mix your metaphors. You even get something into those technical articles—something human, warm—like yourself," she added seriously.

Toby howled. He was bouncing up and down in a market basket set upon the office floor. Mary had always carted him around in baskets. He wore as few garments as possible, and was sun brown. He lived, weather permitting, out of doors, in and out of the basket, which was generally occupied as well by Tabitha the cat, or one of her inevitable kittens. Mary removed these guests when it appeared necessary. Otherwise she didn't bother much.

Toby had a sleeping porch built off his parents' room. This had been Mary's suggestion when the carpenter hadn't been able to pay his doctor bills over a long period. "Take it out in trade," advised Mary practically, "we can buy the lumber." So the sleeping porch came into being.

Toby howled again. His father picked him up. "Your mother," he said, "flatters me basely. But she's pretty nice—if managing."

Less than a week later, on Sunday the twenty-eighth of June, Graham escorted the twins to evening service, feeling very superior. His father had been called on an emergency case some ten miles away and Mary had gone with him. It was a warm day, and very beautiful. There were buggies and runabouts and surreys hitched outside the church and a brave showing of automobiles. Graham put his money in the plate with all the noble sensations of the wage earner, as, following his father's example, he had taken a position in the drug store where, in addition to helping compound prescriptions under guidance, he also mixed sodas, in a white jacket, and fluttered more than one maidenly heart.

Returning home he vanished into his attic while Anna immersed herself in a novel, something that would not have been permitted in her father's generation, and Matthew went out to wait for his father's return and light a lantern over the barn door.

The car drove up and Matthew ran out to scan it for dents or mud or dust. He took care of it, groomed it as carefully as a race horse and regarded his father's rather erratic driving with a troubled eye.

"Hey, supper's almost ready," he told them.

Mary climbed out of the car, and David drove it boldly into the barn. "Some day," prophesied Matthew gloomily, when the engine was shut off and his father reappeared in the yard, "some day you're going clean through the other side of the barn."

David draped an arm about Matthew's shoulder. "What's for supper?" he inquired. "I'm as hungry as a wolf. And don't worry about my driving, Mat, I'll get there."

"Yes, but how?" inquired Matthew, "right side up?"

On Monday when the New York newspapers reached David, he learned without enthusiasm that Jack Johnson had retained his championship by a decision over Moran; with faint interest that two Mexican generals were discussing war; and with no concern that an Archduke of Austria had been murdered during a state visit to Serbia, by a schoolboy. Of more immediate importance were the doings of the Bull Moose Party and the threatened ill health of Colonel Roosevelt. He tossed the paper over to Mary, and settled to rereading a letter from Heng-ong which had reached him by the same mail. Mary, glancing at headlines, laid the paper aside and regarded him with intent, frowning face. "What is it?" she wanted to know.

He told her briefly that the Commission was well under way, that by now Heng-ong would be working, doubtless under the greatest difficulties, in Manchuria. He put the letter aside, after a time, and sat staring at the familiar furniture in their living room. Mary said nothing. She knew how for days after a letter from China reached him he would be restless, and even irritable. She understood, and made no comment. He had talked to her a good deal about China since their marriage, as well as during the years before. She sometimes felt as if she had been there with him, so well could she visualize much that he remembered.

Later, during the evening, she asked him, her thoughts returning to the papers, "Just what does all this Serbian-Austrian business mean?" and he answered, immersed in a medical journal, "Nothing much, I suppose . . . just more trouble in the Balkans. They're always stewing around over something. It needn't concern us. . . . What I wonder is, if we'll be drawn into this new mess down in Mexico?"

"Hardly, if we're sensible," answered Mary absently, wondering if she could commit the extravagance of a new linen duster. Driving along the dirt roads was fatal to dresses, she reflected. And there were many times when the buggy was indicated, for the imminent changing of a tire involved a good deal of precious time. In winter, of course, horse and sleigh was the only practical measure. She didn't suppose that automobiles would ever be adapted to country roads in the winter.

Summer wore on. The Gateses bought a new pianola and Anna went on a visit to Carthage and spent most of her time in a nickelodeon. Graham, increasingly aware of his coming importance as a Yale freshman, fell in love with a visiting girl from

Syracuse and began to wonder if, after all, a romantic elopement were not to be preferred to eight years' preparation for a career. At that rate, he decided gloomily, I'll be an old man before I can get married!

On July 28, Austria declared war on Serbia and other declarations followed one after another until, following that of Great Britain, President Wilson proclaimed the neutrality of the United States. "And a good thing too," agreed the cracker-barrel oracles at the corner grocery, "it ain't any of our business, is it?"

It was severally conceded that it was not.

Here and there in various of the villages and towns one noted the absence of a familiar face, some unimportant farm hand or cobbler or houseowner had quietly shaken the dust of the United States from his feet and departed, by circuitous and difficult, and not always successful routes, to his country. His name in such cases was a German name.

In the fall when Graham went off to Yale the Juggernaut had gathered momentum and was under way. Liège had been taken, the Austrians had entered Alsace, the British Expeditionary Force had landed in France, between the sixth and the tenth of September the Battle of the Marne was fought, and trench warfare began. The Germans were in Antwerp, the Germans took Saint-Mihiel and on the eastern front there was desperate fighting at Tannenberg and Lemberg. British and German ships were sunk and, on August 23, Tsingtau was bombarded by the Japanese. David, flinging down the paper which contained this news, lifted a drawn face to his wife. There was no end to the misery and folly and wastefulness of this war madness, he declared bitterly. Mary nodded. He said, a moment later, "If we should get into it —have you considered—Matthew and Graham?"

They wouldn't get into it, she declared stoutly. Why should they? . . . it wasn't their affair!

This war could not touch them except with the impersonal emotions of horror and pity, they thought. Yet it did touch them. They had Canadian friends, and those friends had sons, husbands, brothers. John Gregory wrote that while he was too old to serve his adopted country and his son was too young, he would of course offer himself in some civilian capacity. Richard Wright's brilliant boy, already in his third year in college, and only a little older than Betty, had left his university to volunteer in Canada.

There was a curious tensity in the atmosphere; friendships were broken as unwitnessed battles were fought over and over again, in people's living rooms, in business men's offices, outside the wide doors of churches, in peaceful back yards. Red Cross units were organized to make bandages for the soldiers and such a one was organized by Mary Condit. She said to David, coming home at night, fagged out, "I keep thinking—if they were for one of ours . . ."

Although war raged in Europe and rumors like flung stones rippled the pool of America's peace into ever-widening circles, life went on and death went on, just the same. David worked, in his usual routine, and found that he had fear to combat as well as disease. A sick woman would lose her grip on life wondering if . . . if anything would happen to us, to her, to her grown boy? And more and more such boys were crossing the border and volunteering. People who lived along the border knew more of war than those in other parts of the country, the troops marching became familiar sights to them, and the sound of feet tramping and of drums beating struck sparks and set a flame burning.

"It can't last," David said over and over again, "it must be over soon."

In the spring of 1915 Mary's second child, a girl, was born. Unlike Toby's entrance into the world, this was accomplished with danger and difficulty. Mary had fallen, tripping on a loose board on the stairs, several weeks before the baby was expected and David took her to the hospital in Watertown where Herbert Woodruff attended her.

She was very ill for some time. When she was better and able to sit up and smile at David and Woodruff and to see her baby, she mourned over the smallness and fragility of the child. "Poor scrawny little thing," she said soberly. "I'll have to do better next time."

There wouldn't be any next time, they were forced to tell her, and after Woodruff had left the room she put her hand in David's and smiled at him, although her eyes were brimming. She said, "Funny, what crocks most nurses are when it comes to this business; almost every one I've known has always had a terrible time. But, perhaps it's just as well," she added valiantly, "we've a houseful as it is, and I'd probably put you in the poorhouse, David, if I went on being prolific."

He said, "I've got you, that's all that matters, now."

In May, Mary and the baby, Lee, went home. "Lee's a boy's name," wrote Graham from New Haven, "what's the idea?" But Mary replied serenely that she'd always wanted a girl baby named Lee; and as Lee's father had no objection, Lee's brother shouldn't complain.

Toby received Lee without much enthusiasm, and tried to murder her several times out of simple curiosity, to the horror of the nurse, who returned home to care for the delicate baby until Mary herself was strong enough. Anna adopted her as a new sort of doll and Matthew was totally indifferent. The twins had been very much alarmed at Mary's illness and absence and now that she was home again they would have suffered her to bring a dozen picayune babies with her, so long as she returned to them.

Mary had been home for two weeks and the nurse had gone when she first asked David what had changed him, what was wrong? For he had changed. Perhaps it was her imagination that there were new lines in his face, that his shoulders stooped slightly. She had seen this at once, in the hospital, and had laid it to his anxiety for her and the baby. But she was home again and well, the baby would be all right, so it could not be that. One evening, sitting alone with him on the porch, feeling the security of her home and its background, her two babies sleeping, the older children's voices reaching her, the scents of flowering shrubs and vines and grass in her nostrils, she said, "David, has something happened which you haven't told me—something you've been keeping from me?"

He was glad to tell her then, it had been hard to endure alone. Heng-ong had died, in the line of his duty; few would mourn him save those who had loved him. The Commission would carry on. . . .

CHAPTER XIII

"You shouldn't have kept it from me," Mary told him, after a short silence. There was no word of comfort she might bring him, so she attempted none. David took the hand she offered and kept it in his own, deriving some unconscious consolation from the firm, living touch of her loyal flesh. He said presently, "You were so ill, Mary, and later you needed all your strength and courage to become strong again. You had to think of yourself, and not of me."

"Isn't it the same thing?" she inquired.

He leaned over to kiss her cheek in the darkness, and answered, "You're very sweet, Mary," yet he thought, it isn't, it can't be, that's what we have to learn as we go along, no amount of loving or nearness can make it so.

Mary said, "It's as if the last link which held you to China has snapped." She said it sorrowfully, grieving for him. She felt him stir beside her, lift his head. He answered:

"No, that isn't so, Mary. Not really. The bond isn't composed of the people I've known and cared for. I sometimes wonder if it was wholly due to the accident of birth. Oh, primarily, of course, there's no getting around that. I'll never go back, I suppose. I'll forget names and places, the atmosphere, the feel of things, gradually . . . as I'll forget the language. I've already forgotten a good deal. Or think I have. But it's all there, part of me, even if I can't discipline my memory to chapter and verse. I wish Heng-ong might have lived to see his work accomplished. But I can't be sorry for him, dying the way he would have wished to die. Other men will carry on, his purpose will one day be accomplished. That's the way with the men who blaze the trails, so few of them ever live to see beyond the first clearing."

He was silent, thinking, why am I sitting here, secure, protected, plodding my daily round, doing the things thousands of men could do as well or better, taking this easy and monotonous road to the grave, having made no stir while I live and destined to make none when I die, save in the hearts of those who care for me? Heng-ong was needed. I am not. He had a singleness of purpose which could not be deflected. I had it too, once, but I could be deflected because it wasn't in me to be steadfast.

He held no resentment against Adeline and her part in his desertion, nor had he for many years. Had he been other than he was, less swayed by emotion, by the unhappy faculty of seeing the other person's viewpoint, however mistaken he might think it, a dozen Adelines would not have brought him home again. Nature, he considered, without bitterness, took no concern for a man's purpose in life. His purpose, so far as she was concerned, was purely biological. Now and then it appeared to amuse her to arrange things with an almost conscious cruelty. On one and the same evening he had met Adeline and Anna. Nature had seen to it that it was Adeline who took his heart, and his senses, by storm. It probably did not suit her that a man should have any other consecration in life beyond the primal fulfillment.

Mary spoke at his side, quietly.

"You've never been completely happy since your return to America, have you, David?" she asked.

"My dear child!" He pulled the wicker chair around so that he might see her in the faint light from the living room behind them, "of course I have been. Never more so than you've made me. Have I impressed you all these years as a man with a secret sorrow? I can't imagine anything more abject or more in need of a good hearty kick where it would do the most good."

"I didn't mean that, you idiot," she told him, "I don't believe I would have fallen in love with a martyr. I'm trying to say something and I'm doing it very badly. It's this, I suppose. For so many years there was just one thing you wanted to do—you made yourself ready for it, almost from childhood. And before, you might say, you were well started, you had to give it up and turn to something quite different. At least, you think it's different. Is it, really? Isn't there need here, haven't you filled that need, haven't you justified yourself?"

David said slowly, "So that's it. I've been deluding myself all along that I was the round peg in the square hole, here. I don't know, Mary, maybe you're right. I was just thinking a little while back that a few thousand men, a hundred thousand if you like, could do the job here as well as I—or better. I suppose I didn't finish the sentence in my mind; if I had I might have been telling myself that I could do the other job better than most men. That wouldn't be true, and sounds like a bad case of swelled head. You haven't looked over the books I got from New York this spring, have you? Brill's translations of that Austrian fellow, Freud? I've seen indications that our bunch seems to be coming around to feeling that he's got hold of something pretty sound. If you apply some of his theories to me, you get a good case of a damned fool who had been doing his job pretty badly all these years because of some jackass notion that he's been frustrated . . . !"

"Here comes someone," Mary said quickly, "I heard the gate shut."

David rose and went to the steps. James Miller and his stout, pleasant wife were on the path. "Come aboard," invited David cordially; "hotter than it should be, isn't it?"

"We wondered if anyone was at home," Miller told him, "we wanted to see how Mary was getting along."

"She's as good as new," declared David. "Come up, sit down for a while. The children are either sleeping or subdued, it's been an uncommonly quiet evening."

Mrs. Miller arranged herself next to Mary and fanned herself with a palm leaf. "What do you hear from Graham?" she inquired.

"Plenty," responded Graham's father grimly, "he has a genius for getting into trouble. Oh, nothing serious," he added hastily, "just general devilment. He manages his work, however; I am afraid he is cursed with facility. Things come to him too easily."

"It's a curse I would have welcomed in my own university days," Miller told him. "Betty all right?"

"Splendid. Finest husband in the world, most perfect child, you know the general tenor," David answered, laughing.

Mary rose and slipped into the house to fetch a frosted pitcher of fruit cup from the ice box and a plate of cookies. When she returned with the tray she found her husband and their guests deep in discussion of the sinking of the *Lusitania*.

Little else had been talked of since May 7 in this or any other American town reached by newspapers and telegraph wires. Miller was saying earnestly, "It was a wanton and deliberate destruction of life—"

David said slowly, "Perhaps. I don't know. The mind halts, imagining it. Yet the passengers were warned—"

"My dear David, surely you don't take that attitude!"

"I don't take any attitude," denied David; "the whole thing has made me sick. It simply doesn't bear thinking about, from the humane point of view. But when you begin to argue ethics— war hasn't any ethics, my friend."

Miller warned, "You'll see, this is the beginning, we'll be brought in as sure as sunrise . . ."

"I hope to God we won't," said David.

Miller peered at him in the darkness, and set his glass down with a slight clatter. "You're not trying to tell me you're a pacifist!" he exclaimed.

"I hadn't put a term to it, Jim," David told him, "but, you *should* be, you know, if only by reason of your cloth."

Miller snorted. "What has that to do with it? I'm a man, and an American, and there's nothing in my creed to suggest that men should not do battle for righteousness, in His Name."

"There's 'blessed are the peacemakers,'" David reminded him mildly.

Mary said, "It's no use, Mr. Miller, you won't get a convert . . . you're not the first that's tramped up these steps since the sinking of the *Lusitania* and tried to enlist David, you know."

"I won't be the last," said Mr. Miller. "And I can't understand you, David. You've a reputation of spoiling for a fight most of the time, you know. I've seen you myself, so far as that goes."

David laughed. "Not this kind of a fight, Jim," he said.

"If we go into it, you'll sing another tune," the clergyman cautioned him, and his wife said soothingly, "Goodness, James, don't go getting yourself all worked up, it's bad for your liver!"

Even Miller joined in the little ripple of laughter, and David said, when it had subsided, "I suppose I do take an unpopular viewpoint. It's just that I don't seem able to see right or wrong in this. It's all wrong, so far as I am concerned."

"The Allies," argued Miller stubbornly, "have right on their side, they are on the side of God and the angels."

"How do you know, for certain?" David inquired. "Don't you suppose the Germans believe that too?"

"David," said his friend, "you're impossible, and you disappoint me, very much."

"Not more often than I disappoint myself," David assured him. "Look here, Jim, if we went to war to-morrow, I'd go along, in whatever capacity they'd have me. I doubt if they'd let me shoulder a gun, my job would be patching up the mess guns had made. I couldn't go to the Spanish War, although I wanted to; my father couldn't go to the Civil War, although he believed that he could be of some service. He wasn't interested in guns either, he was interested in souls. I'm interested in bodies. I can't look at this business from any other viewpoint than that of the physician. All I see is ugliness and waste, the loss to youth and to other generations. All I can see is the fine bodies shattered, death and worse, a sort of blind, destructive madness . . . the young men who won't return, the young men who will return, some in worse case than those who died. All I see is cruelty and a terrible squandering . . . It's not alone the destruction of boys and men, it's the destruction of potential life, of the sons they might have had and won't . . . ever think of that?"

Mrs. Miller was slightly shocked. She spoke brightly and hastily to Mary. "Do you think you'll be able to come to the sewing club meeting next week? We do count on you. And can't I see the baby?" she asked.

"It's about time for her ten o'clock bottle," Mary told her. "Want to come in with me?"

As the women left the porch Miller said heavily, "I don't need to warn you that if President Wilson sees fit—as I hope he will—

to enter into this because of the murder of our citizens, you'd be advised not to talk too freely about your views, David."

"No," said David, "you needn't. Yet I suppose I'll talk anyway, Jim. Here, let me fill your glass." He added, in a moment, "Peaceful here, isn't it? Quiet. Begins to feel, and smell, like summer. All over America it's like this, I suppose, in some measure. Won't be, for long, if what you want happens. There'll be few people able to sit quiet, like we're sitting . . ."

Miller said doggedly, "The world must be made safe from aggression."

"By aggression? What about those who live by the sword— perishing by it? That's sound enough. Look here, Jim, I can't believe any cause is great enough to excuse slaughter. I can't bring myself to it. History is written in blood and a fruitless sort of sacrifice. Fruitless because history always repeats itself. We don't seem to learn from one war to the next. France and Germany didn't learn, in the seventies—"

"What about the Revolution?" asked Miller triumphantly, "the American Revolution, or for that matter, the French?"

David chuckled. "That's a smart blow," he admitted. "You want me to announce that I'd rather we'd stayed a colony than struck the blow for freedom? I can't, honestly, I've never been noted for consistency. But I do maintain that, in this instance, the issue is clouded. The cause *seems* clear enough . . . Belgium . . . the protection of the rights of the small states. But is it entirely that, Jim? Aren't a good many people making money out of this war—weren't we all getting a little envious of that *Made in Germany* mark?"

"It's marked on this war too," said Miller.

"Perhaps. I don't know. We'll never know, in our time, and maybe not a hundred years hence. There doesn't seem any purpose in it, Jim, and life has to have a purpose, and a meaning. Whatever it is, it isn't war. If I came to believe that I'd no longer believe in God, I think, and I've believed in Him for fifty years."

The women came out on the porch, Mrs. Miller exclamatory. She had seen the baby, it was wonderful, how she gained, every day. Mary said, standing with her, a little apart, "I wish I could have nursed her. Still, we've found a formula that agrees with her."

When their guests had gone David, standing at the steps, stretched his arms and yawned. "I'm half asleep," he announced, "hope there'll be no night calls . . . let's go to bed."

As they went up the stairs, his arm around her, he said, "I've lost another friend to-night."

"I don't think so. It's just that people have been so edgy since the *Lusitania*. And you will speak up!" she said, laughing.

"I know. Would you rather I didn't?"

"I can't answer that," she told him; "it wouldn't be you, if you held your tongue. But it might be more comfortable."

"You're a practical little piece, Mary," he said, laughing, and thought, silently, women are funny, pretty unscrupulous when they love you—want you to make things easier for yourself rather than harder. Perhaps they're right, I don't know.

Graham, arriving home for the summer six weeks later, had startling plans. Why couldn't he join up with some ambulance unit, he demanded, or what was the matter with the Foreign Legion or the Canadian Army? There was a fight on and he wanted to get into it.

"It isn't your fight, Graham," his father reminded him.

"It's every man's fight," shouted Graham, his fair skin flushed. "You can't in decency believe anything else!"

"Can't I? At any rate I believe this. You're nineteen years old. You have completed your first year at college. You have three more years ahead of you, and your medical school and interneship, as well. During that time I am expected to support you, at a not inconsiderable sacrifice. If you go leaping off to drive an ambulance for Italy or England or any other country, you won't be back for some time—if at all," said David steadily, "and when you do come back in a year, perhaps, or even longer—who knows?—you'll expect to pick up your life where you left off. You won't be able to, of course. No one can. It isn't fair to yourself or to me, Graham."

"Oh, all right," said Graham sulkily, forced to agree. It took money to serve in the gallant adventure, as an outsider. He added, "But if we go in, you can't expect me to be a quitter!"

"I don't expect anything of you," said his father, "except a little common sense, and it looks as if I'm overoptimistic there. I believe, however, that you will best serve your country, although without medals and parades, if you finish your studies and enter with merit into the profession you have selected."

"He's an old man," Graham afterwards confided to Mary, "he doesn't understand, he couldn't, not possibly. There's no sense of adventure left in him, he's just rooted."

Mary said, after a minute, "There's as much adventure for him in this everyday life of his as there is in a hundred years of war, more in some ways. He's bringing life into the world, he's saving it, whenever humanly possible, isn't he? Perhaps he doesn't see it that way any more than you do, I've only just begun to see it that way myself."

Graham went back to college, where he managed to skim through his courses and make a name for himself on the football team and the months marched along, so slowly while one lived them, so swiftly when one looked back. Matthew, through high school in the summer of 1915, had elected for an agricultural course at St. Lawrence University. He had always wanted to be a farmer. Now he was going to be one. Graham laughed at him. "A farmer!" he derided. "Coming home nights stinking with manure, and never satisfied with the weather! Farmers never are, it's always too hot or too cold, too wet or too dry!"

Matthew argued that Graham would stink of worse things than manure when he was through and that there was as much nobility in the farrowing shed as in the delivery room. David listened to the arguments, grinning. But his grin faded as he realized, not for the first time, how integrally antagonistic the brothers were. Graham was quick, very nearly brilliant, extremely egotistic and extraordinarily handsome. He had Adeline's coloring and clear-cut features, made masculine. Matthew was slower, less easily roused to anger, dogged, a big, rather awkward boy with no distinction of appearance or manner. He was in his way quite as stubborn as Graham. He had also what Graham lacked, an ally in his twin sister. Anna adored him, gave in to him at every opportunity. Graham had never been very close to any member of his family, save possibly his mother. He stood always, in a sense, alone.

In the autumn of 1916 Mary, looking about her unusually empty house, told herself, "I feel really alone with David for the first time." She caught herself up on that, frowning, examining into her own thoughts in the prying way she had, as often irritating to herself as to others. It was not that she did not love Adeline Condit's children. She did. She was loyally, if not passionately, devoted to them and she had not had to learn devotion, having always been fond of them. Of the four, Matthew and Anna were her favorites and she admitted it to herself, and to David, freely enough, although she tried not to make any parade of her preference. It wasn't in nature, certainly not in her nature, to be as fond of them as of her own engaging pair, nor did they expect her to be, she supposed, if ever they'd given the matter any thought. She had not come into the house as their father's wife until all four were well grown, and the transformation from familiar friend to stepmother had been easy enough, except in Graham's case, and that had not been hard to accomplish.

Now, she and David and their two were alone. Graham and Matthew were in college, and Anna had gone West on a long visit to Betty. She had a feeling that she was whole again, not jerked this way and that by conflicting demands which compelled her most careful consideration, her sense of justice and power of reasoning. She had to be so much more cautious in her decisions concerning another woman's children.

At Christmas they were all home again except Anna. Betty, expecting her second child, had implored her sister to remain with her, and Anna, torn between her desire to see Matthew and her instinct for sacrifice, finally agreed. After the holidays David and Mary and the two youngsters once more "rattled around in the house," as he remarked the day following the boys' return to college.

It had been an occupied holiday, with plenty to do, dances, parties, a great deal of amusement and an increasing rumor that war was a matter of a few weeks or months away. David said, looking around the breakfast table, "I'm always glad to see the kids come home but darned if I'm not glad to see them go again! I wouldn't dare breathe this to anyone but you, Mary, it's heresy. But they're so young and so cocksure and they settle any problem in the twinkle of an eye. Hope Graham gets over it. If he doesn't, he'll kill more than his share of patients. The worst Mat can do is lose a few crops. By the way, where in time does he expect to get that farm? 'When I have my farm,' he says, like a lord, 'and Anna keeps house for me!' College is all I can do for him. Toby'll probably grow up a happy ignoramus. Legacies don't last forever."

"I'll be a little sorry for Mat's wife," said Mary soberly, "when he gets one. Anna will make her life miserable!"

"I'm sorry for Anna," David declared. He looked across at his youngest daughter. She was not yet two and, superbly proud of herself, sat in a dilapidated high chair and beat upon the rim of her tray with a spoon. She was a pretty baby, small and delicate seeming, yet sturdy enough to relieve her parents of their early anxiety about her.

Toby, dark and active, had succeeded in crawling out of his chair without mishap during the discussion and was eating the leg of the table with a dogged determination but some disappointment. The flavor wasn't quite what he had expected. He was something over three years old, a relentless and wayward young man. Mary rescued him, regarded his egg-decked countenance, hugged him soundly, and called Janet, the amiable maid of all work, to take him away and wash him.

David said, "These kids—make me feel young again, somehow. So little responsibility, beyond their small digestions and that sort of thing. But the others! I thought as one's children grew up one would grow up too and discover wisdom, ready made when it came to dealing with them. It's a base lie! I sometimes wonder at the careless way one undertakes the responsibility . . . I knew a lot more about child raising when the other four were Toby and Lee's age than I do now."

"I know," said Mary. She lifted her curiously-hued, clear eyes and looked at him. "It's easier for me to deal with my own, of course. I can spoil them or be unjust to them, and take the blame. With the others, it's different. You see that, don't you?"

"I do. You're a wonder, Mary," he declared, "how in blue blazes you ever persuaded yourself to marry a man with four children, heaven only knows! I don't. But I'm grateful. And so, I believe, are they."

He looked at his watch, pushed back his chair. "Have to be off," he said, "don't wait lunch for me."

He kissed her, tweeked a red-gold topknot which curled like a feather on Lee's small head and went out of the room. Janet came back with a clean, but not subdued, Toby, and presently Mary had them settled on the porch, Lee in her carriage, Toby in his play pen, bundled up like a couple of young ski-jumpers, rosy cheeked, and perfectly happy.

Since the boys had left, since Anna's departure, their step-mother had been considering something of the utmost importance to herself, to David and to their children. She had turned it over and over in her mind. There were times when she shrank from it, times when she told herself that it was too late, that it would be to no purpose; times when she thought that David would believe her insane for considering it. She went now into his office, with a duster in her hand, and looked with tolerant resignation at its disorder. She knew better than to remedy it. To dust and air and clean, so much he permitted, but no more. She took down the image of Kuan-yin and turned her in her hands. The feel of the porcelain was smooth and cold, the goddess wore a smiling face of impersonal benevolence, her hand, raised in blessing, was static . . .

On the wall was a silken scroll, red, with the happiness character—Fu—embroidered upon it. David had told her that years before. She stood considering it. Happiness, in gold, on scarlet . . .

She thought, I won't decide at once . . . possibly after Betty's baby is born? I'll have to think about it. It means so much to all of us. I can't decide all at once . . .

She generally did decide "all at once." This was new to her, this groping and examining of a purpose, this questioning.

In the early spring, she reached her decision. She was impelled to it, not by any event, but by a sentence David spoke one night in his office.

The children were asleep, the windows open to a cool wind from the mountains. April was green on the hills, and in the pastures. The first unintimidated flowers thrust up their green spears through the brown earth which still held the remembrance of winter. David, washing his hands at the little sink, spoke to her over his shoulder.

"Thanks," he said; "plucky kid, wasn't he?"

He spoke of the patient who had just left. Mary had helped him do the dressing. She nodded, standing by the window, looking out. David said, after a minute, "I had a letter from Sia Homei to-day."

She had seen the letter, with the Chinese stamp. She asked, "Had he news—?"

"Not much. He is a very old man, his writing is shaky. I don't expect he'll live long. Heng-ong's death took the tucker out of him, somehow. I think he loved him almost more than he does his own sons and grandsons."

"How old is he?" asked Mary.

"I don't know—my father's age, or thereabouts. Must be eighty or over. He says . . . if he must die without seeing me again, he goes to his grave with his eyes open . . . Poor old fellow," said David. He added, drying his hands, "He always believed I'd come back. Heng-ong didn't, you know."

He walked over to her in his shirtsleeves. She turned and looked up at him briefly. Yes, he'd grown very gray in the last year or so. There were lines about his eyes, but were they not of laughter, of concentration, of vigil? He carried himself strongly, his shoulders were broad, and when they stooped, as they did now, he realized it, and squared them.

"Want to have a little walk before we turn in?" he suggested.

"No. Wait a minute, David. . . . There's no reason now why you can't return to China, if you wish to," she said.

"No reason—" he began incredulously, but she interrupted him, speaking rapidly.

"No, none. I've been thinking about it for—oh, six months perhaps. I hadn't any right to suggest it earlier, to transplant another woman's children, to reorder their lives. But don't you see, David, they're grown up. Betty's married, the boys are in college, Anna could make her home with Betty. It would all work out. And we'd go with you, Toby and Lee and I—"

He was too astounded to be deeply moved at the moment. That would come later, and shake him with an inexpressible gratitude. He put his arm about her, and said:

"For six months . . . and you never told me! But you might hate it, Mary."

"I might," she said, "but I don't believe so. Not if you were there. And I could help—"

"And the babies? You've heard all the arguments, the risks, the dangers," he told her slowly.

"I know. But they're my children," she reminded him. "I've a right to decide for them. I'm not worried about them, David. You can go back, and we'll make a home for you, and there will be plenty for you to do. There'd be a place for you, there are all the new hospitals you've told me about, there's the research work your friend died for—"

"To go back," he asked, "with you?" His wonder broke, his amazement vanished. He took her shoulders and shook her slightly, and his eyes blazed suddenly into her own. He looked very young, at that moment, and almost terrifyingly alive. "Mary," he said, "do you know what you've given me?"

He released her and began to plan, walking around the room, the words pouring from him. He knew just the man who would take his practice, he would sell the house, he would write to this person, consult that one. He would go to New York and see the Secretary of the Foreign Mission Board. He would make certain inquiries. It could be arranged, just as she said. Betty would be glad to have Anna with her, the boys were old enough to shift for themselves, perhaps Alex could arrange to have them board nearby during their holidays . . .

Once he stopped and planted himself in front of her as she sat quiet on the sofa, and demanded, "Do you think they'll believe me too old?"

"No," she said, "I don't. If they could hear you now they'd think you were about Matthew's age!"

"I mean, seriously? I'm fifty-three. With any luck, I've twenty years ahead of me. Good years. And if I went back? I will go back," he said loudly. "Heng-ong thought I wouldn't. But I shall. He'll know."

She thought, if only it isn't too late, if only it won't be strange to him, if only he doesn't find that, perhaps, after all, he's lost touch . . .

At the end of two hours he was still talking, planning. She said gently, "Come to bed, it's awfully late. You have to go to Watertown to-morrow, you know. And you may be called out to-night."

He went obediently enough, and later when they were together in the friendly darkness he took her into his arms with a strength of passion and of gratitude she had never before experienced. He said, "I believed you'd done all any woman could do for a man's happiness—but I was mistaken. Look here, Mary, if you've the least doubt, the least uncertainty, we'll say no more about it. But I'll always be grateful to you, my dear. Only don't let me be entirely selfish."

"I haven't any doubt," she assured him. "You'll have to consult the children, of course, Betty and Anna and the boys. That's only fair. But I don't believe they'll stand in your way."

Presently he believed that she slept. He lay beside her thinking of her, her quiet ways, her unspectacular loyalty. Then, his thoughts swung backward. Once more, for the hundred thousandth time, but clearer than of late, the pictures unrolled before him upon the sensitive screen of his mind, detached, yet blending in the familiar pattern: a plum tree in blossom . . . a pagoda crowning a hilltop . . . the bronze bell of a great temple . . . the wild coast line . . . the fishing boats sliding by . . . the yellow waters of the Min. He saw the green marvel of the rice springing from the mud and the bending blue of a spring sky. He saw Mi-daik's face, as he had last seen it, and as he would never see it again. He saw misery and suffering and patience and hard, unremitting work.

I'm too old, he thought.

No, he was not too old.

Mary? Was it fair to her? Was it fair to Toby and to Lee? Had he any right . . . ?

But the temple bell spoke and the kites flew high over Black Rock hill, he heard his mother's laughter from the courtyard and his hand was a little hand suddenly, clasped in a stronger . . . and Heng-ong spoke and said to him, "Some day I shall be a doctor—"

He was dreaming, and did not know he dreamed.

In the morning he woke and lay quiet a moment, wondering what had happened to him. This was his room, and this his bed, and Mary slept beside him, her short thick lashes quiet on her cheeks. Lee woke, too, and cried from the sleeping porch, and Toby added his clamor to hers. Mary opened her eyes without shock, smiled at him, swung her slender legs to the floor and reached for a dressing gown. But he held her back, with one hand. He asked, "Did I dream it, Mary—all of it?"

She said, "No, you didn't dream it, David. Listen, that's the office bell, isn't it?"

David got out of bed, and went to the hall. Janet had answered the bell and he heard a man's voice. He said, getting into his clothes, "Better call Watertown, I may not be able to get over . . . tell Herbert . . . I wanted to see that operation," he grumbled, "but it looks as if the Fitch baby was about to make its appearance."

He clattered downstairs. Mary, busy with her small fry, hoped that despite the anxiety of the moment the Fitches would remember to give him coffee.

When he came home he was very grave. He said briefly, "It looks as if it were war, Mary. We've been fooling ourselves, with hope, all along . . ."

It was the second of April, on which day President Wilson asked Congress to declare a state of war with Germany. Four days later the declaration was made but Graham's wire, on April 3, was explicit enough. "Will join up in event of war," it said.

Other wires were reaching other homes, all over the United States. There was as yet no word from Matthew, but that word would reach them eventually. Mary said, with trembling lips, "Oh, but, David, to throw it all away, everything he's worked for—can't you persuade him?"

"No," said David, "I can't. I shan't try, again. It's out of my hands now." He turned the wire over between his fingers and laid it down on the desk. He said, "We won't be going to China, Mary . . ."

He had dreamed it, after all. But it had been a good dream. He looked at the yellow slip of paper thrown down on his open books. So many yellow slips of paper . . .

He had answered the telegram, he'd said merely, "Do as you believe best." There was no use saying anything else. To-day was April 7 and the United States had been, for twenty-four hours, at war. He remembered Jim Miller plodding up to the house the evening before, crying, "What did I tell you, David, what did I tell you?"

Mary said, standing beside him, "It may not last, David, it may be over before Graham has a chance to get there, it may be over in a few months. Of course it will, and then—"

He said, "No, we'll stay here. I've known it all along, I suppose. There'll be plenty for me to do. They won't send me to battlefields, I suppose, or base hospitals, but there'll be the camps . . ."

Someone knocked at the office door. A girl opened it without waiting for permission, and looked in, her face wild with a sort of unbelieving anxiety and rebellion. She said, "Oh, Dr. Condit, if you'd come, right away—"

"What is it, Catherine?"

"It's mother. She's just had word that Frank—with the Canadians. And before the message came Pete wrote that he was enlisting, in New York. Please hurry," she urged, weeping.

David touched Mary's shoulder briefly and went out with the girl. She was sobbing. "I ran, all the way."

Three houses down the street, and a woman who had lost a
son, and who feared she would lose another. Mary drew the
shades in the office windows and went upstairs alone. She stood
for a long time by the cribs on the sleeping porch, looking down
at Toby's dark small face, relaxed in slumber, at Lee's small rosy
mouth, molded to a smile. . . . These two, she thought, were
safe. But were they, was anyone safe in a world where such things
could happen, a world which could go mad, without warning?
Or was it just that one couldn't read the portents?

She went downstairs into the living room and took up a basket
of sewing. David, she thought, her head bent, was terribly hard
on socks. . . . People went by on the street, there was talking,
she heard cheering, faintly . . . She heard a piano being played,
almost savagely . . . She heard a boy's exultant shout . . . and
a woman cry out hysterically . . .

David's dream was ended, it had been a long dream, and yet
very brief. Somewhere, stripped of martial music and drumbeat
and weeping and exultation, there was a reality. She thought,
weaving the darning cotton in and out of its little window-like
pattern, he's needed here, that will help him . . .

Three houses away, a woman said to David Condit, "It's so
hard. I don't see what I've done that I should have to bear
this . . ."

David didn't see either. When, after a long time, he left the
house her husband went with him to the steps. He said, brokenly,
"It's pretty tough, Dave. Thanks for coming . . ."

"There was very little I could do," David told him regretfully.
"She'll sleep through, until morning . . . It was all I could do
for her."

"We couldn't get along without you," said the man, who had
lost one son and believed he would lose another.

David walked up the street toward his house. He, too, heard
the sound of singing and of shouting. People passed, stopped to
exclaim, to clutch his sleeve, to talk, to hurry on again. He paused
at his own gate and looked at the four-square house, light stream-
ing from it. He could see the shadow of Mary's bent head on the
drawn shade . . .

He told himself, these are my people. The dream, the stubborn dream, must die. There would be so little time for dreaming, now. Perhaps there never had been.

He went up the steps and into the house where Mary waited.

BIBLIOGRAPHY

A partial list of books which I read or reread during the writing of this one must include such contemporary history as Mark Sullivan's *Our Times* (Scribner's) and Arthur Train's *Puritan's Progress* (Scribner's) as well as innumerable novels written during the years 1862-1917, or more recently and reconstructing earlier eras. I have consulted books on costume, and files of photographs such as those contained in *The American Procession* by Agnes Rogers and Frederick Lewis Allen (Harper's); and must also mention a *History of Agriculture in the State of New York* by Ulysses Prentice Hedrick, published by the State, and a *History of Jefferson County* by Dr. Franklin B. Hough, published in 1854.

There are also the many books on clipper ships, including Captain Clarke's *The Clipper Ship Era*, Basil Lubbock's several volumes, published by Lauriat. Lack of space precludes the entire list of these and other books but my shelves contain a complete *Valentine's Manual*, edited by Henry Collins Brown, and the source of my information on the Collegiate School in New York City came from a book which was lent to me by the present Headmaster.

The books on China, exclusive of fiction, have been numerous. Many were lent to me, others are in my possession. A partial list of these includes: S. Wells Williams' *Middle Kingdom* (Scribner's); *Nathan Sites*, S. Moore Sites (Fleming Revell, 1912); *Manual of the Foochow Dialect*, Rev. C. C. Baldwin (Foochow Mission Press, 1871); *Manual of Chinese Metaphor*, C. A. S. Williams (Commercial Press, Shanghai, 1920); *Chinese Proverbs*, Scarborough Allen (Shanghai, 1926); *Social Life of the Chinese*, Justus Doolittle (Harper's, 1867); *Life Among the Chinese*, Rev. R. S. Maclay (Carlton and Porter, 1861); *A Course in the Analysis of Chinese Characters*, R. B. Blakney (Commercial Press, Shanghai); *Two Gentlemen of China*, Lady Hossie (Seeley Service and Co., London, 1924), and *Portrait of a Lady*, Lady Hossie (William Morrow and Co., New York, 1930); *Half a Century in China*, Archdeacon Moule (Hodder and Stoughton, London, 1911); *Fukien, A Survey*, by the Anti-Cobweb Club (Shanghai, 1925); *Lady Fourth Daughter* and *The Moon for Planting*, Mary Brewster Hollister; *Folk-*

ways in China (London); *Along River and Road in Fukien,* Edwin T. Dukes (New York Tract Society); *Historical Sketches of the Foreign Missions of the M. E. Church; Rethinking Missions* (Harper's, 1932); *Chinese Verse,* Fletcher (Shanghai, 1918).

There were many more; and I am grateful to all of them. And I make an acknowledgment to the New York Public Library for use of the files of the N. Y. *Herald* for the month of June, 1862; and for the photostat of the *Hotspur,* now in my possession. As consultants on costume of the various periods I have *Costume and Fashion,* Norris and Curtis, Vol. 6 (Dutton, 1933), and *Modes and Manners of the 19th Century,* Fischel and von Boehn, Vol. 3 (Dutton, 1927); as well as a bound volume of *Leslie's Ladies Magazine* for 1864 and other sources.

Charles Dudley Warner and Louisa M. Alcott were taken down from my book shelves in order to catch a glimpse of the youth of their eras; while Constance Woolson and other contemporary writers supplied a more adult fare.

There were other books. Some were useful, some were not. But all interested me and made me dull company for my family during the months they littered my desk and stimulated my mind.

Included in this company are several fine autobiographies by living medical men and a *History of Nursing* by Lavinia Dock (Putnam).